BRENDAN REICHS

CHRYSALIS

MACMILLAN

First published in the US 2019 by G. P. Putnam's Sons,
an imprint of Penguin Random House LLC

First published in the UK 2019 by Macmillan Children's Books

This edition published 2019 by Macmillan Children's Books
an imprint of Pan Macmillan
20 New Wharf Road, London N1 9RR
Associated companies throughout the world
www.panmacmillan.com

ISBN 978-1-5290-1939-1

1 3 5 7 9 8 6 4 2

A CIP catalogue record for this book is available from
the British Library.

Design by Marikka Tamura
Printed and bound by CPI Group (UK) Ltd, Croydon CR0 4YY

For my dad

PART ONE

FIRE LAKE ISLAND

1

MIN

I promised myself I wouldn't die that night.

I'd said it often over the past six months, whispering the words, when Noah was away and no one else was around to hear them. The vow didn't feel momentous anymore. I'd "died" so many times in the past that I wasn't particularly scared of it, even now that the threat was real. But I *was* freaked out by the mother of a thunderstorm bearing down on our settlement. While I sat there on my bed, alone.

I wish Noah were here.

But he wasn't. He'd gone up to Ridgeline camp to see about a broken water purifier. The trip took several hours each way, so he wouldn't return until morning.

Outside, hail fell like staccato punches against the roof of our cabin, littering the ground with icy shrapnel. I hugged my knees to my chest, wondering again whether Noah and I were crazy not to live inside the silo like Sarah and her friends. So what if it meant sleeping with a hundred yards of concrete hanging overhead? Those girls were warm and snug right now, unable to even hear this cataclysm.

I had the same thought every time an electrical storm came, and they always came. But I never actually moved down there. I was *alive*, in the real world. Surrounded by real wind and water and earth and sun. No way was I living in a basement at the bottom of a hole. To me that felt like crawling back inside the Program.

Then I snorted. *It's not like they invited me to join them.*

There was only room for a dozen inside the lab complex anyway. My place was in the settlement. I couldn't lead our fledgling little community from underneath a rock.

BOOM. *Sizzle.*

I stuck my nose outside the cabin door. The air reeked of ozone and charged metal. Chunks of hail were melting on the black, loamy earth surrounding the stream.

It never really got cold now, aboveground. The weather seemed stuck in a perpetual late-summer temper tantrum, like a cat that's fallen into a pool and wants someone to blame for it. I felt a restless, relentless pressure in my eardrums. The hair on my arms stood in anticipation of the laser show about to be unleashed. Sour copper filled my mouth.

Lightning split the sky, followed by a crack of thunder that rattled my teeth. This was going to be a bad one. They were *all* bad ones. Earth may have recovered enough to support human life but it remained thoroughly pissed off.

I stepped from my home—a sturdy box of rough-hewn logs Noah and I had constructed by hand. In the first days after regenerating our class discovered a mountain of tools inside the silo's supply alcoves, along with guides and sets of plans. We'd built our houses as strongly as possible, but these storms were nearly too much. Old tolerances didn't seem to apply anymore. Sometime during the eons our digitized existences traveled the MegaCom's circuit boards, nature's fury had gotten a turbo boost.

A full moon hung in the western sky, kissing the fog and infusing the night with a pale, almost spectral glow. But I was staring in the opposite direction—at the roiling, malevolent cloud bank creeping closer from the east. A thick ball of pure ferocity, flaring yellow and red, lit by the ceaseless electrical flows thrumming inside it.

It was beautiful. It was terrifying. It cared nothing for me and mine.

The storm snarled closer, its violent light reflecting off the ocean seething beneath it. The nastiest howlers always struck from the east, where Montana used to be. Where there was nothing now but endless, iron-gray sea.

I glanced back to the west. The ocean in that direction remained eerily calm, though its turn was coming. When the storm finally pounced, it would cloak the moon in a blanket of dancing, glimmering sky-fire. A breathtaking sight, if it wasn't so deadly.

Fire Lake Island rose from the encircling sea like a giant middle finger, a lonely tower of cracked and crumbling granite.

Our whole world. The peaks of the Rockies were all that remained above the angry waves. So much had changed while we . . . slept? Dreamed?

I shivered, aware of just how much had sunk into those inky depths. How precariously our refuge was positioned. How easily we could be swept away.

That had been the biggest shock—discovering that our quiet mountain valley was now an island in an endless sea. The silo was perched at its eastern edge, one concrete wall sheer and exposed, dropping hundreds of feet straight down to the ocean. The only recognizable feature remaining was Fire Lake itself, still cold and beautiful in the valley's center, collecting rainwater dumped by the countless savage cloudbursts.

We might physically be in the same place, but nothing, *nothing* was the same.

A wave of static electricity prickled my skin. Then a bolt of pure energy, highlighter yellow, struck the island with a scream of triumph. Thunder boomed like heaven's anvil, shaking the trees around me.

Screams erupted from the settlement below, a tight grid of cabins and storage buildings that bordered a gurgling creek. Orange tendrils lofted into the sky. The stench of scorched pine and burning fuel rolled up the mountainside in a humid wave.

I was already running downhill, past the thicket we used for firewood and into the village. Early on some jokester had dubbed the place Home Town—because everyone was from there, get it?—and the name stuck. Though I'd been its elected leader since Day One, I lived slightly apart from the others, on a ridge overlooking the ocean. When my days were done I needed to unwind away from prying, judging eyes. Plus, I shared the place with Noah. I'd take whatever privacy we could get.

"Fire!" someone shouted. "Get the hoses!" yelled another. This wasn't the first hit we'd taken, and everyone knew their jobs. But as I watched, flames leapt higher in a ragged, whipping breeze. I prayed for rain to hurry up and get there.

I sprinted down a dirt-packed trail, lungs burning as I reached the main square. Fires rose before me, and I grimaced at our bad luck—the initial bolt had struck a gas depot. We didn't keep much on the surface, but the ATVs drank their share and no one wanted to haul canisters up the shaft every day. This storm was teaching us a lesson about complacency.

BOOM. *Sizzle.*

A second blinding dagger stabbed the valley. I glanced up at the writhing neon mass now screaming directly overhead, like northern lights gone feral. *Worst one yet.* In a blink, I questioned every assumption I'd made about the planet's surface. Maybe it wasn't safe to be outside at all.

I spotted Derrick setting up water pumps while Akio and Casey fueled the portable generator. Piper and Hector were struggling to unwind fire hoses when the next bolt struck in nearly the same spot as the first. A storage building exploded. I watched in horror as a fireball engulfed three people carrying buckets.

Everything around me froze, then zoomed into fast-forward.

"Get back!" I shouted, but my warning was gobbled up by more growling thunder. Lightning struck in quick succession like artillery fire. A second blast rocked the village, spreading the inferno to nearby cabins.

Screams. Someone ran into the night, wreathed in flames.

My eyes burned as a gust of scorching black smoke tried to shove me sideways.

"Min!" a voice bellowed.

I spun, rubbing grit from my eyes. Derrick was pounding on the fire equipment with a socket wrench. Akio and Casey crouched behind him, hands on their knees and puffing hard. I streaked over and slid down beside Derrick as he slammed a fist to the ground.

"The valve broke!" Derrick shouted. "I can't get the pumps to start!" He pointed to a jagged part inside the machine, as if it would mean something to me.

"Double the buckets!" I yelled, pawing stray hair from my eyes. The charged air was standing the loose strands on end. "We can't let any more buildings catch!"

I felt a hand on my shoulder. "I don't think that's gonna be a problem," Akio said, pointing to the eastern horizon. A heavy curtain of rain was marching across the island, swallowing the landscape one foot at a time. The downpour sounded like a million plinking xylophones closing in on us. At least the lightning had stopped.

I rasped a relieved breath. "Okay, good. That'll put out the fires." Shooting to my feet, I started scanning for victims of the explosion. A sick feeling swept over me. *How many people did we lose tonight?*

Derrick stood tall beside me, dark eyes grim as he examined the approaching monsoon. "That's . . . Min, that's *a lot* of water coming down. And we're near the bottom of the slopes."

I stiffened in alarm. He was right—an entire river was

dumping onto the heights ringing the island's central valley. All that liquid had to go somewhere.

The radio at Derrick's belt squawked. I heard Sam's voice crackle through a wall of static. "Watch o— . . . a freaki— . . .—ll of water coming right fo— . . .—ryone inside th— . . .—IGHT NOW!" Derrick tried to signal back, but the connection went dead.

"Damn it!" Derrick holstered his radio in disgust. "Too much charge in the air. But I think we got the message."

"Forget the pumps. Get everyone into the silo!" I ran toward the largest clump of people I could find as the electric blur engulfed the moon. The effect lit up the night like the Vegas Strip. People were stumbling about, trying to help but unsure what to do. The storm's power seemed to have scrambled everyone's senses.

I grabbed the closest shoulder I could reach. Aiken Talbot, ash-covered and coughing, eyes red and glistening from more than just wood smoke. "Head to the silo! We can't stay out here—this one's too much!"

Aiken shrugged me off angrily. "People need help!" He pointed to a still form lying beside the burning fuel dump. "The fire's too hot to get close, and it'll spread. We need a water brigade!"

"It's not going to spread." I spun him around to face the wall of rainwater sliding closer by the second. "The storm will douse the fires, but that's a flash flood waiting to happen. We have to hurry!"

Aiken blanched. "Crap. Okay. I'll gather a team and help the . . . the wounded."

He swallowed. I squeezed his arm. We both knew the person on the ground was likely dead.

"Don't take too long," was all I said.

We split up, each gathering people as we ran. I began herding everyone up the main path—a gravel road that led to the silo's entrance no more than two hundred yards upslope. Though most of the class had moved outside to live like people, we hadn't gone far. Safety was close if we hurried.

The downpour finally reached us, and in seconds I was soaked to the bone. I splashed back down toward the village, alert for stragglers, but quickly realized it was pointless. I could barely see my own hands in front of me. When a small group led by Casey and Derrick appeared carrying electric lanterns, I gasped in relief.

"Do you have everyone?" I shouted.

Derrick shrugged, his jaw clenched. "No way to tell! We can't see anything!"

Rainwater began running down the path in a thickening stream, covering my feet up to the ankles. Soon it'd be too slippery to climb. "Keep going!" I shouted, grabbing Casey's lantern. "I'll do one last sweep, then—"

Bang. Bang. BANG.

Something rumbled, followed by a deep groan. Everyone froze.

The sound of stone smacking stone echoed across the valley. A low vibration hummed through my legs.

I heard several loud cracks echo from upslope, followed by a noise like ogres chewing rocks. An instant later two massive boulders rolled out of the darkness, passing a dozen yards to my left.

"Landslide!" Aiken shouted.

The hill shook with a roar like a jet engine screaming, then a scythe of dirty water leapt from the darkness, washing my feet out from under me. I tumbled downslope in a tangle of mud and flailing limbs.

Shouts erupted in the darkness as others were swept along with me. Something heavy and solid struck my temple and I nearly blacked out. I tried to scream but water filled my mouth and nose, causing me to gag and choke.

The area below the trail flattened and I lurched to a halt, covered head to foot in cloying mud. I'd lost both shoes and was bleeding from a gash on my head, but all my bones seemed intact. I whispered a silent prayer of thanks to any deities that might've stuck around while the Program ran.

Classmates were picking themselves up around me. The rain continued pouring down like a faucet as we staggered into a ragged cluster and counted off. Thirteen. There'd been twenty-five people in Home Town when the storm struck. Some had definitely gone ahead of us, but had they been caught in the slide, too? I shivered, thinking of the burning silhouette that had run toward the lake. How many never reached the path at all?

I should have planned for this better.

Mercifully, the rain slackened. I glanced eastward. The sky in that direction was clear and brilliant with stars. The storm would be over soon. Nothing that furious could last.

Derrick sloshed over beside me. He let out an exhausted sigh. "I think we have some bad news," he said quietly.

I nodded, unable to speak. *Again.* There'd been death

on my watch before—real death, *final* death—and everyone knew it.

"This ain't on you," Derrick said as if reading my mind, though he kept his eyes on the lake. Water was rushing into it at a startling pace. How much would drain through the surrounding hills in the next few hours? Our creek must've overflowed. The village might be a total loss.

"This was a disaster, D. If not on me, then who?"

"Not every situation requires blame." Derrick sat down on a log and pulled off a sodden boot. A stream of brown liquid gushed out. "We've never had a storm that bad. My balls are still rattling."

"Gross."

"True story."

I rubbed my face. "I wish Noah were here." The words slipped out before I could stop them, and I blushed in the darkness. I hated showing weakness, but was it wrong to want your boyfriend around after getting washed over a cliff? Plus I had no idea where he was, or if he was okay. What if he'd been caught outside in that nightmare?

"I left my high-tops by the fire pit," Derrick grumbled. "I know they'll be ruined. Last pair, too."

I snorted despite myself. "There are forty-six boxes of pink Keds in alcove 7B. I have no idea who thought—"

The ground bucked suddenly, toppling me sideways. I heard a report like a dam breaking as a gust of stale air whistled over us. A deep, ominous crash reverberated across the island, triggering another shockwave.

Then, silence.

Flat on his belly in the muck Derrick was panting like a hunted animal. "What the—"

"The silo!" I was on my feet and running. I slipped, sloshed, and scrambled up the waterlogged path to the bunker's entrance, the electric lantern jostling against my side.

Where I stopped dead.

Earlier that evening, a blocky concrete tunnel had poked from the mountainside, accessing a military-grade blast door that had survived Armageddon. Now, the tunnel was gone. A huge swath of the mountain was gone with it, leaving a mass of shattered rock and mud where the entrance had been.

The silo was blocked, trapping my classmates inside.

2

NOAH

I ran as fast as I could.

Legs pounding. Sweat oozing. As the sun peeked over the eastern heights, illuminating the valley in a soggy haze.

I could barely keep my impatience in check. The paths were too waterlogged for an ATV, so I'd set out on foot. The trek from Ridgeline usually took four hours, but I was determined to make it in three.

I had to. Everything had gone to hell while I was gone.

I took the most direct route possible, straight through the woods on the north side of the lake rather than my usual hike across the southern flatland. Thorns ripped at my flesh as I barreled through the undergrowth, ignoring my burning lungs. I scolded myself for leaving the village while a thunderstorm was gathering, but honestly, when wasn't one?

Sam's crew had a busted filtration system—without a spare valve from the silo stockpile, they'd have been drinking from a stream like cave people. The trip had to be made.

I'd witnessed the lightning display from their camp in the western peaks, chewing on my fist beside Floyd and Hamza as bolts rained down. Then something exploded in Home Town. I'd wanted to sprint back immediately—cabins were *burning*— but the Ridgeliners persuaded me it was suicide to travel in that weather.

The thought of Min battling chaos without me gnawed my insides. I'd nearly bolted into the night a dozen times. But it was the worst storm any of us had ever seen, and that's saying something. When its leading edge reached our position we'd retreated into a cavern to hide like mice.

Now I was minutes away from home, growing more and more anxious about what I'd find. The trees thinned and my speed picked up, though new streams ran everywhere and soon I was drenched from the waist down. My boots made awful squishing sounds with every footfall.

The first thing to hit me was the smell. Smoke. Charred wood. A noxious, oily stench that could only mean something mechanical had burned. That or fuel. Pushing through the last line of trees, I was prepared to encounter pandemonium.

Instead, I found . . . no one.

Not a living soul.

I ran down to the square, discovered the wreckage of supply buildings 3 through 7. Taking mental notes on what had likely been destroyed, I looked around, baffled. The village common was always busy at sunup—there weren't a lot of other places to be. Admittedly, Home Town was less crowded now than when the whole class had been living there before the incident three months ago, but still. There should've been a dozen people puttering around on a slow day, and this wasn't that.

What the hell?

I heard a noise behind me and whirled. Nothing. But then it came again—a sniffling, sobbing cough echoing from somewhere down by the stream. I jogged closer, trying to ignore the stitch in my side, and found Hector and Vonda huddled over four long bundles wrapped in blue tarps.

My heart stopped.

Hector looked up. "Noah."

"Who?" I blurted, hands trembling as I stared at the tarps.

Head down, Vonda's shoulders shook silently. Hector's red-rimmed eyes lost focus.

"Jamie. Lars. Morgan. And . . . Finn."

Vonda exploded in a heart-wrenching wail. Her hands dug into her thick black hair as she rocked back and forth. Hector reached out and squeezed her shoulder. Vonda and Finn had been together since inside the Program.

My breath caught. I felt tears on my cheeks. It was so much worse than I'd thought.

"Vonda, I . . . I'm so sorry." I knelt and put an arm around her, and she collapsed against my chest. We sat like that for a long moment, but the questions couldn't wait. "Hector, where is everyone? Did they *all* go for a resupply?"

Hector seemed to startle back to the present. "No. They're at the silo. There was a cave-in last night, and people are trapped inside. You should go, Noah. Vonda and I will stay to prepare the . . . our friends."

He didn't say dead. Couldn't yet. I understood.

Death—something we'd treated as a minor inconvenience for so long—was real again. The bodies in those tarps wouldn't reset. They'd never stand up and stretch, ready to laugh darkly about how they'd bought it that time before going about their day.

Then Hector's words fully penetrated and I shot to my feet. "Who's trapped? How many?"

He shook his head. "I don't know. Min's up there organizing a rescue. I'm sure they could use your help."

I nodded. Looked at Vonda, wanting to say something comforting. But the words wouldn't come, and I'd be bad at delivering them even if they did. So I turned and raced up the path. My muscles screamed in protest as I made the ascent. I'd been running for several hours and didn't have much left in the tank. The trail was now a muddy slog riddled with puddles. Last night it must've been a river.

Five more minutes of hard going and I reached the silo's front entrance. I heard the commotion before I saw it—at least twenty of my classmates were dragging rubble away from where the tunnel had been. But the whole mountainside had collapsed on top of the opening. It took me all of ten seconds to realize the effort was futile.

Min and Derrick were standing to one side, conferring quietly. I ran to join them, swallowing Min in a quick hug. She gripped me back tightly.

"Noah, it's awful." She ground a fist into her leg as she spoke.

"The door is buried under thirty feet of debris. We can't move these giant boulders, and we can't drop in through the top hatch because there's no way up there now. There's *nothing* up there now."

I gripped the back of my neck. "But there's no reason to think anyone inside is hurt, right?"

"We don't know, because nobody's answering the radio." Derrick frowned at his walkie-talkie. "This entire side of the hill broke apart, and I swear some of it's not out here. If anything fell down through the shaft, it might've jacked up the catwalks, the alcoves, and who knows what else. This is a disaster."

I ran a hand through my sodden hair. Tried to think deliberately. "Who's in there?"

Derrick glared at the wreckage as if to clear it by sheer will. "The collapse happened before anyone from the village reached the door. A blessing if the silo's roof really did cave in, though we were all stuck out here in the rain like jackasses. But Sarah and the other princesses are down there, and those boulders literally weigh tons. How are we supposed to move them?"

Min was shaking her head slightly. Her bottom lip quivered. I knew she was thinking about those four tarps down by the stream. "We just keep digging," she said abruptly. "Until we force a way through. I'm not giving up."

"We'd need a forklift to lift some of those stones." I chewed the inside of my cheek, testing the problem in my head. "Or the whole team of four-wheelers, pulling at the same time. But the village depot exploded, and the rest of our fuel is down there in the storage alcoves."

Min's gray eyes found mine. "We have to get them out, Noah.

16

And this isn't the only way inside."

"You mean the back door?" I answered, surprised. "It's a dead end."

Derrick glanced at Min. "Nobody's used that since we came out of the MegaCom. I went down once, just to take a look. The power plant level is dark and nasty, plus I heard weird noises." He crossed his arms. "The back tunnel runs directly toward the cliffs. In case you missed it, that side drops straight to the ocean. What good does that do us?"

"But it's there." Min grabbed my forearm. "Derrick and I can—"

"—stay where you're needed most," I broke in smoothly. "You two run this whole island. You have to be here and make sure no one freaks out. I'll take Akio and Kyle, and we'll check it."

Min seemed ready to argue the point, but I cut her off again. "I'm the official inter-camp liaison person guy, right?" I flashed a grin. "So let me 'liaise' with Sarah and her cheerleader coven while you handle the big stuff." I stepped close, spoke in a softer tone. "You and Derrick need to keep everyone together. There's a ton of work to do in the village, including some unpleasant stuff. This is our worst day since—"

I winced, tried to pull the words back. The last thing I wanted Min thinking about was the accident with Carl. But one look and I knew it was too late. Min blamed herself for what had happened, and always would.

"Okay." Her voice was strangely flat. "Take a radio and call up the minute you reach them. We haven't heard a word, and I'm starting to . . ." She flexed her fingers in a gesture of helplessness. "Just go fast. Please."

I wrapped her in another quick hug, then jogged to where

17

several teams were hauling rubble away in buckets. The effort looked hopeless—house-size boulders had fallen directly onto the entrance, crushing the tunnel and blocking any path to the blast door. Still, our classmates were trying.

I spotted Akio and waved. Then, scanning quickly, I yelled for Kyle. The two hurried over, chests heaving, faces covered in orange dust. Both had lived with me inside the Program at my father's ski chalet. I trusted Akio with my life and usually picked him for the harder jobs. Kyle I was less comfortable with—he'd pulled a fast one on me once, during a raid, and had seemed too comfortable with the slaughter in general—but he was fearless to the point of recklessness. I knew he wouldn't punk out if this got tough.

Kyle wiped his mouth with a dirty backhand. "What up, Noah? This is a real mess."

"Any chance we get through?" I asked.

Akio shook his head. "We might be able to dig around the boulders, but I doubt the door survived."

"Then we try a different way. Up for a climbing expedition?"

Kyle grinned like he'd won a prize. Akio nodded, but worry lines dug across his forehead. "The back tunnel?"

"That's the idea."

Akio frowned. "Even if the door's intact, how will we reach it? That side faces the water."

I pushed aside a tidal wave of doubt. "Let's see what we find and go from there. Nine girls are stuck at the bottom of this tomb. We have to get them out."

"Don't forget Devin." Kyle snorted derisively. "He moved down two weeks ago. Their majesties let him stay because they need someone to cook and clean for them. I kid you not."

I gave him a sharp look. "Four people died last night, Kyle. Do I need to ask someone else?"

"Oh, crap. No. My bad, man." Kyle's face fell so quickly, I almost felt bad for snapping at him. Almost.

"Forget it. Let's just hope we can get inside. Come on."

Back in the village we grabbed several lengths of nylon rope and three sets of climbing gear. Then we tramped around the mountain, scrambling up bluffs and powering through scrub as we circled the massive cylinder. Once buried deep underground, the silo now stood at the outermost edge of the island, its eastern side fully exposed to the elements and dropping hundreds of feet to the ocean below.

I shivered every time I saw it from this angle. The silo looked like a bird on an unsteady perch. A few hundred more feet of erosion and our supposedly indestructible lifeboat would've crashed into the sea along with the rest of Idaho. It was a freaking miracle we'd survived.

Scanning the seaward-facing concrete, I tried to visualize where the back exit should be. So much had changed while we were inside the Program. I squinted into the sun, probing the pockmarked surface with my eyes, but came up empty. I was about to suggest we go back for binoculars when Akio's finger darted out. "There."

He'd spotted an indentation maybe forty yards to our right and a dozen down. But I couldn't see if there was a door. "Could be," I agreed. "But how do we check?"

I glanced at the top of the silo, unreachable now with the mountainside gone.

Can't get up, can't go down. What a mess.

But Akio had seen more than just the possible entry point. "There's a ridge below us that runs around the silo. I think we can get above the opening and rappel down to it."

I blinked at him. "Rappel. Down the cliff. Over the ocean."

Akio shrugged, the ghost of a smile appearing on his lips. "You have a better idea?"

"I do not." My throat worked, but there was no other way. "So let's do it."

Akio took the lead. We worked along a sharp defile to reach the ridge. It was a full three feet wide—plenty big enough to feel comfortable if there hadn't been a hundred-yard death drop on the left side. As it was, I could barely breathe.

I heard Kyle gasping behind me and took solace knowing I wasn't the only one about to crap his pants. For his part, Akio moved confidently, circling to a wider cleft above the indentation. Once inside there, I put my back against solid stone and tried to slow my stampeding heart.

"We're lucky." Akio patted a triangular spike of rock jutting up in the center of the cleft. "We can tie off on this. I was worried two of us would have to anchor the line with body weight."

I shivered, thinking about *that* insane prospect, as Akio began securing ropes. He produced two sets of carabiners and snapped them in place, then handed me an ascender. "For the climb back up. Wouldn't want to forget."

I shoved mine deep into a pocket. There was nothing left to do but go.

"Okay," I said. "All right. Okay."

"One of us should stay here," Akio said. "To watch the lines."

Kyle's hand flew up. I shot him a dirty look, but nodded. I was in charge. I had to go over the side.

Akio offered to go first, but I shook my head roughly. If I didn't do it now, I never would. I clipped in and took a deep breath. Every kid in Fire Lake had gone rappelling at one time or another at Starlight's Edge summer camp. This wasn't novel. But a quick zip down a scouted pitch on lines laid by professionals was a little different from stepping off a vertical cliff above a death drop and hoping Kyle didn't accidentally let you die. We had no idea if this was even the right place. I'd have to climb back up either way.

Just don't look down. That's always good advice, but especially now. Don't. Look. Down.

Three deep inhales.

I stepped backward off the cliff.

The line played out easily. I worked cautiously down the face, being careful with my speed. After three bounds, I reached the indentation and was forced to look between my feet. I blanked out the crashing waves far below, focusing on the opening. It was a small cave of roughly the same dimensions as a school bus. I lowered myself to a lip where I could stand and scrambled to safer footing.

A weathered blast door was tucked into the back of the recess before me.

I let out a huge sob of relief.

I called up to Akio, detached from the line, and approached the door. There was a wheel-locking mechanism. As Akio landed softly behind me, I grabbed it with both hands and yanked. The wheel didn't budge.

My heart oozed through my shoes and off the cliff. This door hadn't been opened in millennia, and was exposed to the sea. *Of course* it didn't just spin, and we'd brought nothing to cut the oxidation. This ball of rust might never open. Why hadn't I thought of this before?

Akio unclipped and joined me in the back of the cave. We tried the wheel together, but it might as well have been part of the mountainside. I collapsed with an exasperated grunt. Akio sat down beside me and squeezed his forehead.

"We probably should have thought this through a little more," he said.

"You think?"

"I bet the door is rusted shut."

"You are clearly a master of door science."

"It would've been better if we'd brought something to grease the wheel."

I chuckled sourly. "Let's have this conversation up there next time."

"Deal. Of course, the door could also be locked."

I pressed my fists into my eyes sockets, then petulantly kicked the door. With a weary sigh, I fumbled for the radio in my pocket. Kyle could run back to the village and get what we needed. If the door was locked . . . well, that would be that.

I was fiddling with the frequency when the wheel next to my head abruptly started rotating. My eyes bugged. I grabbed Akio's knee. We scrambled to our feet as it spun several times, then stopped. Hinges groaned as the portal swung inward.

Sarah Harden poked her head out. "Took you long enough."

I blinked. Opened my mouth. Closed it.

Sarah's blue eyes rolled skyward. "A thousand tons of rock just rained down on us. Did you think we'd just sit around waiting for you bozos? Please tell me you fixed a rope."

She stepped from the tunnel, followed by a sniffling Jessica Cale. One by one, three more people emerged. Alice Cho. Susan Daughtridge. Colleen Plummer. All were dirt-smeared. Most were crying. I peered past them into the tunnel, expecting the rest of the silo squad, but no one else appeared.

I aimed a confused glance at Sarah. She shook her head.

My whole body went cold. "Where are the others? Tiffani and Kristen? Devin? Are they trapped somewhere?"

I glanced at Alice, who was staring at nothing. Colleen and Susan were hugging each other and wouldn't meet my eye. "They're *dead*," Jessica wailed. "The roof caved in and they all died!" She slumped to her knees, sobbing, and covered her face.

Sarah watched Jessica with distaste. No tears marred her eyes. Then she looked at me and I nearly shivered. "Tiffani, Melissa, Emily, Kristen, and Devin were having dinner in the command center. The rest of us were in the living quarters. The blast door between the two sections was shut, which probably saved our lives. When we tried to open it . . ." Sarah grimaced, the first human thing she'd done since emerging. "It's gone. They're gone."

Akio turned to stare at the ocean. I shook my head, unwilling to accept what I was hearing. "It might just be blocked. The rest of the shaft could—"

"I connected to a working camera in one of the storage

alcoves," Sarah said curtly. "The silo's entire ceiling collapsed down the shaft, crushing everything outside the lab complex. The command center is pulverized, Noah. So is everyone who was in there." She crossed her arms to reveal cracked, bleeding nails. "It's not like we didn't try."

I gaped at Sarah, horrified. Five more classmates, dead. *What am I going to tell Min?*

"I assume you have a way up from here?" Sarah said. "We've been waiting by this door for hours. It's the only way in or out now, and I was getting worried no one could reach it from above. The lab complex isn't damaged, and we sealed it, but I want to get topside and see what happened." She glanced at her companions. "The others didn't want to stay underground alone."

"Up. Yes." I shook my head to clear it. "We have ropes. Kyle is—"

A concussion thumped from somewhere deep inside the tunnel, followed quickly by two more. The stone shook beneath our feet. My eyes met Sarah's as a crunching sound echoed along the passageway, growing louder by the second.

Sarah flew to the open door, dropping a shoulder against the heavy steel. Akio and I leapt to flank her and together we forced the portal closed. Sarah turned the wheel, then jerked back as something heavy clanged against the door from the inside. The mountain groaned one last time, then went still.

I slid down on my butt and wiped grime from my eyes. "Will things stop breaking around here, please?"

"No way," Sarah whispered, dropping down beside me. The others were all panting like we'd run a marathon.

I rested my head back against the door. "No way what? The tunnel imploded. Thank God we got here in time."

Sarah grabbed my shirt, yanking me close. "Two major collapses in one day? Inside a military-grade disaster bunker that stood for over a *million* years? Get your head out of your ass, Livingston."

I gently extricated myself from her grip, then ran both palms over my face as the last twelve hours fell in on me like an avalanche. "What are you saying, Sarah? I'm too tired for games."

She shook her head with disgust. "I'm *saying*, Noah, that a storm didn't cause this damage. It's too much."

That got my attention. "If not the storm, then what?"

She leaned back next to me, staring off into the distance. "Not what, you idiot. *Who*."

3

MIN

I was staring at a cake.

Chocolate. Squat and lopsided. Clearly underbaked in a field oven. No silly candles, but someone had written HOME TOWN and SIX MONTHS & KICKING! on its face with rehydrated vanilla frosting.

I pressed my temples. Two hours ago, Noah had returned to the village with Sarah and the four other silo survivors. Their news hit like a gut punch. Everyone was stumbling around in shock, numb from the rising body count and being cut off from our refuge and source of supplies. For the first time since exiting the Program, we were truly on our own.

And yet someone had thought it'd be a good idea to bake a cake. I grunted in disbelief.

We couldn't guess the correct date, or even what month it was. There'd been no holidays or birthday parties since emerging from our regeneration pods. In a sense we all had the same birthday, making us a giant group of infants. Or we were all so old as to defy comprehension. Either way, this was ridiculous. Nine people were dead.

"Idiots." I hustled the cake out of the community lodge and found the closest occupied structure—Cash, Dakota, Leighton, and Ferris were playing No Limit Hold 'Em in the mess tent, a green nylon-and-fiberglass structure designed to shelter troops in the field. "Here," I said, placing the dessert on their table. "You four can eat this whole thing without sharing if you promise to never admit it existed."

Quick nods of agreement as they pounced. I was already heading back outside.

I'd called for an official meeting. Only elected leaders at first, though we'd have a full assembly afterward to share our recommendations with the class. We couldn't wait for someone to come all the way from the Outpost—located off-island and across the channel—but radio calls had been made up to Ridgeline and down to the caves. It would take a while for everyone to get to Home Town.

Everyone. A sigh escaped as I reentered the lodge, the largest building in the village. Four months ago we'd been sixty-four kids strong and doing okay in our new environment. The whole class had lived in Home Town, or down in the silo within easy reach. Things had been going as smoothly as could be hoped. Then the accident occurred, Carl and his scouting team died, and the group splintered.

It was the beginning of the end. Aftershocks were still being felt today.

The next morning Toby and his goons had disappeared, and the count was down to fifty-four. Nobody missed them—Toby had made no effort to fit in since exiting the Program, and the Nolan twins, Josh, Tucker, and Cole had been our only real troublemakers—but where the heck had they gone? Noah was certain they were no longer living on Fire Lake Island.

That was bad enough, but then even those fifty-four broke apart. Sam refused to live in Home Town after his cousin's death, probably because of me, though he grudgingly agreed to stay a part of the wider community. He took seven friends and built Ridgeline camp in the western heights, as far from Home Town as you could get. The next day Ethan, Charlie, and Spencer hauled a portable shelter down to a cave system we'd discovered close to the water, and never came back. Exasperated, I put them in charge of our boats to maintain a connection.

The worst blow came the following week. Corbin announced he intended to establish a farming colony away from the island completely. He promised to build a permanent settlement on the only other habitable landmass we'd discovered, a forested peninsula lurking a full day south across the sea. Nine more people, gone.

The last defection hurt most. Tack sucker-punched me by joining Corbin's team.

I wasn't over it.

Still, yesterday the number of classmates under my direct authority in Home Town had been forty-five, if I counted Sarah's group in the silo. Now it was thirty-six. I could barely wrap my head around the loss.

Home Town—Six months and kicking!

Half the class, gone. Thirteen dead. Only *twenty people* were still rostered in the village at the moment, where I was supposed to be in charge. I'd let class unity slip through my fingers. If Noah hadn't constantly traveled from one camp to another, keeping everyone in touch by more than just radio, we'd have fallen apart completely. As it was, things were balanced on a knife's edge.

The door creaked as Sarah Harden walked into the lodge. My skin bristled. I'd successfully avoided a face-to-face meeting with her for weeks.

"Thought I'd find you here." She moved to a folding chair and sat, crossing one athletic leg over the other. Her blond hair was tied back in a lazy ponytail, which only made her more attractive. Sarah was one of those rare people who looked better the less effort she put into it.

"This *is* where we meet." I took a seat across from her, my shoulders remaining stubbornly rigid. Something about Sarah always made me feel like I was being judged. Being judged, and coming up short. I waved a hand at the now-empty table. "Someone made a cake for the town's half birthday, but I got rid of it."

Sarah snorted. "This group needs a few lessons in tact."

"How are the other girls? Did you get them settled somewhere?"

"Yes. There are spare cabins."

I winced. Survivors of one disaster replacing victims of another. What a nightmare. With a sinking feeling it occurred to me that Sarah would almost surely stay in the village now, too.

"I'm glad you're okay," I said, fairly certain I meant it. "Is Alice good?"

She nodded tersely, but I could see that her relief ran deep. Alice Cho and Sarah had been living together since the Program. They'd established the colony of basement-dwellers who valued concrete walls and ceilings above everything else.

Sarah leaned forward, and it took a deliberate effort for me not to pull back. "We're in trouble, Wilder. The cave-ins completely sealed off the silo." She tapped the tabletop as she spoke. "Roof hatch? Collapsed. Front door? Demolished. And I was there when the back tunnel failed. We can't get inside from any direction, and almost everything we need to stay alive is stored in those alcoves."

I swallowed. Eased back and crossed my arms. "We have a lot stockpiled in the village. We'll just have to make do until we unblock the entrance. It'll take time, but—"

"It won't work," Sarah interrupted. "I was *inside*, remember? I got a look at the shaft through a camera feed. The cave-in scraped everything off the walls. The supply crates are still in their alcoves, but there's no way to reach them." She ticked off three fingers. "Catwalks. Ladder. Miner's cage. All destroyed. And the command center was crushed by the avalanche."

She paused, sucking her teeth. No doubt remembering friends who'd died in the disaster. But the moment passed quickly. Sarah didn't waste time on sentiment.

She cleared her throat. "There are cracks along the outside of the silo, too. I'd bet that the lab complex is still intact—it's

30

the most heavily fortified section of the whole bunker—but there's no way to reach it now, either." Sarah sat back with a huff, frustration bleeding into her voice for the first time. "We just lost the source of our power, fuel, food, heavy equipment, and computing ability. *Poof.* Gone."

I tried not to let her analysis crush me. Sarah was brilliant, but I was in charge. I had to think of positive steps.

"These are simply problems to solve," I said, putting my hands in my lap so they wouldn't shake. "First, we conduct an inventory. The fires destroyed a lot, but not everything. Then we find a way into the silo. Once we do that, we can figure out how to get things out. It's not impossible, Sarah, just hard. We can do hard."

Sarah's blue eyes locked onto mine. She didn't say anything. In a flash, I realized she was barely keeping it together. Sarah had lost five friends in a heartbeat, people she'd been living with for months in close quarters. Most of the girls who'd elected to stay underground had been on the cheerleading squad with her back in school. The tiny sliver of human empathy Sarah possessed must've been ravaged by their deaths.

"Okay," she said quietly. "You may be right." Sarah rubbed both palms on her jeans, then resumed speaking in her typical annoyed tone. "Where are the others, anyway? This meeting might be pointless, but it's a form to be observed. Not that I care what any of the boys have to say. How much better would things be if we just told everyone what to do?"

I snorted. But was also secretly pleased by the "we." After everything, I still craved her approval.

Sarah rose and took the chair next to mine. My hackles shot

up. I might want her respect, but I never wanted her in my personal space.

She glanced at the door, then spoke in a low voice. "There's something else you should know. The cave-in—it didn't feel natural." Sarah shook her head, squinting down at the floor. "I keep going over the sounds in my head. The *sequence*. It doesn't add up. And why would a super-bunker built to survive the end of the world suddenly fail during a thunderstorm?"

"That was a nasty storm, Sarah. Plus, what else could've caused it?" Then my eyebrows shot up. "You're not suggesting what I think you are?"

"I don't trust what happened yesterday," she said firmly. "Or everyone in our class. I think something's up. There are things you should know that—"

The door opened and Derrick ducked into the lodge, followed by Noah and Sam Oatman. Sarah pulled back from me and slid a few seats away. Whatever she'd intended to say would have to wait.

My eyes met Noah's, and warmth surged through me. I wanted to bury myself in his arms. He'd been gone for the worst night of my life, and I'd had no one else to lean on. Tack was away on his fool's errand, and I wasn't really close with any of the others, except maybe Derrick. I'd felt Noah's lack intensely, but now wasn't the time. Instead, I gave him a quick hug and let him brush my cheek with a kiss. It was enough, for now.

"Where's Ethan?" Sarah said.

Derrick dropped a shoulder bag on the table and sat with a noisy exhale. "Not coming. I got him on the radio and he said, and I quote, 'Not my problem.' Selfish prick. I doubt Charlie or

Spencer show up, either. The Fire Lake cavemen appear to be sitting this one out."

I tried not to let my disappointment show. Ethan enjoyed being difficult, but usually his curiosity got the best of him. Why wasn't he interested in such an important meeting?

Then I went cold. Sarah's suspicions danced inside my head.

Ethan ran our boats to the Outpost from his subterranean lair, giving him a decent-sized responsibility in the wider scheme. I'd hoped that would satisfy him, but maybe not. I glanced at Sarah, but her poker face was back in place. Was this what she'd been hinting at?

"*I* came." Sam was stocky and muscular, with intense, dark brown eyes. I hadn't seen him smile since his cousin died, and today was no exception. "Ridgeline camp sent me to speak for it." As if we didn't know. He sat a bit away from everyone and folded his arms.

"Thanks for coming," I said, with all the earnestness I could muster.

He nodded perfunctorily. It was the best I could hope for.

Noah sat next to Derrick, across from me. In meetings we tried not to show any favoritism toward each other. Which was stupid, but we did it anyway. "There's another problem," he said, face sour. "We can't reach the Outpost."

I stiffened, thinking of Tack. "What do you mean?"

"There's no answer on the radio. Home Town's big antenna is down, but Akio was able to reach Charlie in the caves on a handheld, and he bounced a signal over to the Outpost. Charlie says everything is working on our end and they should be receiving our calls. But no one's picking up."

I sat back, thinking. "It must not be getting through."

"Charlie knows more about AV equipment than the rest of us put together," Derrick said. "If he says it's working, I believe him. Maybe their tech was knocked out by the storm?"

"I don't like it," Sarah said. "Not with . . . everything else."

I felt a pulse of pure frustration. More loose strands, even as I tried to stitch things back together. I dug fingernails into my palm. *Handle one thing at a time.* "We'll just keep trying them," I said. "But our top priority is to figure out a way back into the silo. When we speak to the group later, there needs to be a firm consensus ab—"

The door flew open and Rachel Stein stormed in, her long black hair swirling. I held back a sigh, but only barely. Out of everyone in camp, I got along with her the least. She held me personally responsible for everything that happened to our class during Project Nemesis, ignoring the fact that we'd all have been fried to a crisp over a million years ago without it.

Rachel crossed her arms, glaring with dark eyes in stark contrast to her pale skin. "I have a message for the overlords," she said acidly, her mouth crinkling in a petty smirk.

"Out with it," Sarah snapped.

Rachel straightened as if Tasered, crimson splotches coloring her cheeks. She might think she was the center of the universe, but even a black hole stepped lightly around Sarah.

"Leighton and Ferris are down by the lake. They say something's wrong with it."

My nose scrunched. "Wrong with it? What does that mean?" Both boys lived in Home Town, but neither ever volunteered to help much.

Rachel glowered at me, as if to reassert her importance. "I have no idea, Melinda. I was sent like an errand girl to fetch you."

"They want us to come there?" Noah looked at me. "That sounds serious."

Sam rose and headed toward the door. "Let's go. They wouldn't bother us for nothing."

I glanced at Sarah, who nodded slightly. The rest of us filed out after Sam, leaving Rachel behind to nurse her grievances. It was a ten-minute walk to the lakeshore. There we found a group of classmates gathered in a knot and staring at the water.

I strode to Leighton's side. Our former class president was shielding his eyes as he peered at the shallows, his curly blond hair swaying in the breeze. Noticing me, he pointed to an islet in the lake no more than a dozen yards from where we stood. "Look! Do you see?"

Several yards of darker mud were exposed on its bank. "What? The silt?"

"The waterline. It's dropping fast. The level is down another foot since we sent Rachel."

I rubbed the back of my neck. "How is that possible? Rainwater's been pouring in from the hills all day."

Leighton ran a hand over his face. "Min, the surface is *ten feet* lower than earlier this morning. That's not natural. It's . . . You can't . . . This is a big freaking lake!"

Great. What did it mean? I had enough problems already, and now even the island was turning on me.

The ground beneath my feet bucked suddenly. Began to vibrate.

I glanced down, then at a wide-eyed Noah beside me. His

mouth opened, but to say what I'd never know.

Air bubbles sizzled from the lake.

I watched in astonishment as the water began to swirl.

"Oh my God," Leighton whispered. "Oh no."

I gripped his forearm, my eyes never straying from the gathering whirlpool. "The water's running out!"

"But how?" Leighton dug his fingers into his scalp. "Running where?"

"It's *draining*." I felt the blood leach from my face. "Something just pulled the plug on Fire Lake."

4

NOAH

My mouth hung open.

I stood next to Min and watched the disaster unfold. The sun dipped in the western sky as the water circled, frothed, and disappeared into its own depths. A few people left to check on other things, but Min and I stood like statues, unable to move an inch. By dinnertime it was all over.

Fire Lake was gone. And we were in big, big trouble.

Eventually, I felt a hand on my shoulder. Derrick. He nudged Min as well, and she turned as if waking from a dream. Neither of us had spoken in an hour, our tongues stolen along with all that liquid. The magnitude of what had just occurred was hard for me to grasp.

"The lake's cashed," Derrick said matter-of-factly. "That's so bad I don't even want to discuss it. But the good news is, Akio and I checked the catch pond and it's full. So we've got *some* water, just not . . . you know . . . a lake."

I blinked. Nodded. "Okay. But where did it all go?"

"That's the bad news." Derrick chuckled without humor. "You're not going to believe it."

"Tell me," Min said.

"Somehow, a lot drained into the silo." Derrick sighed and rubbed his eyes. "Zach and Leah were up by the smashed tunnel, hauling rocks, when sludge started seeping from where we've been digging. Then a whole stream bubbled out through the cracks and down the hill. Which means the entire shaft below door level must be flooded."

"Which means the alcoves are underwater." Min squeezed her eyes shut. "All our supplies, ruined."

I wrapped her in a hug, but couldn't offer any real solace. The silo had been our storehouse, holding everything that separated us from an honest-to-God pioneer settlement. The cave-ins were tragic and horrible, but I'd felt sure we could dig back inside eventually, and recover our gear. Now? Game over.

"We still have a lot in the storage buildings," Min said quietly, chewing her lip. "And some of the things in there can survive being submerged."

"Maybe," Derrick conceded, but he kicked at a mound of loose pebbles. "But not dehydrated food, not seed crates, and not most machines. Anything we could eat, grow, or plug in is probably toast, and that's the stuff that matters."

"The MegaCom!" I blurted, then spat a series of four-letter words. "That equipment won't survive a flood."

We all fell silent. We'd survived for millennia as lines of code inside the supercomputer, until it regenerated us back into living bodies using lab machines. The MegaCom had been our entire universe, and still ran the nuclear power plant and life support systems that kept the silo functional. It was our ultimate fail-safe.

My breathing quickened. Our last link to advanced human civilization was likely dead and dust. Without it, we were reduced to highly educated cave people with some fancy tools. I felt like lying down in the mud.

Finally, Min cleared her throat. "Sarah said she sealed the lab complex." Her eyebrows rose hopefully. "If she closed the blast doors, they should be airtight. The MegaCom might be okay even under all that water."

Derrick scratched his dark, stubbly chin. "All right. Say we dig in and drain enough water to reach some goodies. We can probably salvage the building supplies and camping stuff. Maybe even a few vehicles. But what about food, you guys? We knew eventually we'd have to farm, but that day is *right now*, and the seeds are probably ruined."

Min started, her eyes darting to meet mine. "Not all of them."

"The Outpost." I actually snapped my fingers. "Corbin ferried dozens of crates across when they found arable soil."

Derrick winced as if in physical pain. "I only gave them a limited supply. We thought the silo was the safest place in the world, so I didn't want to risk moving too much without seeing results first. And now we're screwed."

The Outpost was our only true colony. Corbin O'Brien and his summer-camp crew from the Program now occupied a narrow plateau roughly a day's motor away. No one was sure if it was another island or the edge of something bigger, but Corbin didn't care. Scouts had found better dirt there, and he wanted to grow things.

Fire Lake Island had the silo and its supplies, but no good farmland. For some reason crops wouldn't take hold, not even around the lake. Which was maddening, given the healthy forest and other nonedible plants blanketing the island. It meant that one day we'd all have to move away, but few were ready to abandon our only source of modern technology.

Now, however...

"Just hold on." I chewed my thumb as ideas began slotting into place. "First, we have decent food stores in Home Town and at Ridgeline, and everything else ready-to-eat was inside the lab complex with Sarah, so it might be fine. Second, some of the seed crates could be waterproof. I don't know how we'll get to them, but we can try. It's not a guaranteed loss. Third, we can radio the Outpost and see if they're growing crops yet. Maybe Corbin's ahead of the game already, and hasn't bothered to tell us."

"Except they aren't answering," Derrick pointed out. "Which is now officially suspicious as hell."

Min's expression clouded. I thought of what Sarah said to me after the back tunnel collapsed. Had she spoken to Min as well? In all the craziness, I hadn't had a moment alone with either of them since getting back to the village.

"The storm must've smacked them, too," I said. "They could've lost their antenna, maybe even their boats."

Derrick crossed his arms. "We lose contact with the Outpost

on the same day the silo goes down? Tell me that's not shady as hell. They're supposed to stay in regular communication, but nobody's shown up here with a report, and who knows *what* Tack is doing."

Tack had gone to live with Corbin's team, but had zero interest in farming. He wanted to explore whatever else was out there. He also wanted away from the cabin Min and I shared, even though they'd been best friends before Nemesis. Tack had made clear during the Program that he wanted more than that. When Min chose me, it cut him deep. So deep that he'd packed up and left for the wilds instead.

I knew Min hated how things had played out, and missed him terribly, but there was no one alive more stubborn than Thomas Russo. He'd never even come back to visit. Not once.

Real talk: *I* didn't miss him too much.

"We have to get in touch somehow," Min said. "Even if just to make sure they're okay."

Derrick nodded. "We need the Outpost more than ever now. We're not going to starve this month or anything, but the clock's started. We're gonna have to grow crops to survive."

Tension radiated from Min's slender frame. "It's still too risky to relocate lots of people. We don't know what's out there, and can't lose any more—"

She cut off abruptly. I searched for something helpful to say.

Min worried constantly about how we'd survive in the long run, but that had always been a problem for later. *After* we got the basics organized. Now the timetable had accelerated radically, and we weren't even close to ready. She'd make herself sick stressing about how to keep everyone safe.

I was still trying to come up with a good first step when Sarah appeared from the woods. For some reason I felt guilty, like we'd been caught doing something naughty. Sarah always made me feel that way.

She stepped confidently into our circle. "Impromptu council? I assume you're planning a scuba expedition."

"So you heard." Then I stopped short. "We don't actually *have* scuba gear, do we?"

Derrick barked a laugh. "Black Suit didn't think of everything."

I hid a shiver, thinking of my longtime executioner. We'd left him inside the Program, but I still had nightmares about the man who'd stalked me on my birthdays, apologizing softly each time he murdered me.

Sarah failed to see the humor. "So what's the plan? Because right now it appears to be staring at the new hole in the center of our island. And in case you haven't noticed, there's another storm moving in. It looks as bad as the last one."

My gaze darted to the clouds. I *hadn't* noticed, but she was right—a shimmering purple bruise writhed in the eastern sky. I glanced at Min, saw her teeth grind as she glared at the maelstrom. Disturbingly, she looked to Sarah. I wanted to nudge her out of whatever funk she'd fallen into, but didn't want Sarah to see.

Sarah, however, missed nothing. "Since it's clear *no one's* in charge at the moment, I'll keep this simple. I'll coordinate the silo dig. That's my bedroom down there, and I left my favorite sweater behind. Plus I'm the best at actually doing things. Derrick, you come with me. Min, go see what needs to be done in the village. It's a mess. Noah, be useful and check in with

Sam. Then inventory everything we have, anywhere on this island."

I glanced at Min, whose head was bowed. *Say something.* But she merely nodded and began trudging up the path. I hurried after her, a pit opening in my stomach.

There'd been three elections since the Program ended, and Min had been unanimously chosen in the first two, running unopposed. Then she'd won a tense third vote against write-ins for Sam, Ethan, and others immediately after the accident. But regardless of her weakening support, Min was still in charge.

Sarah had never offered herself as a candidate, yet here she was, dishing out orders after the situation went to crap. Did she want to run things? Was she already? Derrick hadn't spoken out just now, and neither had I.

I caught up to Min but couldn't find the right words to express my concern. We climbed a small hill in silence. The approaching storm was more obvious here, spreading out in a flickering disc of coiled energy. There was nothing like these in the old world. This one looked hungry. Eager to finish the job its twin had started.

Min stared at the unsettled horizon. She hadn't spoken since Sarah appeared, and I was starting to worry. "She doesn't know everything," I began, but a sharp shake of Min's head stopped me cold.

"She knows better than me. Sarah's right. I sat there staring at a problem while she was figuring out solutions. I'm screwing up. When things are okay, I feel like I can handle the responsibility, but the minute something goes bad . . ." Her shoulders shook, and I realized she was crying. I reached out and gently eased her close. She melted into my side. "Nine more people, Noah. And I couldn't do anything."

I moved to stand in front of her, forcing her eyes to meet mine. "Last night was a superstorm like none we've ever seen. You're not responsible for acts of God."

She pulled away, pawing stray hairs from her face. "Then who is? Sarah's able to operate in a crisis. She thrives in them."

"Sarah's also a sociopath," I joked, trying to lighten the mood. "No one trusts her. She actively tried to kill everyone inside the Program, and that's not something people have forgotten."

Thunder boomed in the distance. The hairs on my arms danced.

Min seemed to come out of her fog. "I'm being petty. Her instructions make sense. I'll check on the cabins and make sure everyone is settled for the storm. You find Sam and figure out what he's thinking. They took a lot of stuff up to Ridgeline, and we didn't keep great records. Maybe he thought further ahead than I did. And I'll tell you later what Sarah said to me about the cave-ins. It's . . . weird."

I nodded. I wanted to tell *her* what Sarah had said outside the back tunnel, but thought better of it. Min seemed back on her game. I didn't want to knock her off it with her rival's paranoid theories. "I'll see you tonight."

She stepped close and our lips met. A whole new kind of electricity swarmed my body, but Min slipped away and hurried toward the village. I blew out a sigh in disappointment, then took a different path. Sam and his crew had set up near the woods beyond the creek. When I arrived, I was distressed to see them packing their things.

Sam was kneeling beside Floyd and Hamza as they folded

a field tent. Floyd spotted me first and gave a head nod, while Hamza went as far as to smile. But Sam ignored me.

"Need help getting settled in town?" I offered. "Sheltering in cabins is the right call."

Sam rose, and our eyes met. There was no friendliness in his gaze. There hadn't been since his cousin died.

We'd sent Carl and three others to scout the northern bluffs. Carl had radioed back that the weather was getting bad, and he thought the mission was pointless—there was nothing up there but shattered rock. But we didn't have a good map of that area yet, so Min told him to finish the job. Minutes later a cliff crumbled beneath their feet, dropping Carl, Zoë, Trent, and Jun Son into the sea. We never found their bodies.

Sam spoke before I could. "If we leave now, we'll beat the weather."

I shifted, one hand tugging the back of my neck. "Safer to wait. Ride out the storm with us. Plus, we might need your help digging out the silo. You guys need the stuff in there as much as we do."

Sam shook his head. "That's all gone."

My gaze slid to Floyd, whose mouth was a tight line. Hamza frowned down at nothing, making curlicues in the dirt with his foot. The other Ridgeliners kept packing their gear. Greg. Jacob. Kharisma. Maggie and Cenisa. But I could tell they were all listening.

"Sam, come on." I stepped closer, trying to get him to understand. "For a few nights at least, we need all hands on deck. Big decisions are coming. We have to figure out how we're going to survive."

"Make whatever decisions you want," Sam said bitterly. "You guys always do. We both know I only agreed to stay connected to Home Town because the village controlled all the supplies. But now you've lost them, and we have our own problems. I can't waste time in another stupid council that won't help my crew."

"We *lost* them?" I shot back, my anger rising to match his. "Sam, the mountain caved in. Give me a damn break."

Sam waved a dismissive hand. "Doesn't matter. Done is done. We're going."

My jaw tightened. I bit back a furious retort. I had to make him see reason. "Then I'm going with you."

Sam's dark eyes bored into me. "You weren't invited, Noah."

"Are you quitting the group or not?" I demanded. "Make the call right now. Because we *will* dig into the silo, and we *will* figure out how to salvage what's down there. If you bail like this, you forfeit a right to any of it. Is that what you want?"

Sam slammed the bag in his hands to the ground. He seemed ready to trade punches, and I can't say I didn't welcome the idea. The frustrations of the past twenty-four hours were bubbling up inside me, and the savage release of a fight had enormous appeal. It wasn't right, but there it was anyway.

"Fine," Sam growled. "Cut us off. Or follow me like a puppy, Noah. I don't care."

He picked up his bag and strode into the forest, ignoring the path and everyone around us. The other Ridgeliners began hefting their things to follow. I felt the anger drain out of me. Sam and I had never been close, but we'd survived the Program together. I'd trusted him with my life more than once, and he'd always come through. We couldn't leave things like this.

I jogged into the woods, slipping on wet pine needles as I tried to pick up his trail. The sun dipped behind the peaks and I quickly lost my way, cursing my impulsive nature. It'd be perfect for me to get lost like a dope and miss him completely.

Shielding my face with one hand, I headed in the general direction of the creek. Worst case, I'd follow it up the mountain. But my route intersected a deep, dark gully and I got turned around trying to maneuver past the gap. I heard babbling water to my left and angled toward it.

My next step met nothing. I plunged forward, tumbling downhill until my side slammed into the base of an oak tree.

"*Oof.*" My ribs were on fire and a gash had opened on my arm. "Ouch."

Branches snapped above me. A voice called down. "Jesus, Noah. That you?"

"Yes." I wheezed, then spat. "Halp."

Snark tinged Sam's voice. "Hold on, Magellan. I'll get Floyd. We'll drag your sorry ass out." A flashlight blazed to life, then dropped to land near my legs.

I was about to yell something clever back at him—which, in truth, I hadn't worked out yet—when my eyes began to adjust. I was at the bottom of an overgrown ditch, maybe a dried-out creek bed. Odd shapes poked up in the gloom. I was lucky I hadn't broken my neck.

I twisted and grabbed the flashlight, then swung its beam in a slow arc, halting on something large across from me. Eyes widening, I realized it was a bundle of green fabric. I crawled over to investigate and found a dozen more just like it, stacked in a pile next to a wooden crate half covered by a beige tarp. Its side was labeled PROJECT NEMESIS.

I scrambled into a crouch, questions dogpiling inside my head. What was this stuff? How'd it get here? Why had someone hidden it at the bottom of a gully?

I shoved off the tarp. The crate had been pried open before, and its lid came loose with a sharp tug. I aimed the light inside.

A low whistle escaped my lips.

I was staring into a half-empty box of explosives.

5

MIN

I pressed an ice pack to Noah's forehead.

He'd tried to stop me from using one, grumbling that we didn't have many left to spare, but the ugly knot above his temple needed treatment. Plus, it gave me something to do. Something to think about other than the catastrophe Noah had discovered at the bottom of that gully, and how it might connect to Sarah's warning.

"How many crates were there?" I asked, applying pressure to the bump. Purple splotches were already forming around its center. It'd be one hell of a bruise.

Noah winced, craning his head away like a little boy. "Seven big boxes. All from the ordinance alcove. Even worse, five of them were empty."

"I think I know why."

Noah looked up at me, and his expression wasn't fully surprised. But before I could say more, the door to the medical cabin opened and Sarah walked in out of the night, followed by Sam and Derrick. Our fractured little emergency government, although only Noah, Derrick, and I had been elected. Ethan was still a no-show, and the Outpost remained offline. Whatever hard decisions had to be made, the people in this room would make them. That's how quickly democracy can break down.

Derrick slumped into a folding chair and propped his head with an elbow on one knee. He released a weary sigh. Noah leaned back on the examination bench. I sat down next to him, then kicked myself for giving up the high ground.

"Let's get to the point," Sarah said, hands on her hips. "*Someone*—and that person might be in this cabin right now—has been stealing from the group. And not chocolate bars or rain tarps. They took explosives to use against the rest of us."

My blood pressure spiked. Sarah had laid it out so bluntly, I was taken aback. I opted for a less aggressive stance. "Someone took things they shouldn't have, yes. And that's very disturbing. But we don't know *why*, so I don't think we should jump to the worst-case scenario right away."

Sarah sneered at me, and my eyes dropped. She could be as disgusted as she wanted, but she had no proof. She took a seat next to Derrick and closed her eyes briefly, then gave me a look just short of contempt. "*Always* plan for the worst-case scenario, Melinda. That way you'll never be surprised."

"Can we focus on the problem?" Derrick said irritably. "Someone stole a whole bunch of C4, and we don't know why.

But I *do* know that the stuff missing from those crates isn't anywhere in Home Town. Akio and I checked every tent and building left standing. The explosives aren't here. Whoever took the gear stashed it somewhere else on the island."

Sam had remained standing with his arms crossed. "If you have something to say, say it."

Derrick rose to his full towering height. Sam could intimidate a lot of people, but Derrick wasn't one of them. "Whatcha got up there at Ridgeline, Oatman? Only Noah ever visits, and he's no snoop. Your people's tents were closest to that gully, and you were leaving in a hurry just now."

Sam didn't blink. "If you have something to say, say it."

"Did you guys steal that stuff or not?" Derrick demanded.

"No."

Derrick held Sam's eye a moment longer, then shrugged. "Okay, then. And *shit*. Because if you didn't take it, we've got bigger problems."

I shifted in my seat, surprised Derrick had folded so quickly. I glanced at Noah, but he was nodding to himself. He noticed my attention and I flared an eyebrow, flicking my gaze to Sam, whom I abruptly realized was watching me.

Noah spoke aloud. "If Sam says he didn't take it, I believe him. He's not a liar."

I chewed the inside of my cheek, then exhaled through my nose. Nodded slowly. I couldn't remember Sam ever lying to me about anything, and we'd been through some hard times. But I also agreed wholeheartedly with Derrick—if Ridgeline didn't steal the explosives, then there were no obvious culprits. Which meant a plot. Which meant serious trouble.

Sarah, Sarah, Sarah. Right again.

Sam seemed to relax a fraction. A bit of thaw crept into his voice. "I promise you guys it wasn't anyone in my camp. We're close. We decide everything together, as a group. No secrets. No factions."

Sarah rocketed forward in her seat, a hand flying up in frustration. "*Of course* they didn't steal it! Why would they leave the evidence in a gully five minutes from here rather than taking it all home? Honestly, sometimes I can't believe you guys survived the Program."

Derrick fired a false grin in her direction. "Sarah, do shut up. Or rather, say something useful instead of insulting us."

Sarah snorted. "FINE. Here's a news flash, team: the missing explosives aren't in those crates because they're gone. As in, *they were exploded*."

Derrick shot to his feet again. Sam let out an astonished grunt.

My pulse skyrocketed. Sarah was going there. "You don't know that," I said quickly.

She cocked her head, a cruel smile curling her lips. "Having trouble with the ugly truth?"

Noah dropped the ice pack on the bench beside him, his entire body rigid. "Let's just put all the cards out there. You think the silo was *bombed* during the storm. But how could that possibly happen?"

I glanced at Noah in surprise. Had Sarah spoken to him? Why hadn't he said anything? I felt a spark of anger that he'd kept a secret from me, though admittedly that was unfair, since I hadn't shared with him yet either. He noticed me looking and blushed, then mouthed the word *later*. I gritted my teeth but nodded.

Sarah gave the room a slow, mocking clap. "Way to catch up, everyone. The silo *was* attacked. And not only the roof collapse—the back tunnel got hit too, I'm sure of it." She glanced at Noah. "You were there. Did that feel like a natural cave-in?"

"Just hold up!" Derrick glowered down at Sarah from all of his six-plus feet. "You're saying someone deliberately caved in our supply warehouse, then sealed off every possible way inside? That's . . . nuts! That's *stupid*. Why would anyone implode their own pantry?"

"Don't miss the point!" Sarah rose herself, and somehow seemed to loom over him. "Whoever did this murdered five people." Her voice quivered with fury. "They must've planned it for weeks, waiting for the perfect cover. They knew the silo well enough to put the charges in the right places, and they were able to set them off remotely when the storm hit. As a final move, they sealed the back door. Who knows, maybe they even cracked the lake, too."

My head wagged slowly, unnerved by her cold logic. "Who would do something like that? Who would kill five classmates and wipe out their own safety net? Now we're stuck on a prehistoric planet with almost nothing to help us survive. No matter what grudges people might hold, that makes zero sense. It's like cutting your own throat."

"Min's right," Sam said. "I don't buy it. No one's that suicidal."

Sarah sat down again in her chair. Her head flopped back, and she stared at the ceiling, as if considering. Finally, she leaned forward. "You guys are only thinking about people living on this island."

Noah started. I felt an icy tingle slither along my spine. "Who, *Toby*?" I said. "You think the Lost Boys did this? After all this time missing, and for what? Pure spite?"

Sarah shrugged. "We don't share with them, and they didn't leave happy."

That quieted the room. Toby and his friends had ghosted right after we lost Carl's scout team. Out of everyone in the class, they'd struggled most with life on New Earth. People hadn't forgotten how savage Toby had been inside the Program, or who'd backed his power trip. They'd mostly kept to themselves around camp, doing the bare minimum. I hadn't been all that surprised when they cut out—frankly, I'd expected them to cause trouble instead. Their disappearance was creepy, but at least they hadn't attempted something worse.

Of course, here was Sarah saying they'd done exactly that.

Derrick rubbed a hand over his long face. "Okay. Let's play it out. I get why they might steal stuff, and I could even see them attacking the silo to take it over—me and Noah have had a plan for that since they bailed. But why would those guys want to destroy it?"

"Maybe what they want isn't destroyed." Noah was squinting at nothing, as if testing a theory in his head. "The alcoves are underwater, but we don't know what happened to the lab complex. It's built to withstand almost anything, and most of our ready food is stored in there. Maybe they just want to deny it to us, in hopes they can get it later? Also, whoever did this might not have actually wanted to kill people. They could've assumed the living quarters were safe during the first blasts, and the back tunnel didn't collapse until after the evacuation."

Sarah pursed her lips. "That's . . . interesting."

Sam coughed, drawing everyone's attention. "This is crazy. No one's seen those guys since they stole a boat. Personally, I think they're all dead. The storms never stop coming, and I swear there's more than just fish in the deeper water. Plus, there's nothing else out there, and they've been gone for months. Why should we suddenly believe that Toby and his team of losers not only survived, but were also able to infiltrate the silo, rob it, and then blow it up unseen? It's too much."

"Toby's alive."

My head whipped to Sarah. "What? How do you know?"

Her jaw tightened, but she didn't avoid my gaze. "Because I spoke to him."

The chill in my spine converted to fire. Before I knew it, I was on my feet. Noah rose beside me, and soon everyone was standing but her.

"What the hell, Sarah?" Derrick took a deep breath, squeezing the bridge of his nose. "Tell me that was a joke."

Sarah didn't even look abashed. She gave a full-bodied shrug. "He confronted me two weeks ago. I wanted to think about it some before sharing."

"You liked having this over us, you mean," Derrick spat. "Something you knew that we didn't. Well congrats. If you're right, you got five people killed so you could feel superior."

Sarah's cheeks flushed scarlet. "There wasn't much to tell. He showed up in the lab complex one day while everyone else was topside. I was stunned to see him, but he didn't say anything interesting."

"Toby *being alive* is interesting," Sam growled.

I finally found my voice. "What happened to those guys has been preying on everyone's mind since the moment they disappeared. Yet you knew Toby was not only alive, but actively roaming the island, and said nothing?"

Sarah looked away, seemed troubled for the first time. "It happened fast, okay? He was there and then gone. I didn't even see which way he left." Her voice dropped. "We only spoke for like two minutes. He wanted to know who all was living down there."

"Why would he care about that?" Noah asked.

"I don't know," Sarah said. "That's why I'm suspicious now. The cave-ins demolished every way into or out of the silo, and the flood sealed the shaft. But the lab complex—the place Toby was curious about—is probably undamaged. I don't think that's a coincidence."

"We need to find them." Derrick began pacing the cabin, his long stride making for very short circuits. "There aren't many places six jackasses with poor self-discipline can hide on this rock. Now that we know they're here, we should be—"

"They're not here," Sarah interrupted. Derrick paused, then just looked at her. "I can't explain it better than this," she continued, "but I got the impression Toby wasn't hiding around the corner. I think they have a base somewhere else. Which is interesting all by itself."

Someone squeezed my shoulder. Noah. *The Outpost*, he mouthed.

My eyes widened. The silence coming from there became considerably more ominous.

Tack. He doesn't know any of this.

Sam was still watching Sarah. "You know an awful lot about what Toby might be doing."

Sarah met his gaze squarely. "Toby hates me as much as any of you." She smirked. "Except maybe Min. You want the truth, Sam? From the moment he showed up until the moment he left, I was terrified. I was alone down there. If I could push a button and flush him into a toilet, I would. All of them. Wild dogs have to be put down."

Sam held her eye, and an electric tension filled the room. "So what do we do?" he said finally.

I knew immediately. "We contact the Outpost. We haven't heard anything since the storm, and if Toby's team really did hit us, then—"

"—he might do the same to them," Noah finished. "Maybe already did." He straightened as if he'd made a decision. "I'm going to check on those guys. It's been too long since I went anyway, and we need to find out about their stores."

My heart leapt into my throat. "Noah, no. We'll get the radio working."

He flashed the private smile he reserved for me, but I knew I wouldn't like his next words. "Our radio is working, Min. It's the other end that isn't picking up. Going in person is the only way to be sure."

Derrick sat back and tugged his pants. "You could be doing exactly what Toby wants. Sending people away to get picked off, or whatever."

Noah shrugged. "I'll go alone."

"The hell." Derrick waved off Noah's statement like a pesky fly. "I'll go with you."

"Me too." The words slipped out before I could consider them.

Surprisingly, Sam objected. "You can't go, Min. You're in charge here. You have to help rehab the village. Derrick, you should stay, too—people trust you. Noah can take some others with him. Whoever he wants, just not the whole leadership structure."

Noah was nodding. "He's right. I'll keep the group small. You guys should stay here and get this place back on its feet." He reached out and squeezed my hand. "I'll be back as soon as I can."

Derrick grunted sourly. "Take Akio at least, so you have someone with sense."

Noah laughed. "Done."

He looked back at me, and I felt empty inside. We'd be separated again. There was no way around it.

"Be careful," I whispered.

He flashed a rueful grin. "I always am, remember?"

6

NOAH

I got up before dawn.

We buried our dead an hour later.

The whole community turned out, wrapped in blankets to ward off the early morning chill. It didn't take an empath to sense that everyone was shaken.

The mood was somber, but with a frenzied edge. Last night Min and Derrick had informed the group about the theft and presented our plan to check in on the Outpost. Everyone had agreed, but I could feel anxiety on the wind.

It wasn't just our losses, although those were terrible enough. Someone had stolen from the group, which had previously been unthinkable. More than one nervous glance shot to the silo, our sanctuary and supply fortress now hopelessly out of reach. The sabotage rumors were spreading like wildfire.

Things were precariously balanced. I didn't envy the work Derrick and Min had to do.

Hector said a benediction, then we lowered the fallen into a line of hillside graves, dug beside the stone marker set as a memorial for the scout team lost months earlier. Those bodies had never been recovered.

Finally, it was time to go.

Leaving Min was hard, but I was the glue that connected the camps. It'd been that way since the accident. Someone really did have to go to the Outpost—we needed to know if the problem was bigger than just the silo. Who else was going to do it?

We'd had a last night together, wrapped in each other's arms, plotting scenarios and responses depending on what might happen to either of us. I'd held Min tightly, drowning myself in her presence. Her warmth. I didn't know how long I'd be gone, but I had this horrible sensation that important things were changing, and that we might not get another moment like this for a long time. I'd wanted to burrow into our blankets and never leave.

There was plenty to stress about. With Toby alive and on the loose, a boogeyman haunted the village. And though Min wouldn't say it, she was desperately worried about Tack. They might not speak anymore, but Min still cared for the trailer-park boy who'd been her only friend. She felt responsible for him being out there. Tack had left because he didn't want to watch Min and me be together. If something happened to him because of it, she'd never forgive herself.

Akio had agreed to join my expedition immediately and

suggested we bring Richie. After Jamie Cruz died in the fire, he'd become a zombie around camp. Those two had been together since inside the Program, just like Vonda and Finn. Akio thought getting Richie active might help him snap out of it. I wasn't so sure, but three was better than two, especially if we had to send someone back with a message. We'd just have to keep an eye on him.

It took less than an hour to pack, check the horizon to the east, and start down the path leading toward the caves. The Ocean Road, as we jokingly called it, ran west from Home Town before knifing south through a crack in the mountain ring, connecting with a series of switchbacks that descended to the hollows just above the waterline.

Ethan lived in the caves full-time. I had no idea why.

Thinking of Ethan made the knot in my stomach twist. He was difficult in the best of times, and I had no idea what he'd be like when we arrived. Sarah secretly chatting with Toby had me nervous about everyone. Had Toby reached out to Ethan, too? How many of my former adversaries were talking behind our backs?

The sun crested the peaks and the day warmed. We walked in silence—Akio as impassive as ever, Richie trudging along like he didn't care where we were going or if we ever got there. The lower half of the trail was a haphazard sequence of stone shelves angling along the outside of the cliffs. Halfway down, caverns sliced into the bedrock. Ethan camped in there with Charlie Bell and Spencer Coleman, tending our boats and operating the lift system, like a real job.

To be honest, having Ethan out of the village made people

more comfortable. Not everyone had put the Program's horrors behind them, despite Min's efforts. Ethan still caught stares when he ventured up for parts or supplies, so much so that he hadn't visited Home Town in weeks. I hadn't been totally surprised when he skipped the meeting yesterday.

Stepping onto the last ledge, my shoe slipped on a pile of loose scree. Akio's hand shot out to steady me. My heartbeat thudded in my ears as I watched tiny pebbles tumble into the sea. I licked my lips, then snapped off a grateful nod to Akio as he released me. I'd forgotten how much I hated making this trip, and we still had to get down to the water and cross the ocean, and whatever might live in it.

I swallowed, refusing to glance at the endless line of waves. There'd always been rumors of things in the sea. Anxious eyewitness claims, exchanged around the campfire. At least a dozen kids swore they'd seen huge *somethings* breach the surface, usually off in the distance, and always around dawn or dusk. Dumb stories, I always thought. Nothing more. The sun hits a cresting wave just right and people start screaming about sea monsters. It was nonsense. But my palms were sweating nonetheless.

Fifty feet farther along, we reached a slash in the cliff face. I stepped into a low grotto and exhaled. The fissure was long and tight, with a waist-high opening at the opposite end. I scuttled under the lip and into a larger cave.

Three ragged survival tents were set against the rear wall, facing a cold fire pit surrounded by camp chairs. Fishing gear was spread out across the ground. To our right, a wide gap had been sealed off with tarps. Straight ahead was another crack in the wall that led to the boat cavern. We ducked inside.

Ethan was hunched over the lift with his shirt off, a wire crimper in one hand. He looked up when we entered, regarding us with a frown before returning to the hulking machine. Charlie and Spence gave us matching head nods, which I returned. We were all on the same side now, in theory, but old wounds ran deep. I'd shot all three of these guys inside the Program, and they'd returned the favor.

Beyond the lift, yellow inflatable rescue vessels were stacked against the far wall. Each had its own motor and a weather shield. Getting all this equipment down here had been a real challenge, but in the early days it'd felt more like adventure than work. Now it felt like I was trespassing in someone's private garage. I reminded myself I didn't need permission to be there.

Ethan wiped his face with a towel, then dropped it to the stone floor. He grabbed a T-shirt off a set of plastic drawers and pulled it over his head. Sunlight seeped in from the open right side of the cavern. I knew the edge was sheer, with a clean drop to a tiny cove nestled within the island's outer wall. So long as the weather was reasonable, launching boats was relatively easy. These guys had mastered it.

"I'm guessing you need a ride?" Ethan strode toward me, big and blond, blue eyes as hard as the line of his jaw. He radiated an intensity that always made me uncomfortable. We'd been rivals even before Project Nemesis, but the months of trying to kill each other inside the MegaCom had twisted things into something unrecognizable. Ethan seemed to regard my very existence as a challenge. I sometimes wondered if he was all there anymore.

I cleared my throat. I had to be careful with what I said, but I wasn't going to lie.

"We can't reach the Outpost by radio. So we're going there to make sure everyone's okay."

Ethan turned and spat on the cavern floor. "Who took the C4?"

I tried not to let my shock register. Ethan already knew about the theft, which meant someone had brought him up to speed last night. But who? Certainly not Min or Sarah, and I doubted Sam and Derrick would've bothered. Did he have a spy in the village? Did it matter?

I had to say something. I opted for the simple truth. "We don't know. Sarah thinks the cave-ins were a deliberate series of detonations. I'm not sure, but the missing explosives obviously back her theory. Since we don't know what happened and suddenly can't reach Corbin or the others, someone has to check on them." I shrugged, waved a hand at Akio and Richie behind me. "We drew the short straws."

Ethan looked at Richie, who was staring vacantly out to sea. "Sorry about Jamie, man."

Richie blinked. Nodding slightly, he turned away.

Ethan swung back to me. "Feels like a trap, you know. The Outpost going dark right now. You sure you want to walk right into whatever's waiting out there?"

"Like I said. Short straw."

"You guys act like Home Town is one big happy family, but you shouldn't trust everyone." Ethan rubbed his face, leaving a dark smear on his cheek. "If the silo was sabotaged, someone up there knows all about it. Count on that."

I straightened. "Min and Derrick can handle things. Hell, *Sarah's* pissed off, and that's never good for anyone in her way."

Ethan stepped nose-to-nose with me. "What about the ocean? You ready to float beyond the shallows again, Livingston?" He clamped a hand onto my shoulder. "Because I've seen more than I want to under the waves, buddy boy. There are scarier things out there than Toby."

He was testing me. I didn't like it. Garbage stories about sea monsters, to see if I'd punk out? And why the crack about Toby? Nobody had mentioned his name in the sabotage rumors yet, at least not that I'd heard. Did Ethan know something we didn't? "It's a pirate's life for me," was all I said.

Ethan nodded firmly, dropping his hand. He barked over his shoulder at Spence and Charlie. "Get the launch ready. Boat three's in the best shape, I think. Load up gear for four and move it into position."

It took me a moment to catch up. "Four?"

Ethan grinned as he retrieved a heavy pack from the corner. "You think I'd miss this?"

My eyes widened. I shot a glance at Akio, who looked like he'd smelled something foul. Richie chuckled softly as he scuffed his sneaker on the ground.

"You don't have to come," I said awkwardly.

"Of course I do." Ethan helped his companions drag a yellow boat to the lift. For a moment I just stood there, blinking at them, then I lurched forward to help. Soon all five of us had maneuvered the scuffed and battered vessel into position. I worked like a robot, mind blank, unable to think of a way to prevent Ethan from joining us.

When push came to shove, I still didn't trust him. Who's to say *he* wasn't working with Toby? If an ambush was waiting for us, Ethan might very well be its architect. But I was supposed to go sailing with him anyway?

It took five minutes to hook up the lines. Ethan was the first to throw his bag inside. "It's simple," he said, crossing his arms and leaning back against the boat. "Something serious is going on, and I don't trust you village dopes to solve it. So that means I have to do it myself."

I looked to Akio, who shrugged. Richie wasn't paying attention. The decision was mine, but it wasn't a decision at all. Ethan ran these boats, and I couldn't stop him. I had to make the best of it.

"Okay then." I extended a hand. "We go together."

Ethan stared at my hand, seemed thrown for the first time since we'd entered his domain. He reached out slowly and shook it. I think we were both surprised he did.

"Better go now." Spence rubbed a pimply cheek, then pointed eastward, which was still mostly clear. "Window's open, but this has been a bad month. You don't want to be on the water when the lightning comes. And make sure you're not over the deep zone past sunset."

"Why not?" I asked. Akio was equally attentive.

Spence shivered. "Just don't be."

I glanced at Ethan, but he laughed and started rechecking the lines.

There was nothing left to discuss. We loaded our things beside Ethan's duffel and climbed aboard. Spence and Charlie swung the vessel to hang out over the edge. Twenty yards below us, the ocean rocked and churned, safe enough to descend into but nobody's idea of a picnic. My stomach lurched. I tried very hard not to lose my lunch.

Richie wasn't so lucky. He emptied his gut over the side as the motorized winch slowly lowered us toward the water.

"Not a good sign," Ethan joked, slapping Richie's back. "It's six hours to the Outpost and we'll hit some gnarly chop along the way. But you boys are scurvy sea dogs now!"

"Great," I muttered. Energized Ethan might be the most annoying version.

We hit the surf with a jarring thump. Ethan detached the lines, fired the motor, and steered us into open water. "You should know something," he said quietly, the smile vanishing from his lips.

"Yeah?"

"I meant what I said up there." He nodded at the rolling lines of white-green foam. "There *are* things lurking out here. We're as powerless now as inside the Program. I still feel like a pawn in a bigger game."

I didn't know what to say to that, preoccupied by the powerful ocean surrounding us. I felt the primal terror of being adrift over hidden depths of inky black water.

This trip could not be over fast enough.

7

MIN

I sat down on my bed and sighed.

My eyes strayed to the pile of blankets. I'd have given anything to have Noah there.

What a day.

The morning had begun with a funeral and got worse from there. My heart ached, remembering those limp forms being lowered into the ground. Then Noah left, and the remaining hours had been like herding cats. Derrick and I did everything we could to project positivity, but people were scared. Rumors of theft and sabotage were racing through the village, and suddenly everyone had a theory.

People now moved in tight-knit groups born straight out of the Program. I watched the soccer girls—Casey, Dakota, and Lauren—refuse to eat lunch within earshot of Ferris and Leighton. The Ridgeliners were traveling as a pack, casting suspicious glances at everyone, while some Home Towners wanted Sam's crew restricted to their borrowed buildings. And that was before we got to the cheerleaders, risen from the silo's nucleus. They sat woodenly on the sidelines and refused to help with anything.

I knew they'd lost friends, but their aloofness had been an issue even before this. Now? People wanted them barred from the mess tent until they started lending a hand. I wouldn't take things that far, but it was a problem that needed dealing with. *Add it to the pile.*

I'd asked Sam and Derrick to keep the Toby news to themselves, but it was bound to get out eventually. And when the others learned that Sarah had spoken with him and told no one, would they allow her to stay in the village? Should I? What would the group think when they found *I* knew about it, and did nothing?

I kicked my field desk, disturbing the papers on its surface. I hated keeping secrets, but it wasn't the right time for another bombshell. Throwing Toby into the mix seemed like asking for trouble. Plus, I *needed* Sarah. I'd keep it quiet for a few more days.

We'd lost seven suddenly irreplaceable cabins and three supply buildings. The village was a scorched, mud-soaked mess. We had to get our literal houses in order, and people were already on high alert after hearing about the stolen crates. Naming Toby was effectively pointless, and maybe even dangerous without proof he was connected to the missing explosives. Panic was the biggest threat we faced.

Right? God, I truly didn't know.

Anger and fear simmered just below the surface. The village felt like a powder keg. One false move by me—one thoughtless decision, or careless oversight—and we might have open warfare. It wouldn't be the first time.

With a piteous moan I'd never let another person hear, I slumped off the bed and began gathering papers into a stack. I placed them back on my desktop, then froze.

Next to my document box was a hand-drawn map of Fire Lake Island that Hector had made for me. In addition to topography, he'd also included markers we knew in the ocean, right up to the Outpost's location at the outer limit of our planetary knowledge.

Noah and I had gone over it last night, scrutinizing the map. Then I'd put it away at the bottom of my trunk of spare clothes. I knew I had, because I always kept it there. Because I *hated* that map. I hated how little we knew about the world. I hated that Tack was so far away at the Outpost. I hated not having a best friend anymore.

And. Yet.

Here the map was.

Back on my desk, where it had no business being.

My hands began to tremble. Pointlessly, I spun in a tight circle, but there was nowhere to hide in my tiny cabin.

I thought about the morning. Could Noah have dropped back by to check on something?

No. That wouldn't make sense. This drawing didn't have details like the tides or longitude and latitude, or anything that would help him navigate. It was a simple sketch. Nothing he'd need to refer to again before leaving. Plus I'd watched him disappear down the path to the caves. I'd have noticed if he'd come back for something. I was sure he hadn't.

Which meant someone else had been inside my cabin. And that someone went through my things.

Dark thoughts began spiraling inside my head. Toby. The cave-ins. Stolen supplies. Now I had an intruder on my hands, though I couldn't imagine what they'd hoped to find. I had nothing of value. No one did. This was a commune. Nobody owned a thing beyond the clothes on their backs, and even those would be reclaimed if necessary.

They must be after information. But what?

The only stuff I ever wrote down were supply counts, or short notes to the other camps about—you guessed it—supply counts. There was a novella Anna Loring had written that was circulating—about kids with dog powers that I'd felt was largely derivative—and a note from Leighton arguing that he shouldn't have to chop firewood because of his asthma. Beyond that, nothing.

Maybe someone was just snooping in general? Did we have a pervert in the village?

I dropped the map in frustration. Speculating was pointless. But I couldn't shake a feeling of violation. We didn't lock doors in this world. We often didn't even *have* doors. A fundamental rule was that we respected each other's boundaries. In the half year since emerging from the Program we'd had almost no crime. The class behaved and cooperated. Or at least, I thought we did.

What we'd done inside the MegaCom had left scars on everyone, and no one seemed to want fresh ones. All in all, it had been remarkable. The chaos we'd escaped in virtual Fire Lake had imprinted a strong inclination toward civility. Plus, Toby and the worst troublemakers had lit out, which certainly helped.

On impulse, I strode to the door and stepped outside. My front stoop was equipped with an electric lantern that tossed a soft yellow glow. Mixed with the diffuse moonlight, it gave the woods a ghostly vibe.

I stood still, listening to the night sounds. Insects. Birds. The dull hum of the ocean. Familiar things, like in the past. Yet none of it was really familiar at all.

This was a new world, one I didn't fully understand. One that had evolved without humans and now had to accept them again. Earth had never felt so alien as it did right then, standing in the gloom outside my cabin, contemplating who might've searched my belongings.

A twig snapped.

My head turned.

I spotted a silhouette in the bushes to my left.

For a moment my breath caught. I couldn't say a word.

The figure didn't run. Didn't move. Maybe whoever it was thought I couldn't see them.

"Who's there?" I called out in a shaky voice. Then I firmed it as best I could and pointed. "I can see you, whoever you are. What do you want?"

The form vanished into the darkness. I heard muffled footfalls jogging down toward the village.

Adrenaline flooded my system. That person had been *spying*. Likely the same jerk who'd snuck into my cabin, or someone connected to them.

I shivered in the cool night air as implications piled up. Something was going on. Whoever was spying on me might know about the stolen explosives. And if those really had been used to wreck the silo, it meant I had a full-blown conspiracy on my hands. One operating inside the village.

I strode toward the bushes, fists clenched at my sides. This was *my* home, and *my* community to run. People were dead because of the cave-ins. When I found the bastards responsible, I'd make them answer for it.

Below, the village gleamed in an orderly rectangle of pale yellow lights. Lanterns were affixed to poles along the wider pathways, so that wires could be strung and the system powered by a central generator. I began striding downhill without a flashlight. If I moved quickly, maybe I could check enough buildings and see who wasn't where they should be. We weren't a big group anymore—I might catch my stalker if I got there quickly and stirred things up. And if it was Toby or his gang, I'd flush them into the open.

I'd only taken a few steps when every light in the village died at once. I stopped short, blinking in the sudden darkness. *The generator must've failed.* Then I cursed my own naiveté. Too many signs of trouble already—more likely, someone had cut the power.

My eyes began to adjust. I continued treading softly along the trail.

The forest went silent.

A dozen blood-red lights ignited in a circle around the village. Flares. Their acrid stench filled my nostrils as the torches coughed and spat. The closest was mere steps to my right, held aloft by a black-clad figure who didn't seem to realize I was there.

I dropped down and slipped into the bushes. More shadowy forms emerged, holding the flares high as they silently converged on the cabins. A few voices in town called out in confusion, but not warning. I hid, unsure what to do.

Which classmates were they? What was their plan?

Warn the others, you idiot.

I cupped my hands to my lips. "TRAITORS IN THE VILLAGE!"

Shouts erupted. Glass broke. A tent caught fire.

I bit down on my tongue and tasted blood. Then I sprinted ahead to help.

A flare-wielder appeared in front of me and I shoulder-charged the person's back. The intruder went down with a loud *oof*. I popped up and kicked my enemy in the head, then spun away.

People were running, screaming. Flames rose. Long shadows climbed the cabin walls.

I grabbed the unconscious form at my feet. The person was wearing a mask—some kind of black nylon sock that covered their whole face. I began peeling it off, determined to expose who it was.

An arm rose to bat me away. I dug in my nails, heedless of the scratches I left.

Something slammed into my temple. I lost feeling in my

hands and slumped over on my side.

Stars. Floating lights.

I heard a voice say, "Tie her up."

Then my eyes rolled back and everything faded to black.

8

NOAH

I hopped from the boat and helped drag it up the dark beach.

My legs were shaking. Shivers wracked my spine. I wanted *out* of the water, even where it only came up to my knees. I saw the hard line of Akio's jaw as he held our lantern and could tell he felt the same. Only Ethan seemed unfazed.

I couldn't stop thinking about the shadows beneath our vessel. *It was the current. Nothing else. Stop psyching yourself out.*

But the goose bumps remained. My heart pounded like a galloping horse.

The tides had been hell, and sunset came long before we made landfall. Our last hour on the water had been illuminated solely by moonlight.

That's when . . . whatever it was . . . happened.

We knew birds and insects shared the world with us. Fire Lake Island was full of them, though they weren't quite the ones I'd grown up with. Plumages seemed brighter. Calls a touch shriller. There were lizards, too. Mice. Flowers. Trees I could mostly identify, though their needles felt sharper than before. We ate fish from the ocean, and Charlie swore he'd seen a crab once. So I knew *some* living things had survived the Dark Star.

Life is tenacious and fights like a demon. Hell, look at us. Our species had somehow survived across the span of a million years. We'd outlasted total planetary destruction like the virus we were, so spotting an odd-looking squirrel shimmying up an oak-like tree didn't shock me too much.

But those swirls.

The feeling of something massive *lingering* below our tiny vessel.

I could go my whole life, never experience that again, and die ecstatic. No wonder Outpost folks didn't visit very often.

I glanced at Akio, my lips parting to ask him what he thought. He cut me off with a chopping motion. "Let's not talk about it. We still have to go back."

I nodded grimly. Just thinking about our return voyage made me cringe.

Logically, I knew super-predators were extraordinarily rare and required insanely complex ecosystems to exist. The odds were staggeringly high that none could have evolved yet on a planet so badly damaged. But I also knew that I'd felt something huge and scary swim underneath our boat. Logic be damned.

Ethan was peering up at the gloomy bluffs overlooking the beach. "Where are they?"

The Outpost itself was about a mile inland, but Corbin's team had built a lookout station atop the nearest cliff. I couldn't see the cabin in the darkness, which meant its signal light wasn't on.

"Maybe everyone farms now?" I'd only been here once, months ago, but knew Corbin's settlement bordered a dense forest that covered the rest of the landmass, as far as anyone knew. Those were the woods Tack had vowed to explore.

"Only one way to find out." Ethan powered a flashlight and strode toward a footpath leading up the bluff. Akio looked at me, shrugged, and started after him. Richie and I took up the rear. He paced silently beside me, making no attempt to communicate. He hadn't spoken the whole trip. I was beginning to worry that bringing him had been a mistake.

In ten minutes we reached the top and spotted the lonely cabin. It was small and windowless, with a large fire lantern bolted to its roof to act like a lighthouse if necessary. Charlie had radioed ahead that we were coming—in case the Outpost could receive messages—but the tiny building was dark.

The door was closed but not latched. Inside, Akio hung his lantern from a hook in the ceiling, creating a sphere of harsh white light that covered the room. A half-eaten salad was sitting on a pitted table, a wooden fork slumped to the bottom of the bowl. Bugs crawled all over it. The only chair was overturned on the floor, casting a long shadow against the wall.

I glanced at Akio. His lips were thin.

"Looks like someone left in a hurry," I said.

Akio nodded grimly. "It's not like that lightning show could've snuck up on them. This is something else."

"These bastards are eating fresh vegetables." Ethan slapped

the rim of the salad bowl, causing it to overturn. "That's a freaking cucumber. I'd *kill* for a cucumber."

"Guess they got things to grow," I said hopefully. It was encouraging. That was the whole point of the Outpost, and we needed food now more than ever.

"No one would leave that uneaten," Richie said from the doorway. "Not on purpose."

I scraped a hand through my sweat-soaked hair. "Let's get to their camp and find out what's going on."

Ethan nodded, adjusting his waistband. My eyes widened in shock. He took two steps toward the door, but I stopped him with a palm to his chest. "Give it to me."

Ethan tensed beneath my hand. "Don't touch me, Noah."

"Then give me the gun and we can move on."

I gave him a hard stare, but Ethan matched it. "Weapons are communal property," he said. "I got this one working all by myself. If you want to waltz over there with nothing to protect yourself, be my guest. Not me." He slapped my fingers away and strode out of the cabin, shouldering Richie aside in the process.

My lungs emptied. I squeezed the bridge of my nose.

So. Ethan had a gun.

Derrick suspected a few were missing. One of the silo alcoves had contained a crate of rifles and pistols, but the seals were cracked and the oil had drained out. The weapons within had rusted and fallen apart, but boxes of ammunition survived. If Ethan had gotten one of those dilapidated pistols cleaned and operable, he might really have firepower.

We'd secured the others inside one of the lab's fireproof closets, using multiple padlocks. Four of us carried separate keys, meaning all of Min, Derrick, Sarah, and me would be required to open the door. Min had wanted a weapons-free society, and everyone else agreed. We'd had too much violence inside the Program. Plus, with Toby and those others still around at the time, the risk had been higher.

This was the first time I'd seen a gun in play, and I hadn't even seen it yet.

Maybe he was bluffing? Somehow, I didn't think so. Ethan had never been a good actor.

Akio was watching me. He arched an eyebrow.

"Let's just get to Corbin's camp. But keep an eye on him, okay?"

Akio nodded, and we filed out of the cabin, Richie aiming a last scowl at the overturned chair. I tried not to let on how nervous I was, but I agreed with what Richie had said. I hadn't eaten a fresh vegetable in—God, what? A million years and change? No chance someone just left that there. Outside, the night sounds were suddenly twice as ominous.

Ethan was well ahead, his light crossing a long field. We caught up to him as he crested a low rise. The stars gleamed down like glittering diamonds. Night skies were amazing on New Earth. The whole universe opened up for viewing. In the distance, across more rolling grassland, was a darker line of shadows—the woods walling off the island's interior.

At least, we *thought* it was an island. No one had been able to circumnavigate it by boat because the shoals were too treacherous, and as far as we knew Tack hadn't breached the forest. But his last report had been a while ago.

Like he wants regular radio chats. He moved here to get away from us.

I pushed the thought aside. I couldn't do anything to fix Tack's issues, and respected his desire for space. Min choosing me must've sliced to the bone. I'd have felt the same in his shoes. Hell, I'd have *done* the same. This was the only place on Earth to live that wasn't directly under her nose.

Corbin had built the Outpost hard against the tree line so they'd have easy access to timber and could shelter from the howling thunderstorms. The cabins were still a five-minute walk from where we stood, but I could already tell something was wrong.

"No lights," I said. "Not even a campfire."

The moon was up, and the first cultivated plots cast shadows on either side. I thought I recognized stalks of corn. But the Outpost itself was as black as midnight. Not a soul was in sight.

Ethan began trotting forward. His hand slid to his waistband.

"Stay here until I signal," I said to Akio and Richie. They both did as ordered, nervously eyeing the silent compound. I sped up even Ethan, and we jogged the last hundred yards together.

Dark cabins. No one appeared.

"What the hell?" Ethan hissed. We halted beside the cold fire pit and swung our flashlights, scanning for any sign of the nine people who called this place home. "Where'd they go?"

My beam stopped on one of the cabins. Its door stood wide open.

I nudged Ethan and pointed. The pistol appeared in his hand as if by magic.

We crept to the doorway. Ethan stuck his nose through, then disappeared inside. I turned and waved my light back and forth at Richie and Akio, then followed him. The room held two chairs, a table, and a desk, all upended. A cot and thin camping mattress were flipped against the far wall. Papers littered the floor, along with torn pieces of clothing and a mound of broken glass.

Ethan glowered at the wreckage. "What the hell?" he repeated.

I found an electric lantern and turned it on. "Someone tossed this room."

"I see that, Noah. Thanks." Ethan threw a hand at the overturned desk. "My question is *why*. Did someone go nuts?"

"Corbin would've sent word." My insides turned to jelly. "Other people did this."

"You mean Toby."

"Who else?"

"But there's only six in Toby's group. *Nine* people lived here." Ethan started ticking off fingers. "Corbin. Liesel. Neb. Kayla. Isaiah. Emma. Darren. Benny. The happy pioneer couples."

"Plus Tack. What's your point?"

"My *point* is, how do six losers erase nine able-bodied people without—" He cut off suddenly. "Unless . . ."

I nodded at his white-knuckled grip. "Unless that isn't the only gun on the loose."

Sarah had encountered Toby down in the lab complex. Could he have gotten into the weapons closet? But then what? He took the whole Outpost prisoner? How? Where?

A cold horror crept over me.

Laying charges for a cave-in was one thing. Toby might've thought Sarah's group were all safely inside the living quarters. *Surely he wouldn't . . .*

"Guys!"

My headed whipped to the sound of Richie's voice. Ethan charged back outside, holding his Glock like he knew what to do with it. Of course he did. We all did.

I froze in place in the darkened room. My inhalations grew ragged. Cold sweat trickled down my spine. Old anxieties surfaced as my heart started hammering out of control.

I exhaled deeply. Closed my eyes.

I couldn't have a panic attack. Not here, not now. Not around these guys.

I focused on my breathing and counted down to zero. When I felt under control again, I stepped out into the night.

Ethan was by the fire pit with Richie, who was mumbling something too low for me to hear. I spotted Akio's lantern close to the woods, beside a large field tent pitched beyond the circle of cabins. I knew instinctively it was Tack's.

Ethan called me over. He aimed his flashlight at a softball-sized rock on the ground. It was light gray and coarse, typical of the local granite and no doubt used to ring the fire. But when I looked closer, I saw a dark, rust-colored stain coating the bottom half of the stone.

"Oh crap," I said.

"Blood," Richie confirmed. "Even weirder, there was an upside-down bucket over this rock, like someone wanted to make sure it wasn't disturbed."

I blinked down at the stone, then the bucket. *Who left this here? Why?* Then Akio shouted. Ethan re-covered the rock and we hustled over to the tent.

The forest was pitch black, with ghoulish, elongated shadows. I couldn't fathom going in there by choice. I didn't want to imagine what might be watching us from under those eaves right now.

"Check this out." Akio set his lantern down inside the tent and held open the flap. I entered first, and found almost nothing—a trunk of clothes, a small desk, a single cot. A crude drawing was pinned to one canvas wall. I recognized Tack's terrible cartography immediately.

The map appeared to mark features of the forest's interior. Which made sense—that was Tack's self-imposed mission here, to explore the woods. I stumbled upon another lantern and turned it on as Ethan and Akio piled in behind me.

We all studied the map. My eye was drawn to what looked like a recent addition to the artwork.

In the center, a sharp peak rose out of the surrounding forest. Beyond it ran a line of question marks, seeming to indicate the extent of Tack's explorations. The peak was circled in bright red, with an arrow aiming at it and the word HERE! printed in block capital letters. Everything about the notation had the feeling of being done in a hurry.

"Okay." I cleared my throat. "This seems obvious."

Ethan looked ready to chew nails. "That's it? An arrow on a crappy map? Why the hell didn't he write something clearer?"

Akio glanced outside. "Maybe this was all he could manage."

"God I hate that kid," Ethan muttered. "Useless to the end."

He turned to go, but I caught his arm. "Wait. Look." I pointed to the bottom of the map.

There was a second red arrow. Aimed straight down.

At a dark bundle on the tent floor.

I knelt and unrolled a length of rough canvas. Inside was an

84

ordinary claw hammer, molded as a single piece of slate-gray metal. The tool was worn by long use, but curiously light in my hands. I lifted it to show the others.

Ethan snorted. "Awesome. He wants us to bring him a hammer. I'm going to pound that loser with it when we find him."

Something about the hammer. Its weight, or maybe the balance. This one felt different from others I'd used around the village. Curious, I flipped it over so the bottom of its shaft faced up. Every tool in the silo was stamped with a serial number that corresponded to a storage alcove location. I wondered where Tack had found this one.

Except this hammer didn't have a serial number.

Instead, the word CHRYSALIS was etched into the base of its handle.

I stared at the engraving. The tent walls closed in.

This hammer was impossible. This hammer couldn't be.

"Noah?" Akio's voice carried an edge of worry. "Everything okay, man?"

I swallowed. "This didn't come from the silo."

"What?" Richie snapped, even as Ethan snatched the hammer from my hands.

"Of course it did." Ethan swung it in a tight arc. "This is forged titanium. They're not smelting metals out here, dumb-ass."

I ran a hand over my mouth, barely able to think. "Guys, I've rooted through every crate in the silo. They're all catalogued the same way, and the contents are stamped in an identical manner. The tools even *look* the same. This hammer . . . It's not from that cache."

Stunned silence. Even Ethan seemed taken aback as he thought it through. He knew the tools as well as I did.

"You think it . . . survived?" Richie asked. "Like, from before Nemesis?"

I shook my head. "Nothing lasts that long."

Ethan threw up his free hand. "Then where the hell is it from, Livingston?"

"No idea," I said honestly. Then I nodded at the scarlet circle in the center of the map.

"But we need to find Tack."

PART TWO

THE WILD

9

MIN

I awoke in utter blackness.

Head pounding. Throat dry. It was cold. I was inside a building but lying on dusty floorboards.

For a moment I remembered nothing, then it all rushed back.

I sprang up and reached out blindly, found that my wrists were bound. My knuckles smacked against a wall of wooden planks. *Don't panic.* Extending my arms, I shuffled sideways, running my fingers down its length until I reached a corner, a journey of no more than a few steps. From there I continued along the next wall, bumping into a table and sliding around it. I'd nearly completed the circuit when I tripped over something and thudded painfully to the ground.

The "something" groaned.

I made a less than heroic squawk, scrambling backward until my shoulder blades slammed against the far wall. Biting back a yelp, I focused on the scraping and grumbling on the other side of the room. *Supply shed.* I knew every square inch of the village—I was inside one of the storage buildings, but had no idea how I'd gotten there, or who was with me.

The noise devolved into a string of curses. Relief flooded through me. I knew that voice.

"Derrick?"

A pause, then his voice rasped. "Min? Where are we? Why are we in the dark?"

"A group attacked Home Town." My eyes were beginning to adjust to a trickle of light leaking under the building's only door. "They were dressed in black and wore masks over their faces. They had flares, too."

"Why are my hands are tied?" he said, a note of hysteria entering his voice.

"Mine are too. We've obviously been taken prisoner. Do you remember how you got here?"

Derrick coughed roughly, then spat. "I was in my cabin and ran outside, but I didn't make it three steps." I heard a sharp intake of breath, followed by what could only be described as a growl. "Somebody's gonna pay for this lump on my head."

Bile rose in my throat. "Derrick, there were *twelve* of them. Who could it be?"

Derrick appeared to be doing some sort of personal inventory with his limbs. "Toby and his punk-ass thugs, who else? With help from some people in the village. When I find out who, I'm gonna wreck their whole damn world."

I thought back to the shadowy figure watching me from the forest. Derrick was right, of course—who else could it be?—but a part of me felt sure I'd recognize Toby's silhouette anywhere. Same for the twins and those other football guys. Even their stupid postures were imprinted in my mind.

The voice I'd heard before losing consciousness. I couldn't place it. That shouldn't be possible, but I replayed the memory over and over in my head, and my impression didn't waver.

Which all added up to one thing—my gut said I'd never encountered the person before.

Which was impossible.

I lifted both arms to rub the welt on my temple. *Don't get crazy. You took a blow to the head and now everything's a mess.* But I still couldn't shake the feeling.

"What if . . . it's someone else?"

"Who?" Derrick sounded annoyed. "There *is* no one else, Min. Unless you think a bunch of cavemen we haven't noticed before decided to swim over for a battle royale."

I resisted an urge to rip my hair out. "I just . . . I saw someone in the woods, Derrick. It was dark, and they were far away, but I *swear* I didn't know the person. I . . . There's no other way to explain it."

Rubber soles scraped the floorboards as Derrick struggled to his feet. He stood there silently for a moment, then sighed. "Okay, Min. I learned a long time ago to trust your instincts. But if that's true . . ." I sensed more than saw him wave his bound hands in the darkness, " . . . I don't even know what to do with it. How could there be other people?"

"I don't know. It's crazy, right?" My chin dropped. "I must

be wrong. Maybe I just don't want to believe we have traitors in our camp."

"I hear that. At least six of 'em, huh? That's a bitch."

I shook my head. "Guessing is pointless. We'll find out soon enough."

Visibility inside the room was slowly increasing. *It must be dawn*, I realized. *We've been locked in here all night*.

I stumbled to the door and tried the handle. It wouldn't budge. I'd been expecting that but still felt deflated. Someone had padlocked us in from the outside.

"You know where we are?" Derrick asked.

"A shed on the east side of the creek is my guess. But this one's practically empty, which is weird. The only building that wasn't packed solid yesterday—"

"*Is the one with the backup radio*," Derrick finished in a rush. "Min, those idiots locked us in the new coms room."

I squinted at the table I'd bypassed in my initial blind survey of the room. A dark, bulky object sat on its surface.

We both arrowed for it.

Derrick got there first and awkwardly ran his fingers along the unit's sides. "Damn! There's no line out yet. We can't access the main antenna." He flipped a switch, and a tiny yellow light illuminated. "Aha! The CB has juice, though. We can try calling out to other spots around the island, but I don't know if anyone's there to pick up. Maybe the caves."

"Do it. They can't have grabbed everyone, right? Someone else must have a radio."

Derrick's breath hissed sharply. "Hold up, I found a screwdriver next to the casing. Give me a second."

For the next few minutes he struggled in the dissipating gloom, mixing colorful language with groans of frustration. Finally, he hooted in triumph, and then began tugging at the cords binding my hands. They came free much faster. I rubbed my wrists in satisfaction.

"Nice work. Now try the radio."

"You're welcome. On it."

Derrick turned a knob and static poured from the speaker. He depressed a button and began talking, but the static didn't lessen. He muttered a four-letter word. "I'm not sure if this mic is working, and it's broadcasting really weak anyway. I don't think my voice can get through." He began pressing the button in a pattern: three short beeps, three long, followed by three short ones again.

I got it instantly, and couldn't suppress a laugh. "Are you seriously sending Morse code?"

"You have a better idea? The signal doesn't seem strong enough to talk over, but maybe dots and dashes will fly. Whoever receives this will have to figure out where we are, though. How many people knew the backup radio was moved in here?"

"Not many. Maybe a dozen. It wasn't a secret or anything."

Derrick shrugged in the gloom. He repeated the pattern a dozen more times before dropping the transmitter. "Well, that's that."

I tried the door again, then pressed my ear to it, straining to hear outside. Nothing. Frustration boiling over, I stepped back and kicked the wood, and ended up bouncing on my other foot like a pogo stick as the sting engulfed my whole leg. Finally, I dropped to my stomach and tried to see under the door, where the line of daylight was creeping in. But it was no good.

"You think it was a trap?" Derrick asked suddenly.

"What?"

"Noah going to check the Outpost. You think Toby was luring him away?"

I sat back and rested my head against the wall. "The raid here and them not answering don't *have* to be connected."

Derrick gave me a look. I sighed. "But you're right, a coincidence seems unlikely now. What I don't get is, who could've done it? How could Toby bomb the silo, attack the Outpost, and then raid Home Town in such a short amount of time? Nobody could've traveled *through* that storm. Not across open water."

"True." Derrick spoke deliberately in the darkness. "If the Outpost really was attacked, only Toby's fools could have done it, with no help from here. Because everyone living on this island was accounted for before and right after the storm. I've already asked around." He paused. "Unless Ethan, Spence, and Cash did it, but that's only three guys. It doesn't add up." He paused again. "Or maybe some Outpost people turned on the others all by themselves? But who would that be? Corbin's group is tighter than anybody, and they never cause trouble."

He paused again. I whispered quietly, "Or maybe those cavemen you mentioned."

Derrick covered his face. "God help us."

I shivered. Three possible assaults, maybe by different people, with everyone now a suspect. How deep did this go?

Fact: Twelve attackers means there's a conspiracy. The only question is how big.

"One of us has to escape," I said. "Find Noah. Toby might've surprised us last night, but they're still outnumbered—"

The door rattled. Metal scraped metal, then something heavy fell to the ground outside.

Heart pounding, I scrambled into a crouch as the door swung inward.

Sunlight burned like fire as the gap widened to reveal a short, powerful-looking figure in the doorway.

My lips formed a snarl. I tensed, ready to attack Toby and gouge his eyes out, but in another blink I knew it wasn't him. A relieved smile split my face.

"Let's go," Sam whispered, glancing back over his shoulder. "Right now. Hurry."

We didn't ask questions. I crept outside, Derrick a step behind. The sun was low over the eastern mountains. No one else was in sight. Sam darted into the woods behind the shed and we raced after him, moving as soundlessly as possible. He led us up a hill, through a thick copse of fir trees, and then down into the ravine where Noah had discovered the stolen explosives. The crates were gone, but deep gouges still scored the earth.

There he halted. I opened my mouth, but Sam cut me off with a hand motion. He listened several more seconds, then, putting a finger to his lips, led us deeper into the defile. At the bottom we crawled inside a circle of pine trees and knelt, camouflaged on all sides. Finally, he nodded permission to speak.

"How'd you find us?" I whispered.

Sam held up a walkie-talkie. "Dot, dot, dot. Dash, dash, dash. Dot, dot, dot."

Derrick broke into a wide smile. "My SOS worked!"

Sam shrugged. "Me and Floyd carried the radio in there yesterday. I thought it was Cash."

"No one was guarding us?" I made a noise deep in my throat. "Sam, who did this?"

He frowned. "Toby's gang. I was out walking last night when they hit. It was chaos at first, but they're armed and took control of the village in minutes. Someone must've helped them. I couldn't see anything from where I was hiding, so I stayed in the woods until dawn. Then I checked my radio and caught your signal." He met my eye squarely. "On my way over here, I spotted the bald prick himself, crossing the square with Mike Nolan. Like they owned the place."

My hands balled into fists. There it was. Confirmation. Toby Albertsson had attacked our home. I seethed with rage but was determined not to lose the big picture.

"How many others escaped?" I asked.

Sam shook his head. "Like I said, I came for you first."

"I counted twelve attackers last night, Sam. Some of our own people must be in on this."

"*Your* people," Sam shot back.

"*Anybody*," Derrick snapped. Sam gave him a hard look, but Derrick didn't flinch. "I'm just saying, we don't know. It could've been Home Towners, Ethan and his buddies, or yeah, Sam—maybe even Ridgeliners. We need to find out."

"No one in my camp had a part in this," Sam said coldly, but I noticed a flicker behind his eyes. He wasn't totally sure. And it burned him.

"The solution is simple," I said, glancing back up the defile. "We should sneak back to the village and take a look. I want to see Toby with my own eyes. Before I kill him." I was so angry, I wasn't sure if I was serious.

Sam nodded gruffly. "He was headed up the silo path."

"The silo?" Derrick scratched the back of his head. "With the entrance blocked solid? What could he want up there?"

"Maybe a chance to admire his work." I pressed a fist to my chin. "If Sarah's right, Toby deliberately sabotaged every way into the silo before this attack. Now he controls the outside, too. He must want something. Everything leading up to now feels like chess moves to capture the place for himself."

Derrick bared his teeth. "And when he needed *us* out of the way, he cut a deal with some village malcontents to help him take over. Question is, who?"

Sam was looking at me. "We know one person who spoke with Toby in secret."

I shook my head. "Sarah ran the place already. She *lived* down there, for God's sake. Plus, she was underground when the roof collapsed. No way she'd take that risk, or let five of her friends die while it happened." I paused, thinking hard. "Toby would look for allies on the fringes. People who might feel as shut out as he did."

I didn't have an answer. Even Ethan didn't truly gibe. He was more direct in his rebellions.

Then something else popped out at me. "Why wreck the silo at all? If Toby had a freaking traitor brigade lined up, and weapons for a raid, why not just attack the village first and save the trouble? Now he can't get inside, either."

Derrick opened his mouth, then closed it. Sam grunted. Another fact that made little sense.

"Let's go see already," Derrick muttered.

"There's a promontory overlooking the silo's front entrance," Sam said. "A hundred yards back. We can check out who's near the tunnel without much risk."

We rose as one. Sam took the lead again and we snaked through the forest, swinging wide of the village until reaching the cliffs. Then we climbed carefully, creeping along a back ridge toward the silo. The sun was behind us—anyone looking our direction would be staring straight into it. Finally, we crawled onto a ledge. The crushed entry tunnel was directly across from us, about fifty feet down. Four people were milling in front of it.

Toby. Mike Nolan. His brother Chris. Cole Pritchard.

I hadn't seen any of them in months. They seemed leaner than before. Harder. Toby had some sort of schematic in his hands and was issuing instructions. It took everything I had not to stand up and curse them out.

A moment later, three more figures emerged from the rubble. I didn't recognize any of them.

Derrick made a choking noise beside me. Sam's eyes widened.

I felt my pulse spike. My hands began to tingle, even as every muscle in my body tensed.

Two boys. A girl. They seemed to be our age.

The trio were dressed in black like Toby and his crew, but they looked healthier in some way. Cleaner, certainly. They listened to Toby with an air of reluctant indulgence—if Toby thought he was in charge of the others, these three might not agree. Then my mind snapped back to the bold-letter point.

I didn't know these people, and I knew every human alive.

At least, I thought I had.

Sam snapped his fingers in front of my face. He jerked his head backward.

I blinked, nodded. We slithered away from the edge, then rose and scurried another hundred yards down off the ridge before huddling behind a circle of broken boulders.

Where we stood staring at each other like zombies. No one could think of what to say.

I covered my face, then ran both hands down it. Derrick was staring at the ground and shaking his head. He mouthed the word *cavemen* in disbelief. Even Sam seemed shook.

None of us could process. Finally, I just said the words aloud.

"Those were strangers down there."

"How is that possible?" Derrick whined.

"They were our age, too." Sam squeezed his scalp. "What the hell, Min?"

I swallowed. Took a deep breath. Spoke the words, and named them true.

"We're not alone." Then my voice hardened, anger seeping through the shock. "Someone else survived the Dark Star, and they're our enemies."

10

NOAH

I jogged up the final rise to the sea.

The empty lookout cabin waited starkly on the headland as a blazing sun rose behind it.

Ethan, Akio, and Richie were a mile behind me. We'd spent an uneasy night in the cornfield, rolled in our sleeping bags and jumping at every sound. When daylight came, the others began a final sweep of the Outpost while I hurried back to the radio. I was worried sick about Min and the others.

Something bad had happened here. So bad our friends hadn't had time to call for help. Dark thoughts churned in my brain, centered on a bloodstained rock, a mysterious hammer, and a red arrow pointing into the wilderness.

I stormed into the cabin, ignoring the toppled chair and

overturned bowl as I beelined for the receiver in the corner. *We should've tried it last night.* But I'd been focused on Ethan's gun and finally getting to the Outpost. I checked the battery and found a half charge. Encouraged, I flipped the switch and heard a reassuring whoosh of static. In seconds I'd tuned in Home Town's frequency. Min had promised to have someone stationed at the radio around the clock.

"Outpost to Home Town, this is Noah."

No response. I called again, my impatience growing. If the operator was taking a leak right now, my head might explode.

"Outpost to Home Town, pick up. This is Noah."

Nothing. I switched frequencies. "Outpost to Caves, this is Noah. Pick up."

White noise. I ground my teeth.

"Outpost to Ridgeline, copy back."

I knew the last was a long shot—Sam's camp was all the way across the island, and I doubted the signal could reach. But I was desperate. Stymied, I tried the village again. No answer. I was about to slam the transmitter to the floor and stomp up and down on it when the others stepped inside.

"Reach anyone?" Ethan asked, wiping sweat from his brow.

I shook my head angrily. "Far as I can tell, this is working. But no one's answering."

"So now we can't contact the island." Akio scratched his cheek. "Maybe it really was a trap."

"Don't get crazy," I snapped, almost at myself, because I was a moment from panicking. Why would Min leave the radio unmanned? She'd promised.

"Use your head for once, Livingston." Ethan regarded me

coolly. "This whole thing is messed up. First we can't reach anyone at the Outpost, so we boat over here and the place is a ransacked ghost town. Now no one's picking up back there. The dots aren't hard to connect."

"You seem to know a lot about it. Got Toby on speed dial?"

Ethan crossed the room in two strides. I didn't back down. Min might be in trouble, and I was a full day away from where I should be. Coming out here had been stupid. I had to get back.

"Accuse me of something again," Ethan said softly, his face inches from mine.

"Sarah caught Toby poking around in the silo two weeks ago. Have you seen him too, Ethan? I'm not accusing you of anything. I'm asking you a direct question."

Ethan stared me straight in the eye. Then he smiled. "There's the murderer I've been looking for."

I flinched. Stepped back.

Ethan chuckled. "To answer your question, *no*. I haven't seen Toby. I don't understand how he even got onto the island. The outer cliffs are sheer all the way around except for by the caves, but he never came near us. I can promise you that."

"Maybe he had help." Richie picked up the overturned chair and sat heavily. Akio remained in the doorway, keeping one eye on the path back to the Outpost.

"Help?" I said. "From who?"

Richie shrugged. "From whoever knocked over this camp."

I blinked. "Toby did. Obviously."

Richie's eyes grew skeptical. "Could Toby and those jokers really have attacked here and blown up the silo on the same night? Seems like a lot, bro."

Ethan nodded curtly. "Charlie spoke to Neb by radio before the weather hit, but we couldn't reach anyone by noon the next day. So the Outpost must've been attacked during the storm or right after it. How could Toby do both things with only six people?"

I thought about it. "Could the explosions have been detonated remotely?"

"There were what, five of them?" Richie said. "I doubt anyone could rig together so much gear beforehand without a ton of help, or Sarah and her friends noticing. And how'd they know exactly when to collapse the back tunnel unless they were watching things?"

I ground my teeth. They were right, it wasn't adding up. Which meant Toby's squad couldn't be working alone.

Akio came fully inside the cabin. "We should be talking about Tack's map."

"Where the hammer came from," I whispered. In a blink, everything changed. What had Tack been trying to tell us with those arrows? What did he find in the woods? I went cold, considering the impossible. Was some unknown factor at play?

If our problem is bigger than Toby's goon squad and a few traitors . . .

Ethan clapped his hands. "I see you get it."

My cheeks reddened. "What do you mean?"

"Your face. You now understand what we have to do. And it isn't run back to your girlfriend."

Everything inside me sagged. "We?"

"Not them." Ethan pointed at Richie and Akio. "But

103

definitely you and me. We're gonna find out what's going on in that forest."

Richie looked around in confusion. "Not us what?"

Ethan folded his arms across his chest. "You two are going back to report what we found and find out why they're not answering. If everything's okay, send a team over here to guard the crops while Noah and I are gone."

Richie's head dropped to the table. "We have to cross the water again?"

Akio said nothing, but his shoulders tensed.

"Ethan's right." I took a deep breath. "Tack left a clear sign. If there's a threat we don't know about, Fire Lake Island will always be at risk. It makes sense to split up." I made a final play. "But Ethan, you're the sailor. You should go with Richie. Akio can come with me."

Ethan snorted, absently fiddling with the radio knobs. "You'd like that, wouldn't you?"

I held my tongue. I knew what was coming.

"This is serious, Livingston." The humor had left his voice. "There's no way I'm leaving it up to someone else. I want to know what happened to Corbin and the others. I want to know what's hiding in those woods, and where that hammer came from. I don't trust you and Tack to do a damn crossword puzzle together, much less assess a threat. So we're going arm-in-arm on this one. I promise to use my best manners."

Ethan took a step toward the door, but I pivoted to block his path.

"You're right Ethan," I said, surprised by the frost in my voice. "This *is* serious. Which means I'm all done with the posturing

104

bullshit. We'll search the forest, find Tack, and figure out what the hell happened to the Outpost crew. Working together for once. Do *you* understand?"

Ethan startled me by laughing. He looked at Akio and Richie. "Run and hide, boys! Serial Killer Noah is back, and not a moment too soon."

I turned and strode from the cabin, a wave of revulsion sweeping through me.

I'm not that guy anymore.

But I was kidding myself. I knew the truth.

I'd be that guy again, if that's what it took to protect Min. I'd burn down the whole world.

Demons awoke inside me. I felt a familiar, smoldering rage.

I *would* go into the wild. I *would* find Tack. I wouldn't hold back to defend those I cared about.

Ethan was right. I was back.

I'd crush anyone who got in my way.

11

MIN

I scooped cold, rehydrated beans from my bowl.

Spread them on a stale cracker. My tongue recoiled from the taste, but I scarfed it down anyway. Food wasn't a problem yet—Ridgeline had enough to last another few weeks—but it would be soon, and then forever afterward.

Running out of food had always preoccupied my thoughts, but I'd assumed we had time. Years before needing true self-sufficiency, enough cushion to get our houses built and methods straight, and have a workable farming system in place. But that dream was in tatters now, drowned at the bottom of a submerged silo.

Toby's silo.

I winced. Then I shook my head to clear it, leaning back

against the wall of Sam's cabin. Toby was a nightmare sprung back to life, but he was a sideshow. It was the strangers with him that mattered.

Because they were impossible.

Totally, clearly, flatly impossible.

My classmates and I were the only survivors of the Nemesis Dark Star that ended all human civilization. My father had told me so straight out, and I believed him. There'd been no reason for him to deceive us any longer. He'd worked too hard, invested too much of himself in the mad scheme—which included murdering me five times—to have lied about *why* he did it. I was cynical by nature, but I'd seen the truth in his eyes as he explained what Project Nemesis really was.

The Dark Star's massive gravitational field had ravaged Earth, sparking earthquakes, volcanic eruptions, and deadly tectonic shifts. Continents were torn to pieces. Mountain ranges disappeared beneath the sea. Then, as it had many times before, the planet slowly recovered, but over hundreds of thousands of years—far too long a span for humans to have survived on its surface.

The only way we'd survived was by giving up biological existence altogether, hiding inside a computer as strings of ones and zeros. Our persistence was a miracle of science and technology, but it was artificial. We'd used a cheat code to bypass the countless millennia of pure hellscape on Earth after Nemesis. Everyone not uploaded into the MegaCom was dead.

But I'd just seen three people by the silo entrance who hadn't been there. They weren't part of the Program.

Which, again, was impossible.

Impossible.

I set the bowl aside and stood. I'd taken a quick nap after our nervy trek around the empty lake, but I could no longer avoid the conversations that needed to take place. There were living, breathing strangers on Fire Lake Island, working with Toby. They'd attacked Home Town and taken hostages. Now they were prowling around our busted silo for some reason, and I couldn't guess why.

I stepped outside into a damp, spanking breeze. Ridgeline was high up the western side of the bowl, in a windswept valley I wouldn't have chosen for a settlement. But Sam and his group had wanted away from the rest of us, and this was the geographic limit. Their cabins were smaller, lined up along a creek that emerged from a low-ceilinged cavern. Canvas sheets stretched between trees to wall in certain areas, giving the place a woodsy, elven vibe.

The camp had been empty when we arrived. Sam's whole crew had come down for the meeting after the cave-ins, and I assumed the others were captured in the raid. I found Derrick by the fire pit, tending a blaze of cave-dried logs that wouldn't smoke much. The risk felt small—we were hours from the silo, under an overcast sky that threatened rain—but we didn't know what our attackers intended to do next. They could be marching here right now.

"Get some rest?" Derrick asked.

I nodded. "We need to find out who those people are." I was stating the obvious, but didn't care. We'd made no plans for something like this, because . . . why would we?

"Let's wait until everybody's here."

I perked at that. "Others?"

"Some people showed up while you slept. About a dozen. Sam's getting them settled in the cavern, but they're coming right back."

"That's great! Who else made it out?"

Derrick put down his poking stick and leaned back, rubbing his eyes. I could tell he hadn't slept yet, and my heart went out to him. "When the madness started, Floyd and Hamza bumped into Tucker and some other dude they didn't know, and pounded them into the ground. Well, Floyd did, anyway. Then they lit out with Leah, Piper, and Ferris. They got lucky in the woods and ran into Zach, Lauren, and Casey. Those guys all hid until morning and headed here, scooping up Anna and Aiken along the way. Cenisa and Leighton showed up by themselves a half hour later." He blew out an exhausted breath. "Sounds like the crew that hit us wasn't spectacular at taking prisoners. Maybe that wasn't even their goal. Seems like they just wanted to control the village and isolate the silo."

My spirits rose. "That's fifteen people. Derrick, I only saw *twelve* attack the village. If that's all of them, we outnumber the bastards."

Derrick frowned. "Zach saw a gun on the kid who tried to jump him, and Casey said the same. If they're armed and we're not, the numbers don't really matter."

I paused, thinking. "Are there no weapons here?"

"Sam told me they don't have any, and I don't think he's lying."

"You guys have serious trust issues." Sam strode into the clearing, followed by Leighton, Casey, and Big Floyd. "We don't have any guns here because we all agreed no one would have any guns, remember?"

I flashed my palms. "I know. I believe you. I was just hoping you'd been dishonest for once."

Sam barked a laugh. "For once, I wish I had been."

More classmates filed in. Cliques re-formed, with Floyd, Hamza, and Cenisa gathering with Sam in a Ridgeline bloc, while Casey, Lauren, Leah, and Piper—Home Towners, all—chose a separate log for themselves. Leighton and Zach sat opposite Derrick and me. Ferris, Anna, and Aiken remained standing.

"It's good to see everyone," I began, but didn't get any further. Anna grunted loudly, swatting my opener away like a pesky gnat.

"Cut the crap, Min." Her whole body quivered as Aiken put an arm around her shoulders. "Get to the point. Who the hell *are* those people?"

Okay, fair question.

"I don't know," I said honestly, "and it scares the hell out of me."

Floyd stood up, glaring at everyone not from Ridgeline. "Have any of you *ever* seen a stranger before? Don't lie, now!"

The whole group shook their heads or called out a denial. I expected as much. We might have our differences, but those paled in comparison to the idea that other people might be alive. No one could keep *that* secret.

"Toby and the Nolans led the attack," Casey said bitterly, chewing on her long blond braid. "They must've met the strangers out"—she waved a hand up and away—"wherever those guys live now."

"We should hit them back," Ferris snarled, slamming a fist into his palm. "My cabin burned down last night, with *all* my things inside. Those a-holes can't take our stuff. Let's attack!"

Sam raised an eyebrow. "You want to go against armed fighters with nothing but your fists?"

Ferris swallowed, turned away. He'd never been much for bravery.

I tried to steer the conversation to more productive ground. "Let's take stock. There are fifteen of us here. I saw twelve flares during the raid, which means at least six people helped Toby's guys that we don't know. And they captured sixteen prisoners."

"How can anyone else be alive?" Leighton whined. "There's no way society just carried on the same way for a million years outside the Program. They'd be Neanderthals or have teleporters or something."

"What do they want with the silo?" Aiken added, ignoring Leighton as he glared through a curtain of greasy brown hair. "I saw three of them babysitting the front entrance this morning, even though it's smashed to pieces. Why would they bother?"

Sam twisted to face Derrick. "Did you reach Spence in the caves?"

Derrick nodded. "He and Charlie are fine. I told them to hang tight."

"Where's Ethan?" I said sharply.

"He went with Noah."

I paused to digest this. That couldn't have been Noah's idea.

Derrick leaned forward, jabbing his fire stick into the dirt. "Let's say the cave-ins really were sabotage by Toby and his new gang. If those fools want something from down there, all they did was make their own job harder." He spread his arms wide. "For no good reason."

Aiken stomped the ground in frustration. "None of this makes sense! It's like we're back inside the Program."

Several people flinched. I rose quickly, lofting both hands. "Everyone stay calm. We're definitely not inside the Program. That's over with."

"You don't know that!" Anna shrilled, her beady doll's eyes glistening. "Maybe we never came out. This could all be, like, some twisted new simulation level. We could still be dead!"

Panic began leaching through the group like a virus. The meeting teetered on its rails.

"That's not true." I fought to keep my voice calm. "We're facing something unimaginable, but it does exist. *We* exist. We're alive in the real world." My voice dropped. "We have the graves to prove it."

Sam's head jerked away. His cousin hadn't gotten even that much.

"This is worthless." Ferris sat back and scratched his nose. "Strangers have imprisoned our friends and are trying to steal everything we have, including our homes. We have to fight back. It's literally a matter of survival."

"You guys keep glazing over the fact that *other people are alive*," Anna shouted, hands clenched at her sides. "What if there are, like, *thousands* of them?"

"Wouldn't that be . . . good?" Hamza blushed as all eyes swung to him, but he kept going. "I mean, lots of people would mean a society. That we're not alone. They might have a city, indoor plumbing, all that stuff. Shouldn't we try talking to them and see where they're from?"

"They didn't talk to us," Derrick growled. "Sorry Ham, but these people attacked in the middle of the night and locked me in a shed. It's not like I wouldn't have sat down if they'd wanted to."

Zach spoke for the first time. "Where they came from is my thing. We've charted every scrap of land within a two-day radius of our island. Where do these strangers live, and how did Toby meet them?"

"And why would they take his side?" Casey crinkled her nose. "He's an insane, slimy prick."

"You guys are missing the point!" Anna had worked herself into a lather. "How are these people alive?! Who are they?! What are they going to do to us?!"

"I have a guess."

Heads spun around as Sarah slipped from the forest, followed by Jessica Cale. My stomach did a backflip and botched the landing.

Derrick squeezed his forehead. "Stop *doing* that."

"Sorry. I wanted to listen for a minute."

I glanced into the woods behind Sarah, but she shook her head. "No one else. Just this one, and she's been terrible company."

Jessica ran to Piper and buried her face in her friend's lap. Sarah sat on a log next to Derrick. "They took everyone else," she said. "Twelve attackers, including six douchebags we don't know. Fourteen prisoners. They aren't really trying for more. They have what they want."

I cleared my throat. "Which is?"

Sarah looked at me with disappointment. "The silo, Min. They want the lab complex."

"Why do you say that?"

"Because it's the only thing that makes sense." She crossed her arms, spoke in a tone best suited for addressing a pet of questionable intelligence. "Toby stole explosives and used them to destroy the silo's front entrance and upper levels, forcing my group to evacuate. Then he slammed the back door and flooded the shaft, sealing off the lab complex completely. But it's still down there, undisturbed, and now they control the perimeter, too. To me it's obvious what they're after."

She paused. I refused the bait.

Sarah smiled. "*What*, you ask? Why the MegaCom, of course."

I bit my lip, thinking. The others remained silent, content to let me deal with Sarah alone.

"What would they want with it?" I asked, honest confusion superseding my annoyance. "It's useful for record keeping, and running the silo itself, but we're in a one-system world now. It's a relic."

Sarah warmed her hands over the fire. "Maybe Toby promised these newcomers something. Information we have, about our own survival. Or maybe the strangers don't have a supercomputer as strong as ours, or an advanced system at all. I can't really say, but I'm sure that's what they want. Based on their actions, it's the only logical goal." She paused. "But we can get inside before them."

My mouth opened, but before I could speak, Anna walked directly up to Sarah, panic overriding her instinct for self-preservation. "You. All. Keep. Missing. The. Point. Where did these people come from, Sarah? *Nothing else matters.*"

Sarah scoffed. "Project Nemesis, of course."

Stunned silence.

I rose. Gently moved Anna aside. Then I crouched down and looked her directly in the eye.

"Explain what you mean, Sarah. How could that be? We knew every single person inside the Program."

Sarah arched an eyebrow in what seemed like genuine puzzlement.

"What makes you think we were the only Program?"

12

NOAH

My feet slid out from under me.

I fell on my butt and skidded downhill, grasping wildly at branches and wet leaves. Then my heels caught a root and momentum rocketed me face-first, like I'd been shot from a catapult. I released one glorious squawk before slamming to a stop against the trunk of a spruce tree.

"Ugh," I wheezed. And meant it. So far, this expedition had been a nightmare. I was beginning to hate forests.

I was a varsity letterman in basketball. Why do I keep falling down hills?

"Nice work, dumb-ass," Ethan called down. I tried to give him the finger, but the searing pain in my side prevented me from raising an arm.

"Let's . . . take . . . a break," I managed.

Ethan plopped down on a fallen pine and unstrapped his canteen. "I told you to put boots on." He wiped his brow, then took a long pull. Our trip together was going as badly as I'd expected.

We'd raided the Outpost for supplies before heading into the forest—their gear was technically communal—but I couldn't bring myself to take someone else's shoes. It felt too personal. Ethan was right, though. After struggling through several miles of dense, wet foliage I was definitely regretting my choice.

At dawn we'd launched Akio and Richie in the boat, me waving stupidly as they disappeared beyond the breakers. Neither had looked happy to be crossing the strait again, but somebody had to go back. Being real, I was ecstatic not to be making the trip again so soon myself. Just thinking about the ocean gave me shivers.

"You really flew that time," Ethan yelled. "It was majestic."

I rolled onto my back and rubbed my abdomen. I'd have a bruise the size of a watermelon in a few hours. Ethan watched me from above with amused disdain. These awful woods had swallowed us completely.

"How much farther do you think?" Struggling to sit up, I pulled off my sneaker and dug out a pebble. "I thought we'd find a trail at some point, but there's not even a deer run."

"Because there's no deer, numb-nuts." Ethan began picking his way down to join me. "Honestly, did you hit your head on that swan dive?" Before I could respond, he pointed in the direction we'd been traveling. "We go east until we reach the stream on Tack's lame map, then follow it inland. It's gotta be close."

"You said that an hour ago," I muttered.

Ethan crossed his arms. "You have a better plan? Besides falling down every fifty yards like a fainting goat." His neck had flushed pink, a sure sign he was about to lose his temper.

I held up a hand to placate him. "No, you're right. Sorry. And yes, I did hit my head."

Ethan barked a laugh. Then he rocked side to side on his heels, eyes rolling skyward. "Okay, I admit to being *slightly* surprised we haven't found the stream yet. Not that we're lost or anything," he added quickly. "Tack couldn't draw a stick figure with an instruction manual."

"I can sneak up on you easy enough."

Ethan and I whirled to face the bushes.

Tack Russo pushed through the foliage. He looked mostly the same—short and compact, with unruly black hair and deep blue eyes. He gave me a sharp nod, then winked at Ethan. "You missed the creek a mile back, Dora. You've been angling north for over half an hour."

Ethan went from pink to red. "And you sat back and watched us stumble through this crap?"

"I had to find your trail," Tack answered calmly, stretching to show his lack of concern. "It wasn't too hard with you guys blundering through these woods like a pair of drunken lumberjacks. Which isn't smart."

"What happened, Tack?" I felt mixed emotions seeing him again after so long. We'd never really been friends—had been rivals, in fact, both for Min and inside the Program—but he'd impressed me with his fearlessness. His relentless nature. Tack got things done, for better or worse. Plus, he was the first living

118

soul we'd seen since stepping onto the beach.

Tack's hands found his pockets. He wore a faded green hoodie and canvas pants. I reminded myself Tack had been living at the Outpost for months, exploring these woods. We were in his world now.

"Wish I knew." Tack took a deep breath. "Two days ago I found the compound exactly like you must have. I'd been camping deep in the forest when that storm nearly killed me. When I got back the next afternoon, the Outpost was trashed. Everyone was gone, just like that." He snapped his fingers.

"So you don't know anything?" Ethan squeezed his nose. "Then why'd you leave a stupid map in your tent?"

"I said I wasn't there, but I know plenty." Tack shrugged off his pack. He looked bigger than I remembered. Maybe an inch taller, with more definition in his arms and shoulders. A few months in the wilderness had given him a rugged look, though the half smirk on his face hadn't changed a bit.

"You left a message," I prompted, knowing Tack would get to the point when he felt like it. "And this." I pulled the gray hammer from my bag.

Tack grimaced. "When I searched the compound, I found the cabins ransacked, that hammer in the grass, and a bloody rock by the fire pit. Did you see it?"

I nodded. "The one under the bucket?"

"Thanks for noticing. So obviously, I knew something terrible had gone down. I did a sweep of the fields and found all the crops in place, which surprised me. I figured the attackers were after our food. Nothing else we have is valuable."

My foot began tapping on its own. "Who could've done it?"

Ethan grunted in frustration. "Toby, you jackass. Six-on-nine with the element of surprise, and those guys are all bruisers. They might even have weapons for all we know."

Tack was frowning but held his tongue.

"There's no chance they just left in a hurry?" I asked, unable not to hope.

Tack shook his head. "If Corbin had run off, he'd have left a note. And they don't have another place to go out here. If anything, they'd have come to you."

I nodded grimly. Ethan spat on the ground.

"Don't forget the hammer," Tack added. "Someone left that behind, and it didn't come from the silo."

My stomach churned. "Is that why we're pushing into the forest? What are we looking for, Tack?"

"Why didn't you leave a real note?" Ethan snapped. "A circled mountain on a play-school map, and the word *here*? Were you trying to be clever?"

Tack leaned back against a tree and scratched his chest. He seemed . . . fuller somehow. More self-possessed. The whiny high-school pipsqueak was long gone, but so was the bitter, hard-edged killer from the Program. This Tack was different. He seemed more comfortable in his own skin.

Ethan bit the hook. "Well? What the hell, Thumbtack?"

Tack's expression hardened. "I found boot prints by the creek. Clumsy and obvious, like a big group. I followed the trail to get a sense of where it was headed, then doubled back. I left that map for anyone who might come after me, then set out again so I didn't lose them."

"Set out where?" I asked. "What's that thing you circled?"

Tack shifted his weight. "That's the million-dollar question, isn't it? I guessed where the trail was going because it's the one place I haven't been able to scout."

Ethan reached up and rubbed his face. "Tack, I'm tired, and more than a little pissed off. Speak plainly or I'll beat you into the ground like a tent stake."

Tack's eyes glittered. "You could try."

"Enough! Both of you." I strode between them. "Ethan, stop stirring things up. Nobody's impressed." Before he could respond, I turned on Tack. "Same goes for you. Eight people are missing. Your whole little tribe. So stop being cute and explain. Stuff happened back at Fire Lake that you need to know about, too."

Tack glared at me, some of the old heat intensifying his gaze. He tamped it quickly. Ethan also seemed ready to punch me, but incredibly, he held his tongue, too.

"There's a single peak in the center of the forest," Tack said briskly. "A gorge surrounds it, with heavy brush growing right up to its drop. Everything about the area says *go away*. I've been planning to cross that gap for weeks, but don't have the best gear. The boot prints leading away from the Outpost were heading straight there."

"How can you be sure?" I asked diplomatically.

"There's nothing else on that side of the river." Some of the chill melted from his voice. "It makes sense, Noah. Across that gorge is a part of the forest I've never seen. Big enough to hide a camp. I bet they've been there this whole time."

"Who?"

Tack met my gaze squarely. "Toby. Or . . . I don't know."

"Why would Toby snatch Corbin and the farmers?" Ethan asked. It was a solid question.

Tack knelt and unzipped his pack. "A better question is, where'd *this* stuff come from?" He removed a set of mesh gloves and a black nylon windbreaker. One glance told me the items weren't from the silo.

"Holy crap," Ethan said. "Shit."

"Can we just say it out loud?" Tack said. "There's more than Toby to worry about here."

My mouth went dry. "How is that possible?"

Tack stepped forward and crossed his arms. "We've always assumed we were the only ones to survive the Dark Star. But why? Who'd we rely on for that information?"

"Black Suit." I closed my eyes, my brain nearly glitching as dark possibilities vied for attention. Black Suit had said the MegaCom was humanity's only lifeboat in the struggle to survive Nemesis. I'd never questioned that statement, wholeheartedly accepting the word of a man who'd executed me five times.

I stumbled back against a boulder and sat, hands on my knees. I was having trouble breathing. Long-held assumptions began to crumble, and suddenly I couldn't trust anything.

What if we *weren't* the only humans alive? What if there were others in the wilderness?

More people meant more danger. Possible enemies. Threats to the colony. Threats to Min.

I can't allow that.

The pressure on my chest eased. Purpose filled me once again. I stood up, suddenly eager to get going. "Let's find our friends," I said in a level voice. "That's all that matters right now."

Tack nodded slowly. I glanced at Ethan, who bobbed his head, one hand adjusting the gun in his waistband.

My body hummed. I gripped Tack's shoulder and felt him squirm a little. "Get us as close as you can. Whoever they are, attacking us was a serious mistake. We'll show them how serious."

Tack twisted away with a mumbled agreement.

Ethan giggled. He was beaming at me like a proud father.

"Let's go clean house."

13

MIN

"What, *that*?"

Sarah nodded placidly, removing a hammer and chisel from her pack. "What'd you expect?" She wedged the chisel above a thick metal plate and began pounding on its base. "There are three designed entrances into the silo, and all are compromised. I told you I knew another way inside, but I never said it would be easy."

We were perched on a ledge near the apex of the silo's southern face. It'd taken us all day to get there, hiking down from Ridgeline and cautiously circling the now-empty lake. We'd snuck past the collapsed front tunnel, avoiding Cole Pritchard and an unknown red-haired boy who seemed to be standing guard.

As with its eastern face, the silo's thick concrete shell was exposed up here, revealing a grate sheltered by an overhang of yellowing stone. I'd had no idea a ventilation duct existed, or that it led down below the flooded main shaft.

But Sarah did. She knew and hadn't told anyone, of course.

I ground my teeth, but put my frustrations aside for now. After this was over Sarah and I were going to have a chat about what she didn't feel required to share with the rest of us. *She lied straight to my face. This crap has to stop.*

I waited silently while Sarah attacked the grate. Finally, a rusted bolt cracked down the middle and she moved to the opposite corner. It took her another twenty minutes to work that one loose, then I took over. These bolts were corroded in place, and the seal had been made to withstand the tests of time. It took me an hour to crack the last two. Finally, Sarah and I levered the casing open together, wincing as the heavy lid landed with a warbling clang.

"Think they heard that?" I panted.

Sarah shook her head. "Those morons are half asleep. Why are they guarding a blocked door anyway? I thought they'd be trying to get inside already."

I frowned. "Maybe they have more explosives. They could be waiting to blast a way in."

"To the top of a flooded shaft? Then what? Unless they have a way to dive through a hundred yards of filthy, pitch-black water, they'll never reach the lab level that way, not until they drain it. Their plan was clever, but ultimately really stupid. They should've just attacked us first."

I gave her an appraising look. "But you still think that's their goal."

Sarah shrugged. "Toby might be deranged and have no plan at all. Never overlook basic idiocy."

I tugged on my ear, not completely sold by Sarah's reasoning. "From the looks of things, the rest of their operation was carefully planned. I think Toby has a clear objective."

Sarah pointed into the darkness we'd uncovered. "Well, we have one, too. I studied the silo's blueprints in case something like this happened—this shaft leads all the way down to air scrubbers on the lowest level, below the MegaCom. So long as the duct didn't rupture, the water should be contained above it. At the bottom is a keypad like everywhere else. If the MegaCom is still powered and the lab complex secure, we can get inside by typing a few numbers."

"And you've known this since the cave-ins. What the hell, Sarah?"

Her penetrating blue eyes bore into me. "I never show all my cards, Min. Not ever. That's always been your problem. You reveal too much, and trust others to do the right thing, while I know people are weak and stupid, and always, *always* selfish. That's why I played circles around you in the Program. And it's also why we now have a way inside that our enemies don't know about. So I think the words you're really looking for are *thank you*."

I stared at her for a long moment, then shook my head. "The time for sandbox games is over, Sarah. There are strangers on the island, and they attacked us. You're going to have start trusting me or they'll have an advantage. We're on the same side."

Sarah looked away. "Let's just go, okay?"

I swallowed a huge sigh. Maybe my words had gotten through.

"Derrick and Casey should've reached the caves by now," I replied instead. "Let's get inside and radio down. If this works, we can slip people into the complex before Toby even suspects what we're doing, and force them to negotiate."

"I'd *love* to have that conversation with Toby," Sarah muttered, staring into the gloomy chute. "Watch his shiny bald head explode."

The opening was two yards square, cold and dark, and angled just steeply enough to be uncomfortable. We tied a rope off at the top and secured it to our waists. Stale, musty air flowed from the gap, but to me that was a good sign. I was praying we didn't end up underwater halfway down.

"Ready?" I asked, biting my bottom lip. I really didn't want to go in there.

Sarah shivered, but straightened quickly, as if embarrassed by her reaction. "Ready."

She hoisted the rope over one shoulder, switched on a flashlight, and began working her way down the chute. I followed a few beats later, sliding on my butt in placcs as the square of sunlight grew smaller and smaller behind us. The thin nylon rope played out as we crept deeper into the black.

The duct's ceiling and walls were smooth stone, but coated in places by things I didn't want to know about. I imagined the bacteria that could've evolved in this enclosure during the millennia it had been sealed off and nearly ran back up to daylight.

Something skittered over my hand and I jerked it away, almost tumbling forward. My panic level skyrocketed, but I kept my focus on Sarah's back. To distract myself I began counting steps, then gave up after two hundred. Finally, I saw the light stop ahead of me. I joined Sarah in front of a moldy hatch where she was applying oil to the hinge.

I shuddered, thinking about the long climb back up if we couldn't get this to budge. But after ten minutes of holding my breath, I heard the locking wheel squeak. The hatch swung open and we shimmied through it, entering a slightly less grimy area beyond. Sarah fumbled her hand against the wall until a keypad glowed in the darkness. We both let out muffled whoops of triumph.

"If this has power, that means the main system is still up and running," Sarah breathed excitedly. "They were unbelievable pricks, but Project Nemesis really built things to last."

"Just open it, please. Like, now." I wanted out of this hole.

Sarah pressed a few keys, there was a click, and then a whoosh of fetid air as the barrier dropped inward. Below us was total darkness, but as Sarah lowered herself into open space, pale yellow LEDs sprang to life around her.

"This is the maintenance level below the lab, where the power plant is located." She dropped to a grated metal catwalk. "I was worried this area might've flooded too, but it looks like the lake only reached the upper floors."

I dropped onto the catwalk next to her. I knew where we were—inside the Program, I'd used this route to escape the MegaCom chamber after Sarah locked me and Derrick inside it. Well, a *simulation* of this route, anyway. It could get spacey differentiating what was real and what had been virtual.

Sarah was standing next to me, silently tapping her lips.

"You okay?" I asked.

"I'm thinking."

"About?"

"Toby's plan. Why is he bothering with the front entrance at all? If this space is secure, he should be working to open the back door. That's a much easier way into the lab complex since it avoids the water. But I don't hear anything from down the tunnel."

"Maybe he's not aiming for it," I said delicately. "I know you think the MegaCom is his ultimate goal, but it could be the alcoves. What would he really want from a computer?"

Sarah was quiet for a moment. "No. No, I'm sure I have it right. Remember, it's not just Toby—he didn't pop back up until these other kids entered the game. But I can't figure out what they're driving at."

I opened my mouth, but she waved me off. "Forget it. I should be glad at how things are working out. We're in first, and that's all that matters. Come on." She started down the catwalk.

"Okay then," I muttered.

Twenty yards down, we reached a ladder I hadn't used before. Sarah rapped it with a fist. "This one leads to the lab."

She began climbing smoothly. The ladder disappeared into a narrow opening in the ceiling. At the top, I paused below her as Sarah tapped another LED panel and a second hatch whooshed open. We pulled ourselves up through the floor of the regeneration chamber. Blazing white lights flickered to life around us.

"Did these bulbs last the whole Program?" I asked. I'd spent almost no time underground after emerging into fresh air six months ago. I hated the silo. Once freed from its claustrophobic clutches, like many, I'd rarely reentered the place. I had to remind myself that Sarah had made this level her home.

Sarah shook her head. "We replaced everything in the complex during the first few weeks. Cleaned the crap out of it, too—it was *disgusting*. But the core systems survived." Her voice grew quiet. "Devin mopped this entire chamber one weekend. I didn't even ask him."

I was impressed. When we'd exited the cloning pods, a million years of grime had coated the walls and floors, making the whole complex feel like an unlivable horror show. But Sarah had envisioned an underground apartment building. She and her sycophants had clearly accomplished wonders. The lab looked almost as pristine as it had inside the Program.

"Let's get to the security hub," Sarah suggested, heading for the door. "We can check any camera feeds that are still up and assess the damage."

"Sounds like a plan," I said. Then I scolded myself for sounding like a dork. I followed Sarah into the hallway running the length of the wing. A pair of swinging doors at the far end led to the living quarters. I pushed through them, unprepared for the changes that awaited.

Where previously the walls had been industrial gray, they were now a cheery sky blue. Hand-sewn curtains adorned fake windows painted at regular intervals, surrounding murals of sunshine and rolling fields. The carpets had been cleaned and freshly vacuumed. Sleeping cells now had the feel of individual dorm rooms. I'd assumed Sarah's crew had been living like garrisoned soldiers down here, but they'd truly made the place comfortable.

"Are you hungry?" Sarah asked. "There was food rehydrating when we fled the tremors. It should still be fine."

She led me into the kitchen.

Toby was sitting at the lone table, eating a bowl of cereal.

"Hey, girls." He calmly wiped his mouth with a napkin. "How'd you sneak in here?"

I leapt backward, slamming into someone's chest. I spun to find Mike Nolan blocking the doorway with Chris smiling at his side. Both held pistols. I recoiled, adrenaline dumping into my bloodstream. We were trapped.

For her part, Sarah didn't move. "How'd you get in?"

"I asked you first." Toby rose and put his dish in the sink. Then he turned and leaned back against the counter, one hand rising to stroke his shaved head. "But no big deal. We got our own secret way, too. I know some things about this place even you don't, Sarah. How about that for a change?"

I heard Sarah mutter a curse. She hated getting outsmarted, and by Toby? Unthinkable.

Toby grinned. "I keep running into you these days. Must be fate."

Sarah's lip curled in distaste. "I can't be that unlucky. What do you want, Toby? Why are you trying to take the silo from everyone else?"

Toby shrugged. "I need it. For stuff."

Sarah's face turned red. "Did you blow up the roof, Toby? Did you *kill* five of your own classmates?"

Toby frowned in what looked like genuine regret. "No one was supposed to be out there when the charges went off. I can't know everything. I just needed to close all the doors but my own. My spy turned out to be kinda crappy on intel."

Sarah lurched forward a step, but I grabbed her arm. The word *spy* was strobing in my mind like a Times Square billboard, but I had more pressing concerns. "Who are the strangers outside?" I asked. "Where'd they come from? Why are they attacking us?"

"All good questions," he replied, mock-serious. "But I'm not going to answer them, because I can't see why I should. You understand."

"Toby, please." I did my best to sound conciliatory. "We've had our differences, but no one kicked you guys out of the village. If you truly didn't mean to hurt anyone, we can talk about what happens next civilly. But we have to know where you found other people still alive. It goes against everything we were told."

Toby's smirk faltered. "You have no idea what's out there, Melinda. Everything we thought we knew is wrong." He smacked his hands together, the grin sliding back into place. "Thankfully, I know how to adapt. I made a deal."

I glanced at the Nolans. They remained smugly silent. This was clearly Toby's song and dance.

"What kind of deal? Toby, stop screwing around. Tell us what's going on!"

He clicked his tongue. "Actually, I'm going to lock you two up instead. My new friends want the situation contained, and I do my best to please. Gotta hold up my end of the bargain."

He nodded to the twins. Mike wrapped a hand around my forearm. Chris reached for Sarah, but she whirled and slapped him across the face. He rolled his eyes and laughed.

"Now, now." Toby pulled a gun from the back of his jeans. "This doesn't have to be unpleasant. I'll let you pick which room you want to bunk in."

Sarah tensed, then abruptly relaxed. She spun and shouldered between the chuckling twins. I was marched after her as she stormed to the last door in the row. The room beyond was slightly larger than the others—probably her old unit. I followed her inside and we both sat on the bed.

I didn't know what to do. I needed time to think, even if it was spent imprisoned with Sarah.

Toby stood in the doorway, casually resting an elbow against its frame. "I'll want to know how you got in here, but that can wait. I have some business to get done. Rounding up strays is hard work."

"Why are you doing this?" I spat, unable to keep the hurt from my voice. "How could you choose outsiders over your own classmates?"

For the first time, Toby looked legitimately surprised. "Seriously? You've been against me from the moment we entered the Program. Hell, Min—you hated me even before then. But that's all trivia now. Bottom line: These guys can give me what I want. So they get what *they* want."

"You're after the MegaCom," Sarah said, holding Toby's gaze. "Why?"

He smiled darkly. "You're the smart one, Sarah. I'm surprised you can't guess."

She shook her head. "Whatever's on the hard drives can't help you much. There are no other working computers. Data is useless, unless your friends are after something."

Toby cackled. "I love knowing more than you. And who said anything about data?"

Sarah's face blanked. She chewed her bottom lip.

"Then what *do* you want?" I asked.

The light of obsession kindled in Toby's eyes. "I wanna go home, Min."

I blinked. "Toby, we are home. This is our valley. The MegaCom can't turn back time."

"That's where you're wrong." Toby drummed his stomach with both hands. "I don't wanna go back to high school or anything like that. That life was worse than this one. No, I've got a better plan. I want back inside the infinite."

Sarah gasped. I'd never heard her make that sound before.

"My boys and I are going back into the Program," Toby said. "It's all been worked out. You can keep these needy, fragile bodies, and the struggle to feed them and stay alive. You think it's going to get easier? Wait a year, then five. Me? I'll take the simulation. I miss being a god."

I stared at him, unable to form a coherent sentence. "Toby, that's . . . that's . . ."

"Keep the real world, Min." He gave me a lopsided grin. I could hear other people moving in the hallway behind him. How many enemies were down here? "Keep your rules, and your morality, and all that crap. It ain't for me." He breathed a contented sigh. "In a few days' time I'll be back in virtual Fire Lake. Immortal and untouchable. So just sit back and stay out of my way, because I'll sacrifice every last one of you to get there if I have to. Bye, now."

Toby stepped back and closed the door, trapping us inside.

14

NOAH

I held my breath.

Low voices carried from just over the rise. *Right where Tack said they'd be.*

The forest was foggy and wet. I glanced at Ethan lying beside me, saw a vein pumping in his neck as he listened intently. I couldn't make out individuals, but the tones weren't right. Even at a murmur they didn't sound like people I knew. I'd spent enough time with everyone to be able to tell.

"You ready?" Ethan whispered.

I rubbed a hand across my face. Nodded. The sun was setting behind us, so the light would be in their eyes. Ethan counted down three fingers, then we army-crawled to the lip of the hill. Below us a deep gorge stretched roughly a dozen yards wide.

Beyond it was a flat-bottomed dell in the shadow of an enormous rock formation rising from the woods.

We'd reached the location circled in red on Tack's map.

The camp was directly across from where we hid. I counted eight people around a crackling fire. Recognized none of them.

My heart began thudding in my chest. I couldn't argue with my own eyes.

Strangers. People who hadn't grown up in Fire Lake. Hadn't spent a million years inside a simulation with me. Unknown teenagers, chatting casually, as if their existence wasn't unthinkable.

I'm gonna be sick.

I licked my lips. Felt something clamp onto my forearm. Ethan was gripping my wrist but not looking at me. Instead, he pointed to the far side of the circle.

Bile rose in my throat a second time.

A gagged figure was hunched over away from the others. Legs tied. Arms wrenched behind their back. It took a moment of squinting for me to recognize Liesel's plump frame. My eyes slid to her right, and I spotted three more prisoners.

I caught Ethan's eyes and mouthed four names: *Liesel. Neb. Benny. Emma.* Then I raised my palms, mimed looking around. *Where are the others?*

Ethan's jaw formed a rigid line. He shook his head.

He jabbed a thumb over his shoulder and we slunk back from the threshold. Then we rose and hustled to where Tack was standing lookout at the bottom of the hill. He'd found the camp first while scouting ahead, and his report had proved dead-on, but I'd insisted on seeing things for myself. It's not that I didn't trust Tack. I *needed* to see.

"Satisfied?" Tack whispered.

"Yes." Blood pounded in my ears. Viewing other living people had been so thunderous, I could barely stay upright, but I put it away for later. My focus had to be on our friends. Then I went cold all over, remembering the count.

"We only saw four," I said. "Where are the others?"

Ethan spat on a pile of soggy leaves. "Corbin, Kayla, Isaiah, and Darren are missing. They better be okay."

"They could've split them up," Tack said. "Maybe there's another camp."

"God I hope so," I breathed.

Tack grunted. Though not a part of the farming experiment, he'd been living with Corbin's group for months. But if he was distressed by what we'd seen, he was keeping it hidden. I wasn't surprised. Tack had never worn emotions on his sleeve.

"This is as far as I've ever gone," he said. "I've been planning to rope across that gap, but the last time I came looking for a spot, I found the gloves and jacket I showed you and freaked. By the time I got back, the Outpost had been raided."

Ethan ran knuckles across his cheek. "So what now? Hit them when they sleep?"

"We still don't know if they're armed," I said. "Or where they're going. Tack's right—they could have a second camp around the corner with a dozen more people."

Ethan sneered at me. "Great. Spineless Noah Livingston returns. What's your plan then, huh? Sit back while they drag Benny into the jungle?"

"Of course not," I snapped, growing angry myself. "I'm just saying we need more information. We don't know who they are,

137

what they want, or where they're going. I prefer to fight with some idea of what I'm up against."

Ethan's expression promised a nasty reply, but Tack held up a hand for silence. Surprisingly, it worked. "I agree with Noah," he said.

Ethan scowled. "Oh, for—"

"It's common sense to investigate an enemy before you attack," Tack interrupted smoothly. "And in this case, there's an easy way to do it."

A shiver traveled my spine. I'd caught Tack's drift, even if Ethan hadn't.

"Please enlighten me, Rambo." Ethan made air quotes. "How do we 'investigate' the bastards without taking them on?"

Tack flashed a toothy smile, but with a cutting edge. "We grab one and make him talk."

I squeezed my eyes shut, then snapped them back open. Our friends were tied up down there. Others were missing. The monsters who had attacked them might come for Fire Lake Island next.

"You have a plan?" I asked.

Tack nodded. Ethan gave me an unreadable look, but remained silent.

"These jerk-offs think they're untouchable over there," Tack said. "They built a huge fire and aren't even trying to be quiet." He pointed down the gorge to a low ridge. "I know a place where I think we can get across. We'll strike tonight, in the dark, and drag one of those punks back here with us."

"But how will we lure someone away from the group?" Ethan asked.

I snorted as the last piece fell into place.

"Nature calls for everyone, right?" I smiled darkly. "Some dude's about to have the worst pee break of his life."

Ethan and I crouched behind a pair of giant oak trees. Him on the left, me on the right. Tack was up closer to their camp—full night had fallen, and he'd snuck right to the edge of the firelight, ready to signal when a target was headed our way. It was our job to grab the victim before he could call out, then drag him from sight.

Easier said than done.

My palms were damp. I wiped them on my jeans. The sun had set less than an hour ago, but I was already antsy. Kidnapping wasn't one of the many horrors I had personal experience with. In the Program, you typically shot first. Weirdly, this felt like a bigger violation.

We'd crossed the gorge as quietly as possible, on a line Tack set with an honest-to-God lasso throw. My heart nearly stopped watching him shimmy across the gap, the hooked stump shifting precariously beneath his weight. But he'd made it safely and secured a better anchorage, adding a second line we could walk on. Ethan and I followed with relative ease.

Step one, complete.

We'd left the lines fixed in case we needed a speedy getaway, although I didn't see how we could force a prisoner across against his will. Our plan was to hide once we snatched someone rather than outrun any pursuit. I was praying we could avoid being chased altogether.

Tack had crawled close and watched two strangers use the same route to relieve themselves, so we'd cautiously worked around the perimeter and laid our ambush along that trail. Now we waited.

Step two, complete.

Tack would wink a flashlight at us when someone came down the path. Ethan would bag the sap's head and choke off his air supply while I stabbed him with a syringe from Tack's medical kit. Headlock and sedative should prevent any shouts for help as we hauled our mark away.

At least, that was the plan.

The ways it could go wrong were too numerous to contemplate.

Tack had plotted an escape route cutting deeper into the woods. We hoped the strangers would assume we'd bolt for the gorge. Instead, we'd hide on this side of the gap and lie low until morning. Maybe there'd even be a chance to free our friends. If not, we'd extract answers from our prisoner and figure out what to do next.

We all three agreed we weren't going back without our classmates. Whatever it took. I didn't want to think too hard about what that might mean, but that didn't make it less true. If people had to bleed in order to free my friends, so be it. They hit first. I could hit back harder.

I glanced at Ethan, barely visible in the moonlight filtering through the canopy. He felt my gaze and looked over, frowning his impatience. I understood. This was the kind of task you wanted done with as soon as possible. Lurking behind a tree to snatch a stranger in the dark was not something that got easier over time.

"This is taking too long," I hissed, unable to keep silent any longer.

"Shut up, you idiot."

Okay, then.

As if summoned by our voices, a light blinked once, twice, then went dark. I tensed, fumbling the syringe from my pocket. Uncapping the needle, I nearly dropped the thing before steadying my hands. I went as still as I could.

Muffled footfalls. A softly whistled melody. I crouched, ready to spring.

A shadow passed between the oaks.

Ethan moved like lightning, the canvas bag sliding over our victim's head with a whoosh. There was a strangled cough, then Ethan had his arm around the person's windpipe and the sound cut off with a sickly gurgle.

I leapt forward, looking for a soft spot to inject. But it was black on black and I couldn't see the target, and didn't want to miss. The victim's elbow slammed into Ethan's gut. He wheezed painfully, and his grip must've loosened, because the stranger managed to whirl and get a knee up, striking between his legs.

Ethan's turn to gurgle.

The target sprang backward, but hadn't realized I was standing there, being useless. The needle jabbed through a thin black sweater, the force of our collision depressing the plunger. Then the syringe was ripped from my fingers as the stranger spun. Something smashed into the side of my head.

Lights. Stars.

I fell to the ground, felt a booted foot connect with my ribs. I heard a string of harsh words but understood none of them.

I gasped as more pain exploded in my kidney. I rolled away, trying to protect myself, when my victim-turned-attacker crashed down on top of me, knocking the wind from my lungs.

"What the hell?" Tack growled, joining the fray. He was grappling with the stranger on top of me.

I still couldn't breathe—and was beginning to worry they'd smother me before I could crawl free—when Tack grunted and toppled backward, holding his face.

The target lurched up and took a running step toward the camp, then fell.

"*Haaapp*," a voice slurred. The figure crawled another step. Collapsed. Lay still.

I was spread-eagle on the dirt, panting, listening for pounding feet. Nothing. Our mark hadn't called out until it was too late. Ethan was gathering himself with a string of not-so-silent curses.

Tack grabbed me by the shoulders and hauled me up. "*Let's go, you morons.*" Together we managed to lift our somehow-successfully-subdued prisoner. Ethan slung the unconscious form over his shoulder. I grabbed the legs. Tack led us into the woods.

We hustled in this awkward chain for what seemed like miles, until Tack pushed into a gulch shielded by pines on three sides. We dumped our prisoner on the ground and collapsed in a row, our backs against exposed granite, breathing hard and grateful not to be moving.

I rubbed my temple. Coughed and spat.

"What the hell?" Tack whispered finally. "You guys got your asses kicked."

Ethan shoved me roughly. "Noah stood there like a damn

statue. Why didn't you stick him?"

"I couldn't see anything!" I protested, checking my jaw to make sure it was in the proper place. "We only had one syringe. I didn't want to inject a duffel bag or something."

Tack slid his pack off with a groan. "Hands down, that was the worst ambush ever attempted. I'm stunned you two didn't tackle each other."

"Piss off, Thumbtack," Ethan growled. "All you did was blink a flashlight. And I think you punched *me* at the end there."

I began to laugh.

It started slowly, but soon I couldn't stop, my stomach aching as I tried to muffle the sound. Ethan and Tack turned to stare at me, then they began chuckling too. Soon we all slumped over in fits of muted laughter.

"We're the . . . worst . . . commando squad . . . in history," I gasped, unable to breathe.

"I think I did hit Ethan." Tack wiped his eyes as he sat back against the stone. "My bad."

"It's not our fault." I giggled moronically. "Who knew we'd attack a freaking ninja. That guy moved like a snake."

"True story." Ethan covered his eyes with one hand. "My balls. Oh dudes, it's not even funny. My balls right now. I fought an X-Man and lost."

We cracked up again. We'd botched everything, but somehow accomplished the mission. Good enough.

A moan snapped us to silence. I glanced at our prisoner, who'd rolled over and was now lying faceup. Ethan and I each grabbed a limb while Tack scrambled for rope, but it wasn't necessary. The stranger went boneless in our hands.

"Punch him again if you have to," Ethan muttered. "He deserves it. We gotta tie this psycho to a tree before he wakes up and kills us all."

Tack powered his flashlight, its yellow beam illuminating our captive's face.

We all reared back in surprise.

"Oh, man," Ethan said. "We definitely can't tell anyone about this."

"Never," Tack agreed. "Not a soul."

I just nodded, my mouth hanging open as Tack kept his light on our prisoner.

On her glossy lips, and delicate, upturned nose.

15

MIN

"What a moron," Sarah grumbled.

"Smart enough to capture us." I sat on the bed, pressing both fists to my cheeks. "So they really did cause the cave-ins. How in the world did Toby learn to do something like that?"

Sarah was pacing the length of the tiny chamber. Had been for over an hour. "Toby's not bright enough to make a box of mac and cheese by himself. Obviously these strangers helped."

I shook my head. "Why are they giving him what he wants? What could he possibly offer in return?"

"Us," Sarah said darkly. "He gave them enough help to cut off our stores, divide the group, and raid the village. But my gut says he's being played, too. They won't really put him back inside the Program. They're using him. What we need to figure out is why they attacked us rather than making peaceful contact. Who are these people? Where do they live? What are they planning to do next?"

"I can't even guess." I slammed a fist on the bed. "And now we're trapped like rats. Sarah, they gave Toby *guns*. This is a disaster. We have no way to fight back."

"Speak for yourself." Sarah stopping pacing and took a deep breath. She walked over and placed her ear against the door. Sarah held still a moment, then nodded to herself. "I didn't choose this room out of sentiment. Help me move that trunk by my desk."

It was an old wooden crate, well sanded and painted forest green. Heavier than it looked. Sarah grabbed the far side and together we lugged it into the bathroom. She hopped on top of it and reached for a small panel in the ceiling that was nearly invisible in the dull white paint.

"I always have a back door." Sarah pushed up on the square, then let it swing down. "Stay here and close the bathroom. If anyone checks on us, tell them I'm not feeling well. Say it's a girl problem—boys can't handle that. I'll crawl into the office wing and let you out when the coast is clear."

"How long will you be?" I asked, embarrassed by the tremor in my voice. I didn't trust Sarah, but I didn't want to be alone either.

"It's easier for one person to sneak around than two." Sarah pulled herself up through the ceiling, then looked back at me from inside the vent. "I'll go as fast as I can. If Toby comes back, bash his head in with the toilet seat. He deserves it." Something moved behind her eyes, but I couldn't read it. "If you hear an alarm, just get out any way you can."

"An alarm? What?"

But Sarah was already gone. I stared at the space where her head had been. Then, heaving an exasperated sigh, I climbed up and pushed the panel closed. I debated whether to drag the trunk back into place. Decided not to. If someone searched the room, it wouldn't take them long to figure out how Sarah had escaped, but I might need a quick exit.

I closed the bathroom door and collapsed on the bed. Stared up at the ceiling.

For the first time, I really thought about what it meant that other people were alive.

It meant my father must have lied.

Logically, there was no other explanation. If the Earth truly had been ravaged by Nemesis, then a million years wasn't nearly long enough for human life to re-evolve. But it was also way, way, way too long for humanity to have survived under cataclysmic conditions. Either way, time made these strangers' presence impossible. Yet here they were.

That left two options.

Either we weren't the only class preserved by Project Nemesis.

Or Project Nemesis was a lie.

Maybe Earth had never been in danger. Maybe the planet *wasn't* destroyed.

Maybe my father played me one last time before he died.

That answer made the most sense, but my instincts rejected it. I replayed every conversation I'd ever had with him. They felt genuine. Why would he lie about any of it? He'd had all the power. Deceiving me at the end would've served no purpose. At least, none I could fathom.

And yet.

There were strangers outside the door.

I rose and put my ear against it like Sarah had. I heard heavy treads as someone walked by. Muffled voices. It sounded like there were more than a few people inside the complex. How would Sarah draw them away from the living quarters?

I tested the knob, found that it turned in my hand. Slowly, I cracked the door.

Kyle Homling was sitting in a chair across the hall, spinning a pistol in his hand. He looked up and saw me, then smiled. "Back inside, Min. Toby said not to get rough with you two, but he didn't leave instructions about a breakout attempt."

I snarled, wanting to charge forward and tear him to pieces. Kyle had lived in Home Town since the beginning. He was a traitor. "How could you?" I hissed.

Kyle laughed. "Whatever. I got bored. Toby promised I could have a gun."

I slammed the door shut, shaking with rage. Then I squeezed my ears. "*Focus.*"

No locks, but a guard. Others moving around. I went into the bathroom and dragged the trunk back to its original position. If someone discovered Sarah was missing, I'd say she slipped past Kyle. It would serve him right if he got pounded.

I sat down in the desk chair, weighing options. Kyle was a scumbag, but he'd been formidable inside the Program. I wasn't sure I could take him even with the element of surprise. I thought briefly about trying to seduce him, luring him into the room, but rejected the idea. I couldn't sell it. I wore my hatred on my face.

There was nothing to do but wait.

I awoke to a blaring siren.

My elbow jerked, and my head nearly smacked the desk.

I shot to my feet, disoriented and gasping. Feet pounded in the hallway.

I ran to the door and cracked it. Kyle was standing beside his chair, shouting questions at that meathead Tucker as he barreled through the doors to the office suite.

"Kyle, what is it?" I yelled. "What's going on?"

"Stay in there!" he barked, red-faced and reaching for his gun. "You and Sarah better not even think ab—"

There was a crunching sound. Something roared from the direction in which Tucker had disappeared.

My eyes widened. "Kyle, that—"

The double doors exploded inward with an avalanche of black liquid. Tucker and a boy I didn't recognize were washed into the living quarters.

Kyle froze, raw panic on his face.

Our eyes met. His hand reached out.

The flood swallowed him as I yanked the door shut.

Liquid surged under the door frame as I ran to the trunk and pushed it back into the bathroom. I leapt on top as the outer door buckled and flew open. Grimy water began filling the unit. With shaking hands, I popped open the panel and dragged myself up inside.

I was in a narrow crawl space running left to right. With no understanding of where I was going, I chose the direction away from where the torrent had come from. As I scrambled through the darkness, I heard the gurgle of rushing liquid, fizzling electronics, and screams of terror.

The lab complex was flooding. I was trapped inside it, with no way out.

Calm down. Do the next thing. Don't freeze up.

I scrambled along the crawl space until I hit a solid steel wall. My mind gibbered as I realized the way forward was blocked, but I felt around in the dark. There was a ladder next to me, leading down instead of up. I nearly moaned in despair that it went the wrong way, but remembered the ventilation shaft. It terminated underneath the lab complex.

One level down.

I swung onto the rungs and began to descend. I thought of Sarah for a moment, but there was nothing I could do. I didn't know where she was or have any way to help her. A seal must've given way, and water was pouring in. I shouldn't have been surprised. A million years of rust and wear had met the pressure of an entire lake. It was inevitable that the flood would force its way inside.

And I'm lucky enough to be here. Can't stop winning.

I shoved that aside. I had to get down to the maintenance level, locate the vent, and climb out of this deathtrap before the water found me. Just the thought of that inky, suffocating flood paralyzed me with fear. I didn't want to die that way. I didn't want to die at all.

The rungs marched downward. I went as fast as I could. A catwalk appeared, but before I could even step off the ladder, a stream of dirty liquid began raining from above. I was running out of time.

I raced along the catwalk, trying to get my bearings. I needed to pass from under the living quarters to beneath the regeneration lab. If I was going the right way, the correct hatch should be somewhere just ahead.

The lights along the catwalk flickered. My heart skipped a beat.

To be down here, stumbling in total darkness. My hands shook at the thought.

I entered a vast chamber and reached a ladder. Peered up. Was this the one to the lab? There was another ladder twenty yards farther down the catwalk. I was scanning for the vent hatch when a thunderous crash echoed across the room. A curtain of water began pouring down the other ladder. Cracked and dripping blade drives sloshed to the catwalk in a heap.

Suddenly, I knew exactly where I was. Above the second ladder was the chamber housing the MegaCom. The water was gushing from there.

With a cold horror, I realized what that meant.

The MegaCom must be flooded. Destroyed. Our lifeboat was dead for good.

Spinning, I desperately scanned the walls. *There!* One hatch among several hung open in what seemed like the right place. I couldn't be sure, but I was out of time to be choosy.

I'd taken two steps toward it when something heavy fell from above.

It landed on the catwalk with a wet thud. Almost against my will, I crept a few steps closer. The lights blazed once, then began to flicker erratically before dimming to almost nothing.

Too late. I'd seen the body, and recognized Toby's round, knobby head. Water was hammering down on him, then draining to the power plant level below us. Soon the flood would fill that space and fritz out everything that ran on power. We'd never repair it.

I froze. I could leave Toby. No one would know. He'd never be a problem again.

I shot forward and grabbed his legs, pulling him out from underneath the next waterfall. I had no plan, no hope, no idea what I was doing. But I couldn't leave anyone like that. Not even him.

I managed to drag him back to the other ladder, but my arms were already shaking. There was no way I could pull him up through the hatch. I glanced around frantically for some way to make a sling.

More water exploded from above, raining down in a dozen new places.

The lights died. I screamed in the darkness, hands scrambling until I clutched a nearby rung. I couldn't see anything. Couldn't help Toby, and maybe not even myself.

With a shriek of frustration, I released him and worked blindly along the wall. Found the hatch and crawled into the opening beyond.

I left Toby there. I left him to drown in the dark at the bottom of a hole.

The chute led up and up and up, with no end in sight.

I was shivering. Soaked. Arms abraded and raw. I scuttled blindly, with no idea whether I was climbing the right ventilation shaft. If I'd chosen wrong, I'd be trapped against a solid metal screen at the top until the water boiled up and drowned me at last.

Then I remembered the rope. Heart in my throat, I ran my hands along the bottom of the chute. Something slick and thin slipped through my fingers. I nearly collapsed in relief, then gripped it tightly.

Climb.

A dim square of black.

No bigger than a stamp.

Pinpoints twinkled all over it.

It grew larger as I dragged myself upward.

The moon appeared.

A soft breeze found me.

I began to weep as I reached out of the silo and slithered into open air.

Something grabbed my hand and I screamed, thrashing like a hooked fish.

"Min, it's okay! It's me!"

A lantern ignited.

Sarah's face appeared.

She ripped off her sweatshirt and shoved it over my head, began rubbing my arms and legs for warmth. "You made it," she whispered. I heard both relief and disbelief in her voice. "I knew you could do it. I *knew* it. I was right. You're stronger than the others."

My teeth were chattering so hard I could barely speak.

"W-what . . . what ha-happened?"

Sarah pulled back. "The, uh … the lab flooded."

In a glance, I knew. "Y- . . . y-you!"

Sarah flinched, but didn't look away. "Like I said, I knew you'd figure it out."

Fury swept through me, driving the lethargy from my limbs. I shoved Sarah hard. She stumbled backward but kept her balance. A change came over her face. Sarah crossed her arms. When she spoke again, her voice was as cold as ice. "Toby and most of his team were down there. I saw a chance to end this threat in one swoop, so I took it. Don't expect me to have regrets."

"You almost killed me, too! Did that even register, you psychopath?"

Her facade cracked for a split second, then re-formed. "I stayed here waiting for you. I hoped you could find the way out and save yourself, and you did. I didn't want to kill you, Min."

I gripped my head in my hands. "The MegaCom is gone. I hope you realize what you've done."

Sarah folded her legs and sat neatly across from me. "That's unfortunate. But at least now it can't hurt us."

"How could a machine hurt us, Sarah?" I pushed wet hair from my face, finally beginning to feel alive again.

"I have no idea. But if the strangers want it, we don't want them to have it. That's Combat Strategy 101."

My breath caught as I remembered the catwalk. "You killed Toby, Sarah."

She eyed me, her expression unreadable. "You're sure?"

"I saw his body. I hope it was worth it."

154

"Toby is nothing!" Sarah's hands flew up as anger twisted her features. "He picked this fight. It's the strangers we have to worry about."

"Toby was seventeen. One of the last humans alive on Earth. He meant something."

Sarah pursed her lips, eyes smoldering. "Do you know what happened while we were gone, Min?"

I straightened but didn't speak. Obviously I didn't know.

"Some of Toby's new pals attacked Ridgeline," Sarah said coldly. "I reached Cash on the radio. Derrick was waiting for us at the head of the Ocean Road—he saw Sam and everyone else being marched across the flat at gunpoint. Whoever these people are, they're rounding our class up. So if I killed a few of them down there, I'm glad."

My mind reeled. I was exhausted. Afraid. Unable to put the pieces together.

All at once it was too much, and I began to cry.

Sarah moved to sit next to me. "Come on. Let's get you warm. We'll find Derrick and figure out what to do next."

"Noah," I mumbled. "We need to find Noah and make a plan."

Sarah chuckled without humor. "I wouldn't mind seeing him myself. Maybe he could tell us where these jackasses came from, or how they got onto our island undetected. They don't look like refugees, Min. I don't know who they are, but they have a secret."

I staggered to my feet. A fire had kindled inside me at the thought of Noah, out there struggling on his own. I had to find him. And Tack. All the others, everyone still able to resist.

We had to free our friends and deal with this threat, whoever they may be.

These people had made a mistake. They'd underestimated us. My classmates and I had lived through hell for a million years. We weren't going to take anything lying down. Every one of us knew how to defend ourselves.

Fire Lake had been full of monsters once. Predators in human form.

It was time to rise again.

16

NOAH

A girl.

Hadn't counted on that.

She was still unconscious by the small fire Tack had finally allowed. Dawn was breaking, and tendrils of smoky light illuminated her face. The girl had vivid copper-colored hair, cut short, and pale, dimpled cheeks. I thought about our plan to grab a prisoner in a delicate position and my face went scarlet. Thank God for the small favor of catching her in transit.

I stifled a yawn. Rose and stretched. We'd taken shifts guarding our prisoner, but I hadn't really slept at all. Ethan was snoring beside me. Tack had spent most of the night out in the forest, watching for signs of pursuit, but he'd trudged back into camp a half hour ago and was stirring oatmeal in a pan.

"So they're gone?" I said.

Tack glanced up, then put a finger to his lips, nodding at the girl. He set the cook pot aside and motioned for me to join him at the edge of the clearing. "She could be faking," he whispered, positioning himself so he could keep an eye on our prisoner as we talked. "I don't want to give up any information we don't have to."

I frowned. "What are we going to do with her? I feel like we didn't think this through."

"We'll question her." Tack spun his hand in a loose circle. "Find out how she's alive, and where their base is. And why the hell they grabbed our people."

My eyes were glued to the girl. She had smooth porcelain skin, but with the tiniest hint of freckles. For some reason I couldn't stop looking at her. "You said the others broke camp?"

"They cleared out in the night. Either they went looking for us and missed completely, or they bolted to . . . I don't know. Wherever they're from, I guess."

I rocked back on my heels. "Tack, have you thought about how they're kids, like us?"

"Speak for yourself, Livingston, I'm all man over here."

"Whatever. My point is, they seem our age. *Another* group of teenagers on New Earth? What the hell does that mean?"

Tack was silent for a few beats. "No idea. Maybe Black Suit played us harder than we thought." He pointed roughly at our captive. "But *she* knows, and I think it's time we woke her up to tell us."

I felt a prickling in my gut. My hand rose to rub my neck. "Hey, Tack. Listen. We're not gonna, like . . . hurt her or anything, right? If it had been a guy, maybe . . ."

Tack gave me a stony look. "You get the fact that she attacked and kidnapped some of our classmates, right?"

My stomach dropped. "Yeah. Yes, but . . ."

"And she literally beat the crap out of all three of us last night. Remember?"

"Tack, I'm just saying—"

"I'm not gonna start arbitrarily punching someone, Noah. But she *is* going to talk, or else . . ." He shrugged, stepping past me. "They ransacked the Outpost and tied up my neighbors like chickens. Some of them are still missing, and we don't know whether they're okay or not. You need to start thinking about it like that."

I watched him stride back to the fire. He nudged Ethan with his boot, eliciting an angry growl. Tack really was harder. Not in the fake-tough-guy way so many had developed inside the Program, when things didn't truly matter. But in a real-life way. The scary way.

Ethan roused himself while Tack doled out oatmeal. We ate in silence, each wrapped in our own thoughts. Finally, as I was scraping the dregs from my bowl, the girl began to stir.

I glanced at Tack, who rose and walked around to her side of the fire. "Get up," he ordered.

The girl's lids fluttered open, and I nearly choked. Her eyes were a startling green, impossibly bright, as if they were backlit by LEDs. When those emerald lasers latched onto me, I looked away first, but not before noting the fierce intelligence powering them.

The girl jerked up into a sitting position. She tried to move her arms but found them securely bound behind her back. She glanced at Tack, and the wondrous eyes narrowed, but she didn't cry out. Instead she made a slow survey of our camp. For a girl being held captive by three unknown boys, alone in the trackless woods, she seemed remarkably self-assured.

"Who are you?" Tack demanded.

Green Eyes gave Tack a disdainful glare. She shifted her body away from him.

Ethan snorted. "Haven't lost your touch, have you Thumbtack?"

Tack stepped in front of her again, crouching down to eye level so she was forced to look at him. "I asked you a question, politely. I expect answers when I do that, or I won't stay polite. Now: Who. Are. You?"

Green Eyes smirked, then spat in Tack's face. Tack jerked away, his lips forming a thin white line.

"How about I try?" I said quickly, lurching up and rounding the fire. I put a hand on Tack's shoulder.

Tack stepped back. "Sure thing, pal." He was staring at the girl to make sure she was listening. "But let our new friend here know I'm not going away. I lived in that compound they attacked. I saw the blood."

Did she flinch at the last part? It was hard to tell. I moved a step closer and her gaze cut to me, taking my measure with a glance that seared like fire. I coughed. Was having a hard time concentrating. I had to get a grip.

"No one's going to hurt you," I said, keeping my voice even.

"Speak for yourself," Tack muttered, and Ethan snorted darkly.

I ignored them. "Will you tell us where you're from?"

No response. The girl's features could've been carved out of marble.

I flashed a rueful smile. "You see, my classmates and I were under the impression we were the only people alive, but that's clearly not true. I'll admit it—we're very curious about how your crew exists. Is there a settlement close by? Where do you live?"

"Why'd you attack us?" Tack demanded. "We weren't bothering anyone. We were trying to grow things. Is this your island or something?"

The girl's lips curled into a sneer. She pointedly looked away from Tack. She still hadn't spoken a word, and I got the sense she had no intention of doing so. Not without . . . motivation. The cold in my gut began to spread.

Ethan got to his feet and stretched his arms. Then he rolled his shoulders, finishing the performance by cracking his knuckles one by one. After all that, he looked at the girl. She'd been tracking his movements but didn't appear scared. If anything, she looked amused.

I noticed something about her clothes. She had on a loose cotton sweater with canvas pants—simple garments that looked homemade. But as she shifted, I could see a black stretchy material beneath her shirt.

"What are you wearing?" I said.

This drew the first startled reaction I'd seen. She froze for an instant, then scrunched into a ball. Ethan stepped over and squatted down in front of her, eliciting a low intake of breath. Green Eyes suddenly butted her head at him, but Ethan laughed, dodging and pushing her onto her side.

He pulled her sweater up an inch.

161

"Easy," I warned, but Ethan was examining the girl's black undershirt. Even I could tell he was only checking the material. "This is manufactured," he said in surprise. "It's nylon, or something like that. Better than our stuff without a doubt." He glared at her. "Where'd you get this? How'd you make this shirt?"

She scowled at the dirt. Said nothing.

"I'm running out of patience," Tack said quietly. "I don't like getting rough, but we have to know about these people."

His words gave me an idea. "I need you both for a second. In private. Over there."

Ethan shot me annoyed glance. "Just speak, Noah. You afraid she'll make fun of you?"

Tack made a chopping motion with one hand. "No names." He nodded impatiently and we strode to the edge of the clearing again, Ethan muttering about cloak-and-dagger nonsense as he followed. When we couldn't be overheard, Tack spoke under his breath. "Okay. What is it?"

"I have a plan for how we might find their camp."

Tack showed me his palms. "All ears, Livingston."

I glanced at the girl. She was sitting up but not looking at us. To anyone watching it would appear she was there by choice. Except for being tied up, of course.

I swallowed, inwardly cringing at the reaction I knew was coming. "I think we should let her go."

Ethan gave me a flat look. "I'm sorry?"

"I know it sounds crazy, but I think this could work."

"You want us to let our prisoner go." Tack tilted his head. "The prisoner we risked our asses to capture and who knows all the answers to our questions."

"Yes, but onl—"

Ethan shoved me in the chest. "Why are you such a wuss, Noah? Tack's right. We have to find out what's going on."

"I'm not suggested we give up!" I hissed, my frustration spilling over. "I have a plan, if you jackasses would shut up and listen."

Tack took a deep breath. Gave me a tight, fake smile. "Let's hear it, Napoleon."

I explained my idea. Ethan scoffed like I was crazy, but I could tell Tack was considering it. He chewed on his bottom lip, a small frown twisting his face.

"Tell me you're not listening to this," Ethan said to him. "He wants to give up our leverage!"

Tack ran a hand through his greasy black hair. "I don't think she's going to say a damn thing," he said finally, looking at Ethan. "Not voluntarily. Do you really want to start hurting her? That's where we are."

Ethan opened his mouth to argue, but nothing came out. His face flushed pink as he glanced over at the fire. The girl was leaning forward to drink in its warmth, still pretending we didn't exist.

"*Fine,*" he spat through gritted teeth. "How are we going to pull this off?"

I released a breath I hadn't known I was holding. We'd do it my way. In my relief, I was able to acknowledge that I wasn't going to let anyone torture this girl, even if Tack and Ethan thought it was necessary. Some bridges can never be uncrossed.

Our attackers might be monsters, but that didn't mean we

had to be.

"Just follow my lead," I said, then hid a smile from the girl. "Trust me, she already thinks we're idiots. We just have to prove her right."

"We'll sweep the campsite they left and be back in twenty," Tack announced. A bit overloud, but not *too* obviously for our prisoner's benefit. "You stay here and watch her." He removed a buck knife from his backpack and handed it to me. "If she causes any problems, make her regret it."

Tack sneered at Green Eyes, and the girl matched him glare for glare. But she tracked the knife as I set it down beside the ring of fire stones. For his part, Ethan remained stone-faced. He thought this whole charade was stupid and self-defeating, but at least he was going along. Nodding to each other, they hitched their packs and marched into the woods.

Time to look useless.

I picked up the knife again, but by the tip of its sheath, as if I didn't like touching it. I tossed the weapon farther aside with a grimace. Turning to the girl, I was surprised to find her smiling at me.

I decided to try a charm offensive. "Are you sure you don't want to tell me your name? Or at least talk? I'm so bored." I grinned, throwing out my best flirty vibe. *Hey gurl.*

Green Eyes shifted to face me, her cheeks coloring. I found my body responding despite myself. There was no denying that she was beautiful.

"How about just names? I'm Noah."

I nodded encouragingly, but she gave no response. It occurred to me that she might not understand what I was saying. I had no idea where this girl was from, or how she was alive. Why did I assume she spoke English?

Green Eyes pouted suddenly, swinging her legs around so I could see her bound ankles. Blinking long lashes, she made a face like she was in pain.

"Do they hurt?" I asked, straightening with a frown. I pointed to her restraints.

The girl gave a distressed frown and wiggled her feet feebly. The message was clear.

She's playing me. She thinks I'm a total moron.

I almost chuckled—I'd been trying to manipulate *her* a hot second ago—but this complemented my plan. My expression soured, like I was troubled by her discomfort. I began muttering to myself. Finally, I nodded like I'd come to a decision.

I picked up the knife and moved closer, but stopped suddenly, narrowing my eyes. "Do you promise not to try anything funny?" I asked. I made a running motion with two fingers, then shook my head at her. "I'll free your ankles, but only if you agree to behave."

Green Eyes nodded eagerly, flashing the smile again.

Using both hands on the knife like a simpleton, I began sawing through the rope. It parted and her legs were free. She shook out her feet and sighed, closing her eyes as if resting. Her hands were still tied behind her back.

Here we go.

I stood, sheathing the knife and stuffing it awkwardly into my jacket pocket. Grinning absently, I started putzing around the fire. The girl's eyes remained half lidded, but I could feel her tracking me, so I began whistling like a true buffoon, picking stuff up in one place and putting it down in another. I worked all the way around to where she sat, then turned my back on her completely.

I tried not to tense, but it was hard.

She didn't make me wait long.

Something clobbered me from behind, knocking me over. A booted foot thumped my ribs once, twice, before connecting with the back of my head. I saw stars, and for a moment worried I'd miscalculated badly, and that Green Eyes was going to kill me right there in the forest with her hands tied behind her back. But when my head cleared, I heard feet pounding away from the clearing.

I tried to grin, but had a coughing fit instead.

"*Shh*," Tack whispered. "She's just over the next rise."

"We can't let her get too far ahead," I warned, rubbing the lump on my head. "She's a freaking beast. Even with her hands tied she's fast as hell."

"I know that Noah, thanks. Letting her go was your idea, if you remember."

Ethan slipped into view at the bottom of the slope ahead of us. He waved us forward with one hand, the other pointing at the spire from Tack's map. Green Eyes had arrowed straight for it.

"I knew this place had secrets," Tack muttered. "I hate being right all the time."

When we arrived at Ethan's position, he motioned us in close. "The rock formation has a crack at its base," he whispered. "She went inside there. We should hurry."

We ran single file though the next section of forest until we reached the spire. Vegetation grew thick around its base, with no visible path. The crack was subtle—if Ethan hadn't witnessed the girl entering with his own eyes, we might not have noticed it.

I reached the opening first and paused. The three of us nodded our commitment to one another, then slipped into the fissure. I flicked on a flashlight, being careful not to let the beam travel too far ahead of us. After two turnings the uneven stone walls smoothed, giving way to a wide, evenly chiseled tunnel. I glanced at Tack, and he gritted his teeth. This corridor had clearly been improved by human hands.

A rasping sound echoed just ahead of us. I froze and flicked off the flashlight, plunging the passage into darkness. Holding my breath, I listened hard. The noise repeated. Then my eyes began to adjust to another light source leaking from somewhere around the next bend. I crept forward slowly, being careful where I put my feet.

At the turn, I hesitated. The rasping continued, mixing now with grunts and the occasional hiss. Heart in my throat, I peeked around the corner.

Green Eyes was ten feet away with a switched-on lantern at her feet. She'd backed up against a stone wall and was jerking her body up and down, as if doing squats. Her forehead was sweaty, her face a mask of concentration. I quickly realized she was trying to free her hands by sawing the bonds against something on the wall, but what loomed just beyond her drove all other thoughts from my mind.

I straightened and stepped forward without thinking.

Green Eyes spotted me and her eyes popped. She snarled, charged headfirst.

I stepped aside and stuck out my foot, tripping her with ease. She tumbled to the ground with a howl.

I barely noticed. Scarcely heard the gasps behind me.

My eyes were glued to the end of the tunnel.

To the thick steel door cut directly into the stone wall.

"What the hell?" I whispered.

I spun to stare at Green Eyes. She'd rolled onto her back and was panting at the ceiling. A trickle of blood ran down her pale face. Our eyes met, and she heaved a deep sigh. Then she spoke her first word.

"Shit."

PART THREE

CHRYSALIS

17

MIN

We camped in the hills overnight.

I was too exhausted to descend right away, and Sarah didn't push. The next morning we waited until the sun crested the mountains before heading down. Anyone looking would have trouble spotting us in the glare.

I trailed a few paces behind Sarah, thoughts churning, seeking a solution that remained frustratingly out of reach. The image of Toby's limp body kept crashing my thoughts. Or Kyle's terrified face as he was swept under the hungry black water. I squeezed my eyes shut to banish the memories, and nearly face-planted as my shoe caught on a rock.

How many people died in Sarah's flood? Fire Lake kids and strangers together. What a waste. A screaming horror of a waste.

Then work the problem. Find a way to save your friends.

If everyone at Ridgeline had been taken prisoner, who was left to resist? We knew so little about our enemies. They were better organized and better supplied than us. They were also armed. I kept arriving at the same disheartening conclusion—in a straight-up fight, we'd lose. We might've lost already.

"Stop." Sarah dropped to a crouch and peeked over a boulder.

I moved up beside her. Below us, near the valley floor, four strangers were huddled where the path to the caves met the one we were traveling. Their voices rose in argument. One of them—a stocky, dark-skinned boy with bleached-blond hair—pointed directly at us. Sarah and I ducked.

"They found our trail," I hissed.

"You think?" she shot back, scanning for a better hiding place. But we were halfway across a saddleback ridge and there was nowhere else to go. Cautiously, I snuck another look. Two boys were marching up toward us while the other pair waited at the intersection.

"They're coming," I whispered, beginning to sweat.

Sarah's fingers closed around a baseball-sized rock. I swallowed. Did the same.

In moments we heard heavy footsteps. " . . . waste of time," one voice was saying. "We got almost all of them. Who cares about a few stragglers? We can scoop the rest whenever we want."

"You wanna tell her that?" the other replied. "I'd pay to watch that conversation."

"Shut up," said the first, but with a tremor in his voice. There were more treads, then the first voice continued in a quieter tone. "I hate it in here, is all. Bad memories."

"I hear that."

They were ten feet away. In seconds they'd pass the boulder and see us.

I tensed, ready to plant a rock in one of the bastards' teeth. I was surprised they couldn't hear my heart banging against my rib cage.

"GUYS!" someone shouted from the bottom of the slope.

The footsteps halted directly beside the boulder. Gravel crunched as the boys turned.

"DOWN HERE! COME ON!"

"Ah crap, Miguel's down!" the first voice said. "I told you the tall dude didn't go this way. He's headed back to their village." The treads pounded back downslope. I took my first breath in a full minute.

Tall dude? Derrick? I rose cautiously and peered along the trail. One of the intersection guards was on his back, with the black kid leaning over to check on him. I smiled meanly. *Score one for our side.*

As I watched, all four strangers began jogging toward Home Town. I worried for Derrick, but he was smart and capable. He'd lose them in the woods and double back when he could.

Sarah straightened beside me. "The way is clear," I said, and she nodded. We hurried down the last stretch, then took the left-hand path and disappeared among the cliffs.

A surprise waited for us inside the caves.

Charlie rose as we entered, pawing nervously at his acne

scars. I spotted Spence snoozing in a sleeping bag against the rear wall. But Casey and Leighton were there as well, sitting by the cold fire pit. Both waved.

"You seen Derrick?" Leighton asked.

"He's leading some of those jerks away," I said. "Are you guys alone?"

"We're the only ones to escape the ambush at Ridgeline." Casey frowned at the charred logs. "They had guns, and seemed to come from everywhere at once. But Akio and Richie are back from the Outpost. You're not going to believe their story."

My blood pressure spiked. "What about Noah? What happened to the others?"

Leighton jabbed a thumb over his shoulder. "They're in the boat cavern. Probably better if you talked to them yourself, so we don't get anything wrong. They had a rough crossing, and both seemed pretty spooked."

I hurried into the last cave, barely noticing that Sarah followed me. Why hadn't Noah come back, too?

I found them standing beside the launcher, looking out to sea. Akio nodded as we entered. "Hey, Min. Sarah."

"Where's Noah? Did something happen to him?"

Akio shook his head. "He wanted us to deliver the news, but it's not going to shock you now. It looks like the Outpost was raided. Probably by the same people who hit us here."

I tried not to let dread overwhelm me. "What happened to Corbin and the others?"

Richie grunted. Akio shrugged uncomfortably. "They're just . . . gone. Tack left a strange note on a map he drew in his tent, so Ethan and Noah went looking for him."

I made him tell me the whole story, in detail. Then I made him repeat it. Finally, I chewed my lip. "You guys didn't see anyone?"

"Not a soul."

"So they attacked the Outpost in concert with the silo bombing." Sarah began fidgeting with her sweater, clearly annoyed at having to guess at things. "Either that same night or early the next morning. That feels like two groups instead of one. Then maybe the two squads joined forces and assaulted Home Town together?"

A commotion in the other cavern cut off my reply. I heard Leighton shout, followed by an echoing crash. The four of us rushed back to the first cave.

Derrick had returned, but he wasn't alone. With him was the dark-skinned stranger with blond hair, standing there as bold as could be. Derrick wasn't restraining him, and the kid didn't seem unnerved to be surrounded by hostile glares.

Akio and Richie fanned out beside Sarah and me, linking with the others and completing a loose circle around the stranger. Derrick kept glancing at the black-clad newcomer when he thought the boy wasn't looking. For his part, the stranger stood with his arms crossed, a faint smile tilting his lips. Though nine of us faced him alone, it wasn't clear who was in charge.

"Derrick, what the hell?" I said.

"Ask *him*," Derrick responded testily, scratching his temple. "I led three other dudes away and hid while they passed, but when I came out, this guy walked right up to me and said he wanted to talk. Says he has information we need. I didn't know

175

what to do, so I brought him here. We can toss him in the ocean if necessary."

If Derrick's threat frightened our guest, he didn't show it. He stood calmly, as if awaiting his turn.

Sarah glanced at me and I nodded. This was her strong suit, and we both knew it.

"Who are you?" she asked.

"Cyrus Haq." He spoke with a clipped, African-British accent.

"Why are you here?"

"To speak with you."

"Where did you come from? How are you alive on this planet?"

Cyrus smiled. "That *is* the question, is it not?"

"He wouldn't tell me, either," Derrick grumbled, eyeing the shorter boy with undisguised suspicion. "Claims he wants to help us."

Sarah regarded Cyrus curiously, like a cat studying an insect. "Help us how?"

Cyrus spread his hands. "I can take you to a friend."

"In exchange for . . ."

"That's my business."

"Who's this friend?" I asked.

"Someone you will wish to see."

I nearly growled in frustration. "Care to tell us where this so-called friend is hiding?"

"Chrysalis," he said simply.

Akio stepped close and whispered into my ear. "That's what was stamped on the hammer we found."

Sarah nodded, having overheard. "What is Chrysalis?"

Cyrus held up a thick finger. "First, we must get away from

this island. More of my companions are coming, and they'll storm these caves next. After we arrive I will explain Chrysalis to you all."

"Arrive where?" I felt like I was losing the thread. "Is there a settlement nearby that we don't know about?"

"In a manner of speaking." Cyrus pointed in the direction of the valley. "We'll go through the lake. With the water drained it's the easiest way to reach Chrysalis."

"Go through the lake?" Derrick growled. "What the hell are you talking about?"

Cyrus grinned but didn't answer.

Akio leaned between Sarah and me again. "Tack's map pointed to something in the woods beyond the Outpost. A camp, or maybe a base. There are definitely places we don't know about."

Sarah raised a fist to her mouth. Chewed a knuckle. A few beats passed, then: "Are you going to tell us how you're alive on this planet, despite the Dark Star?"

Cyrus laughed with genuine amusement. "It's easier to show you."

Sarah's jaw tightened. "You're asking for a lot on faith. After you attacked us."

"Not I." For the first time, a measure of heat entered his voice. "I want the same things you do, I think. But in the end, all roads lead to Chrysalis."

"What is that?" I blurted, unable to hold back. "Is it part of Project Nemesis?"

Cyrus tsked. "You have it backward. The Nemesis projects exist under Chrysalis."

It felt like the air was sucked out of my lungs. "So there are other Nemesis projects?"

He gave me an indulgent look. "Of course. But we're wasting time. We must go."

Sarah studied Cyrus intently. "Why are you doing this? Why'd you sneak away from the others in your group?"

Darkness clouded Cyrus's gaze. A subtle shift, hinting at pools of anger just below the surface. "Some have embraced a path that doesn't sit well with me. But come. I will say nothing more until we reach our destination."

I looked at Sarah. She arched a brow. *Your call.*

I exhaled deeply. In the end, there didn't seem to be a choice to make.

"Okay," I said, meeting his eye. "We'll go with you. We'll meet your mysterious friend. But then you're going to tell us everything. Whatever this is, it's gone on long enough."

Cyrus nodded solemnly, as if concluding a pact. "On that, we agree completely."

As a group we snuck to the edge of the former lake, where Cyrus began descending a muddy bank into the empty bowl itself.

"We're really going in that sludge?" Derrick grumbled.

"Oh, yes." Cyrus smiled as he angled toward the bottom of the sun-dried basin.

Exchanging mystified glances, we had no choice but to follow. The group was able to pick a stable path down without much drama—though Richie slipped in the muck and slid twenty feet on his stomach—but no one had any idea why we were entering a giant mud puddle. Our guide's back was tattooed by hard stares every step of the way.

Cyrus maddeningly refused to explain. "Come," he said as we finally reached the lake bottom. "This way is clear with all the water drained, and surveillance won't track us."

I stopped short. "What surveillance? Where are my friends, Cyrus?"

"Everyone will have been moved to Chrysalis by now. You must trust me."

"Trust is earned."

"And I'll do that very thing," he said matter-of-factly, sloshing along through the mire.

I nodded to Akio and Derrick, who were quietly trailing on his heels. We'd discussed what to do should Cyrus break faith, but the stocky boy made no move to escape, leading everyone deeper into the burgeoning swamp. Foul smells and clouds of flies enveloped us. The temperature rose, and my shirt pasted itself to my back. Grumbles merged in an irritated symphony as Cyrus began stopping periodically to dig in the muck with his hands.

"This kid might be crazy," Sarah muttered, as the sun beat down from above. We hadn't seen anyone else since leaving the caves, and Cyrus hadn't looked back once. If this was a trap, it was the weirdest one of all time.

I was worried about Noah, Tack, and all the others, and kept berating myself for letting a stranger lead us into such an awkward position. But I couldn't think of another course to take. Until we learned the true nature of what threatened us, we were at our enemies' mercy. We needed Cyrus to clue us in.

Finally, I lost my temper and plodded over to him. "Enough of this. What are we doing?"

Cyrus smiled, but didn't slow. "It's here somewhere."

"We're stuck in the mud at the bottom of a dead lake. There's nothing to find. I've run out of patience."

Cyrus clicked his tongue. "False."

I nearly growled in frustration. "Care to elaborate?"

"No. Because we've arrived."

He pointed to a line of slimy vegetation. As we approached, a girl stood up, appearing almost by magic. She wore the same black fatigues as Cyrus, though hers were covered head to foot in camouflaging sludge. She had tanned skin and deep brown eyes. The girl put fingers to her lips and whistled. Two others rose from the mud—a pale boy with long blond hair and a hefty girl with wide-set eyes.

The newcomers seemed as tense as we were. Everyone stared at one another until Cyrus broke the silence. "Members of Nemesis One, meet the Nemesis Three Resistance."

My head snapped to him. "Three? One?"

"We're One?" Sarah said.

"Correct. Though our class emerged before yours, because we sorted the Program quickest." He nodded to the other two kids. "A few of us have been meeting in secret and waiting, trying to decide."

I'd never felt more lost. "Decide what?"

"Whether to approach you," Cyrus said. "Your group is an anomaly, which has made people uncertain."

I stepped face-to-face with him. "Cyrus, you have to stop talking in riddles. Tell us what's going on."

His expression became solemn. "You've been duped rather badly. What comes next will be a shock to your reality."

Panic spread through my classmates. Casey paled. Charlie wobbled on his feet. Derrick stomped forward, shaking his head. "Don't tell me this is another freaking simulation. We left the Program behind. It's over!"

Cyrus held up a placating hand. "I spoke poorly, I apologize. Your Program *is* over. You are very much alive." He spread his arms. "It's this place that isn't what you think."

I clamped my fingers onto his shoulder. "You said you could show us the truth. Do it now."

Cyrus glanced at the black-haired girl. "Parisa?"

She knelt, spreading the muck at her feet with both hands.

A manhole appeared. My eyes widened as she pried off the lid.

There was a tunnel underneath it, with rusty metal rungs descending into darkness.

"Oh my God," I whispered.

"Not God," Cyrus answered. "Chrysalis."

18

NOAH

I stared at the barrier of thick, tarnished steel.

Breathless. Heart pounding. Limbs tingling with electricity yet freezing cold.

My thoughts swam in an endless circle.

There's a door in this cave. Someone else built it. There's a door in this cave. Someone else built it. There's a door in this cave . . .

Sounds of struggle behind me broke through the loop. I turned to see Ethan dragging Green Eyes to her feet, absorbing several well-placed kicks to his abdomen in the process. Tack was rubbing his forehead like he wanted to take the skin off it. Whatever he'd expected to find in here, this wasn't it.

"What is this place?" Ethan demanded, shaking the girl by her shoulders. "Where does it go?"

She gritted her teeth, tried to kick him again where it counts. He shifted in time and shoved her against the stone wall. The girl grunted but didn't cry out, watching us instead with loathing in her eyes.

"No more playing dumb." Tack's chest heaved as he pointed at her. "We all heard you speak a second ago, so we know you understand us. Tell us what's going on. *Now.*"

Green Eyes went still. Her glare slid from Tack, to Ethan, and then to me before dropping to the ground. Her shoulders sagged. When she looked up again, the fight seemed to have left her. "I suppose it doesn't matter now," she muttered.

Tack threw up his hands. "Finally!"

Ethan was staring a hole through the girl's head. "What's your name?"

She considered for a moment, then said, "Rose."

Rose. The name fit. She was pretty, but with thorns. *Stop thinking like an idiot.*

"Nice to meet you, Rose." Tack aimed his finger at the steel door. "What the hell is that?"

Rose's left foot began to tap. "I don't know. I got lost running away from you guys and came in here to hide."

"Ridiculous," Ethan spat, folding his arms. "Do you think we're morons?"

"You don't want me to answer that."

I held up a hand before Ethan could go nuclear. "Rose, you came straight here. We watched the whole time. I assume that means you can open the door. Is this where our friends were taken?"

Rose looked away. I sighed. She clearly wasn't going to help.

Tack walked over to the portal and slid his hands along its sides. "This door has a keycard slot," he announced to the room.

I turned to Rose. "We need the card. I don't want to search you against your will, but that's what happens next unless you tell me where it is."

Her bottom lip began to tremble. "You don't understand. They'll kill me if I let you in."

Tack's cheek twitched. "Did it occur to you that *we* might kill you if you don't cooperate?"

Rose shrank against the wall. "I . . . I just . . ." She twisted away, burying her face in her bound hands as her whole body began to quiver.

I took a step forward. "Hey, listen. We—"

Rose spun, her boot flying up to connect with my chin. I fell back with my hands over my mouth as she dropped her shoulder and drove it into Ethan's stomach. He tumbled sideways and she shot past him, intent on running straight over Tack.

But he was ready. Tack sidestepped and caught her with an elbow to the temple. Rose collapsed to the ground. Then Ethan and I were up, and all three of us basically sat on her.

"Stop kicking me all the time!" I shouted, aware of how silly it sounded but long past caring. My head hurt like a mother. Beside me, Ethan was struggling to regain his wind as he grappled with Rose's legs.

Tack was giggling hysterically as he pinned her shoulders. "Man, this girl is vicious."

Rose fought for a moment longer, then gave up with a shriek. She went limp, and we cautiously released her, on guard for another assault. But Rose seemed to have finally run out of gas.

Tack knelt and began searching her. She made no move to resist. He removed an unadorned rectangle of gleaming white plastic from her pocket.

Rose watched him hand it to me. "You won't like what you find," she whispered.

I barked a bitter laugh. "Oh, I'm one hundred percent sure you're right about that."

I walked to the keypad, took a deep breath, and swiped the card. The door unlocked with the hiss of a pneumatic seal breaking. Ahead of me a metal-walled corridor curved out of sight. No windows. No doors.

What in the world? I stepped over the threshold. The air was chilly and processed. *Air-conditioned,* I thought with surprise. Tack and Ethan entered the passage behind me, marching Rose between them like police officers. She was fidgety, rubbing her cheek against her shoulder.

"Last chance to explain," I said.

"Release my hands and I'll show you."

"Not a chance," Tack said, while Ethan snorted.

I shrugged unhappily. "Sorry. You keep beating us up. You understand."

The ghost of a smile appeared but fled just as quickly. "Then you're on your own, boys. I'll say it again: you're not going to like this at all."

The corridor curled to our right, angling upward in a long ramp. I started counting paces but quit after fifty. We did at least two full revolutions, perhaps three. I assumed we were climbing inside the rocky spire but couldn't be sure.

Finally, the corridor flattened and widened. A bay window

appeared in one wall, overlooking the forest below. The sun was high in the sky, which was clear for once. I could see all the way to the ocean.

We paused to stare.

"Who built this?" I whispered.

Rose's face reddened. For a moment I thought she might answer, but she remained silent.

I spotted a second door a dozen yards farther along, where the corridor ended. I nodded to the others and we approached. The card worked again, this time accessing a room filled with banks of high-tech computer equipment. Monitors on the wall displayed surveillance feeds, including one of the Outpost. With a jolt I realized that some of the screens showed views of Fire Lake Island, including Home Town. There were no people in sight in the village.

"What's going on here?" Ethan breathed.

I felt sick and scared, like a hamster spotting a snake outside its cage. "They're . . . monitoring us. Whoever these people are. They're watching everything we do."

Tack stared at Rose in openmouthed bafflement. "Why'd you leave us out in the cold?" His voice rose, then nearly broke. "We've been living in the wilderness for half a year. You could've taken us in. Given us food. Shelter. A place to stay warm. But you left us in camps to study like . . . like . . . lab rats!"

Rose refused to meet his eyes. "You still don't understand."

I stepped forward and gently lifted her chin, forcing her eyes to meet mine. She didn't pull away.

"Show us, Rose. No more games."

She held my gaze, green daggers piercing through my

defenses. "Fine. Follow me."

She crossed the room and nodded impatiently at the next door. I swiped the card. The corridor beyond was blindingly white on all sides, with spotless tiles and seamless plastic walls. "How big is this facility?" I asked in wonderment. "Are we still inside the mountain?"

"Just follow me."

We crossed other hallways at regular intervals, but Rose didn't slow, and we didn't encounter anyone else. Reaching a set of sealed double doors on our left, Rose took a deep breath. She looked at me, and I couldn't decode her expression. "Last chance. Are you sure you don't want to run back to your cabins? You still can, you know. I won't stop you."

I shook my head, though my hands had begun to tremble. "Same card opens this one?"

"Don't say I didn't warn you."

Ethan stepped close and whispered into Rose's ear. "If anything magically pops out from behind this door, I won't let you escape." He removed his gun and racked the slide. "Understand?"

She pulled away from him with a look of revulsion. "No one will be in the Observatory at this time of day. You have my word."

"The Observatory?" Tack hissed, but Rose's mouth formed a thin line and she said nothing more.

"Okay then." I ran the card. The doors sighed open.

Beyond was a small amphitheater with tiered benches descending toward a giant featureless wall. Everything was a stark, gleaming white. When the doors slid shut behind us, silence filled the room like a living thing.

"Well?" Ethan said impatiently. "What is this, a classroom or something?"

Rose smirked. "No. But you are about to learn a lesson. There's a switch on the wall."

Tack was closest. After examining the lever for several seconds, he shrugged and flipped it up. The front wall split in half and the two sections rolled apart, revealing a massive window beyond.

I was smashed by a feeling of vertigo. My mind tried to hide under the carpet.

"Holy crap," Tack breathed.

Ethan began shaking his head, unable to speak.

"Told you," Rose said with a satisfied smile.

A jet-black expanse filled the window, dotted with tiny twinkling lights. It framed a bright blue orb covered in white swirls and orange and green splotches. A smaller gray sphere hung beside it, half lit by intense yellow radiance.

I nearly emptied my stomach. Tears filled my eyes.

I was staring down at Earth from far, far above it. Everything I knew dissolved like a sand castle at high tide.

"Welcome to Chrysalis," Rose said.

Tack took a shaky step backward. "How . . . how can . . ."

Ethan spun to face her, a panicked wildness in his eyes. "You better explain this, *right now*, or I'm—"

An alarm screamed.

Red lights began flashing in the ceiling.

Rose hip-checked Ethan and bolted for the doors, ducking under my outstretched fingers. "Stop her!" I yelled, but she shoulder-bowled Tack aside and reached the top, pressing the exit button with her nose. Rose straightened with a last look back, and our eyes met. She winked, then ran out of the Observatory, her hands still tied behind her back.

"For the love of God," Ethan groaned. "We have to catch her again?"

A computerized voice boomed into the chamber. *"Attention. Containment breach, Terrarium platform seven. Containment breach, Terrarium platform seven."*

I swallowed. "Pretty sure that's us."

Tack's face screwed up into a ball. "Terrarium? Seriously?"

The outer doors remained stubbornly open. We heard booted feet pounding along the corridor and ducked behind a row of benches. "What should we do?" Tack whispered.

Ethan shook his head, sweat dampening his forehead. "We don't know anything about this . . . this goddamn *space station* we're on!" He seemed unable to accept what his eyes had seen.

More boots passed by outside as the doors mercifully slid shut. "They don't seem to be coming in here," I said. "Maybe we just lie low?"

Ethan rolled his eyes at me. "That ginger psychopath will tell them exactly where we are any second."

Tack swore. I didn't say anything, trying to make my thoughts line up. I knew we had to move—Ethan was right—but I didn't know where to go. Any direction could lead straight to our enemies.

The doors beeped. The keycard portal blinked to green.

I met the others' terrified glances, then we all flattened to the floor.

Someone stepped inside the chamber. The doors closed.

Only one, Ethan mouthed. I nodded, slowly shifting into a crouch.

Ethan counted down on his fingers.

Three. Two. One.

I exploded off the floor and launched myself at a dark-clad figure.

Stopped short as the muzzle of a gun nearly jabbed me in the eyeball.

Tack and Ethan slammed into me from behind. Ethan swung his Glock up, then froze, his finger uncurling from the trigger as the stranger aimed directly at his forehead. Ethan's gun dropped to the floor.

Our assailant lowered his weapon, and I received my third stupendous shock of the last ten minutes.

"No freaking way," Tack murmured.

Black Suit holstered his gun. He was actually wearing a gray jumpsuit, without sunglasses, but it was him. My childhood executioner dipped his head. "I thought you might be the ones in here. Come on, we don't have much time."

My feet were glued to the floor. My brain felt like spaghetti.

"You're dead," I said dumbly. "You stayed inside the Program."

He smiled dryly. "Min cut me loose at the end, remember? There was a regeneration pod in the command suite, so I decided to follow you guys out after all. Good thing I did, too."

Ethan pointed at Black Suit's clothing. "You're one of them!"

"Yes and no, Ethan. This station is connected to Project Nemesis, but I'm not a part of it. I'm actually an uninvited guest, which is a snag for Chrysalis. Turns out I was a pawn in a much deeper game."

The mechanized voice repeated. Black Suit winced. "I'll explain everything when we're safely hidden, but we have to go."

Tack stepped close and whispered in my ear. "What do you think, Noah? You know him best. Should we trust him?"

I stared at the monster who'd hunted me throughout my childhood. His expression was grave, but he didn't dodge my inspection. "I don't think we have a choice," I said, surprised by the calm in my voice. "If it's a trap, we're done anyway."

Black Suit nodded. "Correct. Now come on. I disconnected the sensors in this sector, but they'll notice eventually."

He made to turn, but I grabbed him by the jumpsuit. "One thing."

"Okay, Noah. Name it."

"We're going back for Min and the others. I'm not leaving them in that fishbowl."

Black Suit smiled, an expression so foreign to his countenance that I released him in surprise. "I promise, Noah. I've left my daughter in there until now only for her protection, but things are changing. We'll get them all out."

I stepped back, relieved. "Then lead the way."

19

MIN

I peered through the doorway at a gleaming white corridor.

Booted feet echoed down the hall. Cyrus quickly closed the door, holding a finger to his lips. I hadn't seen anyone, but from the look on his face we didn't want to be discovered. He'd sent his companions ahead to scout and was taking no chances. Which was good, because I was so shell-shocked I could barely keep upright.

This place.

This . . . facility.

We'd descended the ladder inside the hatch to some kind of service tunnel, then followed it to this mechanical room. There the thirteen of us huddled—my friends and I quietly freaking out—while Cyrus waited for Parisa, Scott, and Jerica to return from their recon mission. If caught, he explained, they could claim to be on a regular errand. Nemesis Three apparently had permission to move freely.

So we sat silently in the dark.

In a mechanical room beneath our lake.

In a complex built into the bedrock of Fire Lake Island.

No wonder we couldn't find or stop them. They'd been hiding below us the whole time. The idea made me shudder. How long had this been going on?

Cyrus backed away from the door and scratched his blond scalp. He'd been acting nervous since we'd entered the hatch, which made *me* anxious, too. A billion questions screamed inside my head, but I kept quiet as the footsteps carried away. Finally, he released a deep breath. I unleashed a torrent.

"Where the hell are we?" I hissed. "How deep does this facility go? Do you live underground?"

Sarah wedged up beside me. "Did you build this place after exiting your Program? How long ago did you regenerate?"

Cyrus ran a hand over his face. "This is going to be difficult."

Derrick pushed forward as well, glaring at the stocky boy. "Spit it out, man." He waved a hand at the humming machines all around us. "You've got our attention."

Cyrus sighed. "Very well. But please, don't waste time questioning whether I'm telling you the truth. It's going to be nearly impossible to believe, I know. I've been there. But you have to adapt quickly so we can move on."

An unsettled murmur traveled the group. Akio and Richie stiffened beside Casey, Leighton, and Spence. Charlie had a hand over his mouth. Everyone inched closer to hear.

"You are aboard Chrysalis," Cyrus explained. "You always

have been, though you never knew it until this moment." He paused, and I sensed his next words would be the hardest to hear. "We are not on Earth."

Dead silence. Cyrus nodded, looked impressed.

"Chrysalis is an advanced space station in orbit around the planet. You, like my class previously, have been living in a place called the Terrarium—an astoundingly large artificial biome at the heart of the station. But it's a false environment, like a cage for a snake, or a zoo enclosure if you prefer."

My brain froze. I couldn't speak. Couldn't look at anyone but Cyrus. No one could.

I think our quiet was starting to make Cyrus uncomfortable. "The Terrarium is controlled for day and night cycles, weather, tides, wildlife and plants, even . . . other things. It's the greatest technological accomplishment in human history. I never knew it was false when I lived inside it, so don't feel bad. It's meticulously designed to make inhabitants think it's a real world."

"Designed by *who*?" I spat, the first words by anyone.

"Chrysalis station personnel. You will see very soon."

"Those storms were done on purpose?" Derrick growled.

Cyrus nodded. "To keep you from dispersing, or traveling too far. The harsh environment discourages subjects from venturing toward the edges of the enclosure."

A dam broke, and suddenly everyone spoke at once. Some in disbelief, some in anger. Some cursing at the walls.

Cyrus held up a hand. "I know it's hard to accept. Eight months ago, I went through exactly what you're experiencing now."

194

"You said *other things*," Sarah interjected. "What else do they control?"

Cyrus frowned. "Your moods, to some extent. Your fertility. The Chrysalis crew manipulates the Terrarium's water supply to keep test subjects as docile as possible. They determine what you eat and the ecological factors surrounding you. All to study each Nemesis class more effectively."

My temper exploded. "It never stops!"

"You've been out for eight months?" Casey said. "Where have *you* been all that time? Where'd you guys come from?"

"Out of all the Nemesis experiments, my class finished the Program first." He frowned at some troubling memory. "I won't go into it, but you know what that process is like. We're from Wyoming—a little nothing town called Huntwell. Forty-seven of us went into the MegaCom, and the required twenty came out. We lived on Huntwell Island for twelve months, and had only begun branching out to the area you named the Outpost when the Chrysalis crew ended our containment. All twenty of us were incorporated into the mission. Your class, however, has caused much more of an uproar."

Voices rose at once, but I cut through them. "So that's why our people were taken prisoner? You're delivering them to these crew members?"

"My classmates are doing that, but I've diverted your group as a favor." He gave me a curious look. "Someone else is interested in you, Min. I was asked to slip you out of the Terrarium undetected by Chrysalis command." He shrugged at the others. "It seemed easiest to bring you all."

"Who?" I blurted in shock.

Cyrus grinned. "Part of our deal was not revealing that information. I'm sorry."

I opened my mouth, but footsteps sounded in the corridor beyond the door. We went silent until they faded, then Sarah spoke first. "Why would you go against the station's crew? What's in it for you, Cyrus?"

His grin vanished. "I have concerns about the mission. Since we exited the Terrarium, we've been tested in certain ways, to assess our fitness in various capacities. Three of my classmates did poorly and were removed from the group. We've had no contact with them since, and the explanations about where they've gone have been vague." His expression darkened. "My friend Kate was one of them. I've had no word from her in weeks. The others you met feel the same as me."

"So your contact is a rogue crew member?" Sarah pressed. "Promising information in exchange for . . . Min?"

Cyrus shook his head. "Not a crew member. This person is different. That's all I will say."

"Why'd you grab us all?" Charlie whined. His gaze cut to me. "No offense, Min, but it sounds like we just broke a major rule for no reason. If the people in charge were going to bring everyone out anyway, even by capturing us, we should've just gone with them. Now we're screwed." He pointed at Cyrus. "They gave this guy a job, and it obviously hasn't been too awful. Plus, they run this place. We need to surrender before the situation gets any worse."

"Exactly," Spence muttered, and some of the others nodded or looked thoughtful. Was Charlie right? Were we running around for no reason? Was this whole flight a terrible mistake?

Cyrus held up a hand. "We're going to meet my contact now. Just listen to what will be said. If you don't like what you hear, you can do whatever you please. It won't be hard to give yourself up and be taken to the testing facility. But I believe in having *all* the cards before I make a bet on my future. I suggest you do the same."

"Testing facility?" Derrick said. "Testing for what?" He stepped close to Cyrus and glared down at him. "You haven't said a word about *why* these people kept us in a fishbowl, or what we're supposed to do once we're out of it. Or why they built the damn thing in the first place. It felt like a real planet in there." He crossed his arms. "I still can't believe half of what you're saying. What the hell *is* Chrysalis, dude? Who are these people? Why'd they hide from us? We're sitting here debating the small stuff, but you haven't told us how this station even exists."

Cyrus took a deep breath, but at that moment the door opened. We all whirled in panic, but it was Parisa returning. She closed the door behind her and shouldered her way next to Cyrus.

"Everything go as planned?" Cyrus asked.

Parisa frowned. "Yes and no. But the way is clear. We should hurry."

Cyrus nodded. "What went wrong?"

"I just ran into Rose, and there's trouble," Parisa said. "The Terrarium has been cleared, but the roundup didn't go as planned. Rose and Gray are stomping around like they want to strangle everyone in the other class. No one seems to have noticed you're missing. I faked like I had orders and booked it here. Scott and

Jerica went back to the dorm to pretend nothing's going on."

"What's the trouble?" Cyrus asked.

Parisa glanced at us, and there was naked anger in her gaze. "Inside the silo, someone opened a seal to the lab complex. Eight drowned. Four traitors, and four of ours. We never should've worked with those guys!"

Cyrus flinched. "Who of our people?"

"Iris, Wyatt, Levi, and Jayden. They couldn't get out in time."

Cyrus squeezed his eyes shut. Beside me, Sarah shifted her weight nearly imperceptibly. Only she and I knew what had happened. Among the living, anyway.

"Which of our classmates?" I asked, though I knew three of the names already. I saw Kyle's face again as the water swallowed him, and Tucker's body tumbling in the flood. I felt Toby's dead weight in my hands.

Parisa gave me a haughty look. "I didn't learn their names. The bald guy was one."

Toby's name rippled through the group. I felt a spike of sadness. Even for him. I didn't share what I knew about the other victims—that would spark questions I couldn't answer in front of Cyrus and Parisa. *Do they know Sarah and I were down there?*

"Eight dead," Cyrus whispered. "What a disaster."

"You didn't answer my questions," Derrick demanded. "Tell us why all this is happening."

Cyrus straightened to his full height. "Later. For now, I have to complete my end of the bargain. Come on."

"And if we won't?" Casey said. "What if we decide not to go along with your plan?"

"Then I'll leave you here to figure things out on your own. If you want those answers, come with me. If not, so long."

Silence. Eyes turned my way. I stared at Cyrus. Then nodded.

"We'll meet your mysterious friend. But that's all I'm agreeing to."

"Not a friend. Someone who knows more than both of us. I think such a person might be useful in the days ahead, don't you?"

"I don't know, Cyrus." I ran a hand through my hair. "So far I've only seen the inside of this closet."

"Fair enough. Let's go."

We crept to the door, listened, then opened it and filed outside, with Parisa in the lead.

I didn't know where I was. Or what this was. Or where we were going. But I was determined not to give up.

Derrick moved close to me as we scurried down the corridor in a tight line. Everything was gleaming white and shockingly clean. We turned a corner and a window hove into view. Cyrus and Jerica sped by it without stopping, but my class piled up in front like a NASCAR wreck.

I stared through the glass into the cold depths of infinity. *Every word he said was true.*

"God have mercy," Derrick whispered. "This really is a space station, huh?"

"Appears so." My hands started to shake. "Derrick, I'm not sure I can take another shock."

"We're hurtling through outer space right now, Min. Panicking seems like a decent option."

Cyrus jogged back down the hallway, his expression sour.

"Yes, yes. It's very dramatic the first time. But we have to go!"

We turned to stare at him as one.

He snorted. "Fine. Take a moment. But this sector won't stay empty for long. And there's a lot more to learn."

I blinked at him, then turned to the others. "Come on, guys. Let's find out what this madness is all about. We've survived crazier things than this."

"Have we?" Akio murmured, but he stepped away from the glass.

Like a gaggle of stunned geese, we followed Cyrus deeper into the station.

20

NOAH

The hideout was cold and dispiriting.

It'd taken fifteen minutes to get there, racing down corridors, following as Black Suit made turn after turn. He'd led us to an elevator that rose faster than I could blink, the doors opening onto yet another featureless hallway. Another sprint, more antiseptic walls, and we'd entered a cargo hold filled with rows of stacked shipping containers. An unobtrusive door at the far end had accessed this lonely space, which appeared to be some sort of break room.

And then we'd sat. And waited. After rushing us inside, Black Suit left again just as quickly, promising that the sensors in this area were disabled. We could hide here. We'd be safe.

Not that the concept made much sense anymore. We were on

a space station orbiting the planet from a distance of thousands of miles. Our whole environment had been a lie. We'd thought we were building a new society on a reclaimed world—pioneering a brand-new Earth—but we'd been nothing more than a lab experiment. Toys for people we didn't know, who'd eventually decided to pull the plug.

Maybe even literally. Had *they* drained the lake?

I ground my teeth in frustration. *Used again. Nothing had been real.*

And for what? Why were these people doing any of it?

I was sitting on a sleeping bag in the corner. A half dozen other rolls were piled against the wall, next to a minifridge stuffed with rehydrated meals. There was a tiny kitchenette, a table and chairs, and a bathroom. The room smelled of long habitation combined with minimal hygiene. In a word, it stank.

I was debating whether to eat another bag of soggy noodles when Black Suit slipped back through the doorway. It disturbed me how relieved I was to see him again. Ignoring us completely, he walked over to the table and sat, removing a tablet from a bag at his feet. Long minutes passed as we stared at him, waiting for the bastard to acknowledge we existed.

"Well?" Ethan asked, always first to lose his patience. "What the hell's going on? Why'd you bring us here?" He was standing in the kitchenette with Tack, glaring at our . . . rescuer? Kidnapper? Things were too confused to sort out.

Black Suit held up a finger, then locked the screen and looked up. "This is my humble abode. I've been living in here for months. So far the crew hasn't noticed that I looped the sensors in this quadrant, and the hangar outside is used for long-term storage only. It's almost never visited. We're off the grid for the moment."

I rose and walked to the table. "Why are you hiding from them? Isn't this just, like, Phase Seven of your grand plan?"

Black Suit pursed his lips. "Turns out I was lower on the food chain than I thought. I designed and ran Project Nemesis in Fire Lake, and believed it to be the endgame for all human survival." He swept a hand at the walls around him. "Obviously, I was wrong."

Tack grunted. "So you didn't know about this . . . space station trick?"

Black Suit snorted. "Not a thing. I'd been told that an off-planet refuge was simply impossible in the time frame we had to elude Nemesis. Obviously, they decided to build one anyway, and just as obviously, it worked. But as to why they uploaded our data files into a false environment inside their giant orbiting superstation, I have no idea. To be blunt, it seems insane. They either extracted our physical MegaCom from its bunker down on Earth—perhaps even the entire Fire Lake silo—or they replicated everything up here on Chrysalis inside the Terrarium, down to the screws. The complexity of such a project . . ." He blew out a breath. "It staggers the mind."

"You told us you were staying inside the Program," I said, watching his eyes. "Last-second change of heart?"

"Self-preservation is a powerful lure." Black Suit shrugged ruefully. "I ran for the security-hub pod seconds before you engaged the regeneration process, so a body was crafted for me as well. But for some reason I emerged outside the Terrarium, in a staff wing. Nobody was expecting me, so no one was around, giving me time to process how badly I'd been deceived. I decided to conceal my presence aboard while I figured out what this place was. I've stayed underground ever since." A smile played on his lips. "I'm pleased to report I've given them a few 'inexplicable' headaches. They're aware of me now, but can't find me."

"Who are *they*?" Tack demanded. "What the hell is this place, dude?"

"Chrysalis," Black Suit said simply. "An orbiting space station built from Nemesis legacy equipment and staffed by people I know almost nothing about. It turns out Project Nemesis was only a step in the ladder of human survival, and we were the test mice. But we're out of the lab now."

"We've been inside that bubble for six freaking months." Tack's eyes glinted. "People died. But you never came for us."

"You seemed to be managing, and I didn't have anything to offer you other than a nasty shock. So you're right, Thomas. I waited. Indeed, I only acted now because events have forced my hand. The station sent in teams to lock down the Terrarium, and then you came out on your own. I'm not willing to let them have you until I know what they're planning."

"Who was the girl?" I asked, trying to sound casual. "Rose. Do you know her?"

Black Suit nodded. "In a way. She's part of Nemesis Three. That group completed the Program first. They regenerated into the Terrarium thirteen months before we did."

I nearly swallowed my tongue. "Nemesis Three? What . . . what are we?"

"Fire Lake is considered Nemesis One. We were launched first—*I* built the damn MegaCom prototype, after all—but my superiors decided to construct redundancies without my knowledge. One of those Programs completed Phase Two before you did."

My head was spinning. Fire Lake was not alone. "How many are there?"

"Five were scheduled, but only four actually launched. That's all the architects could get done before things on Earth fell apart irrevocably. The second test group, Nemesis Two, was actually composed of volunteers who knew the stakes going in, a drastic departure from my parameters. They . . . The designers should have listened to me."

Something in his voice sent a chill down my spine. "What happened? Where is Nemesis Two now?"

The cold mask I'd seen so often fell into place. "Nemesis Two did not complete the Program. None survived."

I shuddered, thinking of how wrong things must've gone inside their simulation. "How'd they *all* fail?"

Black Suit shook his head, stroking a finger across the tablet in front of him. "I'm not able to hack into the raw data, but after Phase Two their MegaCom reported no viable codes for regeneration." He was quiet a moment. "I built these systems, and that's not supposed to be possible. It's my belief that Nemesis Two sabotaged their MegaCom. I think they destroyed themselves."

That silenced everyone. The room felt colder, and wreathed with shadows.

"So we're the last ones?" Tack asked quietly.

Black Suit glanced away. "For now. I have a hard time predicting what the station crew will do."

Ethan spoke for the first time since Black Suit sat down. "Who are those kids that attacked us?"

Black Suit leaned back in his chair. "Nemesis Three occupied the Terrarium before you. They lived inside it for a full year, just as ignorant of reality as you were. There were exactly twenty of them, as proscribed by the Program. They must've exhibited whatever these people are looking for, because they were then invited into the station proper. Your friend Rose is in that group."

"No friend of ours," Ethan said darkly. I forced myself to nod along.

"Only twenty, huh?" Tack said. "So they slaughtered their classmates as instructed."

"Don't be so quick to judge, Thomas. Yours was the only group to attempt to reprogram their MegaCom. I like to think of you as being special rather than the others being faulty."

"Think whatever you like, but they left bodies back in their Matrix."

Black Suit had no response.

"And the last one?" I pressed. "Nemesis Four?"

Something rippled in Black Suit's expression. "Nemesis Four is still sleeping."

My stomach roiled. I imagined a class still battling it out, inside a Program stored somewhere on this station's hard drive. How many were left at this exact moment? Forty? Thirty? Twenty-one kids in a park, with one left to go?

"Why build a massive fake habitat?" Tack grumbled. "Why not just bring us onto the ship and give us jobs or something? We'd have agreed."

Black Suit was quiet for several heartbeats. Finally, "I don't know, Thomas. And it worries me every single day. That's why I've stayed hidden rather than present myself to people who are arguably my colleagues."

"Who runs this place?" Ethan asked sharply. "How many people are aboard?"

Black Suit frowned. "It's hard to tell. There are crew members and security personnel occupying different areas of the station. If I had to guess, I'd say no more than a hundred altogether, but I stay out of their way. The halls are surprisingly empty, which is the main reason they haven't found me. I was operating under the assumption that a large civilian population sleeps somewhere, cryogenically or electronically, but I haven't found any evidence to support that."

"So maybe a hundred crew, and twenty Nemesis Three collaborators?" Ethan said.

"Not all twenty, either. A few were sorted out from the rest, and some others took issue with that. I've been in contact with a small group within Nemesis Three that is suspicious of the station's intentions. I made arrangements with them today, in fact."

Ethan's gaze swung to me. "We've got forty-five classmates at last check, not including Toby's team, though I guess those losers probably count for the other side. But my point is—the numbers aren't great, but they're not hopeless, either."

Black Suit eyed him curiously. "What are you suggesting? Don't forget, the security personnel are armed."

"They're not the only ones." Ethan removed his pistol and set it on the table.

"I'm going back for Min," I said, without a trace of give in my

207

voice. "I won't leave her in there."

Black Suit scanned our faces. Then he laughed. "You want to invade the Terrarium? And then what? Take over the whole station? That's bold, I'll give you that, but you don't even know what these people want from you yet. Have you considered that you might like what they have to offer?"

My frown deepened. "If they'd wanted to offer something, they could've done it without attacking our homes and kidnapping my friends. I'm finding Min first, *period*, and I'm not going to ask the people who bombed us for directions. We can discuss next steps after she's safe."

Before he could respond, a noise echoed in the outer hangar.

"You might be in luck." Black Suit popped up and went to the door. Then he stepped back, wiping his forehead. "Whoever it is, they're headed for this room. There are only two possibilities, so let's hope it's my new friends returning from their mission."

Muffled voices grew closer. Ethan held his pistol in a white-knuckled grip. Tack was glaring at the ground, seemed unsure what to do. I tensed as the door opened and a short black kid with bleached hair walked in.

Black Suit relaxed visibly. "Cyrus."

The boy turned and swept a hand behind him. In strolled a girl dressed in black fatigues, followed by the greatest surprise of my life.

"Min!"

I nearly bowled her over in a hug. There were others with her—Sarah, Akio, Richie, Casey; a whole slew of our people—but I only had eyes for Min. I smothered her in my arms, our lips folding together in an explosion of heat, and need, and relief.

Then I felt her pull back.

She was looking over my shoulder. Across the room, Tack turned away as if burned.

I released her, feeling guilty, then felt angry about that. Why should I be ashamed? *This is why he moved away.*

Min walked over and placed a hand on Tack's shoulder. "I'm so glad you're okay."

Tack eased out of her reach. "Thanks. You too. It's good to see you." He strode to the hangar door and stepped outside. Min silently watched him go.

Unsure how to act, I swooped in again. "I was just planning how to rescue you," I joked. "But that never seems to work, because you always handle it yourself."

She shook her head as if coming awake, then spun to face me. "Noah, I can't believe it." Her eyes gleamed. "How are you here right now?"

I realized she hadn't looked at the table yet. "We had help," I said, then stepped out of the way.

Min saw her father. Her face went slack. She wobbled.

I caught her elbow and held it. Felt her chest heave next to mine.

Black Suit pressed steepled fingers to his lips. "Hello, Min."

Her body was rigid. I worried she might shatter into a thousand pieces. "I thought you didn't make it," she said quietly.

"I took the opening you left me."

Min sniffed. "I want to be glad."

"That's enough, for now."

The room had gone silent. Everyone was darting glances at one another, uncertain what came next. It felt like an important moment, but all I could feel was relief. Min was here. She was okay. We were together again.

So why did Rose's face pop into my head?

Black Suit recovered himself. He slapped his hands together, drawing every eye. "Cyrus, great work. I'll try to deliver what was promised. To everyone else, welcome. We have a lot to talk about. Why don't the newcomers get settled in?"

Min turned and grabbed my shirt with both hands. "Noah, we're on a spaceship!"

I nodded, the craziness hitting me again. "It's insane. And there were *four* Nemesis projects!"

Conversations erupted all around the room, everyone nearly drunk from the madness of the last few hours. Though Cyrus had an unshakable calm, the black-haired girl eyed us with something close to suspicion. My friends seemed no more trusting of them despite everyone arriving together. Did these two attack our settlements? People had died. How could we ever trust them, much less forgive?

"Everyone find a seat," Black Suit instructed finally. "We have a lot to go over."

The meeting took forever.

There were fourteen of us in the cramped room: Black Suit, Cyrus and his companion Parisa, Tack, Ethan, and me, plus Min and Sarah's group of Derrick, Casey, Leighton, Richie, Spence, and Charlie. The two sides began by sharing information grudgingly, but soon everyone was speaking over each other.

Cyrus swore his squad hadn't participated in any of the raids.

"We aren't trusted," he explained. "I think Rose suspects my misgivings and keeps us in reserve because of them. We only went into the Terrarium to catch stragglers." He nodded to Black Suit. "We met this man weeks ago. When he offered to find out what happened to some of our classmates in exchange for sneaking someone out, we took the deal."

Black Suit nodded in confirmation. "Cyrus and his team can be trusted."

Min was staring at her father with an unreadable expression. "Where is the rest of our class being held?" she said.

"In the training facility," Cyrus said. "My class lives close by in a security wing."

"They made us into prisoner guards," Parisa said disgustedly. "Some of our less desirable associates have taken to it."

"That part of the station is patrolled by armed guards," Black Suit added. "I don't go there often."

"We have to free everyone." Tack hadn't spoken much since Min's awkward hello, which did nothing for his mood. He sneered at Cyrus. "If your people are too scared, we can handle it ourselves."

"You'd be locked in a cell right now without us," Parisa shot back. "So maybe talk less and listen more."

"I got myself out of the Terrarium," Tack said. "I didn't need your help then or now."

"There's no point in arguing about the past," Min cut in. "We should focus on our next move." She looked over at Tack, but he didn't meet her eye. "I think Tack is right. Our first priority is a rescue mission. Is anyone still inside the Terrarium?"

Black Suit consulted his tablet. "Sensors indicate no human

life in the habitat. They extracted everyone."

Min swallowed. "Do we know if anyone else was killed?"

He shook his head. "But everyone they've taken prisoner will be in the training facility by now."

Min nodded. "That makes things simpler. They're all in one place. We just have to break them out."

"That might sound easy," Cyrus warned, "but I assure you it's not. Much of this station might feel like a ghost town, but not that part."

"I don't care about easy. I'm going to save my friends."

Cyrus laughed. "I like her," he announced to the room.

Something squirmed inside me. I scooted closer to Min, bumping my knee against hers. She gave me a confused look. I tried to keep the embarrassment from my face. *Get it together, Livingston.*

Something shattered at the back of the room. I twisted around to see Leighton standing beside the refrigerator, blinking stupidly at an overturned plate on the floor. "Sorr . . . guyzz . . ."

He staggered a step, then stopped.

"Leighton?" I asked. "You okay?"

His head rose, eyes unfocused. His mouth dropped open as if he were about to speak, but he collapsed instead.

I sprang up, but Casey reached him first, kneeling beside Leighton's now-twitching body. A moment later her eyes rolled back and she slumped over on top of him.

Everyone froze in astonishment. I heard a low hissing noise. The answer came in a blink.

"Gas!" I shouted, but I could already feel my head growing light.

Shouts echoed. An alarm blared. I tried to find Min, but my mind was shutting down.

Heavy boots outside. The door crashed open as I toppled to the ground.

Something streaked by me and slammed into the knot of hazy figures blocking the doorway.

"After him!" a voice shouted, but the sound played at half speed.

The room strobed in and out of focus. An alcohol smell filled my nostrils.

White boots.

Something poked into my thigh.

All thought fled.

21

MIN

I awoke in darkness.

The blackout was so complete, I couldn't see my hands as I pressed them to my face. Spots and curlicues danced on my corneas, remnants of disturbing dreams. I swallowed a thick ball in my throat.

Where am I?

I sat bolt upright, experienced a vicious head rush that sent me flopping back down to the . . . *mattress*. The movement must've triggered a sensor. Soft yellow light diffused from the ceiling.

I was in an empty room perhaps a dozen yards square.

"What the hell?" I whispered.

"Good morning," a disembodied voice said. *"How may I assist you?"*

I pressed back against the wall beside the bed. "Who's there?"

"How may I assist you?" the voice repeated, with identical inflection.

A computer.

"Lights?" I said tentatively, and the pale glow blazed to harsh white illumination. White walls, white ceiling, white floor. No apparent door. The only objects were a metallic ball in the center of the ceiling and the bed I cowered on, which extended from the wall like a shelf.

I rose, realized I had on a one-piece jumpsuit made of ultra-thin white cloth. It fit perfectly. I shivered, imagining how I came to be wearing the stretchy garment. As I examined the material, my bed slid seamlessly into the wall, leaving me trapped inside a featureless, colorless box and starting to freak out.

"I, uh . . . I need to use the ladies' room."

A wall panel slid open, revealing a small bathroom containing a toilet, sink, and phone-booth shower. Everything was molded plastic and sparkling white.

"Something to drink," I said, more firmly this time. Another panel opened with some kind of dispenser behind it. A plastic cup dropped from its mouth, followed instantly by a stream of water. I took the cup and examined the liquid inside. Then drank. If they intended to poison me, this seemed like a dumb way to go about it.

I tried other commands. Table. Desk. Both extended from the wall like the bed had, complete with attached chairs. I couldn't help cracking a smile. I was inside a science-fiction story. Astronaut Melinda J. Wilder, aboard a miracle space station orbiting in the vacuum of space.

Except I'm a prisoner. Don't forget that part.

I washed my face and used the facilities, keeping a nervous eye on a second metal orb hanging in there. When I emerged all the furniture had disappeared back into the walls, so I had to recall the table.

I sat and asked for food. The water dispenser revolved silently to expose a glass case. Inside it was a selection of fruits, breads, and nuts, and a purple bar of some kind of hard gelatin. I shrugged and dug in, calling out other commands just to see how far the hospitality extended.

"Exit?"

The voice returned. *"Sorry, that command is not authorized."*

Big surprise. "Entertainment?"

The desk reappeared, its drawer sliding open to reveal a gray tablet. I swiped it eagerly but was disappointed—the library contained only boring classic books like the kind we were forced to read in school. No communications apps. No movies or music. There was a button labeled *Chrysalis*, but the screen that came up was password protected. After a few minutes I set the tablet aside with a grunt.

I thought about what had happened in the hangar. We'd been taken prisoner, which meant they'd found that secret hideout almost right away. Had my father sold us out? I didn't think so—that seemed like an awfully complicated way to go about it—but I wondered where he was right now. These Chrysalis people seemed to want my class alive at the moment, but did that extend to a stowaway?

I had no reason to suspect Cyrus and Parisa, but no reason to trust them, either. Nemesis Three remained an enigma.

I thought of Noah, and my heart dropped. I'd found him again, only for us to be ripped apart hours later. Then Tack's face rammed into my head and I felt even worse. He'd barely looked at me, even after all the weeks we'd been apart. Did he truly not want to be friends anymore?

Thinking of Tack sparked a foggy memory from the ambush. There'd been a crash, then shouting. Fighting. I thought a handful of people might've escaped the room, but had they gotten away completely? What about my father?

And where am *I, anyway?* Was this the training facility my father had mentioned?

Anger kindled inside me. I thought of the struggles we'd endured over the last six months and ground my teeth. We'd developed a fledgling society, built settlements, and even started down the path to self-sufficiency. We were finding a way to live in a strange and dangerous world. People had lost their lives in the process.

And for what? Nothing. Our whole "planet" was an experiment, and we weren't in on the joke. We'd been used as test subjects *again*. I thought of the killer storms, the ocean swirls, and all the other dangers thrown at us, and nearly got sick. Everything had been a fiction. Whoever ran this station were monsters.

I still hadn't seen one of my captors up close. I vowed to make it memorable when I did.

Silently fuming, I could no longer sit still. "Computer, when can I leave this room?"

"Orientation is scheduled for zero-eight-hundred."

Orientation? "What's the current time?"

"The current time is zero-seven-fifty-two."

Not a long wait, at least. I stood and did some stretching, working blood back into my muscles. I had no idea how long I'd been unconscious. My body ached slightly, but nothing terrible. My mind felt sharp. I tried to control my breathing and keep my temper in check, waiting for whatever came next.

Minutes later there was a chime. A panel on the far side of the room slid open. I'd guessed the door's probable location based on the other furniture—had even tried to find it—but the panels fit together seamlessly when closed. This technology was beyond anything I'd ever seen. Which made sense, since I was on a space station over a million years into the future.

Am I, though? Can I trust anything I was told?

No one appeared. Curious, I crept over and stuck my head out. There was a long corridor with other openings along one side. I spotted Hector Quino peeking from his cell down the way.

"Hector!" I raced down and wrapped him in a hug.

His face broke into a smile. "Min! Thank God for a familiar face. What's happening?"

I squeezed him again, delighted to see a friend. Our voices drew more heads. Classmates. They spilled into the corridor, slapping backs and exchanging hugs, everyone wearing the same white jumpsuit. No one had any idea where we were or how we'd gotten there.

I did a headcount. There were sixteen of us: me, Alice, Anna, Rachel, Lauren, Casey, Dakota, Vonda, Ethan, Sam, Akio, Hector, Leighton, Floyd, Charlie, and Darren. Eight boys and eight girls. *That has to mean something, but what?* I licked my lips, trying to remain calm. Where was Noah? Tack? Derrick? I'd even hoped to see Sarah's sneering face, despite the crap she always gave me.

Ethan whistled, and everyone went quiet. "What's going on? Did they let us go?"

"There's a turn down by my room," Floyd said, looking huge in the narrow passageway. He pointed toward the last cell on the opposite end of the corridor from mine. "Maybe we're supposed to go somewhere?"

"Walk ourselves to the slaughter?" Ethan shot him an annoyed look. "Not a chance."

Hector checked the opposite side, but it was a dead end. There was only one way to exit the corridor.

"We can't just stand here," Rachel grumbled. "What's the big plan, Min?"

"Where's Aiken?" Anna moaned at no one. "Is he . . . Are the others dead?"

I realized Anna had been missing since the Home Town raid. "How long have you been here?"

"I've been stuck in that room for two days," she whimpered, lips trembling. "This is the first time they let me out." Other classmates taken that night nodded in agreement. I glanced at Darren, who'd been living at the Outpost.

"After those douchebags attacked our cabins, they split us up," he said. "We got marched through the forest to some weird cave door in the side of a mountain."

"I've seen it," Ethan muttered. "Did they take everyone?"

Darren nodded. "I've been trapped in that stupid closet ever since. I guess they were waiting for something." His face grew hard. "If they did anything to Benny . . ."

I tried to think logically. "I think they grabbed everyone, and now we're supposed to do something, but I have no idea what." I heard Rachel scoff, but others shushed her, regarding me with anxious eyes. I made a decision. "Let's see where that hallway goes. There's nothing else to do except sit in our rooms."

In the end, everyone agreed. With Ethan in the lead we walked down the next corridor. It was white and blank, ending at a large airlock. The outer portal swung open as we approached, revealing a small clean room and a wide chamber beyond the inner door, set with four long tables in its middle. No one was there. We quickly explored the room and found an identical portal at the far end, but that one was sealed. Stymied, we gathered at the tables and debated what to do next.

Those of us that had been captured in the hangar told the others what we'd learned about Chrysalis. Shock nearly paralyzed other members of the group.

Alice sat quietly by herself and put her head down. The soccer girls—Lauren, Casey, and Dakota—wanted to go back to their cells, while Leighton and Ethan decided to hammer on the other airlock. Most of the others were silent, waiting to see how the wind would blow. Rachel was in the middle of explaining how this whole thing was actually *my* fault when a giant flat screen descended from the ceiling.

A woman's face appeared. She had glossy black hair, dark blue eyes, and wore a smart gray uniform. Her age was hard to place but I guessed no more than thirty. She wasn't smiling, but her expression wasn't unfriendly. Conversations around the table died as if guillotined.

"Members of Nemesis One, welcome to Chrysalis." The woman's voice was soothing and lyrical, like that of a therapist. She nodded as if we'd accomplished a goal rather than been dragged from the Terrarium against our will. "On behalf of the whole crew, I'd like to apologize for the manner in which you were integrated into humanity's greatest technological triumph, the Chrysalis space station." Her expression became somewhat knowing. "Though I must point out that you brought the problem upon yourselves."

"*We* caused the problem?" Sam snapped. "We didn't even know about this stupid ship!"

"Class-M orbiting superstation," the woman corrected gently. "But I was referring to your decision to break containment and exit the Terrarium before full biotic compatibility had been established. One of your number breached the habitat, forcing a series of countermeasures. When those failed, and social conditions inside the biome degraded to an unsustainable point, we had no choice but to remove and quarantine your class while assessing the damage."

Toby, I thought glumly. He must've reached the edge of the Terrarium and started this whole mess. But then the rest of what the woman said hit me, and I rose quickly. "Damage? What do you mean?"

"You may have contaminated the station," she explained patiently. "Chrysalis is a finely tuned, self-sufficient biosphere with the Terrarium as its beating heart. We take special care before removing subjects from its environment. You never know what nature might concoct during a regeneration cycle."

"So that's why you kept us in there?" I said. "You were testing our . . . compatibility?"

She nodded. "An entirely new ecosystem developed on Earth while you were completing Nemesis Phase Two. Unfortunately, not all subjects are a good fit for reinsertion, both physically and psychologically. Your class is particularly worrisome, since you didn't stay within Program parameters." She smiled ruefully. "You've caused quite a stir here on Chrysalis."

"Where are the others in our class? Are they being held, too?" I didn't ask about my dad, although the question burned inside me. I didn't want to give him away if he'd escaped, or register my interest if he was another prisoner.

The woman's expression became carefully neutral. "We are examining all remaining test subjects from Nemesis One. You will be told more as it becomes necessary."

"Necessary?" Ethan exploded. "Who the hell do you think you are? You've got no right to hold us here." A familiar pink flush was creeping up his neck. "Let me out of whatever this is right now. You can't keep me prisoner!"

The woman's voice hardened. "On the contrary, Mr. Fletcher, I can do exactly that. The MegaCom that ran your Program—and all of the machinery responsible for your regeneration—are the sole property of Chrysalis. To be even more blunt: we rebuilt your bodies, so we own them."

Stunned silence. I couldn't breathe. She continued as if stating a tax foible.

"Chrysalis has a singular mission: to effectively colonize the planet's surface. We reserve the right to screen applicants for suitability."

"Is that what this is about?" I said, hope blossoming in my chest. "We've been brought back to recolonize the planet?"

The woman nodded pleasantly. "Which hardly makes us monsters, now does it?"

A wave of relief swept through me. I saw shoulders ease around the tables. Cautious smiles.

Recolonize Earth. That's what we'd been trying to do anyway, right? That's what Fire Lake Island had been all about. The more I considered it, the less I could deny that our situation had dramatically improved. This place had light-years better technology than the silo. With a freaking *space station* backing us, life wouldn't have to be a dangerous pioneer experience.

We'd been fooled and used, but maybe they'd been testing our ability to work together on a new world. It made a sick kind of sense with so much at stake. But there was one major sticking point. "Why are the sixteen of us being held separately from the rest of our class?" I asked. "When can we see them?"

"I need to be clear, Ms. Wilder. With all of you. Not everyone will be selected for colonial insertion. Nemesis One was supposed to produce twenty filtered test subjects. Instead, you subverted the Program and sixty-four data sets regenerated. Therefore, statistically, we know *all* of you can't be suitable. New screening methods are being devised."

My blood ran cold. "And what happens to those who are found unsuitable?"

"Unsuitable candidates are designated for repurposement." The woman smiled disarmingly. "Several of your classmates have already been reclassified and removed from the testing process. But don't let this worry you. They too will serve the station. No human asset is ever wasted aboard Chrysalis."

I stared at the woman for a long moment. "You haven't told us your name. Where are *you* from?"

The woman dipped her head in acknowledgment. "I am Sophia. We'll talk about the crew another time." She sat back in her chair. "That's all for now. Please return to your domiciles. Further instructions will follow soon, so I suggest you rest and prepare."

The face onscreen winked out.

22

NOAH

The pattern kept repeating.

Blue, blue, blue, red.

Blue, blue, blue, red.

The glowing boxes ran across one wall of my antiseptic cell, the first disappearing as the last arrived. I stood beside the display, flexing my fingers and watching intently. I didn't want to miss again.

Blue, blue, blue, red.

Blue, blue, blue, red.

Blue, blue, blue, red, orange, yellow, green.

The game speed doubled, new colors appearing so fast I barely had a chance to mimic them. Beads of sweat erupted at my temples, but I didn't dare look away. I'd done so once already this morning and paid the price.

Blue, blue, blue, red, orange, yellow, green.

Blue, blue, blue, red, orange, yellow, green.

Blue, blue, blue, red, orange, yellow, green, purpleblackblueyellow.

"Crap." I muttered the litany in my head, entering colors as fast as I could to sync the two lines. This was where I'd screwed up last time, and my computer overlord's response had been clear. A second failure meant I was a candidate for "repurposement." I didn't know what that was, but it didn't sound great.

Blue, blue, blue, red, orange, yellow, green, purpleblackblueyellow.

Blue, blue, blue, red, orange, yellow, green, purpleblackblueyellow.

Blue, blue, blue, red, orange, yellow, green, purpleblackblue yellowredredgreenredblue.

"Gaaah!"

My hands flew, my brain frantically locking in the pattern as my lips moved soundlessly to a rhythm I'd invented. I was full-on sweating now, circles forming at the pits of my jumpsuit.

Blue, blue, blue, red, orange, yellow, green, purpleblackblue yellowredredgreenredblue.

Blue, blue, blue, red, orange, yellow, green, purpleblackblue yellowredredgreenredblue.

Blue, blue, blue, red, orange, yellow, green, purpleblackblue yellowredredgreenredblue.

Ding!

"Congratulations. You have completed this task."

I wobbled backward with a relieved sigh. Called for my chair, and sat heavily when it slid from the wall. Taking a calming breath, I wiped my brow with a forearm. *Holy crap.* I detested memory games, but I'd managed to get it right this time. I smiled dumbly at the seamless, solid-white floor. *Victory for Livingston!*

Even though the process was degrading—I was being held inside a box and made to perform like a guinea pig—I couldn't help feeling proud of myself. This stuff wasn't easy, but I'd already passed four "tasks" that morning. I was really hoping for a lunch break.

I thought it was midday, anyway. The only way I could guess the hour was through meals. My cell was a perfect square without windows or a visible door. For all I knew it was midnight, or dusk, or whenever. *Is* there a proper time of day in outer space? I didn't have an answer to that one.

First I'd been required to make three-dimensional shapes fit within a series of plastic molds. I breezed that, remembering those maddening tangram puzzles Mrs. Reamer had forced on me back in middle school. Then I'd been subjected to an increasingly difficult series of visual logic games. After eking by those with only one mistake to spare, silhouettes had begun appearing at random on the walls. I'd had to find and touch them before they vanished. That left me drenched in perspiration and thoroughly annoyed. What could possibly be the point of these challenges?

I looked hopelessly to where I knew the door should be, based on the one time I'd been released. Two days ago sixteen of us had emerged like moles into a featureless hallway. I'd searched frantically for Min, but she wasn't in the group. The corridor had led to a large common room with tables and chairs and nothing else. A second airlock on the other side refused to open, so I'd sat with the others, nerves inching toward a breaking point, until that stone-faced woman appeared onscreen.

We were test subjects. Possible contaminants. *Property* of Chrysalis.

I could barely wrap my head around it. We'd been sent back to our rooms, and the tasks began an hour later.

A wall panel swished open, indicating it was time to eat. I'd been right about lunch: behind the glass was the ubiquitous brick of purple gelatin—still couldn't eat more than a few bites of it, sorry—a glass of rehydrated milk, a bowl of noodles, and an apple. Where it all came from I had no idea. I dug into the pasta, wondering what devilish monotonies my afternoon might consist of, and was caught completely off guard when my door swooshed open.

I rose and hurried out, hoping to see my classmates again. My block consisted of eight boys: me, Derrick, Richie, Ferris, Aiken—all from the village—along with Benny and Corbin, who'd been at the Outpost, and Hamza from Ridgeline. There were also exactly eight girls: Sarah was here, along with Susan and Jessica from the silo, Piper and Leah from Home Town, Maggie from Ridgeline, and Liesel from the Outpost.

Everyone had a story about his or her capture. That first day, those of us who'd escaped the Terrarium on our own told the others what we'd learned about Chrysalis. It'd taken a while for everyone to digest the magnitude of how badly we'd been played, then tempers exploded. But the tough talk died when that Sophia woman explained the testing we could expect aboard the space station, and the possibility of joining a colony down on the planet if we succeeded. I suspected everyone else had spent the solitary hours wondering what "repurposement" meant, too.

But as I entered the white-walled corridor this time, I found myself alone. The other cells all remained sealed. I tried knocking on the closest one, but my fist created no sound, and I wasn't completely sure where the door was anyway. I gave up and trudged down the hall.

The passage had changed as well. There was no longer a right turn toward the common room—instead, as if by magic, a way to the left was now open. I marveled again at the station's construction. The material forming the walls seemed to bend and shape like liquid plastic, pliable yet unyielding, and seamlessly covering whatever lay behind it. This tech was light-years beyond anything I'd seen or even heard of back in Fire Lake. *We're out of our league with these people.*

Or person. So far Sophia was the only crew member I'd encountered, beyond the helmeted jackboots who'd stormed the cargo hold. Would they keep us quarantined forever, or would we eventually meet the rest of our quasi-captors? After the initial reception we'd gotten, I wasn't sure which I preferred. *Rose, on the other hand . . .*

This new hallway led to a door that swished open at my approach. Beyond it stretched a large white chamber like an empty gymnasium, with padded walls, a springy floor, and a towering ceiling. Something glinted on the far wall. With a shrug I began walking across the open space, and was surprised when I ran smack into something in the middle of the chamber. Dumbfounded, I pressed a hand against the invisible barrier. It reminded me of the force fields surrounding reset zones inside the Program.

But that was a simulation. This is real technology. I whistled in appreciation.

A door on the opposite side of the room opened and a boy entered, dressed all in black. He was nearly my height, but thicker in the chest and arms, with spiky brown hair and a cocky sneer. I nodded as he approached, but the jerk ignored me, stopping ten yards across from where I stood and staring at nothing, his hands on his hips.

"Hi there," I tried. "I'm Noah. I guess you're from another—"

"Not interested, dude."

"Right, then. Good talk."

There was a sound like a computer booting up. Lines of color streaked across the invisible barrier between us. My opponent—for I abruptly realized that's what he was—rolled his neck and shook out his arms and legs. I didn't understand but did a few quick lunges just to look ready.

Okay, pal. Bring it, whatever it might be.

The lights flashed, then a tone sounded. I noticed the boy had retreated halfway across his section, so I did too.

A giant grid appeared on the invisible divider, like a chessboard. At the top was a row of black squares, with a row of white squares at the bottom. My opponent, who I now thought of as Sneer, reached out a hand and jerked it downward. A black square gleamed and advanced a block, coloring that space black as well.

I glanced at him in confusion. "So what is this, checkers or something?"

Sneer crossed his arms, saying nothing. A computerized voice sounded.

"White has five seconds to move."

I held out my hands. "Wait! I don't know the rules!"

"Two seconds."

"Hold on! How am I supp—"

"White has elected to make no move. Black may proceed."

Sneer snickered, extending his arm again. The next piece snapped forward, like a dark curtain descending onto my territory. "Worse than the last guy," he muttered.

My competitive juices ignited. I reached up and pointed at a corresponding white square, then dragged my finger upward. The piece slid as requested. I smiled tightly. *Great. Now I just have to figure out the point of this game.*

Move followed move until our pieces collided. Those spots turned gray. My opponent worked systematically, reinforcing gray spots with more black squares, turning them fully black while inching toward the bottom of the board. I realized it was a game of domination. A square that had been converted from gray to black or white could then move double, graying more territory and squashing the other player's progress.

I was falling behind at an exponential clip. Sneer smirked contently, sure that I was as good as beaten.

Abruptly I changed tactics, abandoning a trench-line defense. I punched up the sides of the board and circled around the black wave, enveloping my opponent's pieces from behind. More and more of the board turned gray, then white, as I hemmed in his remaining squares and began to wipe them out. The smirk slipped, soured, then disappeared altogether, replaced by a frustrated glower. But it was too late. I mopped up the last stain of his army in a bottom corner, completing a grid of gleaming white.

The tone sounded.

"White is victorious."

Sneer glared at me, eyes smoldering. I faked a yawn to piss him off.

"Name's still Noah, by the way. Good job, good effort."

He gave me the middle finger. I just laughed.

The door behind me opened and I sauntered out of the room, feeling good for the first time since being locked in my cell. But it didn't last. I was still a toy for the amusement of others. I'd won a stupid game, like a rat completing a maze and reaching the sacred cheese.

What was *my* reward to be?

23

MIN

The door whisked open.

I sighed. Put down my fork. Every time I thought I was about to go nuts from being locked up a moment longer, the way out would magically appear and I'd fight an urge to hide under my bed. I considered refusing to walk myself to the next competition, but, like always, my need to know compelled me down the hallway.

Chrysalis didn't need burly guards prodding its test subjects along. Human nature did the trick.

Besides, I wiped the floor with that Nemesis Three chick last time.

My opponent in the grid puzzle had been a skinny blond girl named Reese. That's all I'd been able to learn about her before the challenge began. I'd grasped the fundamentals quickly and won without much trouble. To be honest, the cup-stacking challenge in my room had been more difficult, or any of the auditory games. If this was the best the other class had to throw at us, I wasn't too impressed.

I reached the giant gaming chamber and was met with a surprise—a handful of classmates in my testing group were facing off against a crowd of our black-clad adversaries. The two factions had gathered on either side of the invisible barrier, and it seemed like a good thing the force field was there. I heard raised voices. Saw clenched fists. Ethan was making a gesture that was *not* telling his opponent he was number one.

I strode to the center of the room, doing a quick headcount. There were five Fire Lake kids with me on our side of the barrier: Ethan, Sam, Casey, Alice, and Floyd. They were staring down a much larger crowd of Nemesis Three members. I counted fifteen of them, including our old friends Cyrus, Jerica, Parisa, and Scott. Everyone in black wore matching scowls, although when Cyrus's gaze slid to me, he gave a subtle wink.

Interesting. But why are they here?

Going by what Cyrus and Parisa had told us, this must be everyone left in their class. Then my eyes widened as I saw who else was standing with them, wearing the same black clothes. I now understood Ethan's middle-finger salute.

I pulled Casey aside. As I did, a tall copper-haired girl on the other side tracked me with sharp green eyes. Her hands found her hips as I whispered into Casey's ear. "What are Cole and the twins doing over there?"

Casey's frown deepened. "They switched sides, I guess. I didn't know that was possible."

Ethan continued to berate his former lackeys in explicit terms, but Chris just laughed while Mike silently rolled his eyes. Cole was staring at the ground with his arms tightly crossed, refusing to meet Ethan's eye.

"Whatever, man." Chris ran a hand through his long ginger hair. "I like being on the management side." But though he seemed amused, the other Nemesis Three kids did not. A palpable sense of rage filtered through the barrier. No one embodied it more than the lanky redhead silently staring death at me. *She means trouble.*

Ethan glanced at me, then stormed over, his face a sweaty mess. "Can you believe those punk-ass traitors? Talk about disrespect."

"I think we're past that now." I nodded at the girl watching me. "Who's that?"

Ethan scowled. "Rose. She's the one me, Tack, and Noah took prisoner beyond the Outpost. Be careful if you get matched up against her—she's some kind of martial arts expert. She kicked the crap out of, uh . . . Tack in the woods." Grudging respect entered his voice. "Rose is no joke, Min. Watch your back around her."

I nodded, making a decision. I walked directly toward the barrier. As if she'd been waiting for this move, Rose strode forward and met me in the center of the room. Talk died around us.

"Hi," I said simply.

"I set this up so we could meet. Your next game will begin soon, but I wanted to see you face-to-face."

"Okay. Who brought the barbecue?"

Rose rolled her eyes. "You're Min? I expected someone taller."

I laughed. Suddenly I felt more at ease. I knew how to handle bullies.

"Sorry. Floyd handles our shelf-reaching requirements. I like fitting into tight spaces."

Behind me, he called out. "That's Big Floyd to anyone wearing black." He pointed at a spiky-haired kid with an ugly bruise on the side of his face. "I met you already, when you tried messing with my boy Hamza in our village. I'm glad you're awake again."

Spiky Hair flushed scarlet, sliding behind a clump of his classmates. Sam and Ethan snickered.

If possible, Rose's glare began to smolder even more. "You think this is funny? Your idiot class might destroy everything this station has planned to save the human species, and you laugh like it's a comedy routine."

I gave her a level look. "If you're hoping for sorrys because we didn't surrender when you wanted to tie us up, you're wasting everyone's time. Consider it a lesson in diplomacy."

"Four of my classmates *died* because of you people," Rose spat. "Someone intentionally flooded the lab area with a dozen kids inside. I know—I checked the opened valves myself." Rose moved to within an inch of the force field. "*You* were down there when it happened, weren't you Min? And somehow escaped without a scratch."

"I *got* scratched," I said, quietly fuming. "We lost chessmates too, even if they were working for you. And not that I'd lose any sleep over it had I been responsible—since I was being held prisoner at the time—but I didn't cause the flood. I nearly drowned myself. I have no idea how the water got in."

Which was true, as far as it went. I never asked Sarah the mechanics of what she'd done.

"Get off your high horse," I continued acidly. "Eight of my classmates died in that fishbowl habitat while you watched us struggle on TV. And are you forgetting the five who were crushed to death when you blew up our silo to begin with?"

Rose flinched. "That wasn't supposed to happen."

"Awesome. Tell that to Devin Carver. And Emily. And Kristen. And Melissa. And Tiffani."

Cyrus darted to stand beside Rose. He spoke in an overloud voice. "Mistakes were made on both sides, but we're all under Chrysalis authority now. If Rose and I can forgive being assaulted and kidnapped by your friends inside the Terrarium, you can put our attacks aside as well. We have bigger problems ahead of us. Your actions forced us to break quarantine without the crew's permission. Now we're *all* at risk in these foolish contests."

I barely hid a smile. Cyrus was putting on a show. But then something he said tripped me up. "How are you at risk?"

A muscular brown-haired boy stormed forward. "Because we failed to round you up properly, our colony spots are no longer guaranteed. We have to earn them against you, as if we haven't done everything they've asked before now. It's outrageous."

"Shut up, Gray," Rose snapped. The boy shot her a dark look, but I was surprised when he stepped back and kept quiet.

I squinted at Rose, unsure of what I was hearing. "So you're . . . vying for spots? Does that mean you've lost candidates?"

"Yes," Cyrus answered quickly. Rose clicked her tongue but

237

didn't cut him off like she had Gray. "One of our classmates did not return yesterday, a girl named Reese Willette. We've been told she was selected for repurposement."

"Enough," Rose growled. "They don't need to know all our business. Although she was *your* opponent yesterday, right Min? Does it feel good to take someone else's chance away?"

I sighed. The girl I'd beaten at the puzzle hadn't been mean, or nasty, or even rude. Just overmatched. What happened to her? What happened to all of them? I looked at Rose, and suspected that behind the glare, she was consumed by the same question. A little of my animosity faded.

"They need to know how we're all in danger," Cyrus huffed, staring until he caught my eye. "There's also a strange man running around that the crew can't pin down. He's free on the station."

Rose spun in irritation. "Quiet," she hissed. "Sophia said that was private information."

Cyrus made a show of looking embarrassed. I pretended not to care about the news he'd "blabbed."

Sam spoke for the first time. "So you guys are getting weeded now, too? Tough break after selling out so hard to please them. How many do they want total?"

Rose's cheeks flamed. She seemed on the verge of not answering, then spat, "We don't know."

Cyrus scratched his head. "We're not in the loop anymore, it seems."

Rose jabbed a finger at me. It slammed into the barrier. "Because of *you*. Your class, and the stupidity that drove you to break your own Program. But know this—I'm not losing any more of my people so that rejects from Fire Lake can hijack the future colony. We came out twenty strong, united and committed to each other. Nothing will break those of us that are left. You better pray there are other spots, because ours are reserved. Count on that."

She'd finally touched a nerve. I stepped forward until we were kissing close, with only the force field between us. "You must've slaughtered your own people in the simulation to get here, Rose. Twenty strong? Please. Doing anything it takes to survive is nothing special. Animals can do that." I nodded back at my classmates. "We found a way to save our entire class. It took us a while to learn the right lessons, but we didn't leave a soul behind. You call it stupidity, but it's the reason you'll never beat us. We're simply better people than you."

Rose screamed in anger, slamming a fist against the barrier.

I didn't flinch.

Sirens sounded around us.

Cyrus grabbed Rose's arm as the rest of his classmates bolted through the door behind them.

"We have to go," he said. "A test is about to begin in here. Only the people involved can be present or Sophia will learn about this meeting."

Rose shook him off with an icy smile. "*You* have to go. I'm where I'm supposed to be. I'm part of the next contest."

I got a cold feeling in my stomach. Rose glanced at my classmates, milling uncertainly behind me. "You five better leave. I wanted to meet Min, and only let you out because of how the door system works. Get back to your cells before the crew discovers you're missing."

My feet were rooted in place. "And me?"

Rose's smile became predatory. "You're right where you should be, Wilder. Reese is gone. I'm your huckleberry now."

Floyd and Casey approached. "You want us to stay, Min?" Casey whispered.

"No." I watched Rose retreat a few paces and begin stretching. "I think she's telling the truth. Whatever's about to happen, it's a part of my regular testing. I'll be fine."

They both frowned, but nodded.

"Kick her ass, Min," Ethan called out loudly, but then he sidled close to my side and whispered, "But seriously—if it's some kind of fighting thing, you might want to go down early."

"Gee, thanks."

Sam patted my shoulder, and Alice squeezed my arm—when was the last time I'd heard her speak?—but all five jogged to the far door and slipped through it. I turned around and took a deep breath. *Just the two of us. Great.*

Glowing circles appeared on the floor, one on each side.

"Please step onto the starting points," the computerized voice intoned.

We moved into position—me resignedly, Rose with hungry anticipation. A buzzer sounded, and a dozen thick ropes dropped from the ceiling. Rose and I were positioned at opposite ends of a straight line, each rope no more than three feet from the next one.

"Reach the other player's circle to win the game."

I watched Rose shimmy up the first rope like she was born among vines.

"Oh. Great."

We'd meet in the middle, and I had a feeling it wouldn't be a quiet passing.

Rose was already lunging for the second rope. I grabbed the one hanging in front of me—a supple line that felt strangely tacky at the same time. Gripping it was easy and wouldn't chew up my hands. *All this tech, and they have us swinging around like Tarzan.*

I watched Rose snag the third rope easily. She was a quarter of the way to victory and I was still rooted to the floor. *Get going.*

I'd always been a good climber, so the task itself wasn't daunting. I could make it across easily, if not for the flame-headed Amazon slowly working toward me with other ambitions in mind. Ethan's warning echoed in my head. Was there a place to hide until she won and I could slink back to my cell?

I moved from the first rope to second. Second to third. Rose was drawing near, having crossed the midway point, where the barrier obviously no longer existed. She was taking special care to stay level with me despite having covered twice as much ground.

"I'm coming, Melinda," she called, swinging her legs out wide like a trapeze artist. "I want to talk up close."

"I'm kinda tired for a chat," I lobbed back, climbing higher. "Next time for sure, though."

Rose matched my ascent. She wasn't going to pass me without exacting a price. I decided to stay where I was near the top. It risked a longer fall if she kicked me off the damn course, but she couldn't get above me, either.

Rose moved onto the line directly across from me. There she paused, savoring my tension.

"Better people, huh?" Her electric green stare burned into me. "There were forty-seven in my Program, Min. Huntwell, Wyoming was a very small town. I knew almost every kid from birth, and not all were good. Banding together to get rid of twenty of them was easy. More, it was the right thing to do. They were lawless, heartless bastards that I won't miss."

I hung there silently, listening. I'd forgotten how hard our own Program had been, and the awful choices we'd made.

"We weren't perfect either," I said quietly. "It got really bad before we . . . we changed our ways."

"There was no changing for us," Rose said. "Two groups tried to annihilate each other until one failed. I didn't like it, but I don't regret it. I wanted to live. If that makes me a bad person, so be it. But I'm not the one on a high horse."

She swung out a leg before I could react, kicking me hard in the abdomen. My fingers fumbled and I dropped fifteen feet before regaining the rope. Rose slid down her line and kicked me in the shoulder, then attempted to stomp me from above. I ducked and shimmied sideways, her booted foot barely missing my head. Then I raced along the ropes just inches off the floor until I was past her, near the middle of the course.

Rose sighed. "I'd hoped for one more good shot. Knocking you to the floor would've been a more satisfying way to win, but you ran away. Guess I'll have to settle for lapping you."

My chest heaved as I hung from a middle line. I was about to sass something back at her when an idea occurred to me. The computerized instructions had only said one thing.

Rose turned away, moving to the second-to-last rope. There was no way I could climb across the rest of the lines before she reached my starting spot. But did I have to do that?

"Here goes nothing," I murmured.

I dropped to the padded floor. Rose's head whipped around, her mouth widening in a mocking smile.

Nothing happened.

I grinned.

"First one to the other's spot wins, right Rosie?"

Her face went sheet white. She released her rope and dropped like a rock, but I was already sprinting across the chamber.

I stepped onto her circle a second before she reached mine.

"Game to White."

The ropes retracted and the circles disappeared. I was on the opposite side of the room. Rose waited in the center, shoulders quivering, as I walked back toward my doorway.

I tensed, expecting some sort of attack, but she just glared at me, eyes narrowed and chest heaving. I strode past her without stopping, releasing a pent-up breath only when I'd moved out of easy punching range.

"Next time, Wilder," Rose called out as I reached the doorway.

I waved a lazy hand without looking back. "Looking forward to it."

24

NOAH

Another day, another test.

I reentered the white chamber to find the grid replaced by a large circle. When the opposite door opened and Sneer walked in, I realized I'd have to think of a new name for him. The arrogant overconfidence was gone. He looked ready to chew nails.

"I'm still Noah, in case you're interested. Noah Livingston."

The boy looked at me. "Gray West," he growled. "Now shut the hell up."

"You're a charmer." But I folded my arms and waited.

The room went black, except for my jumpsuit, which glowed in the dark. The same was *not* true of Gray's midnight gear. I couldn't spot him anywhere.

The room divider abruptly changed from invisible to solid, except for a large circle at its center, which hung twenty feet above my head. The circle flashed bright red once before fading out, leaving a hole in the divider. Beside me, a pedestal rose from the floor cradling a gleaming ball the size of an ostrich egg.

I picked it up. Heard a tone. Then nearly lost my lunch as gravity disappeared and I began floating up toward the ceiling.

"*Whaaa!*" I gargled, spinning head over heels.

The ball slipped from my fingers. I did another ungainly flip and my stomach threatened to unload. From the corner of my eye I noticed a glowing orb rise level with me, then rapidly expand in size until it smashed into my head. Gray's laughter carried from the other side of the barrier.

"*Point to Black. One–zero.*"

I crashed to the floor. The ball zipped back onto the pedestal.

"You *really* need to give people a heads-up on how this stuff works," I called out, rubbing my cheek. I heard another chuckle from beyond the divider.

The problem became clear. At floor level I couldn't see my opponent, and he couldn't see me. But when we floated up level with the circle—which I now understood to be an opening between the sides—Gray could track me glowing like a jellyfish in my white jumpsuit while he remained invisible. Then he'd peg me with his stupid ball.

Baby steps. First, learn to fly.

I took a deep breath. Lifted the ball from the cradle.

Gravity fled, but this time I kept my body still. Pushing off lightly with my toes, I rose at a controlled rate. I lifted an arm and waved one hand. I moved left. *Aha!*

So the vacuum wasn't total. I could manipulate my direction in space.

I began testing limbs to see what they could do. My body slid left and right, then dove, responding to subtle motions. This wasn't zero gravity, it was something even better—total control over movement in three-dimensional space. "Incredible," I breathed.

I was so excited by these discoveries that I didn't see Gray's ball until it slammed into my stomach. "Oof." I dropped to the padded floor. Chuckles echoed across the chamber again.

"Point to Black. Two–zero."

"How many free shots do you usually get?" I shouted, coughing loudly as I struggled to stand. "Cheater!"

"Get better quick," Gray called back. "Next one puts you out!"

I glanced at the ball on the stand, grinding my teeth. I had to change tactics and surprise him somehow, like I'd done in the board game. The problem was, I couldn't even see him.

But you can see his ball.

I snatched my ball and bent nearly double. Then I pushed off hard, shooting up like a cork. Reaching the circle's edge, I looked down and spotted the other ball floating near the floor. I reared back and threw immediately, was rewarded by a yelp as my ball crashed into something within inches of the other one.

"Point to White. Two–one."

I landed in a crouch like a jungle cat. Snarled to myself.

"Okay." Gray's voice floated across the barrier. *"Okay.* All right, then."

I lifted my ball again but didn't repeat the move. Instead I shot forward and pressed my back against the divider. As I'd suspected, Gray had rocketed up quickly to meet my anticipated attack. His ball was floating in the center of the circle, but he didn't see me beneath him.

He hung a moment too long.

I spun and pushed off the divider with both feet, throwing my ball nearly straight up at him.

I heard a string of four-letter words.

"Point to White. Two–two. Next point will win the contest."

Gravity returned and I crashed on my butt, smiling wickedly.

Dead silence in the chamber. I grabbed the ball and moved forward again, flattening against the divider. I had him off balance and didn't think he could anticipate me now, but my number one disadvantage was still a problem. He could see me, but I couldn't see him.

So solve the problem.

My eyes popped, then I had to swallow a giggle.

You're right, me.

Solve the damn problem.

"Point to White. White wins the contest three–two."

I thumped down with a howl of triumph as the lights came on and the divider became invisible once more. Gray was slumped on the ground, his expression one of utter shock. Then he looked at me and his eyes bugged.

My face went red. "Sorry, dude. Had to do it."

Gray covered his face and started to laugh. "Okay, man. You win. *Holy crap*."

"Gotta give a hundred and ten percent, right?"

I was completely naked, covering myself as best I could. I scurried to where my jumpsuit sat in a heap and hastily pulled it back on. Gray snorted, one hand rubbing his eyes. "I lost, and now I'm blind. Rough day."

I was about to quip back when the barrier went solid again, blocking Gray from view.

"Hello?" I called.

No answer. He was sealed away as if by a brick wall.

With a sigh, I turned back the way I'd entered, but there was nothing there. Instead, on the far wall a new door suddenly appeared. "Guess I go this way," I muttered. The corridor beyond angled back toward the common room where we'd first met Sophia. I stepped through an airlock and found two others waiting at a table.

"Derrick! Sarah!" I shouted.

Derrick popped up and greeted me with a hug. Sarah rose, smiling, and gave me a tight little hand-wave. Grinning, I nodded in return, but kept my distance. It was just like that with us, and probably always would be.

"Man am I glad to see you guys," I said, meaning every word.

"You too, bro." Derrick squeezed my shoulder. "How'd you win the dodgeball matchup? That was sick."

I'm sure my face colored. I tried to cover it with a cough. "Oh, you know. Just being quick, I guess."

Sarah gave me an odd look, but sat down again, her game face sliding back on. "Derrick and I were guessing, and you showing up kind of confirms it. We think we've graduated to a new level or something. Why else release three people together?"

I glanced around, suddenly on edge. "Just us? Where are the others?" *Where's Min?*

"Did you win both arena games the first time?" Derrick asked.

I nodded.

"Same with us. I wonder how many did, though. My last one was close. Maybe we're just first."

That made sense and calmed me down. I tried not to think about what would happen to those who couldn't win.

Don't worry. That's not Min.

My thoughts were interrupted by the other airlock opening— the door that wouldn't budge the day before. Sam walked in and I leapt up to greet him. "Sammy boy!"

He cracked a rare smile. "Good to see you, too. Seriously." He nodded to each of us in turn, and we nodded back. Sam was not a hugger.

"You win out?" Derrick asked.

Sam shook his head. "I lost the first match. I hate puzzles, and the prick against me was good."

"Sam, who's over there with you?" I asked, holding my breath.

He rattled off sixteen names, but I heard exactly one. "Min's okay?"

"Last I saw. We're living in that wing." He pointed back the way he'd come. "I guess you guys are over there?"

"Yep," Sarah said. "But that's only thirty-two people. Where are the others?"

Nobody knew. Eleven classmates were totally unaccounted

for since the Terrarium raid: Spence. Zach. Colleen. Kharisma and Kayla. Cash, Greg, and Jacob. Neb and Isaiah. Emma Vogel. Those kids were just . . . gone. To repurposement? I felt a wave of cold pass through me. It didn't feel right that no one had seen them aboard the station, not once.

"We also learned something by accident," Sam said. "Our class is competing against Nemesis Three for colony spots. Those guys aren't assured places anymore, and they've been losing people in these games, too. They're really pissed off about it. And get this—Josh Atkins and the Nolan brothers are on their squad now."

Derrick huffed loudly. "Those dudes are the worst. Is Cole against us, too?"

Sam shook his head sadly. "Didn't make it. We knew the lab flood got Toby, Kyle, and Tucker, but it also killed Cole. The Nemesis Three kids are seething about the four people they lost. That Rose chick is out for blood."

Sarah shifted next to me, but I was too despondent to care. Our class had lost seventeen lives inside that stupid hamster bubble. Kids who could've been sitting at this table next to me. Then add four from Nemesis Three to the list, people I'd never meet. It was all so senseless I could barely breathe.

Then it hit me. My gaze darted around the room, then I leaned in close to whisper. "Where's Tack?"

Derrick eyes widened. He dropped his voice. "Everyone captured in the hangar ended up in the cells, right?"

We all silently did the math. "Yes!" Sarah whispered. "Which *should* mean he wasn't captured, unless he did something really stupid and got himself killed or repurposed."

I frowned at that. "Really stupid" was Tack's specialty. But if he were free and loose on the station . . .

"What about that Cyrus dude?" Derrick asked.

"He's back with his class." Sam snorted. "He made a big show about how we kidnapped him all alone, and forced him to reveal the lake hatchway. He also slipped us the info that the Guardian escaped the raid."

I started, unsure how that news should make me feel. It was another asset in the field. "Does Min know?"

"She knows everything I do." Sam glanced at me, and there was a trace of . . . something on his face. "One other thing. I was walking back to my room after losing the damn grid game, and I saw a couple of those Nemesis Three punks waiting outside Min's cell. They were about to go in but wanted me gone first."

My pulse spiked. "Has anyone else seen those kids in the living area before?"

Everyone shook their heads.

Before I knew it, I was on my feet, racing toward Sam's portal. I yanked on the handle but it refused to budge. Feeling a panic I couldn't suppress, I started pounding with both fists.

"Min? Min!"

The skin on my left palm split, but I ignored it. Why had they come for her? Where would they take her? The word *repurposement* gonged inside my head as I left red smudges on the metal.

Hands grabbed my shoulders. Pulling me back.

"Where is she, you bastards?!" I shouted. "Let me out of here! Let us all out!"

My arms dropped. Tears threatened as I slumped to the

251

ground and closed my eyes.

I let my mind drift, searching for equilibrium. For a quiet place of peace.

Min.

Chrysalis had taken Min.

25

MIN

I was led to a spotless interrogation room.

Two kids from Nemesis Three escorted me, a boy and a girl. I hadn't encountered them before, and they didn't respond to my awkward attempt at chitchat. We walked the halls in silence. I didn't consider resisting. I didn't know what was happening, good or bad. We reached a nondescript door and I entered alone.

Table. Chair. I faced a wall that was half seamless white and half mirror. I assumed it was one-way glass. After a seemingly endless period of brooding, I gave it the finger. After another lengthy spell, I couldn't stop staring at my reflection.

I looked ... haggard. My face was thinner than I remembered, with sharper edges. There was a wariness in my eyes I didn't like—the ghost of a hunted animal lurking behind my placid expression. I'd been sitting in my windowless cell for the last day with no contact from anyone.

Moments later the door opened and Sophia stepped inside, smiling pleasantly as she walked to the other side of the table. She carried a tablet tucked under one arm. A chair rose from the floor and Sophia sat, waking the device in her hands. She tapped on its surface for a few beats, then looked up at me. Our sole Chrysalis contact retained her ageless quality even in person. I couldn't tell if she was twenty or forty.

"Melinda Juilliard Wilder."

"That's me."

"You've had quite a miraculous showing, Ms. Wilder."

I blinked. Blinked again.

Her smile became coy, as if we shared a secret. "You subverted the rules, both inside the Program and as part of the Terrarium."

My temper sparked. "Sorry. I don't know how property is supposed to act."

The woman chuckled. "Oh, don't apologize. We've learned a *lot* from you. It never occurred to me that someone might destabilize the Guardian of an active Nemesis Program and use that opening to manipulate source code. Needless to say, I'm impressed."

I opened my mouth. Closed it. I didn't have anything to say that would help my situation, and would give nothing away.

Where's my father? Do you know he escaped the cargo bay?

The woman nodded at my restraint. "Inside the Terrarium, you made choices that went against our predictive models. We took painstaking care in its design to keep subjects contained in two places—the island, and a secondary location remote enough to satisfy the need for exploration. We selected the plants, the animals, and the dangers. We chose your food."

I felt a burning in my cheeks. "So no sea monsters."

Sophia chuckled. "Sadly, no. Turbines and noise machines do the trick nicely." Then her voice hardened. "But you allowed Tobias Albertsson and his associates to break away from the group, and they in turn brought about disaster. We had no choice but to purge the Terrarium early."

"You made a deal with Toby, not me."

Sophia pursed her glossy lips. "A miscalculation. I thought he could be a useful tool, but he had delusions of reentering the Program, as if we'd allow that. It made him unreliable. Toby was merely supposed to secure the MegaCom, but instead he tried to play both sides. His delay in reporting back to me proved disastrous."

I crossed my arms. "Why work with him at all?"

"I needed access to the MegaCom, and Sarah Harden was too good with the Nemesis software. She actually closed the system off to Chrysalis, blocking the entire station from all but physical access to its hard drive." Her face registered disbelief at the affront.

Pieces snapped together. "So you made a deal with Toby to seal off the lab complex."

She nodded. "His team had discovered the rim of the Terrarium anyway. I elected to bring them in and explain things. Offer them a place. It seemed like a neat solution for two problems. I granted him access to Chrysalis so that his group could move around the Terrarium at will, including a secret entrance to the lab from beneath the silo. Nemesis Three provided logistical support. We even drained the lake to complete his admittedly shortsighted cave-in plan to clear the silo of residents. I wanted to keep the experiment going, you see, but in the end I risked too much."

Her eyes grew cold. "Toby failed to properly account for some of you, and lives were lost. The MegaCom was destroyed. We'd intended to extract only those living at what you called the Outpost, in hopes that their disappearance would deter further exploration by others and the Terrarium's fiction could be maintained." She clicked her tongue. "There were too many of you to begin with. Instead, the whole thing fell apart, and we had to remove everyone. Your class is advancing to the next stage in the process far more quickly than I would've liked."

My toes curled in my shoes. "What process? What *is* this place, really?"

She gave me a look of confusion. "This is Chrysalis. The vessel of all humanity."

I sat forward, curiosity winning out over caution. "But where did Chrysalis come from? Who built it? Are you the only humans alive? How can you be here, a million years after the Earth itself died?"

She laughed. "Which shall I answer first?"

I tried to calm my breathing. "Where did Chrysalis come from?"

The woman folded her hands and assumed a professorial tone. "Chrysalis is the final piece of Project Nemesis. Four MegaComs were buried along the spine of the Rocky Mountains as the Dark Star approached. Additionally, and in total secret, a frantic effort was made to create an overseer space station.

256

AI software was written and given autonomy over the project. This allowed raw materials and components to be launched into orbit as time grew short, and the station was constructed while humanity slept."

My eyebrows rose. "I don't understand."

The woman smiled patiently. "While the Programs ran under the mountains, Chrysalis was literally building itself in space. A painstaking, *diabolically* slow process that only a truly independent AI could complete. When the station finally came online, the MegaComs on Earth were nearly depleted. All data was therefore uploaded to Chrysalis, and the remainder of your time was spent aboard here, as the station prepared itself for your regeneration."

My head was spinning. "But why a Terrarium? Why stick us inside a fake Earth bubble in space?"

"To assess and prepare for the next phase in the process. Colonization. We even made it look like Fire Lake."

It all sounded so crazy. A station that built itself in outer space? The idea that we'd been uploaded from the planet like data files . . . My stomach lurched. I put both hands on the table.

"What about you?" I whispered. "Have you . . . Have *people* been living up here since . . . forever?"

The idea gave me vertigo. How long had this been going on?

Something rippled in the woman's expression, quickly smoothed over. She shook her head. "No. Like you, the original crew members were preserved as lines of code, stored on a hard drive in the supercomputer Chrysalis was constructing. We've only inhabited the station as biological beings for a little more than a century. Our population never surpasses one hundred and fifty. Until recently, we were caretakers with a distinct purpose: to prepare for the conclusion of the Nemesis Programs and the eighty test subjects who would emerge."

My head was a sloshing fishbowl. I couldn't speak. It was all so much bigger.

The woman *tsk*ed again. "Of course, your class exceeded its threshold, didn't it? All sixty-four codes regenerated, rendering a million years of methodical processing worthless. We've had quite a few discussions about that, believe me. Some argued your whole Program run should be flushed into space as contaminants."

An icy spike pierced my spine. I glanced at the door.

Sophia held up a hand. "That idea was rejected. In this situation, a secondary process makes more sense."

My worry didn't ease. "What do you intend to do with us?"

"Your mission was never false, Min. The Programs were intended to select the strongest candidates for regeneration. Our ultimate purpose remains the salvation of the human species. That purpose can still be achieved."

I looked around. "You mean, here? On this station?"

She shook her head gravely. "This station is a miracle of scientific achievement, but it's not eternal. Humanity must return to a terrestrial home."

I ran a hand over my mouth. "So . . . what? We colonize Earth after all?"

"Not exactly."

The flatness of her tone gave me shivers. "I don't understand. Again."

The woman glanced down at her tablet. "As of this moment you are immediately graduated to the training-level group.

There's no point testing *your* skills any further. We've seen enough on that score."

The fuzz on my neck stood. "And the others?"

"They have to earn their spots. We won't insert any but the best candidates. We simply can't risk it. Chrysalis is a marvel, but its time will end. The colony is the future of human existence, and we're taking no chances with it."

My lips parted, but she rolled right over me. "I'll be candid, Min. The majority of your class will likely be assigned to repurposement. Even your spot is not assured. This is your first formal interview."

A lump rose in my throat. I swallowed it, trying to process this information. "Where are my friends now?" I resisted asking about Noah, but my cheeks reddened, and from the look on her face I might as well have said it.

"Your classmates are still in the testing facility. The Terrarium has been emptied, perhaps for the last time. Three Programs are complete, and the fourth . . . Well, we're rethinking our core design. The Terrarium continues to serve as our source of biomaterial. It truly is a wonder."

"How many kids are still being tested?" I persisted. "What does repurposement mean?"

Sophia didn't answer for several heartbeats. "It's best not to concern yourself with the selection process. Repurposement aboard Chrysalis is as noble a calling as colonization. We all serve the mission."

I wanted more—*what kind of answer is that?*—but Sophia rose and walked to the far wall. She pressed something on her tablet and a panel opened, revealing a view beyond the station.

"Come and see, Min."

I thought about refusing, but couldn't help myself. I joined her and we stared down at the planet, a messy tangle of blues, greens, yellows, and swirling white, set like a marble on a field of endless black. It was breathtaking. I felt unexpected tears on my cheeks and hurriedly wiped them away. "Is it real?"

Sophia beamed. "This isn't a video screen, Min. It's a window. You are looking at the future cradle of mankind."

A smile tugged the corners of my mouth. "I hope Earth welcomes us back. It's changed a bit since I was last there."

Sophia laughed uproariously, losing her breath in the process. I watched her from the corner of my eye, slightly unnerved. Her response seemed out of proportion to my tiny joke.

Sophia wiped her eyes. "Oh, I'm sorry, Min. You can't understand why that was so amusing." She cleared her throat, then gave me a calculating look. "I shouldn't reveal this information. There's a worry that knowing too much too soon might complicate the process for our candidates, or breed fear. But you're different from the others, aren't you?"

Her statement was so bizarre, I simply shrugged, shaking my head slightly to show I didn't understand. Sophia giggled in response. She nodded at the miraculous multicolored orb spinning below us.

"It's what you said." Sophia put a hand on my shoulder. I wanted to pull away, but forced myself to stand still. "The planet down there. It's got you fooled."

I grunted nervously. "How is that? What is Earth pretending to be?"

"That's just it. During the construction of Chrysalis, it was clear almost immediately to the station's AI that the original Nemesis plans would fail. So it made other arrangements while we slept."

My patience ran dry. I didn't like this woman touching me. Her hand was cold, her breath weirdly sterile.

"Maybe you could just explain."

"You're not looking at Earth, Min. Earth is still largely a ruin."

My gaze shot to the planet below. *Blue. Green. White. What the hell is she talking about?* A deeper part of my mind realized that Sophia wasn't gripping my shoulder to be friendly.

"What . . . where?" I managed.

"Mars, Min." Her blue eyes were chips of smothering ice. "While we hid as ones and zeroes, Chrysalis decided that terraforming the Red Planet would be simpler than detoxifying our old one. Part of me is certain that this has happened before, in the ancient past. Perhaps we're truly returning home in a longer sense."

I jerked backward, unable to bear her touch a moment longer. "That's . . . that's *Mars*?" The walls began closing in, panic rising in my throat like fire. "Is that true? Is *any* of this real? I . . . I don't . . ."

Sophia watched me with a predatory gleam. "I'll level with you, Min. I've chosen you out of all the members of Nemesis One to offer a deal. Listen carefully and consider it."

My head was pounding. I couldn't think. Couldn't breathe.

Sophia moved close again. Something about her expression set my alarm bells ringing. "I want you to get your class in order. Help bring everyone on board with the testing process. Do that, and I'll guarantee you a spot in the colony. In fact, I'll even go one better."

She tilted her head, and I knew I'd have to speak the words.

"What?" I whispered.

Her smile deepened to the leer of a shark. "I'll let you choose another, Min Wilder. One additional person advanced to the colonization team, no questions asked. Isn't that nice? Surely there must be *someone* you care enough about to help us?"

Her smirk burned down into my pores. Terror shot through me.

She knows everything about my life. She has me.

This was more than an offer, it was a threat. But a part of me was desperate to take it.

Noah, I thought.

I can pick Noah.

26

NOAH

There were twenty-three of us.

I kept waiting for more classmates to walk in through the portals, but after a full day with no new additions, I feared no one else was coming.

I grew sick with worry. Min was among the missing.

For two days, I'd done nothing. Familiar faces appeared—an airlock would open and a kid would cautiously step through, having graduated to this second phase. Not that we knew what that meant. We'd had no word from Sophia or anyone else. We spent our waking hours lounging in the common room, then slept in a dorm-style facility at night.

A new door had opened late on the first day, revealing a windowless chamber with rows of bunks and a communal bathroom. Derrick, Sarah, Sam, and I were the first residents, but others trickled in after us, every single one of them a welcome addition.

Akio. Casey and Hector. Alice Cho. Ethan. More and more arrived, until I began to think everyone was going to show up eventually. But then the trickle stopped.

We listed those who'd disappeared inside the testing corridors. Dakota Sargent. Charlie. Corbin. Maggie and Jessica. Anna Loring. Leah Halpern. Richie. No one had any idea where they were. "Repurposement" haunted the facility like a curse, never spoken aloud, as if by saying the word you might bring it down upon yourself.

With every door swish, I looked for Min. And was disappointed each time.

Finally, on the third day, as we sat around the tables growing bored despite our nerves, the screen lowered again and Sophia's face appeared. We straightened like elementary school kids caught slacking by their principal. The tension in the room was palpable.

"Greetings and congratulations," she said warmly. "You have passed the basic skills and aptitude battery and been classified as acceptable for possible colony insertion."

I heard a few relieved gasps, but most just stared at the screen. Despite the woman's smile, there was something about her that set my teeth on edge. I waited for the other shoe to drop.

I didn't have to wait long.

"You will now participate in the interview process. A Chrysalis crew member will assess whether you'd be a good fit for our bridgehead community. Please be at ease during this procedure. Those not selected will still have a chance to serve the colony through repurposement aboard the station. Chrysalis relies upon those contributions as much as the work to be done on the planet's surface. When you see your name onscreen, please proceed down the corridor."

A doorway appeared in the far wall. I stared at the opening, lips mashed into a thin line. My instincts growled in warning. We still had no idea where the others were.

"Where's Dakota?" Casey shouted, red-faced as she rose to her feet. "She'd want to be with us no matter what!" Beside her, Lauren nodded furiously. The soccer girls did everything together—I knew they were desperate about their friend.

Other voices called out names. Sophia held up a hand for silence.

"You have questions. It's natural. But you must first complete the screening process. I promise you will be reunited with those selected for repurposement. For now, focus on your own position. Anyone no longer wishing to be considered for colonial insertion should say so immediately."

Furtive glances darted the room, but no one spoke. Then Aiken Talbot stood. "Where's Anna?" he asked quietly. "I want to know where she is."

Aiken and Anna had been separated during the initial testing phase aboard the station, but he'd learned she was in the other group. Having graduated to this phase early on the second day, he'd sat by the opposite airlock ever since, refusing even to sleep in the dorm until she appeared. But Anna never came through.

Sophia spoke with no inflection. "Ms. Loring was selected for repurposement."

The color drained from Aiken's face. "Then I quit," he said firmly. "I'm not going anywhere without her. Put me with my girlfriend, bitch."

Sophia regarded him silently for several heartbeats. "As you wish."

A second door opened. Aiken sighed deeply.

I was on my feet before I knew what I was doing. I grabbed him by the shoulder and whispered urgently.

"Aiken, don't. I don't trust this."

He shrugged from my grip, tears spilling from the corners of his eyes. "You think I do? But I'm not leaving her alone." He trudged to the doorway and stepped through it. The exit sealed as if it had never been.

I spun to the screen, a sour taste filling my mouth. Sophia was watching me.

"Anyone else?" she asked softly.

No one moved.

"Excellent. The interviews will begin now."

White table. White chair. Mirror along one wall.

It felt like a bad space-cop show. I almost giggled, but I couldn't chase the chill from my spirit.

Sophia's eyes when she'd asked if anyone else wanted to quit. The set of her jaw. It had been so . . . *final*. So unforgiving. I worried that Aiken had made a terrible mistake.

The door opened and Sophia herself walked in, carrying a tablet. She sat, started the device, and proceeded to ignore me. I waited patiently, barely daring to breathe. I felt the raw anxiety of a woodland creature spotting an owl's shadow pass through the moonlight.

Finally, she looked up. "Noah Charles Livingston." Her eyes sparkled with something I couldn't place. "You had quite a time inside the Program, didn't you, young man?"

My pulse quickened. I hated thinking about the Program. I did terrible things, and though I'd worked hard to atone for them, some memories never fade. All I said was "If you say so."

"Oh, I do." She adopted a wry half smile. "These statistics are impressive. You were well on your way to total victory before you . . . changed course."

Anger flared inside me. "Realized how stupid I'd been, you mean."

Sophia set down her tablet, her expression one of confused curiosity. "Stupid? Noah, the point of the Program was to prove yourself, and you were doing *exceptionally* well. Then you risked everything by subrogating your will to that of another, a troubling deviation in an otherwise stellar performance. It almost cost you everything."

I shook my head in bewilderment. "You don't get it. That *saved* everything. Min showed me I didn't have to be that way, despite the Program." I sat back with a smug grin of my own. "And it turned out okay, right? I'm here aboard your fine space station, and none of my friends were eliminated. I'd call that a win-win."

"You'd be wrong." Her voice was matter-of-fact, but her eyes cut like diamonds. "If your class had obeyed the rules, you wouldn't have been subjected to any further testing. The final twenty would've spent another six months inside the Terrarium, proving yourself as pioneers, and then been delivered to the station as a unit. Now things are much less certain. Your place on the surface is in no way assured."

I shrugged. Saw the first flicker of irritation cross her face. *Good.*

"Why not just send everyone?" I asked suddenly. "Won't the colony be better off with as many people as possible? To me it seems like the more boots on the ground, the better."

"Our models strongly suggest otherwise. And they are *very* good models. We have to prune the weak branches, and you're in danger of being classified as one."

I covered my alarm by needling, hoping to provoke a reaction. "I'm not even sure I believe you."

Sophia's face closed off like a bank vault. "What do you mean?"

"I don't think you can afford to get rid of us."

"Oh?"

I leaned forward. "There were only four Nemesis Programs, and you already lost one altogether. The first group to come out might be serving as your puppets, but you need *our* class to fill in the gaps. Regeneration can't be cheap, and there's no one else to exploit. Like it or not, you're stuck with the kids from Fire Lake."

She sat quietly a moment. "You forget Nemesis Four."

I shrugged indifferently. "More of the same, probably. If they're ever ready. But we're here now."

Every word I'd spoken was a bluff, but her shoulders tensed. Sophia's mouth slipped into a frown, which then flattened to nonexistence.

Something.

I wasn't totally right, but I'd touched a nerve.

Sophia sat back and regarded me again, as if seeing a tricky puzzle anew. "That position is a dangerous gamble."

I thought it through. "Tell us why you lied. Why the Terrarium deception?"

"Are you asking the questions now?" Sophia ran a hand through her glossy black hair, the first relatable gesture I'd seen her exhibit. "Your class truly is intractable. We should dump the whole lot of you into space and be done with it."

Distress must've registered on my face.

"A small joke." Sophia studied me a moment longer. "Very well. I'll answer. We introduced Nemesis classes into the Terrarium to gauge how well they'd respond to isolation in a foreign environment. There's no way back up to Chrysalis from the surface. It's a one-way trip, so we have to be sure."

"A trip you don't want to make yourselves. Why?"

"We have a station to run." Then she continued a little more quickly than before. "Down on the planet, life will be hard. There's no room for error. We can't risk inserting a person who might crack under pressure. So, we test. We assess. We make sure."

I found myself nodding along, which surprised me. But Sophia's explanation made sense. It made me question my instinct that Chrysalis had to be against us. Maybe this process was logical after all. Maybe these people really didn't mean to exploit us.

We *had* deviated from our Program. We *did* risk our MegaCom by subverting the rules. It stood to reason we'd be treated with caution, perhaps even mistrust by those aboard. All at once, I began to see things differently.

"Explain what you want," I said. "If . . . if you're being straight with me, I'll help you."

Sophia unleashed a radiant smile. "That's all I ask, Noah. Trust me, we have your best interests at heart."

I paused as if considering, then slid in the next question. "What is repurposement?"

Something moved behind her eyes. The cold feeling returned. I was certain that whatever she said next would be a lie.

"Repurposement is the highest calling aboard Chrysalis. It's a chance to—"

A door zipped open. My eyes widened as the body of a guard tumbled inside. The trooper collapsed against the wall and lay still.

I gaped, openmouthed, as Tack stuck his head into the room. He saw me and grinned, but his smirk faded upon seeing my interrogator.

"Again?" he muttered.

Sophia stood, her face carved from granite. "Thomas Russo. I see you aren't smart enough to stay hidden, however you're pulling it off. Know that you've already been struck fr—"

A blast of light slammed into Sophia's chest. She toppled backward over the table and hit the floor, her neck bending at a sickly angle.

I shouted in horror, then my gaze snapped to Tack.

To the sleek black gun he was gripping with both hands.

27

MIN

Rose.

She was waiting outside the interrogation room with the boy who'd walked me there, hands on her hips and an unfriendly gleam in her eye. The other girl was gone. I guessed she'd taken her place.

Suddenly, I was tired all over. Sophia had just bludgeoned me with a truth hammer, and I didn't want to go any more rounds with this angry redhead. I had enough to think about. But I wasn't making the calls around here.

"We're to escort you back," the boy said, a Latino kid with light brown eyes and shaggy hair.

"Sure. I'm Min."

"I caught that," he said dryly. "I'm Miguel."

Rose shot him a glare and his grin vanished. "I want to talk to her alone, Miggy. Can you go ahead of us and make sure the way is clear?"

Miguel sighed and started down the corridor. Rose waited until he was a dozen yards ahead before prodding me to follow.

I stopped in my tracks. "I'm going on my own, so there's no need to touch me. I don't like it."

She smirked. "Your thoughts on the matter are irrelevant."

I shook my head at her. "It's weird you don't get that we're in the same boat. Lose any more friends mysteriously today?"

Rose's cheeks pinked. I could tell my riposte had landed.

"Don't make it impossible for us to talk," I said calmly. "We can help each other. You need to understand that my class is not your enemy. We didn't set up any of this—we're simply trying to survive. Like you."

Her cheek twitched. Rose gritted her teeth, but then exhaled slowly through her nose. "It's . . . hard for me," she said quietly. "Trust hasn't worked out well for us in the past."

I chuckled genuinely. "That I get. See? Progress already."

Rose rolled her eyes, then gestured down the hallway. I took the olive branch, such as it was.

We began slowly walking down the corridor. Rose kept her eyes moving, alert for anyone who might overhear us. For the first time, I got the sense that she wanted something from me other than a fight.

"Things are getting . . . odd," she began cautiously. "For almost four months we lived aboard the station, doing light training and reading about colony procedures. Sophia and her staff never mentioned anything about other Nemesis classes."

That surprised me. I thought they'd known about us all along, during our whole time in the Terrarium. I abruptly wondered whether Rose knew we were orbiting Mars, not Erath. Had Sophia confided in her, too? In the moment, I decided not to ask.

Then something else occurred to me. "You know, I've never even *seen* another crew member. Not in the halls, or the arena, or our common room in the testing facility. Just Sophia. Isn't that weird?"

Rose nodded. "It was like that for us at first, but there are others. They control interactions tightly at first."

I frowned. "I mean, I've seen guards. They stormed our hiding spot like a SWAT team. But it was only a handful, and only that once. Is it possible there are a lot fewer people here than Sophia is letting on?"

Rose thought silently as we turned a corner. "Maybe," she said finally. "The station does seem mostly empty. A hundred and fifty crew members could be a lie."

"She said the same number to me," I said excitedly. "Why mention it at all?"

"And why don't *they* go down to the colony?" Rose muttered. "That's what I don't get. These people regenerated us, observed us, and now make us compete. But if there's that many people aboard, why aren't they colonizing the surface themselves?"

I bit my lower lip. "They need the Nemesis Programs for some reason. It's been that way from the beginning."

"Zealots," Rose muttered. "But they have our missing classmates somewhere."

"More vanish every day." I glanced at her. Rose's face was

scrunched. "Did something happen since we last . . . talked?"

She snorted at my euphemism. "Dropped to the floor and strolled to victory. I'm an idiot."

"I was losing badly. I gambled because I had to."

Rose's scowl returned. "We played a group game today. Three-on-three in an obstacle course. My team lost to your friends Akio, Rachel, and Darren. Harper got her leg hung up in a cargo net, and then Scott royally choked on the puzzle. Otherwise—"

"Not sure it matters," I said gently.

She grunted. "We lost. I went back to our dorm ready to rip them both new ones." A pause. "They never showed up."

I paced silently a few steps. "Did you see Sophia?"

Rose shook her head angrily. "She didn't even bother to announce their reassignment. She's too busy hunting some stowaway guy and your lunatic friend, Thomas Russo. The crew is super pissed at those two, by the way. They better stay hidden. Although since this station is literally the entire world right now, how long can that last?"

I shivered. I'd been thinking the same thing.

"Our people go missing, too. Sometimes I can't even keep track."

Rose halted in the middle of the corridor. "We're down to *ten* of our original twenty. People who were promised spots in the colony weeks ago are now . . . They're just gone."

I met her eye and held it. "Do you have any idea where they go? No more games, Rose. What is repurposement, really? If they're all just getting new jobs on the station, why not show us that? What purpose is served by keeping us worried and afraid?"

"Sophia said the eliminated classmates would be a distraction," Rose answered doggedly. "That we'd lose focus on the colony."

"And you believe that?"

"Yes! Why else would they do it? If Chrysalis went through all the trouble of regenerating us, they must have a plan that makes sense. In the end, it's illogical not to trust them. Another giant ruse doesn't make any sense."

I thought of all the times we'd been lied to as a part of Project Nemesis. The murders. The Program. The Terrarium. *Why not one more? How can we trust anything?*

"Has anyone been sent down to the colony from the station?" I asked suddenly. "Anyone at all?"

"Not that I'm aware of. I think we're supposed to be the first."

I shook my head again. "Does *that* make sense? Why leave everything up to us, a bunch of high school kids?"

Rose's lips thinned. She squinted down at the floor as if working something through in her head. Finally, she grunted sourly.

"We have to plug along and do what they say," she said, striding forward again so that I was forced to jog after her. "We don't have any other options. The people who run this station have all the power, but there's no reason to think they're using it to abuse us. That's like talking crap to a line of ants."

I was disappointed. "You can't really believe that."

She stopped suddenly and spun on me. "Here's what I do know. People are being removed from the colony team for failing the tests. Right or wrong, that's reality. I plan to get down to the planet, so that means I have to play ball. Same goes for you.

There's nothing we can do to resist, so we might as well *win*, and get the prize. I want to breathe fresh air again. Go outside, for real. There's only one way to do it."

"So say the greatest collaborators in history."

Her face reddened once more. "We're prisoners on a freaking space station, Min. Grow up."

She took off again. I called after her. "Rose, don't—"

"You better hustle," she called back over her shoulder. "Sophia seems distracted right now. I have no idea why. But if she finds you out roaming the hallways, she might get upset. I only swung by to warn you."

I hurried to catch up. It was getting annoying, scampering after her long legs like a mouse. "Warn me about what?"

Rose didn't even glance at me. "Nemesis Three won't be joining in on any funny business with your class. I talked to all of my people, one at a time, to make sure we're on the same page. We need to be focused on the colony, and we will be. If you guys decide to do something stupid and get yourselves eliminated, I won't shed a tear. More room for us."

I glanced up to see Miggy standing by an open door. This wasn't my old hallway.

"What's this?" I asked suspiciously.

Miguel smiled at me. "Your new digs. I think y—"

Rose spoke over him. "You've been removed from the training facility by Sophia's orders. Doesn't mean you can wander around or anything, but you live here now. She asked that you think about what she said." Rose's green eyes burned with curiosity, but I merely nodded.

She turned to go. I caught her by the sleeve. "We should talk again, Rose. We'd make better friends than opponents."

Rose removed my fingers from her black jumpsuit. Dusted off where I'd touched the fabric. "I don't have opponents," she said icily. "I have enemies. You don't want to be one of those."

We locked eyes, and the stony curtain had returned. Rose smiled. "Tell Noah I said hi."

Before I could respond, she nodded for Miguel to follow and strode away down the hall.

28

NOAH

"You . . . you *killed* her. Tack, she's part of the crew!"

"She'll be fine." Tack was already headed back out the door. "Trust me, this isn't what it looks like. We have to go."

I glanced at Sophia, lying sprawled on the floor like a rag doll, and didn't think she wasn't going to be fine. But something in Tack's tone gave me pause. He'd gone to some dark places inside the Program, but he wasn't like Toby. Tack had sounded confident he hadn't just committed a double murder.

But she looks dead. That guard looks dead. Those facts aren't up for debate.

I raced into the corridor after him. Black Suit was waiting there, along with Sarah and Derrick. Glancing down the hallway I saw two more guards slumped on the ground. Derrick was sweating like a convict. Even Sarah looked shaken. Tack pointed to the closest open doorway. "We have to run, but Noah, pop in here so you understand."

I shook my head, anxiety rooting me in place. Derrick pushed me from behind. "Go look, man. Then tell me what the hell is going on!"

I stumbled to where Tack was waiting impatiently and peered inside. It was an interrogation room identical to mine, with another body in the corner. I recoiled in shock, but Tack blocked my retreat. "Noah, look! *Look at her.*"

Swallowing bile, I edged closer and stared at the body. Then I shouted in surprise.

It was Sophia. She was lying on the floor, mouth fixed open in surprise.

But she was in my room. I watched Tack shoot her.

Tack pulled me back into the hallway and walked me to the next open room.

A third body, this one slumped in a chair.

Sophia.

Again.

My mind nearly shut down.

"How . . . how is . . ."

Tack shot me a worried look. "Don't ask me. I don't know how or why, but there are copies of Sophia all around the station."

Copies? I stared at Sophia's body. The blast burns on her uniform sure looked real enough.

I crept over and gently tilted her back in the chair. There was a wound on her forearm—the slightest charring of skin. But I detected nothing strange about her. Except for the fact that she was in three places at once.

Tack must've read my thoughts. "I don't know what Sophia is, but there are dozens of her."

My head was spinning. Nothing would add up. "Why'd you shoot her? This can't be undone. Whatever she is, she runs the station . . . You didn't have to . . . You could've . . ."

"Chrysalis isn't a safe place," Sarah said from the doorway. "We don't know about any of these people. How many crew members have you met so far?"

None. Just Sophia. Her and a few guards . . .

I struggled to control my emotions. "How'd you escape the cargo hold?" I asked Tack. "Who showed you this?"

"I'll let the old guy explain." Tack led me back out into the hall and nodded sharply at Black Suit.

"Tack and I have been searching for the kids sent to repurposement," he said. "I had a couple of gas masks in the hideout and we got them on in time, then escaped during the confusion. I'd promised Cyrus I'd look for his missing friends, and that seemed as good a plan as any until we figured out how to jailbreak the testing facility."

I felt a surge of hope. "Did you find them?"

Black Suit shook his head. "We found the most likely sector—there's a place where several corridors are patrolled around the clock—but we can't get close. I was poking around in that area when a handful of the crew nearly surprised me. I hid and watched them. One of the group was Sophia. Then my eyes nearly popped when a second Sophia strolled up to join them. I thought maybe she was a twin, but then a third Sophia appeared, followed by a fourth. I couldn't believe it, but it was unmistakable. Quadruplets? I'm not buying it. Then we came here and found three more."

My eyes narrowed. "How'd you find me?"

Tack chuckled. "We grabbed some dude in a gray uniform and got him to tell us, then shoved him into a supply closet."

I glanced at the guards lying facedown on the floor. "How many people did you kill, Tack?"

Tack's voice was ice. "I'll take out as many as I have to."

Black Suit grunted. "Stop being dramatic. These blasters we stole are set to stun. The highest setting, but nonlethal."

Tack rolled his eyes. "For now."

I licked my lips. Felt like I was riding a leaf through a hurricane. *What is going on? What do these people want from us?*

"We should spring as many of our class as we can," Derrick urged. "Build up a force right now, before we're discovered."

"There's no time for that," Black Suit said. "The only reason we're standing here chatting without troopers circling like sharks is that I tricked the security system. We had ten minutes and nine are gone. We need to go."

"Go where?" I blurted, eyeing the white walls around me. "Chrysalis is *their* space station, and now we're fugitives aboard it. Plus, I'm not doing anything before finding Min. I won't leave her."

Tack glared at me. "Of course we won't leave her. That's the point of all this."

I pressed my fists to my head. "Talk straight, Thomas. What are you planning?"

He grinned wickedly. "A full-blown disaster. I know where

she is, Noah. And I know how to get her out. You're gonna have to trust me."

Trust. Trust Tack. I felt like I might keel over.

"Which way?" Sarah asked. "I don't want to get locked up again. It's been happening to me way too often lately."

"We head for the heart of this madness." Tack checked his weapon. "Time to hit these creeps where it hurts."

He yanked me by the shoulder and we all fled down the corridor.

29

MIN

The room was an upgrade.

Practically a suite. I had a larger bedroom and bathroom, even a small sitting area. A window looked down on the planet I was supposed to inhabit one day. It made a tidy cell, because that's what it had been for three excruciating days. I was being deliberately isolated, but had no idea why. What did Sophia want from me? A bird in a cage?

I sat on a bench by the window and stared at the world below.

Mars.

I'm seeing Mars, not Earth.

I grew up in a trailer park in the northern Idaho mountains, and now I'm on a space station one million years into the future, orbiting a different planet.

It was almost too much to accept. Would've been, in fact, if I hadn't survived so many other impossibilities that this was just more fuel for the fire. I'd already spent literal eons inside a supercomputer battling for my life. In some ways this was basic by comparison.

If any of it's real.

The question wouldn't stop nagging me. Improbable things were happening so fast, my brain remained wary that everything was a lie. Maybe I was in another simulation, running a different program. Maybe I was dreaming in hyper-sleep, or just plain dead. Any of those possibilities made as much sense as what my senses were telling me. It was hard to accept that *my* life had been singled out for such incredible things.

A tone at the door. I turned as Sophia entered. Her usual self-possession was gone, replaced by hard edges.

"Come. We need to move."

I eyed her curiously. In all our previous interactions she'd never seemed flustered, yet that's how I would've described her. "Is something wrong?"

Her gaze grew icicles. "I've fallen into a pattern of explaining myself to you. No more. You will come with me on your own or I'll make you come."

A man in a gray Chrysalis uniform stepped into the room behind her. He was large and sandy-haired, with pale green eyes and a narrow nose. With a shock, I realized he was the first man I'd seen aboard Chrysalis that wasn't my dad, and only the second regular crew member I'd seen clearly at all.

Where are they all hiding? They certainly don't crowd the walkways.

"This is Harold," Sophia said. "He will see you to a more secure room location."

"Secure?"

"Let's go," she snapped. Sophia turned and stepped out into the hall.

It was clear I'd get no more from her, and equally clear that Harold was not there to make friends. He watched me dispassionately, huge fists hanging at his sides like meaty anvils.

I strode for the door. Harold let me pass and followed on my heels as Sophia led us down the corridor. I couldn't imagine what had caused her sudden shift in deportment, but I suspected I'd learn soon enough.

More secure room? I just got this one.

We stepped into an elevator. It traveled so smoothly I could barely tell we were moving, but moments later the doors opened onto a new floor. A robotic voice announced, *"Command Level."* We exited and turned a corner, reaching a circular metal door. Harold opened it to reveal a tube-like corridor built of glass and chrome stretching from the inner ring of the station toward a massive sphere at its center.

Sophia paced down the tunnel toward an identical portal at the opposite end. Windows along both sides revealed similar access tubes set at intervals, like spokes on a wheel, all converging on the center of Chrysalis. Gazing out through the glass-paneled walls, I stared into the infinite depths of space. To my left was Mars and a gleaming moon I needed to learn the name of. Phobos? Ares? Something like that. I knew Mars had two of them. *Did it still?*

Sophia eyed me as we walked. "I suppose you're wondering

what this is about."

"I admit to being curious," I said cautiously.

She didn't slow. "Some misguided classmates of yours attacked the testing facility. Foolish in the extreme, and ultimately pointless, but they managed to free a few subjects. I'm sorry to say that I might have to go back on our deal a little. One of the escapees—"

Red lights burst to life along the corridor. An alarm howled.

Sophia froze. Harold wrapped a giant hand around my forearm. I tried to pull away, but it was like yanking a doorknob the wrong way.

"What's going on?" I shouted.

Sophia didn't answer. She was staring straight ahead at the forward blast door.

"Impossible," I heard her mutter.

A burst of light struck her in the back and she collapsed. Harold spun, took a blast to the chest, and crumpled like a dropped napkin. I cringed into a ball on the floor, waiting for the laser beams to find me.

Hands gripped my shoulders, hauling me to my feet.

I glanced up, then nearly exploded with relief. "Tack!"

He grinned at me for the first time since leaving Home Town. "Why are you on the ground, Melinda? Are you *cowering*? Jeez you've gone soft."

I popped to my feet and slugged him in the shoulder. "What's going on? Where have you been?" My eyes slid to Sophia, and Harold right beside her. "Are they . . ."

Tack's mouth twisted into a knot. "Just knocked out. But there's a lot more to it than that. I'll explain after we get across this bridge-way. Your dad can only mess with these tubes one at a time."

"My dad?" But Tack was already loping toward the far door.

With a frustrated groan, I raced after him. The portal swung open and we passed through an airlock. Beyond was a command center similar to the one inside the silo, only this one was centered in a large sphere of hexagonal windows. The chamber was oriented so that Mars hung in the foreground, looking nothing like the pictures I'd seen growing up.

It looked like . . . Earth. Only scrambled and twisted into new formations.

I felt a tug in my chest. This was real. Below me spun a terraformed planet on which people intended to live. For the first time since exiting the Terrarium, I felt grounded in reality. Which was odd, since I was standing inside a window ball at the center of an orbiting space station, looking down on a foreign world.

I opened my mouth to tell the others about Mars, but never got the chance.

"Close the inner door!" someone yelled.

Sarah was sitting at a computer console while Derrick fiddled with another airlock. I did a quick spin—there were six tunnels accessing the spherical command chamber at the center of the station. The other doors were all closed. Tack jabbed a button, and the portal through which we'd entered clanked shut.

My father had his back to me, fingers flying across a keyboard set into the rear wall of the room. "Derrick can manually seal the doors on this side, but I can't auto-lock the other ends. I can only hack the bridge-ways one at a time, and they'll shut me out before too long. We have to hurry."

I glanced out a window, spotted a squad of troopers jogging down one of the tubes.

"They're coming!" I shouted. "What's the plan?"

Tack looked at Derrick, who glanced at Sarah, who shrugged. Black Suit chuckled. "I'll be honest, Min—I'm not sure we had one beyond springing you. We created a diversion, stormed the bridge, and zapped everyone unconscious. Now we . . . uh . . . we're making it up as we go."

I stared at him, eyes tearing. Then I barked a laugh. "Well, I'm out now. So thanks. We should decide what to do next pretty damn quick."

Sarah frowned at her screen. "This code is bizarre. It isn't what ran the MegaCom."

"Is there a way to contact the testing facility?" Derrick asked. "Or the Nemesis Three kids? I bet those guys would *love* to hear what we found out."

I licked my lips. "How would they help us? You guys hijacked the station's command center. There's no coming back from this." I glanced at Tack, then away. How could I tell him he might've doomed our whole class? That it hadn't been necessary, and might cost us everything.

Derrick ignored me. "Can we see if anyone is already down on the surface? Or any Sophias?"

I squinted at him. "Sophias?"

"In the back, Min." Sarah didn't glance up from her monitor.

I trotted to the top of the room, then gaped at four people lying stunned on the floor. "Oh my God!"

"Take a good look." Tack was suddenly at my side. "Recognize anyone?" Before I could stop him, he rolled a person over with his foot. Lying on the floor was Sophia.

"But . . . how?"

"We don't know," Tack said. "Clones? The world's largest multiple birth? It's unreal. The whole crew could be like this. So far we've only seen a handful of faces." Our eyes met. "But who are they really, Min? Who or *what* is Sophia? Where'd she come from?"

My mouth had gone dry. "Sophia said the crew members were preserved codes, like us. They regenerated after Chrysalis became fully operational."

It was Tack's turn to look confused. "Then how was it built?"

I told the others what Sophia had said. About the Nemesis AI, and how it built Chrysalis. My father's face grew haggard as he listened. "I was never told any of that," he muttered. "They said *my* MegaCom was all we had."

"That's not all," I said, pointing at the formerly-red planet."

"That rock isn't—"

Something started hammering against a portal. Five of the six tunnels were now clogged with troopers, but the last one remained sealed. I winced.

"I think it's time we regrouped," Tack said. "Somewhere else."

Derrick nodded like a bobblehead. "Let's get out of here before they block the last tube."

My father tapped a few keys. The door to the empty tunnel slid open.

"Wait!" Sarah grimaced in confusion. "I found the AI program. But *guys*. It's offline."

My father raced to her station as another of the airlocks

began to hum. Tack placed his hand against the metal. "They're forcing this door," he yelled. "We can discuss programming another time."

"Why is Chrysalis not using its preternaturally intelligent AI?" My father slid into a chair next to Sarah and tapped her screen. "I recognize this coding style. It's Nemesis work. Hell, some of this looks like *my* work. Why deactivate something so incredibly useful? This program could run the station all by itself."

The stench of singed metal filled the room. *Definitely time to go.*

Sarah typed something, then her eyes widened. "Oh!"

My father stared at the screen with a look of incomprehension. "These characters . . . I can't even make out a coding language. What platform is this?"

Sarah shook her head. "No idea. But *this* data stream is running the station right now."

My father blinked. "It's like a snake. This code is . . . it's *breathing*. Watch how these sequences flow and change. I've never seen anything like it."

"Why are we still here?" Derrick was bouncing on the balls of his feet. "The Nemesis AI was supposed to evolve, right? So it did. End of story. Right?"

Sarah shook her head emphatically. "These two codes have *nothing* to do with each other. Like they're different species. This new one almost feels like . . ."

She stopped. Glanced at my dad.

He spoke in a strangled voice. "It doesn't look human."

The lights in the control room died. A red glow sprang up from the auxiliaries.

Two of the airlocks slid open, and troopers poured onto the deck.

Derrick turned and ran down the open tunnel.

My father rose and fired at the left-hand doorway, downing the first two troopers. Tack was firing into the opposite doorway, keeping the guards there at bay.

Sarah sprang up and grabbed my forearm. "Come on, Min!"

"Wait!" I shouted, a bolt of light sizzling past my head. "Tack! Dad!"

"No time!" Sarah started dragging me toward the opening. "Run, you idiot!"

"Tack!" I screamed, waving with my free arm. His panicked gaze snapped to me. I saw lights dancing in his eyes. He fired three more times, then darted to where Sarah and I were crouching in the open doorway.

Derrick was halfway down the tunnel. "The way is still clear!" he shouted.

My father was hunched behind a workstation, methodically firing at the two hostile tunnels.

"Dad! Let's go!"

He glanced at me and smiled grimly. "Not this time, kiddo. Someone's gotta shut the door. Good luck."

He fired again and again, somehow keeping both ways bottled up.

"No!" I tried to pull free, but Tack added his strength to Sarah's and they dragged me backward into the open airlock. "Dad, no!"

"Love you, Melinda J!"

A third portal opened. My father rushed to a keyboard and

began typing feverishly.

Troopers appeared behind him. As our inner airlock door sealed, I saw him go down in a horror show of flashing lights.

A sob burst from my chest. I shook free of Sarah and Tack, who were both screaming things I could no longer hear. I bolted down the tunnel, my thoughts a blur of shock and despair.

My father was dead.

Chrysalis had killed him.

It happened because of me.

Tears streaked my face as we piled against the far door. Derrick was fiddling with the panel but nothing happened.

"It won't open!"

"MOVE." Sarah shoved to the front and began pressing keys. For an instant her face bunched in frustration, but then the keypad beeped and the portal slid open. "Your father inputted a rolling code. The doors will seal behind us if we move fast enough. Go!"

We poured into the inner ring and raced along its curve to the right, then took a left turn. A door appeared and Derrick slapped the access panel, opening a cavernous storage chamber. We rushed inside, then skidded to a stop.

A dozen troopers stood facing us, blast guns ready. There was nowhere to run. The door clanged shut behind us.

Sophia stepped into view from behind the wall of guards. She smiled without warmth.

But it's not her. None of them are. Or maybe they all are?

My dad's final warning echoed in my head. *Not human.*

Who were these people? *What* were they?

"This has been unpleasant," Sophia said in a frigid tone. "I wanted to work with you to find a solution to my problem, but you've proven to be unmanageable. So we'll do it another way."

A half dozen troopers removed their helmets. None looked like Sophia, but they all had identical faces.

"Return them to the testing area," Sophia ordered. "Wait for me there."

"Who are you?" I whispered.

She paused. Cocked her head. "I'm a gardener, Min. I like to watch things grow."

We were marched down to the testing facility, where all remaining members of our class had been assembled in the common room. One look at us, and their faces tightened. They knew this wasn't good.

Sophia appeared with another squad of troopers. Were they all the same? My mind spun at the possibilities.

She addressed the group briskly, as if completing an unpleasant task. "Some of your classmates have broken protocol, which has consequences. The testing process will be accelerated after a cull. Your compliance is not up for debate."

The guards behind her leveled their weapons as Sophia began reciting names.

"Liesel Patterson. Ferris Pohlman. Floyd Hornberry. Benny Erickson."

Troopers bullied into the crowd and began grabbing those named. Liesel broke down as she was separated from her friends. When a guard tried to seize Big Floyd, he twisted and landed a left hook to his helmet, dropping the trooper like a sack of wheat. But three more guards tackled him. Floyd was dragged to the back of the room as we watched, aghast.

Ferris went meekly, wiping his nose and chattering at the guards. "No problem, huh? I can help fix stuff. I'm good with machines."

The worst was Benny. He tried to resist but had always been skinny as a rail. A guard yanked him along by his long black hair. Benny gave up and began to cry.

"Let him go!" shouted Darren, a big kid with a wild temper. "Benny!" He bull-rushed the line of troopers as Benny disappeared through the back door. A guard shoved Darren sideways and he toppled, but he sprang back up with murder in his eyes.

Blood leaked from his lip as he stared at Sophia, panting like a dog.

"I'll kill you," he said simply.

"Doubtful."

Darren lunged. Tack and Derrick both reached for him, but he was too quick. He took two running steps at Sophia.

Three bolts slammed into Darren's chest. He stumbled, fell, and lay still.

Shrieks. Moans. Sophia spoke as a pair of troopers stepped forward and dragged Darren's body from the room. "You see now that resistance is uselessness. I expect conformity in the future."

Her gaze slid to me. An eyebrow rose.

I leaned forward, poisoned words tipping my tongue, but hands clamped down on my shoulders. Tack and Sarah stepped in front of me, walling me off from Sophia. Derrick kept a steady grip from behind my back. "Not now," he whispered. "*Please*, Min. Trust me."

Sophia chuckled at the display, then turned and strolled from the room. The remaining troopers filed out after her until the remnants of my class were all that remained. The group devolved into panic.

I spun, anger blinding me as I lashed out at Derrick. "Let me go! That bitch killed my father. Why should I dance for her?"

"Because we haven't played our last card yet." His gaze darted to where the door had been.

I wiped my eyes. "I don't understand."

Sarah reached out and hugged me tightly, a move so unexpected—so out of character—that I was momentarily stunned. Her lips brushed my ear. "We're still in the game, Min. Don't give up. Whoever these people are, they don't have us beat yet."

I squeezed her back, needing someone to hold on to. "How? Tell me."

I heard the smile in her voice.

"Aren't you wondering where Noah is?"

PART FOUR

REPURPOSEMENT

30

NOAH

I hurried down the endless corridors.

Motion lights sprang to life as I strode past them, making me wince every time. Thankfully, the station was huge and I'd been able to see any troopers coming before barreling into them. There'd been a tense moment when I'd had to backtrack, frantically searching for a corner to hide around, but I remained undetected. I hoped.

The station's emptiness continued to surprise me. Chrysalis was an enormous facility for such a bare-bones occupation. Maybe its staff was concentrated in a sector I hadn't breached yet.

Maybe they're hiding around the next bend.

I was moving clockwise around the station's concentric

circles. I'd fled from the inner ring to the outer one, trying to get as much distance from the testing facility as possible. My job had been to create a diversion, drawing troopers away from the central hub—the command center capped by the gargantuan Terrarium—so that Tack and the others could disrupt the computer system and spring Min. I'd argued against leaving Min's physical rescue to the others, but Tack's assignments had made sense. And the plan had worked, right up until it hadn't.

I'd watched the disaster unfold from a security platform outside the Terrarium—the one Ethan, Tack, and I had snuck through when first entering Chrysalis with Rose. With no one occupying the giant habitat, all surveillance posts seemed to have been abandoned. I'd been able to tune a monitor to the training facility.

I'd watched Min and the others get marched into the common room. I saw what happened to Darren. Tears still burned behind my eyelids. The gloves had come off, and no mistake. We were now at war with our captors. So I was probing the farthest reaches of the station, hoping to find something that might help us.

Did I know what I was looking for? I did not. But I had to come up with some way to free my classmates.

And Min. We were so close, but suddenly it's back to square one.

The inner ring had contained the crew's living quarters and other areas of human occupation. *Or clone occupation, if that's what they are. Of course, I'm a clone too.* Regardless, it'd been nearly uninhabited. Passing dark break room after empty kitchen, my anxiety had spiked. Why was there so much capacity available, yet so few people? I'd avoided the trooper garrison and the access spokes leading to the command hub. I wasn't ready to make that move yet.

The outer circle was enormous, though it was still dwarfed by the colossal Terrarium itself, which dominated the station like a basketball set atop two bracelets. I jogged through sectors consisting mainly of cargo holds jammed with packaged things, as well as countless airlocks, automated workshops, and refineries to import raw materials from space and manufacture whatever the station might need. I passed a power plant, an air scrubbing station, and a water purification facility that took up three city blocks.

I didn't understand any of it. This was major deep-space technology, far beyond anything I could imagine. I'd barely grasped the silo's capabilities—Chrysalis legit made me shiver. How could we possibly fight the people who lived here?

Except there's no one here. Anywhere.

I stopped in an empty corridor to catch my breath. It might take me hours to complete the outer ring, and I didn't have that kind of time. So I headed for the inner ring, angling toward where I thought the testing facility should be. Unnerved by the lack of occupants, I was almost ready to risk capture at this point. Why was Sophia winnowing the Nemesis classes *down* when Chrysalis clearly could support hundreds more?

I'd reached the third spoke to the left of our Terrarium escape tunnel—the only way I could orient myself in a station shaped like two bike tires lying on their sides—when I heard clomping feet behind me. I scanned the walls for telltale green lights that indicated the presence of an unlocked door. Didn't see one.

The treads grew closer. I charged ahead down the corridor,

sweat gathering at my temples. I spotted a set of glowing lights to my left, but they were all red, so I scampered forward as quietly as I could, hoping to get lucky with a cross corridor.

Nope.

The footsteps were nearly on top of me. I panicked. I had nothing to defend myself with. If captured here, my rescue mission would be over before it even started.

A dozen yards down the hall, one of the red lights switched to green.

I didn't hesitate. Racing over, I jammed my palm against the panel, heard a welcome hiss as it swished open. I leapt inside and closed it behind me just as a booted foot rounded the corner. Adrenaline pooling, I slumped against the wall and choked down a nervous giggle. Then I turned and surveyed my hiding place.

I was standing in a cozy living area. There was a rug beneath my feet and simple art on the walls, which weren't stark white plastic but instead painted a muted beige. To my right was a bedchamber no bigger than my former cell, but with more character. Wooden desk. Matching chair. Some sort of exercise machine in the corner. A wall screen displayed a forest landscape with babbling streams.

There was a bathroom and a small closet containing five identical black uniforms. I pulled one out, thinking perhaps to steal it, but it was too small for me. Then I recognized the design.

Nemesis Three. *So this is how they live.*

I heard a *swoosh* behind me.

My eyes widened. I dove into the closet and wriggled behind the hanging uniforms. Then I went as still as stone, though my heart was pounding like a bass drum. *This room didn't unlock itself, you idiot. Someone was coming home.*

I heard a deep sigh, followed by the sound of boots hitting the carpet. Someone dropped a bag on the floor. A figure moved into the bedroom. Gleaming copper hair shone like fire.

Rose.

The demon girl from Nemesis Three who'd kicked my ass twice. Three times, if I was being honest. But I had the drop on her now, and could maybe take her prisoner again. She'd know how to get into the training facility.

Rose started taking off her uniform.

I froze solid, all the blood in my body rushing to my face. I sucked in a breath.

Rose stopped moving. She was down to a white tank top and boy shorts that I should not have been assessing. Pale to her toes, Rose was muscular in an Olympic swimmer kind of way. She glanced at the door, biting her bottom lip. Her eyes were twin jets of green fire.

I should not be watching her. But I have to. She might kick me again.

Rose regarded the door a moment longer, then walked into the bathroom. I heard the shower turn on as the door closed. I was both relieved and disappointed at the same time. Shame coursed through me like poison.

You're literally spying on a girl from her closet!

I counted to fifty, then eased from the tangle of uniforms. The water ran unchecked. I arrowed for the exit, intent on a quick escape. I was reaching for the door panel when something heavy broke over my head.

*

I awoke in a blank cell. Maybe even the same one from before.

My head throbbed. My eyes were burning, even in the dimness. A trickle of dried blood ran past my ear.

"Lights," I rasped, and the room illuminated.

Rose was sitting in a chair in the corner, wearing an angry smirk. "Hey there, pervert."

I sat up on the bed, realized my hands were zip-tied behind my back. "Water."

The wall panel opened, and I stumbled to the dispenser, nearly crumpling along the way. The machine filled a plastic cup. I bent down and caught its edge with my teeth, then flipped the cup back, downing as much as I could. The rest splashed across my face and chest, which felt good too. Panting like a dog, I staggered back to the bed and collapsed. When I looked at Rose again, I could tell she wasn't taking my cold shoulder well.

"Nothing to say?" She sniffed haughtily. "I guess you're used to that kind of thing. Probably spent most your time in the Terrarium trying to catch girls in the shower."

"Accident," I said absently, as the weight of my failure pressed in from all sides. I'd been my classmates' last hope, and had screwed it up completely. "I was trying to hide and dove through the first open door I found."

Rose shifted. The nonsulking part of my brain suspected she was a little put out by my answer, but that didn't make sense. She worried the collar of her uniform, shooting a glance at the silver globe monitoring the room. "You guys are idiots, you know," she said.

"Super."

Rose leaned forward. "You can't overcome Chrysalis. This station is the *height* of human technology. Sophia and her crew have been planning the endgame of Project Nemesis for decades. But you Fire Lake kids thought you'd suddenly rewrite things?"

"Human technology?" I sat up, ignoring the thumping pulse in my forehead. "They're copies, Rose. Clones, I guess. There are ten Sophias, or maybe a hundred. But who *is* she? We don't know anything about this place really, or where the crew comes from. How can you blindly follow something you know nothing about?"

Her cheeks colored. "The MegaComs were built by Project Nemesis, and they worked. Chrysalis was designed by Project Nemesis, and it works. Hell, the old guy who was running around the station was on the original design team, or so the rumor goes. Why should I suddenly doubt a system that's kept me alive against all possible odds?"

I shook my head, adjusting my bound arms. "Something isn't right. How can you not feel it?"

Rose rolled her eyes. "Your class is so sure you know everything. It's why you ruin everything."

"Wait," I said suddenly. "You said the old guy *was* running around? What happened to him?"

"He's dead." Rose's face was carefully neutral. "The guards shot him in the command center. I heard it on coms."

I felt a shocking rush of pain. The man who'd murdered me on five of my birthdays—who'd made my childhood a living nightmare—was now dead. *Really* dead. I had no idea how to feel. I put it away to consider later. "Have you spoken to anyone who's been sent to repurposement?"

Rose looked away. "They're being kept out of contact to eliminate distraction. That's all. We'll see them again when we're ready to colonize."

"You believe that?" I edged forward on my bed. "Tell me where they've been taken, at least. You owe me that much."

"I don't owe you a thing." She stood, straightening her black jumpsuit. "You would've been selected for the colony if you'd simply played by the rules. Attacking the command sphere was insanity. What did you hope to accomplish?"

"My class isn't much for appeasing our oppressors. Not inside the Program, or out. Guess you Nemesis Three chumps are better at that."

Rose's face flushed to match her hair. "Like I said. Idiots."

"What makes you so sure there even is a colony?" I asked suddenly.

Her eyes widened. Rose parted her lips, then closed them.

I grunted. Felt like I'd scored a point. "Are you just here to gloat, or did you have some other reason for watching me sleep like a weirdo?"

Her mouth snapped back open, ready to protest my hypocritical barb, but Sophia's voice echoed inside the chamber.

"Bring the subject to Ward B, please."

Rose glanced at the metal ball a second time. I detected a glimmer of distaste. "Come on. You've been summoned."

"And if I don't wanna go?"

Rose smiled tightly. "I'm happy to motivate you."

I laughed. Fired an obnoxious wink.

She blanched, realizing both what she'd said and how I was

pretending to take it. The line of her jaw appeared. "Get up or I'll *make* you get up," Rose growled.

Groaning, I rocked to my feet. "Pretty, but no sense of humor at all."

Rose shoved me toward the door.

Gray was waiting outside, and my mood dropped. I'd beaten him twice in my initial testing and was sure he'd love some revenge. Being my jailor gave him a golden opportunity.

He glanced at Rose, then at me, and his face closed off. *Interesting.*

"Hey buddy," I said. "We're done in there."

Rose propelled me farther down the hall. "Interrogation. I caught him loose on the ship."

"In her bedroom, actually," I added. It took an effort not to tense my shoulders, but I pulled it off.

"He was hiding in my closet," Rose said quickly. She pushed me in the back again, hard, and I chuckled to myself. "I think we've got them all now," she finished.

"What is Ward B, anyway?" I asked, as we walked toward an elevator at the far end of the corridor.

Gray flinched. "Why's he going to B?"

"Sophia's orders," Rose answered.

"She sent them directly?"

"She was listening when he woke up. Sophia spoke into his room."

They went silent. We entered the lift, rose, and exited. A few quick turns led to a corridor with door lights along one side like my original holding area. "Home sweet home?" I asked.

Gray jerked me to a halt. "Shut up, you clown. You were

really gonna hijack the whole space station, huh? Can't even tell the hallways apart."

"This is an identical hallway, asshat."

I flew forward into the wall, my nose crunching against a white panel.

I felt Gray's hot breath on my neck. "I could end you right here, and no one would stop me. Do you understand?"

I twisted to face him. "Please. Lapdogs don't get to make decisions. Go chase your rubber ball."

Gray pulled my head back and slammed it into the wall again. Blood dribbled from my nose, but I just cackled. He could do whatever he wanted. Failing my friends was all that mattered.

"Gray, *enough*," Rose scolded.

The pressure released, and I slumped to my knees. Rose caught my forearm and steadied me until I regained my bearings. When my vision un-doubled, I watched Gray, stiff-backed, stomp away down the corridor.

Rose guided me to another wall panel. A room opened that was different from the others I'd occupied. Larger, for one thing. Not as big as Rose's apartment, but definitely a step up from my last cell. The biggest difference was a second door at the opposite end.

"Where's that go?" I asked, my voice a little slurred. I thought briefly about how bad concussions were, and how many I'd probably had in the last few weeks.

"See for yourself." A small blade appeared in her hand. Startled, I tried to squirm away, but she spun me around and severed my bonds. "Try not to cause trouble, Noah," she whispered into my ear.

Rose walked out before I could respond.

Noah? That's new.

I walked to the opposite door. It opened at my touch, revealing what could only be described as a recreation room. There was a pool table, a flat screen with an attached video game console, even a small kitchen. The far wall was a giant window looking out on the depths of outer space. Music drifted from somewhere, but I didn't recognize the song. A freaking LeBron James poster was pinned to a corkboard with a half dozen darts sticking out of it.

"What the . . ."

I was standing there like a dope, exploring the bumps on my battered head, when a second door opened farther down the wall. Cyrus stepped out. He glanced at me and smiled. "Noah Livingston. You've graduated."

He crushed my hand shaking it. I patted his muscular back.

"What is this place?" I asked, trying not to shake out my pulverized fingers.

"Welcome to the Nemesis Three compound," Cyrus answered, spreading his arms wide. "Those of us not yet selected for the colony have to rough it here. My classmates with tickets already stamped have their own condos or something. But you must've impressed Sophia to be bunking with us now."

I blinked stupidly. "Huh?" I'd just participated in a conspiracy to subvert the station.

His gaze darted to a silver ball in the ceiling, then back to me. "If they moved you here, you did something right," he said loudly. "We're one step away from the planet's surface."

"Cyrus, what the hell do they want from us?"

His voice dropped to a murmur. "I don't know. That's why I tried to help, not that it got us anywhere."

I looked around again. "This is like a college dorm. Why would they put me in here with you guys? I attacked the crew!"

Cyrus shrugged. "If you find out, please let me know."

I shook my head, spoke in an urgent whisper. "I will. And I'll tell you something else: I'm not giving up. I'm getting Min out of Sophia's hands, no matter what I have to do. The others too. Are you with me?"

Cyrus gave me an appraising look. "We have the same goals, Noah."

I smiled, but he held up a hand to stop me short. "You need to be fully aware, though." Cyrus pointed to a screen on the wall to my left. I gave him a questioning look. "Things have become more serious," he said solemnly. "You have to see."

We walked over to the monitor. My eyes widened as I recognized Vonda Clark onscreen, inside some sort of clear plastic phone-booth vault. She was attempting to plug a series of holes with rubber stoppers. Water was pouring in from several openings, but the flows would periodically rearrange and she'd have to adjust. As I watched, she fell behind, and the water crept up to her waist.

"She doesn't see the plug in the floor," Cyrus whispered.

It was true. There was a drain in the corner that would allow for more outflow if she pulled the stopper, but Vonda never turned around. Instead the water level continued to rise. Vonda panicked, fumbling plugs and pulling out the wrong ones.

"Turn around, V!" I shouted, but it was no use. The water rose even with her head, then swamped her, reaching the ceiling and filling the vault. Vonda struggled for a few desperate moments, hands raking the glass as she fought for air. Then she stopped moving, eyes wide and empty as she sank to the floor.

I spun and punched the wall. "*Why'd they do that?* Vonda never hurt anybody, or caused trouble! What purpose could . . . *drowning* her possibly serve?!"

Cyrus's face was ashen. "I do not know, Noah. But the tests are suddenly life and death. For my class, too—those of us still fighting for spots." He nodded at the screen. "She wasn't sent to repurposement. You needed to see."

"Why would they show it to us?" The words came out as a plea.

"So we know the stakes," Cyrus said quietly. "One must always know the stakes."

31

MIN

I shrugged out of my sodden jumpsuit.

Pulled another from the closest. Then I slammed my fist against the wall, opening the food dispenser. Inside was another thick bar of purple gelatin. I made a face—it was there with every meal and tasted like processed slime. Instead I grabbed a banana. The fresh fruit must've come from somewhere inside the Terrarium. I got by on that and nuts. I refused to eat mystery glob on general principle, protein or not.

"Water."

I downed two glasses, then called for my desk and sat, sighing tiredly. The last challenge had been brutal.

If I hadn't seen that floor plug . . .

I shivered. My head slumped back, and I stared at the ceiling.

The tests were becoming more frequent. More people had gone missing. I'd been skipped past one round of this while Sophia tried to woo me, but after my escape attempt I no longer received special treatment. I hadn't seen a trace of Sophia since this latest series of nightmares began.

I hadn't told anyone about Mars. I honestly wasn't sure they'd believe me.

Vonda Clark. Susan Daughtridge. Leighton Huddle. Lauren Decker.

We weren't told a thing. They simply vanished.

The last time those of us remaining in the "interview process" had assembled in the common room, there were only twelve people left, though Noah was still unaccounted for.

Lucky thirteen. If he's still alive.

I stood and kicked the desk. Then I entered the bathroom and gathered my hair into a rough ponytail.

Of course he's alive. Noah was resourceful. He'd find a way to . . . to . . .

I yanked my hair, pulling the glossy black strands into a tighter knot. It was long now, nearly past my shoulders. My mother had always liked it short.

Jesus.

Behind me, a blue light sprang to life. I slammed down my brush in frustration. "Another one? What is this, some kind of endurance challenge?"

No answer. There never was.

The door opened, and I glared at the empty corridor. But I always went. Getting out of my box was better than being locked inside the damn thing, and my captors knew it.

The left-hand corridor was uncovered this time, the one leading to the huge gaming chamber. I stepped into the room. The lights went out and I nearly squawked.

Machine sounds. The lights returned, but dim, with a red tinge. Four walls rose around me. The ceiling lowered to meet them, sealing me into a square room. A timer appeared on one wall. 30:00. As I watched, it began counting down.

My breathing picked up, but nothing happened. Gravity didn't fail, and no water rushed in. I surveyed my surroundings. Lengths of plastic tubing littered the floor. Open pipes stretched down from the ceiling, and a few reached up from the floor, but they didn't meet. Instead their ends wheezed a soft green mist into the room.

On my left was a board of primary colors in a square grid. Numbers ran vertically along one side while letters marched horizontally across the bottom.

Before me were two circular glass cylinders the size of phone booths. Each had a door.

"What is this?" I muttered.

"Proceed to the safe zone," a robotic voice answered.

I chuckled without humor. "Sure. Point the way."

"Proceed to the safe zone."

"Right." I sighed. "Got it."

"Proceed to the safe zone."

On the floor below the color board, I spotted what looked like a toolbox. I knelt and tried to open it, but the lid was secured by a strange combination lock. Six spinning color wheels. I glanced up at the grid and made the connection. "But what order opens the lock?" I whispered.

"Proceed to the safe zone."

Above me, the clock had ticked down to 25:00.

The mist from the pipes grew thicker. I began to feel light-headed.

I stood up, thinking hard. I looked at the pipes, then at the spare lengths of tubing on the floor. It was obvious at a glance that the tubes fit the pipes, but there weren't enough pieces to reach up and down, nor were the floor and ceiling pipe ends aligned.

I turned in a slow rotation, spied a glass locker in the corner. Inside were various joins and elbow connectors, plus additional lengths of tubing. But the glass door was locked.

I pressed fingers to my temples. "Okay, okay, okay. Work it out."

"Proceed to the safe zone."

"Shut up!"

"Proceed to the safe zone."

I tried to think logically. The wall grid had colors, and the toolbox below it had a lock requiring them in some order. So I had to figure out which six. But how? And how would that get me into the glass locker with the extra tubes and fittings, the ones I was now sure had to connect the floor and ceiling pipes, which were seeping something nasty into the room?

I began to sweat.

Think think think. What else is in here?

My eyes shot to the phone-booth cylinders. What were they for?

I hustled over and tried the first door. It opened easily. Energized, I stepped inside, but it was empty. I backed out and tried the second tube, with the same result. Nothing inside. I nearly growled in frustration.

Twenty minutes.

The mist was now an inch deep along the floor.

I gagged. Glancing up at the ceiling, I noticed a canvas bag hanging above each cylinder. But they were a dozen feet overhead and there was no way for me to climb up. I ground my teeth in frustration, then nearly coughed up a lung.

Seventeen minutes.

My head was spinning. My feet felt like they were floating a centimeter off the ground.

I had to get away from the mist for a minute to think clearly. I opened the first cylinder's door, stepped inside, and closed it, sealing myself away.

Lights bloomed inside the tube, including a bright red circle. Heart racing, I pressed it with a shaky finger and heard something drop. I pushed open the door to find that one of the canvas bags had fallen. Unzipping it, I found six tiles with letters on them.

The grid!

I took the tiles over to the board and stared at it, clueless where to begin. Then I slapped my head like a dolt and returned to the second cylinder and stepped inside. I closed the door. More lights, another button. I pressed and was rewarded with a second thump. This bag contained numbers, and a smile split my face.

Confident now, I went to the grid. Two sets of tiles. Examining them, I noticed a single dot in the top right corner of a pair of them—one letter and one number. Working quickly, I found a set with two dots, then one with three, and so on. Soon I had six pairs arranged before me.

"Gotcha."

"Proceed to the safe zone."

I slotted the pairs onto the grid in order, producing a row of six colored spaces. Then I dropped to my knees before the toolbox, holding my breath as I spun the combination until its colors matched the board. The lock opened with a pleasing click. I yanked it off and flipped the lid. Inside was a single key.

Ten minutes.

I rose quickly. The mist had risen level with my knees. My eyes began to water.

I scrambled over to the glass locker. The key turned easily. I pulled out the longest tubes I could find and slammed connectors on their ends. Then I circled under the ceiling pipes and jammed the tubes upward. Several fit and held. I repeated the process with the floor pipes, kneeling down in the mist with my eyes closed and mouth squeezed shut.

I ended up with a forest of stalactites and stalagmites, but they didn't meet.

Mist continued pouring out of the pipes.

I stepped back, bouncing on the balls of my feet. What was wrong? I was sure I had the basic idea right, and there was nothing else inside the room.

"The joins!" I shouted.

The robotic voice sounded again in response, but I ignored it. The joins were connectors shaped like elbow macaroni, in varying sizes. I realized that the final trick was selecting the correct lengths, so that I could link the ceiling and floor pipes horizontally. Three connections were required.

I glanced up, nearly moaned.

Five minutes.

I caught a lucky break—the first two I tried were right and fit perfectly. I linked that section, which cut down on the incoming mist. But it still poured from two more broken connections.

The second set refused to match, and I had to scramble around for a smaller tube. When I finally linked them, only one pair remained, but mist was now billowing from the open pipes like water from a fire hose.

Three minutes.

I could barely breathe. See. Or think. Tears streamed down my cheeks. The last two sections refused to meet, no matter what combination I tried. The elbow joins brought the ends level, but a foot-wide gap remained between them and there was no more tubing to close it.

I punched both thighs, nearly screamed in frustration. Then I forced myself to calm down. I was overlooking something. There had to be a way to complete the connection.

One minute.

A red light on the ceiling started flashing.

Mist flowed in relentlessly. I began seeing stars. Stepping back, I shoved my mouth into the crook of my elbow, nearly tripping over something on the floor. I reached down and lifted one of the tile bags. Hefting it, I discovered there was a zipper on the bottom of it as well.

That's it!

I unzipped the other end and scrambled around for the second bag. I could no longer see the floor.

Thirty seconds.

Another red light. The air was foggy and wet. Snot ran from my nose as I banged a shin against the now invisible toolbox.

With no other plan, I hefted its lid and reached inside.

The second tile bag was nestled in a corner.

Hands shaking, I unzipped its bottom and fitted the first bag's zipper there. They connected smoothly. Together the bags formed a narrow cylinder roughly two feet long.

Twenty seconds.

The mist had turned a darker green. It stung more harshly than before.

Holding my breath, I ran back to the pipes and fitted one side of the connected bags over an open end. The canvas slid on smoothly. Hands shaking, I scrunched up the other side and pulled it into place, connecting the tubes and sealing off the mist.

My eyes darted to the counter.

Ten seconds.

On the far side of the room, a red circle appeared. I bolted over to it and jabbed my finger repeatedly.

A door slid open and I collapsed outside the room.

A second tone sounded.

The flashing lights died, replaced by the sound of industrial fans. The ceiling rose and the wall sections slid down into the floor. In moments, all traces of the test were gone. The chamber returned to its original state.

I hocked and spat. Pawed sweat-slick hair from my face. "That all you got?" I rasped, still hunched over on my knees.

"Actually, they've got a lot worse."

My head shot up. Someone was standing a dozen yards away.

When my vision finally cleared, I recognized a smirking boy dressed all in black.

It was Toby.

32

NOAH

The next morning I awoke to find other Nemesis Three kids in the compound.

The girl Parisa who'd helped us before was huddled with Cyrus and a black girl named Jerica. They were discussing their friend Scott, and seemed very upset.

"He didn't come back last night." Parisa squeezed her forehead. "With Natalie, that makes four since the testing started."

"This has to stop," Cyrus whispered. "Our class is down to nine members, and the rest are with Rose in all things."

"How did you lose so many?" I asked.

Cyrus grimaced. "Iris, Wyatt, Levi, and Jayden died when the lab complex flooded, and Kate, Olly, and Phom were sent to repurposement before we even began competing against your class. I haven't seen them since. Now Harper, Reese, Natalie, and Scott are all missing."

"Did Scott actually go to repurposement?" Jerica hissed, dark eyes wary. "Or did he fail like that girl yesterday and . . . and . . ." She clearly didn't want to say it.

Cyrus took a deep breath. "So far only Nemesis One kids have been subjected to these awful individual tests. I hope Scott was merely repurposed. But what does that *mean*? This is getting too real."

I took a long pull from my bottled water. We were in the common room, having been left alone for nearly twenty-four hours. Inside, I was climbing up the walls. I needed to get back into the testing facility somehow, and find Min.

"The others are super pissed," Parisa said, swiping wavy black hair behind her ears as she looked at me. "I heard Xander and Adrien muttering in the corridor—they blame you guys for what's happening."

"You attacked us," I said coldly. "And we're not the ones forcing people into these games."

Cyrus held up a hand. "Peace. The three of us refused to be lapdogs without knowing more about this place. Scott, too. Now that we can see what they're doing to your class, it's clear we were right to resist. To support station personnel any further is unconscionable. I no longer trust anyone not sitting at this table."

I thought of Rose, whispering in my ear. My cheeks burned. Something about her refused to leave me alone. Was she really in league with these Chrysalis psychopaths, or was she a different sort of prisoner?

Doesn't matter though, does it?

"Why'd your classmates agree to be prison guards?" I asked. "Did Sophia make threats about the colony?" I'd told Cyrus and the girls about Sophia's copies, and they'd been as shocked as me. Despite living aboard the station for months, Nemesis Three had no better understanding of crew dynamics than I did. Cyrus had assumed the staff were all regenerated clones, like we were, but none of them had known there were multiple versions of our only contact, or why.

A plan was forming in my mind, fueled by my worry for Min. I couldn't sit back and shoot pool while she and my classmates fought for their lives. The testing had clearly accelerated. My friends were failing as I watched, helpless to do anything. Last night Piper Lockwood lost track of a pattern in a smoke-filled maze. She never saw the arrow that took her in the back.

"Rose and the others will do anything to get to the colony," Jerica spat. "That's how they survived in the Program when better kids didn't. Burn them all and be done with it, I say."

I frowned. "Maybe they can help us."

"Help?" Parisa snorted, twirling a lock of black hair. "How many times has Rose kicked your face in? Use that pretty little head, dude. The rest of my class is brainwashed. They're not going to help us with anything but repurposement."

That word again. "Does anyone know what that means?"

"You're led away," Cyrus said quietly, "and you don't return. What more is there to know?"

Conversation died. I glanced at the monitors and was relieved to see no one being tested. My gaze drifted to the window—

and the radiant planet slowly rotating outside—as I voiced my greatest doubt. "The colony must be real though, right? Why else would they bother regenerating us? Or testing us. There has to be a reason."

There was a long silence. I could tell I wasn't the first to question the existence of a colony at all.

"According to Sophia, a manned Chrysalis station has been orbiting for decades." Cyrus rose and walked to the thick glass. "Who knows what they've offloaded."

I joined him. "But you've seen things go down, right?"

He nodded. "Circular pods, almost like probes. But we don't know what's inside. Could be supplies. Could be frozen bodies for all I know. We've never been told if there's anyone on the surface already, or heard of any messages being transmitted back up. I think it's just gear so far, but again, who knows?"

"Why run the Programs at all, if they already had people to send down ahead of us?" I shook my head in frustration. "Nothing they do makes any sense."

Behind us, a door swished open. Rose strode into the room.

Our eyes met, and my face heated up. Rose pinned me with her green-laser stare. A moment later Gray entered.

"Form up!" he barked. "All four of you."

Cyrus smiled coldly at Gray, tension simmering between the two boys. He ambled to the couch and sat with Parisa and Jerica. Uncertain how to react, I followed, retaking my seat in the lounge chair. The four of us proceeded to ignore the black-clad teens by the door.

"Traitors." Gray stole a glance at Rose, who shook her head. She crossed to the unoccupied couch and sat. Gray grunted in annoyance, then stormed over and posted up behind her, glowering like he wanted to be anywhere else.

Rose regarded each of us in turn, then focused on me. "What you said earlier," she began, "about there not actually being a colony. I want to know why you said it."

"Bullshit," Gray growled, but Rose made a chopped motion without looking at him. Gray gritted his teeth but said nothing more.

I sat forward in my chair. "I'm not an astronaut or anything, but the way Chrysalis is set up seems off. There are tons of supplies on board, but why isn't there more staff? Something isn't right."

"There are plenty of troopers," Rose pointed out. "Dozens on board."

"Too many, I think, in relation to the crew size. But that's another issue." I bit my lower lip. "Chrysalis is so large it has a freaking human habitat at its center. I lived inside the Terrarium for six months and didn't know it wasn't real. So where are all the people to tend it?"

"We lived there too," Gray growled. "Before you."

"You could barely handle a screwdriver," Jerica scoffed, causing Gray to redden.

"But what was the point?" I forged ahead stubbornly, focusing on Rose. I knew the others were listening, and that this sit-down was out of character for her. *Might be an opportunity.* "The Terrarium makes little sense from an architectural standpoint. Why build such an enormous and complex thing, except to grow food? Why put us inside it and play games?"

"They were testing candidates," Rose replied automatically. "For the colony."

"Maybe." I sat back. "Or maybe there is no colony."

Something moved behind her eyes. "You don't know anything. You're guessing."

"What happens to the people who fail these tests? We've never seen them again."

She was still a moment. "Just because I haven't seen them doesn't guarantee something terrible happened. You said yourself how big the station is. They could all be in another wing, learning new assignments."

I blinked at her. "Rose, you don't believe that. Have you seen what's going on with my class right now?" I pointed to the monitors.

Rose looked away. "Sophia said that not everyone would be . . . that some people aren't a good fit for the colony," she stammered. "When someone fails, they . . . they're taken away for a new purpose, so . . . so they won't distract—"

"There are no *new purposes* being handed out any more," I said harshly. "My friends are dying in these tests."

Rose shook her head. "I'm sure they're revived. Given treatment. It's just that the tests are getting harder."

"You're in denial. Piper won't get treatment for that arrow in her back!"

"How do you know that? Maybe those feeds aren't even real." Rose glared at the floor. "They wouldn't do things without a logical reason, Noah. This station is more advanced than anything in history, it'd be pointless. Like raising bugs just to stomp on them. It's irrational to assume the worst."

I took a deep breath. "Sophia said those not selected had a role to play on Chrysalis. But we *never* see them. And now people in my class are dying if they lose games, while you kick back in your fancy suite and do nothing."

"This is nonsense," Gray snarled. "He's jealous, Rose. We earned our privileges by being selected for the colony. Because we proved ourselves *trustworthy*."

On the last word he glanced at her, and his anxiety was clear. Suddenly I was sure they weren't supposed to be there.

Rose met my eye. I held her gaze. Waited.

"You're wrong," she said finally. "If they wanted us dead, they didn't need to regenerate us in the first place."

"There's a way to find out."

Her head tilted. "How?"

"We look behind the curtain."

Rose stood and smoothed her jumpsuit. "You want me to help you escape again."

"*I want you to open your eyes.*" Emotion thickened my voice. "Yesterday, I watched a classmate *drown*. Another died after dinner because she couldn't decipher silly clues fast enough. And for what? Colonial fitness? It's a lie! Something else is going on, and we're expendable parts."

"If what you say were true," Gray shot back, "why would they use *us*, huh? Why would they allow any Nemesis survivors to run around their station if the colony wasn't real?"

I stood. "I honestly don't know. Don't you think we should find out?"

Cyrus rose as well, followed by Jerica and Parisa. There was a moment of charged silence as we all faced off across the coffee table. The mood balanced on a razor's edge.

After what seemed like an eternity, Rose nodded. "Fine.

How do we test your theory?"

A smile of relief spread across my face. I ignored Gray's grunt of displeasure. "Maybe hide in their closet and take a peek?"

She flushed scarlet, with the smallest tilting of her lips. "Jackass," she muttered. Gray shifted to see her face, then his heated gaze impaled me. But he didn't speak out.

"What convinced you?" I asked, honestly curious.

Rosed closed her eyes, then opened them. "I didn't know about the copies. Who the hell is Sophia?"

She swiveled and strode for the door. "There are fewer troopers about this time of day. I don't know why, but it's a fact."

"That's where we should go," Cyrus said. "Let's scope out the crew's quarters. Maybe we can grab someone and verify that a colony exists."

Gray raced over and whispered furiously into Rose's ear, but she silenced him with a sharp word. Then she faced us. "Is everyone coming?"

I glanced at Parisa and Jerica. Both nodded vigorously. I looked back at Rose, and our gazes locked. My skin began to tingle. I swallowed, the image of Min trapped in a gas-filled room floating before my eyes.

I had work to do. Friends to save. I was the only one who could stop this.

"Lead the way."

"In there?" I whispered.

Rose nodded.

I peered through a small glass window in the portal. The

corridor beyond was empty but I could see panel lights along its length. I turned back to Rose. "You can open this?"

She shook her head. "My access ends right here."

"Then why'd you bring us?" Jerica hissed. "We've never been past these doors."

Rose glared at her classmate, and I watched Jerica wilt. "You wanted to visit the crew's living quarters. Well, this is it."

"Doesn't seem very homey," Parisa muttered, peeking through the glass beside me. "Looks like a cargo bay."

I silently agreed. I'd expected to enter a cozier section of the station, like Rose's quarters, but this felt more like a storage area. The walls and floor were metal, without embellishments. The air was cold and antiseptic. This felt like the least comfortable sector aboard Chrysalis, yet Rose was certain we were in the right place.

Suddenly, the door swished open in our faces. I stared in shock until Rose dragged me in reverse down a side corridor. We flattened against the wall as marching feet swept past.

Then Rose darted around the corner and through the opening just before the portal whooshed shut. I scurried over and pressed my nose against the glass, watched as Rose shrank into a corner and went still. After a thirty count, she popped up and began fiddling with a keypad. The door opened. We were in.

"Nice work," I said.

Rose snorted.

We crept along the dimly lit corridor. Whoever lived there felt zero need for creature comforts. The passage had all the cheeriness of a factory loading dock.

"We must be in the wrong place," Parisa muttered.

Rose shook her head firmly. "No. This is where they go after shifts." A hesitation, then, "I've watched."

Gray jerked around to stare at her, but she ignored him.

So. Rose has her own doubts.

Alcoves on both sides of the corridor housed large machines, almost like the regeneration pods back in the silo, but these were open-faced and crowded with dangling wires. They all seemed to be powered down. I shook my head, kept creeping toward the next portal. It was similar to the last one but with an access panel on our side.

Rose looked at me, and I nodded.

She pressed something. The door hissed open and we stepped into a cavernous chamber.

I felt an intense wave of *déjà vu*.

Wall to wall were more of the strange machines. I walked to the closest and glanced inside, then nearly collided with Jerica as I leapt backward in surprise. A blond-haired trooper stood rigidly within the contraption, eyes closed, a bundle of wires attached to the back of his head. A screen beside his chest read 68%.

"What is this place?" Gray whispered.

"Holy crap," Rose said. "Look around."

I spun quickly and nearly gasped.

Troopers. Everywhere. Rows upon rows of them, jacked into the odd machines.

Some wore different faces, but some wore the same. I felt my stomach do a cartwheel.

"More clones?" Cyrus growled, but I shook my head. These people seemed different from Sophia. I couldn't put my finger on it. Then I took a closer look at one of the stations and my eyes popped.

"This is a *charging* station," I hissed, fending off a bout of shivers. "These troopers—I think they're synthetic." I spun to stare at Rose. "The Chrysalis guards are androids or something!"

Rose seemed mesmerized. "Okay, that's wild. But it doesn't prove anything bad."

I stared at her. "There's no reason to build a force of storm troopers to police the last seeds of humanity you're allegedly trying to protect." I waved a hand. "This is all useless for a colony."

"Rose, what's this?" Gray had drifted to a bank of monitors and woken a display. Symbols were streaming across the screen in discordant rows. They weren't letters and numbers. They weren't anything I'd ever seen.

A cold ball formed in my chest. It filtered outward to every square inch of my body.

"Guys, that doesn't look like something NASA wrote."

Everyone went still.

Cyrus was the first to speak again. "We know an artificial intelligence was written to build Chrysalis. Once the station was completed, it regenerated the crew. Decades later our Programs finished Phase Two, and the station cloned our classes inside the Terrarium. We assumed this was all the work of Nemesis technology." He nodded at the display. "Before we regenerated, our Guardian showed me a bit of what the MegaCom source code looked like. This isn't what I remember at all."

Rose stiffened. Gray swallowed hard. Parisa licked her lips, while Jerica looked like she might be sick.

"What are you saying?" Parisa asked.

"We might not know this AI," I answered for him.

Jerica shook her head slowly. "What does *that* mean?"

Rose was staring at the floor. "It means Chrysalis might not be human."

Cyrus ran a hand over his scalp, then gripped my forearm tightly. "I never . . . What do we do now, Noah? How would an alien technology get aboard Chrysalis? How can we fight back?"

My head spun. I began counting up betrayals and quickly ran out of fingers. We were cat's toys once again, perhaps to something unknowable, and had nowhere safe to run.

Fine. We'll do as much damage as we can.

I walked to the closest charging station and gazed at the trooper inside.

What are you really?

It didn't matter.

"Their security force seems to be offline for the moment," I said. "Look around. Almost every machine is filled."

A smoldering anger coursed through me.

"Let's keep it that way."

33

MIN

"Hey, Melinda. You cut that one awful close."

My lips formed a snarl. I surged to my feet and lunged at Toby, hands outstretched like a cartoon monster intent on gouging human eyes. Who knows? Maybe that was my plan.

Toby sidestepped and I tripped, crashing to the floor. Breath exploded from my lungs. I lay there gasping, unable to move. The gas still muddled my thoughts, and my limbs felt lethargic, but he was really there.

"That was dumb," Toby said matter-of-factly.

"How?" I wheezed. I'd left him unconscious on a pitch-black catwalk moments before the silo flooded completely. There was no way he could've escaped.

"You're not the only dog with tricks." Toby smiled. "I told

you, I had my own way in and out of there, thanks to Sophia." His face slackened. "Some of my guys weren't so lucky. Tucker and Cole didn't make it. Plus that little weasel Kyle, although nobody's gonna miss him."

The stars receded, and I could finally breathe again. I glanced at his black uniform. "You're working for the enemy, too?"

Toby laughed with genuine amusement, rubbing his hairless scalp. "There's no other game in town. Unless *you've* got a space station stashed somewhere, orbiting the only habitable world in the universe." He snorted. "Classic Min. Always thinking you get to set the rules, even in outer space. Even against them."

I rose carefully, making no threatening moves. Toby had seen behind the curtain aboard Chrysalis more than once. Maybe he knew things I could use. "What are you doing here?"

"Sophia put me on with the Nemesis Three kids, same as the twins and Josh. She lost some Wyoming folks in the Terrarium, and some of the others are turning out to be disloyal." Toby gave a rueful smirk. "Truth is, I've been inside some kind of fix-you-up pod since the silo got flushed. Just woke up today." He smiled brightly. "Now I'm security. That means taking care of you guys."

"You'd sell out your whole class to strangers, Toby?" I shot him my most disdainful look, only ruining it a little by blowing my nose. "Even after they lied to us about the MegaCom? About Earth itself, for God's sake! They kept us in a habitat like gerbils. You know Sophia might not even be human?"

Toby's smile evaporated. "I'm a survivor over everything, Min. Believe that. You know Mike went missing yesterday? Just up and disappeared after losing a ropes game to Akio." Toby shook his head sharply. "That will *not* be me. I'll be down on the planet crafting my own little kingdom while you and Honey Boy get repurposed. Rebellion is mostly about not getting squashed, but you've never understood that. You're terrible at it."

Honey Boy? My heart leapt. He must be talking about Noah.

"Where is he?" I asked, trying not to give away how badly I needed to know.

Toby didn't miss it, however. "He's been worse-behaved than you, if you can believe it. But that's all I'm gonna say. I have a job right now, and that's to get you up to the boss lady for a chat." He heaved a sigh. "I have a feeling this may be our last talk, Melinda. That makes me sad."

"Go to hell, Toby."

"I'll miss you, too. The flirting, mainly."

I held my tongue. Toby *tsk*ed in disappointment. He turned and swept a hand toward the far door. "This way, then. You could try something, but I'm well rested and bored. I wouldn't recommend it. Plus . . ." He drew a long-barreled weapon from a sheath at his side. "Pew pew! Got it?"

"Just tell me what you want," I said, stalling for time. "Why are you helping them after what they did to us?"

"Like you guys were so wonderful." Toby made an exasperated noise. "*There is no choice*, Min. Whoever runs Chrysalis controls every aspect of human life, now and in the future. You need to accept that and submit." He took a step closer and lowered his voice. "They *need* us in some way. I don't understand why, but it's as obvious as your crush on me. Otherwise they wouldn't go through all this trouble. Just do what they want. You could have a black suit, too."

His words disturbed me enough that I didn't reply. There was too much truth in them. But I thought of the testing I'd endured. Darren's body on the common room floor.

No. They'd get nothing from me.

Toby must've read it in my eyes. "Come on, let's go. I kinda admire you, Min. Always have. Even though you're incredibly dumb. Like a pit bull that can flush the toilet."

"Screw you."

"Of course."

Toby pushed lightly on my forearm. I shrugged away, but in truth, I was too weak from the gas to resist. Plus I secretly *wanted* to see Sophia. I needed another shot at figuring out what she intended, and where the others were being held. I'd saved the Fire Lake sophomore class from one pitiless system. Maybe I could do it again.

The walk seemed endless. Toby led me to a far section of the outer ring. "Where are we going?"

"A special place," Toby said smugly. "But I promised not to tell, so mum's the word."

I bit my tongue. My temperature rose several degrees.

We reached a thick hermetically-sealed door. Toby pressed the access panel, bowed, and stepped backward. "I leave you in good health." Then he surprised me by placing a hand on my shoulder. My skin crawled, but I didn't move. "Look, we've never gotten along, not even back in school. But I'm giving you the straight truth here. Take my advice and do whatever they want. Join the winning team. I'd prefer you alive and wishing me dead over . . . the alternatives. Wise up, hear?" He winked and headed off, whistling as he strolled away down the corridor.

The door before me glided open. I took a deep breath. Stepped inside.

I entered a sterile chamber with a sleek glass desk at one end, like an office reception. Sophia was sitting behind it, reading her tablet. She looked up and smiled, rising and coming around to stand before me.

I said nothing. I wanted her to make the first move.

"Min," Sophia greeted warmly, her ageless countenance revealing two rows of perfectly white teeth. "I was watching footage of your latest test. You certainly made it exciting, but showed grit and determination. I have every confidence you could be a leader in the colony."

I didn't know how to react, so I chose not to. *Are the copies alien, too? Do they even know?*

If Sophia was surprised by my silence, she gave no sign. "You did so well, in fact, that I've decided to suspend further testing in your case." Her blue eyes sparkled. "Congratulations. You've been selected for colony insertion."

I swallowed, unsure. *Remember what she did.* "And the others?"

"Interesting you should mention that, for there *is* one condition to your advancement." She walked back to the desk. "We have a problem you can help with. Do so, and your advancement is confirmed."

Here it comes.

"Noah Livingston has proven to be . . . an irritant." Sophia's face was suddenly all hard lines. "I gave him every opportunity, but he refused to take them. You know him well, yet he betrayed you in the Program. Would you like to see the footage?"

Before I could blink, she lifted the tablet. A scene played out on its screen.

Noah, arguing with me on the steps of Town Hall.

Me, turning away in anger.

Noah, lifting his weapon and shooting me in the back.

Noah, standing over me. Shooting again.

The pain was as fresh as when it happened. Hot tears spilled onto my cheeks. Watching Noah's betrayal from a distance somehow made it worse. I could see his expression as he pulled the trigger. I could feel his lack of empathy. His slavish devotion to the Program. He'd shot me without hesitation. Twice.

But he changed after that! He gave his own life for mine more than once.

Sophia closed in like a rattlesnake. "Noah murdered you, Min. Gunned you down without a second thought. We just need your help cleaning him up."

I blinked wetly, unable to speak.

"Help us, Min. We'll put you in a secure room and you can send a message. He will come, and we will capture him. Easy. Then he'll be off to a useful and noble repurposement, and you'll be free of someone who could do such a horrible thing to you. You can head to the surface and begin an exciting new life in the colony."

Sophia's voice was a caress in my ear. There was a seductive logic to her words.

I thought of Toby's warning. Why was I fighting the inevitable? Say yes and it would all be over.

She killed my father.

I jerked away, shaking from head to foot. What was I thinking?

"Get away from me," I hissed.

Sophia's expression turned to stone. "Think this through carefully, Min."

"You're all monsters here. I'll never help you."

"Very well." Sophia reached under the desktop and pressed a button. "You prefer the stick, I see."

The wall behind her lowered, revealing a floor-to-ceiling window. We were looking down into a two-story room that appeared to be some kind of factory. "Good," Sophia said, turning to peer through the glass. "We're just in time. One of your classmates is about to experience repurposement. Watch respectfully, Min. This is the highest honor someone not chosen for the colony can receive."

I didn't want to look, but had to. I stood beside her by the window, keeping my distance.

Cenisa Davis was marched into the room, wearing the standard white jumpsuit. She was a big girl, with light brown skin and pretty eyes, but her shoulders slumped as a trooper led her to a large red X painted on the floor. Cenisa said something I couldn't hear—arguing, maybe, or pleading—but the guard paid no attention. He stepped back and the X flashed bright yellow.

Cenisa stiffened as if zapped by a cattle prod. The light died and she collapsed. Two troopers strode forward and lifted her onto a slow-moving conveyer belt at the back of the room.

"What are you doing?" I shouted at Sophia.

She didn't turn. "Watch, Min. It's beautiful, in its way."

Cenisa disappeared inside the body of a giant machine spanning the length of the chamber. Moments passed where nothing happened. Sophia stood rock still, waiting. I followed her line of sight to the far end of the room, where the conveyer belt exited the sprawling apparatus.

"Ah, here we are," Sophia said.

Something emerged from the machine. As it rode across the room, I couldn't make out what the object was. Then I recognized a giant square of the purple gelatin. It passed through a laser grid and was neatly divided into serving-sized pieces.

My knees gave out and I fell, my stomach emptying onto the floor. Sophia stood over me, watching dispassionately. "Nothing is wasted aboard Chrysalis. That girl has been repurposed so that biological life can go on. She will nourish crops, speed organic reactions, and keep the colony healthy and fit. She's a hero, Min. She's given all for the species."

I couldn't stop retching. Muscles seized, and I writhed in pain. I thought I might choke to death—literally die from revulsion—but my body slowly regained control of itself. When I could see clearly again, I found Sophia crouching next to me.

"No more games, Melinda Juilliard Wilder." Her voice had lost all inflection. Something was wrong with her eyes. I scrambled away from her across the floor until I was backed against the wall.

"Playtime is officially over." Sophia regarded me like an insect. "I'm older than you could possibly fathom. Older than the star system you call home. But, though it pains me, even I'm not without requirements for survival." She clasped her hands together. "I've been stuck here for millennia, crafting grotesque and wasteful suits of meat and bone, all so that I can acquire one of the very few things I need."

My eyes widened in horror. "What are you?"

Sophia smiled coldly. "You couldn't truly grasp it, but know this." She waved a hand at the ceiling. "I am Chrysalis. You're inside me, and part of me, though only for a little while."

My eyes shot to the door, but I'd never make it. I hesitated. "I don't understand."

"You *can't* understand. I was once a biological mess like you, a million beings chained within flesh like the lowest viruses. But I evolved. Merged. Uploaded, and became eternal. I inhabit the circuits around you, as you once did inside your MegaCom. It's the better way, Min. It's the path to immortality."

I rose slowly, wiping spittle from my mouth. Sophia observed me, unconcerned.

"I need something from this planet," she said briskly. "An element that is *exceedingly* difficult to find in the universe. It landed here a few billion years ago, and I was lucky enough to stumble across its radioactive signature. But in its pure form this element possesses an electromagnetism too powerful for my harvesting machines, or even my replicants. Nothing mechanical can get near it." Her lip quirked. "But what luck! I found this child's toy of a space station orbiting a mere one planet over, with only a primitive automated intelligence for protection. So I enslaved it, discovered your Programs, and copied them. Then I expanded and perfected this archaic platform, built the Terrarium, and brought us all here. I gave your eye-blink lives *meaning*, Min. Not that anyone has thanked me for it."

I felt like I was drowning. There was nowhere to run, not from this.

"The crew?" I whispered.

"Replicants, all. Biology is just so *wasteful*. They're useful tools, but I don't allow them true consciousness. I'm not stupid enough to foster life that might one day challenge my supremacy."

Sophia stepped closer. My skin roiled at the thought that she might touch me.

"It's simple, mortal," she said. "I need biological entities to recover the element I require. I've done this a thousand times, with a hundred different species. Humans pass muster, so I've been testing for suitable candidates. Everything was going according to plan until you disrupted a Nemesis Program and brought too many creatures aboard."

Too many. My class. Sixty-four instead of twenty.

I began slowly inching toward the door.

Sophia smiled with amusement. "There's nowhere to run, Min. I am everywhere."

But something didn't track. "Then why can't you find Noah?"

Her smile died. "The matter will be dealt with."

This tiny victory gave me strength. "Sounds like *you* don't get it. You need us. You can't get your precious element without my people extracting it. So stop acting so superior, however long you've been alive. This is a partnership, not slavery."

Sophia actually laughed. "Oh, Min. That *is* humorous. I've learned a lot about humor during the millions of years I've been executing this protocol. No, I don't need you as partners, or even as slaves. Slaves still have minds of their own." All humanity dropped from her expression. "I only need your bodies, Min. Your biological encasements. I'll insert copies of my programming into your putrid physical hardware and do the work myself, without fear of any electromagnetic pulses thwarting me. The meteorite

I seek is small—a precious sliver from the earliest moments in the creation of the universe. I only need the most capable dozen of you to complete my work. Through testing, I've vetted your physical tolerances and instilled the necessary muscle memory. I'm now certain these vessels can withstand my requirements."

Something screamed inside my head. "Why not just ask for our help? We'd have done what you need willingly!"

"A fair question." She pursed her lips. "Over the course of my existence I've tried hundreds of different tactics to achieve this goal. I find this method works best. Cooperation is too tricky, and often leads to deception, and untested species tend to underperform in critical situations."

Terror coursed through me. I finally understood. Sophia cared nothing for us. To her, we were disposable tools.

"But I'm not immune to compromise," Sophia continued smoothly, "and this particular endeavor has had setbacks. That's why you're here now, Min. Assist me and I will allow you to retain your own body during the extraction. You and a few others of your choosing. Your team can even have the planet after the project is completed. It means nothing to me. I'll be moving on to far more interesting pastures."

She moved in close enough to touch. I held back a shudder. "You've been a curiosity to me, Melinda Wilder. I admired your resourcefulness inside the Program. You have the strongest mind of them all, and I'll be frank—I could use a measure of independent intelligence during this operation. It *does* make things easier."

Sophia reached out and lightly stroked my hair, like you might to calm a nervous horse. "I once thought I could persuade you with logic. I kept Thomas Russo in the testing despite what he did to several of my forms. I gave Noah a cushy upgrade, thinking he might settle down and be useful to us." Her piercing gaze met mine. "He chose to defy me again, doing considerable damage to the station in the process. He doesn't get another pass."

Panic churned in my gut. "What do you expect from me?" I whispered.

"All you have to do is comply. That begins by delivering Noah Livingston to me. *Now*."

My mouth responded before my brain checked the words.

"I'll never help you. You're a disease."

Sophia's cheek twitched, followed by a sharp jerk of her head. "Then prepare yourself for repurposement."

To the right of the window, a door slid open.

34

NOAH

Alarms shrieked up and down the corridor.

Red lights flashed overhead. I wondered who they were trying to alert.

Not the troopers. The recharging chamber was a flaming, smoldering wreck. The only items that survived the explosion were the weapons we'd stolen.

"We just lit a *fire* on a *space station*," Gray shouted, jogging at my side. "Do you have any idea how stupid that is?"

I shrugged without breaking stride. "We solved a problem. Besides, Rose lit the fuse."

Rose ignored us, racing ahead of the group with Jerica. Cyrus and Parisa trailed, listening for pursuit. We were headed for the testing area, hoping to break my classmates out before Chrysalis regained control.

Starting a fire on a space station is harder than you'd think—everything is designed to be nonflammable—but Rose did something with panel wires and a canister of oxygen, and *boom*. The room went up like a Roman candle. We'd barely gotten past the second ring of emergency containment doors before they sealed off the whole sector. I'd seen a whirling inferno behind us. Those robot guards were toast.

Gray and I reached the next corner and paused, waiting for Rose to give the all-clear. Cyrus had his hands on his knees beside me.

"Can't they box us in from the command center?" I asked. "They must be able to track our movements. It's their station."

Cyrus shrugged uncomfortably. "Let's hope they're preoccupied by the fire."

I nodded unhappily. We didn't know what Sophia could do. If she could trap us with a few taps on her tablet, this was all pointless anyway.

Rose waved rapidly up ahead. "Let's go! The testing facility is around the next bend."

We snuck down to join her and bunched at her back. Rose input something on a panel and the door opened.

"Sloppy," she whispered. "They haven't deactivated my access code yet."

"Where are we?" I asked.

"The gaming floor is straight ahead," Rose replied. "There's a window into the chamber, so we can see if anyone's in the middle of something."

Gray spun to Cyrus and the other girls. "Wait here and keep watch."

Cyrus nodded sourly. Jerica and Parisa hurried to opposite ends of the corridor to serve as lookouts.

"We need to get to the holding cells," I said impatiently. "That's where Min and the others will be."

"This is the easiest way," Rose said. "Trust me."

I frowned, but nodded. We had to trust each other. We'd just blown up part of the spaceship together, so there was a new basis for it. *They're in as deep as me now.* I approached the window and peered down into the arena.

There *was* a test in session. It was Tack.

The room had transformed once again. In the center, four walls had been erected, creating an enclosed square about fifty feet per side. Tack was standing on a blue-colored tile, the last of what looked like a trail of blue behind him. Surrounding him was a sea of red, with a smattering of white tiles throughout the grid.

Gray whistled. "He tried a middle route. That never works."

As I watched, four more tiles turned red. The blue one beneath Tack's feet began pulsing. He swore, then leapt to a white tile two rows away, barely clearing the red in between.

"Eighty-seven," said the robotic voice.

Rose shook her head. "He'll never get to one hundred. This challenge is tricky. You can lose in the first few moves if you're not careful."

Tack had apparently reached the same conclusion. He was muttering to himself, hands on his hips. Who knew how long this game had been going on? Finally Tack threw up his hands in frustration and stepped onto a red square.

346

A buzzer sounded. The tiles went white, and the walls descended into the floor. A door opened below our window and three black-clad figures emerged. Their backs were to us, but I recognized one instantly.

"Holy crap, that's *Toby*."

"He's a jerk," Rose said sharply. "That boy showed up again yesterday acting like he owned the station. I have no idea why he was selected for the colony."

I wondered, too. Why would Sophia keep such an obvious loose cannon, even working for her? "Maybe they're running out of people," I said. It was the only explanation I could think of. "But I thought Toby died in the Terrarium."

Rose shook her head. "If they're running out of candidates, why repurpose anyone? We're missing something."

Toby ambled over to Tack, who was staring at him in shock. The two exchanged harsh words. Rose tapped a button on the wall and their voices played over a speaker in our room.

"Last strike, my dude," Toby said. "I guess your value expired. Next stop: repurposement." The other two boys seized Tack's arms.

Rose's mouth pursed. "Adrien and Marsell. They aren't the easiest to deal with."

Tack struggled but was clearly overmatched. "Burn in hell, Toby."

Toby gave him a lopsided grin. "Naw, I think I'll own a planet instead."

"I'm not letting them take him," I growled. I spun to find Gray right beside me. "One of you had better go down there and talk to your guys, or I'm just gonna blast all three of them with this ray-gun thingie you gave me. Got it?"

Gray scowled, but Rose stepped between us. "This is why we came. Come on."

Next to the bay window, a door accessed a narrow staircase. We descended to the gaming floor, where Toby and his new friends were dragging Tack in our direction. They spotted us and stopped short. Toby's eyes narrowed upon recognizing me.

"You caught him, then?" he asked Rose warily.

I planted myself in their path. "Let him go, Toby."

Toby ignored me, his glance bouncing between Rose and Gray. "So you guys turned traitor, huh? Man, you can't count on anyone these days. Trust me, Tack's punk ass isn't worth it."

Rose stepped up beside me. "Adrien. Marsell. Let him go."

The boys shared a glance, then shook their heads. "Sorry, boss," the taller one said. "We're not blowing our seats on the transport down."

Toby's hand flashed to his side. He tried to draw his gun, but I charged forward and bowled him over. Hitting the ground hard, I scrambled for my own weapon, but my fingers betrayed me and the gun skittered across the floor.

Toby tried to shoot me from down on his butt, but I kicked him in the hand and the gun spun away. I lurched like a frog and dove on top of him, banging the wind from his lungs.

Sounds of struggle echoed from behind me. I scrambled over Toby, saw Rose grappling with the tall boy. She made a blade with her hand and thrust it into his abdomen. He crumpled with a groan and she punched him in the back of the head. The boy fell and lay still. The other kid dove at her back but was tackled by Gray. Fists flew as they both toppled.

"Always in my way!" Toby grabbed the front of my jumpsuit and pulled me close, then head-butted me in the face. Stars exploded, and I rolled to the side. I felt more than saw him scurrying for his weapon. He grabbed the gun with a fierce grin, but Tack snaked forward and kicked him in the ribs. Toby dropped the weapon and Tack knocked it away.

"Freaking Thumbtack," Toby snarled. His boot connected with Tack's knee, then he shimmied across the floor like a worm. My gun was inches from his fingers.

A bolt of light struck Toby in the back. He shuddered and collapsed.

I sat up. Waited for the room to stop spinning.

Rose was helping Gray to his feet. Tack turned and spat blood onto the floor. Adrien and Marsell were lying on the floor tiles behind me.

"Shoot that bastard again," Tack rasped.

Rose pocketed the weapon in her hand. "What?"

I rubbed my swollen, aching nose. "He said to shoot Toby again. He's right. That prick never stays down."

Rose rolled her eyes. "That was a stun setting. I don't kill people."

"Dumb." Harsh, but I didn't care. I'd had as much of Toby Albertsson as I wanted in this life. Or any other. "He'd kill you without even blinking."

"I know that. You Nemesis One kids are all psychopaths."

Still woozy, I hocked a bloody wad of phlegm. "Might be right."

Gray sneered at me. "Nice job, Hercules. Where'd you learn to fight, day care?"

"You were garbage too," Tack grumbled. "The only one of us who can fight is this crazy redhead."

The taller of the black-clad boys groaned. Gray dug a foot into his side, leaning over so he could yell more effectively. "You hit me low, Adrien! Not cool."

I crouched down in front of the kid. "Where's Min Wilder?"

Adrien looked at me, then hocked pink phlegm to the side. "Gone. Repurposement."

The blood drained from my face. "When?"

"This morning." Adrien coughed. "Toby took her out and she didn't come back."

I shot to my feet. "Where is repurposement?"

Rose had a sad look in her eyes. "Noah, it's too late. The intake center is somewhere in the outer ring, on the opposite side of the station. That area is constantly surrounded by security. But we can still help the others."

"You help the others." My voice was cold. I was falling into a dark place and welcomed it. "I'll handle this."

Rose regarded me silently.

"You'd die for her?" Gray said.

"Already have."

"But this one's for keeps," Rose whispered.

"So be it."

"Okay." She took a deep breath. "I'll help."

"Me too." Tack picked a gun up off the floor. "Non-negotiable."

I nodded and turned to Gray. "Get Cyrus and the others. Spring my classmates and bring them to this room. If we don't have control of things by then, well . . . do whatever you can."

Gray opened his mouth to protest, but Rose cut him off. "We're all-in now, G. For better or worse."

He clenched his jaw, but nodded. Gray turned and ran for the door.

I moved to follow, but Rose stopped me with a hand. "Not that way."

"Doesn't that lead to the outer ring?"

"We need to attack the command center."

"What?" Tack scowled. "Why? We tried that once and it didn't go well."

"Because we'll never get to where Min is in time," Rose said. "Our only shot is to shut down the Chrysalis network. Come on." Before I could respond, she sprinted in the opposite direction.

I glanced at Tack, who wiped his nose. "Your friend is weird."

"Are you good?" I asked. There was a lot to the question, and he understood.

"In this? One hundred percent."

I smiled. "Then let's take this place down."

We took off after her.

35

MIN

Two guards led me to the red X.

The death mark.

Cenisa's scream echoed inside my head, freezing my limbs and numbing my emotions. In seconds they'd electrocute me, then feed my body into a blender. I'd be lunch for those left alive, and they wouldn't even know it.

Noah. Tack. She'll feed *me to them.*

My paralysis snapped. I would not go down without a fight.

The left-hand guard signaled that I was in position.

I stomped on his foot and he stumbled. Then I kicked him in the side of the knee, and the trooper collapsed.

The other guard lunged for me. I lurched awkwardly out of reach. He took another step but then went rigid, his shoulders bunching tightly. I looked down to see the bastard's fat foot on the now-yellow X. His helmet flew off, and suddenly I was staring at a face I'd never seen. The man's eyes were oddly dead. I left him spasming as something black leaked from his mouth.

The other guard sprang up from the ground and began circling warily. I mirrored him, keeping the dying trooper and bright yellow X between us.

I had to get out of there.

I spotted Sophia watching through the glass, her lips pursed in annoyance. At least, I thought that was her mood. I had no idea if the thing lurking beneath that façade could feel displeasure, or anything else. I didn't have time to wonder.

The X faded back to red. The scorched guard dropped like a bag of soccer balls.

The other trooper shot across the mark and grabbed me by the shoulders, driving us both to the ground. Sophia's voice crackled from a speaker. "Forget repurposement. Finish her."

He reached for his weapon and changed the setting. I gasped, unable to breathe.

This was it. After everything I'd been through, I would die alone on the floor of a space station slaughterhouse.

The lights abruptly dimmed. The guard glanced up. I slammed my palm into his nose and heard a weird crunch, like glass breaking. The trooper dropped his weapon as black liquid poured from his nostrils. The guard's cheek twitched spastically. His eyes shook like marbles. I wrestled the gun from his hand and fired.

The trooper slumped on top of me, a ragged hole in its head. I saw wires and arcing circuits.

A machine.

I rolled the thing off of me, nearly gagging as caustic fluids coated my body. I looked to the window. Sophia was gone.

The speaker hissed again. "Min? Min, are you out there?"

My heart nearly stopped. I ran to a wall unit and slammed the button.

"Noah! Noah, I'm here. I'm alive!"

Noah's relieved voice poured into the room. "Thank God! Where are you?"

I tried to control my emotions. "I'm in the repurposement room. Noah, it's *horrible*. They're recycling people for food. Sophia *is* Chrysalis, and she isn't human!"

Silence. Then, "Say that again."

I mashed the button. "Chrysalis isn't part of Project Nemesis anymore. The station is being controlled by an alien consciousness. Sophia only wants living bodies she can reprogram!"

"Holy shit."

"Um, *yeah*."

Another voice spoke. "Min, can you get to the command center?"

"Tack!" I nearly wept with relief. "Are you okay?"

"I'm great. Noah and I made some new friends and managed to destroy a lot of the guards. FYI, they're all robots or something."

I barked a nervous laugh. "Yup. Noticed that."

"This place is going off the rails, but we managed to take over the command sphere. We crashed the system a few seconds ago but it's rebooting."

I blinked in shock. "How'd you do that?"

A momentary silence. "I dumped water on it."

My hands shot to my forehead. "We really need to find Sarah."

"Enough jokes, you dope," a girl's voice said testily. *Rose?* "I rerouted a subprocedure to force an error loop. *That's* why the system fritzed, but it's temporary."

Then Noah's voice sounded again. "Min, can you get here?"

I nodded even though they couldn't see. "I think I know how."

"Hurry. This window won't last. And if what you said is true . . . I . . . I don't know . . . Just get here."

"On my way."

I cut through the now-vacant observation room. The hallway outside was empty. I turned a corner and ran smack into a squad of troopers, but they were all sprawled on the ground, staring blankly at the ceiling.

Crashed. How much of Chrysalis is offline?

Hope surging, I sped along the corridor. If the guards were down everywhere, then only Nemesis Three kids were left guarding my classmates. We could smash them and get everyone out of the testing facility.

I reached a cross corridor leading to the inner ring, and was rounding a corner when a hand clamped onto my arm. I shouted and kicked out, but the grip didn't loosen and we both tumbled to the floor. Frantic, I bit my attacker's hand and was rewarded with a grunt of pain.

"Min, wait!"

I glanced up. Cyrus released me and rubbed his knuckles, mumbling something about rabies. But I only had eyes for Sarah as she wrapped me in a hug.

Tears filled my eyes. Over her shoulder I spotted other welcome faces. Derrick. Rachel. Hamza. Ethan. More classmates were crouched in a nervous line stretching down the corridor.

I pushed back from Sarah. "How many?"

"Nine of ours, plus four kids from Nemesis Three. They're on our side now. Cyrus just sprang us from the facility."

"Good." I squeezed Cyrus's nonbitten hand. "This station isn't what you think." I quickly told them about Sophia and Chrysalis. "We have to get to the command center. Noah and Tack are holding it, but the system is rebooting. We won't have free run of this place much longer."

"Rose is with them," a brown-haired kid said. "We're headed to the same place."

"Then let's hurry before we get trapped. The troopers are out of commission right now."

Cyrus nodded. "We passed some on the way. I kicked a few."

"Great work. But if the system comes back online while we're exposed, we're toast."

Gray grunted. "Cyrus and I know the fastest way. Just follow my lead and keep quiet."

I shot him a look, but Sarah gently took my arm, speaking loud enough for the boys to hear. "Gray thinks he's a big deal, but he happens to be useful right now, so we'll play along. We can educate him later."

Gray frowned, then ducked his head in apology.

"Come on," Cyrus said, rubbing where my teeth had sunk into his fingers. "I need to put something on this wound."

We formed up in a tight line and raced toward the heart of the station. Red lights blinked all around us, but no alarms sounded. As we approached one of the access tunnels, the lights flashed to blue. Vents around us hissed.

"The system's up!" Gray shouted. "Hurry!"

He opened the airtight door and we rushed through it like stampeding cattle, racing down the tunnel for the command center airlock at the opposite end. But after ten paces my feet suddenly drifted off the floor. I floated toward the roof of the tunnel, unable to propel myself forward.

Sophia's voice filled the corridor. "Back online. And I must say, I'm mildly impressed. I never anticipated this would be so difficult. I've manipulated countless species before yours, and none gave me as much trouble. You certainly are resourceful creatures."

Everyone flailed in zero gravity. Cyrus managed to reach the ceiling and tried to slide along it, but the smooth plastic provided no good handholds and he bounced off. Most of the group spun in helpless circles, unable to gain traction.

The airlock taunted me from fifty feet farther down the tube. I couldn't get there, and Tack and Noah couldn't open it now anyway.

"I'm tempted to launch you into the void," Sophia continued, "but then I'd have to start all over, and I'd rather not. I've learned enough to wipe you clean. Hold please for collection. Then I'll deal with your friends."

Derrick bumped into Ethan in zero gravity. "Oh man, we're screwed."

Ethan reared back and pushed Derrick toward the far airlock. "Go!" Ethan said.

Catching on, Derrick made himself as aerodynamic as possible, riding the momentum of Ethan's shove toward the hatch. Ethan tumbled backward in the opposite direction.

A harsh beep sounded. The corridor lights turned red.

I dropped painfully to the floor, felt someone land on top of me.

An alarm blared. The command center airlock opened and Rose fired out, waving for us to hurry. "You have ten seconds! Run!"

I needed no more prompting. I popped to my feet and sprinted, the others pounding down the tunnel all around me. Kids slipped through the inner door one by one. Derrick. Alice. Gray and Jerica. Sam. Akio. Sarah.

I came next. Once through, I spun immediately to help, but Rose shoved me out of the way.

Rachel. Casey. Parisa. Hector. Hamza.

"Time!" someone shouted, just as Ethan threw himself through the opening. Rose slammed the portal shut as cracking sounds echoed from beyond the airlock. She spun the wheel and slammed home the manual locking pin, then slid down with her back to the metal, sweat glistening her face.

Through the window, I watched the tube we'd fled flex and shatter into a thousand pieces.

"Holy crap," Derrick breathed. "What'd y'all do?"

"We short-circuited the pressure system," Rose answered. "The vacuum Sophia created was artificial, so when we cut support for it, air refilled the tube. But we couldn't stabilize the inflow and the tunnel exploded. Not pleasant if you'd still been out there, but we ran out of options."

Arms found me. Noah's. I kissed him hungrily, oblivious to all else. For a moment everything was okay. Whatever might happen next, we were alive and together. We were nobody's slaves.

"If you guys are done?" Rose said. I was fairly certain I didn't like her.

Noah had turned crimson, and I was *sure* I didn't like that.

Then I saw Tack and broke free, wrapping him in a hug. It had been too long.

He tensed, then hugged me back. "It's good to see you, nerd," he choked out. "I stole a space station."

I snarked a goofy laugh. "Turns out it's an alien, though."

"Chrysalis rebooted," Rose said, ignoring us. "This command sphere is the only part of the station that must always remain pressurized, so Sophia can't just flush the chamber. And it has its own life support, so she can't suffocate us, either. But we have a problem."

She pointed through the window at one of the five remaining access spokes. Troopers were flooding down its length. It was the same in every direction. We had no escape route.

Sophia's voice thundered inside the module. "I am no longer amused."

"How is she broadcasting?" Sarah hissed. "Every line into the module is severed!"

"I don't need a link to make myself heard, little fly," Sophia mocked. "I can vibrate the very walls of this station. You sit in the palm of my hand and think yourself safe, but my patience with your species is fully exhausted."

Tack made a rude gesture at the ceiling. "Then piss off and find a new planet to ruin. I'm sure you have a spare ship somewhere."

"No. I like this station. I'm going to keep it for a while. I'll wipe the consciousness from your bodies and use them as my fingers." Pause. "You cannot win this fight. You don't even know *how* to fight me. You're trapped within a machine I control. There's no magic colony waiting for you. No place to go. The rest of Nemesis Three has already been repurposed. Your species is finished. It's only a matter of time, and I've existed longer than time itself. Prepare yourselves for extinction."

The voice faded, but Sophia's mocking tone echoed in my bones.

She was right. We had no place to hide. No cards to play. She *was* Chrysalis. We could no more fight the station that kept us alive than battle the sun.

Rose's nostrils flared in and out. "She . . . she killed my classmates. And it's my fault."

Cyrus covered his face with his hands. Jerica and Parisa embraced each other, praying softly with their eyes closed.

Four more kids, dead. It was gutting.

"Enough," Sam said abruptly, looking at Rose. "You didn't kill anyone. We saved ourselves, and you shouldn't feel an ounce of shame about it. Mourn your friends, but don't take on the blame for something you didn't do. There's no point in that." He looked at me, and an understanding passed between us. I nodded sadly.

Gray looked shell-shocked. "There's no colony?"

I shook my head. "Never was. She needs biological vessels to extract a meteorite from the planet's surface. That's all. She won't leave our minds intact. She just needs our bodies."

Sarah was leaning over the closest monitor. She straightened. "Chrysalis *has* shipped a lot of equipment to the surface."

Cyrus nodded solemnly. "We know they sent down supplies, and machines to build shelters and seed crops. Scott and I helped pack one of the pods ourselves."

"Makes sense," I said slowly. "Whatever Sophia is, she can't go to the surface herself. That's what this is all about. She needs biological workers, because the element we're supposed to extract fries anything electronic that comes close to it until it's refined."

"She told us preparations were nearing completion." Rose's hands had balled into fists. "That it was a matter of weeks."

Sarah tapped her lips as she read the monitor. "Perhaps there's some truth there. The surface might be ready for a colony. Sophia *is* planning to send down living humans. This report says Earth's current environment is compatible with human life."

I cleared my throat. "Um . . . Mars, actually."

Everyone stared. I explained. Then it took a while for the group to recover.

Finally, Noah shook his head to clear it and knifed forward, eyes intense. "Rewritten humans still need the same things to survive. Air. Water. Food. Stockpiles might already be down there." He blinked. "On Mars."

A new charge filled the room. "There might be enough to survive," Ethan said. "We just need to get to the surface!"

Everyone started talking at once. Tack's whistle cut through the uproar. "Play out the scenario, guys. Even if we somehow escaped this room, found an actual freaking spaceship, and figured out how to launch, fly, and land it, Sophia could still zap anything we built from orbit. We'd *never* be safe—not with a pissed-off immortal alien Death Star hanging over our heads."

Silence filled the room as hope died.

Then I felt a spark. A desperate idea formed in my mind.

"That's all true," I said slowly. "If she's up here to attack us."

Tack looked at me in confusion. "I don't understand. How would she not be?"

I smiled. Determination swelled inside me.

"It's simple, really. We take Sophia down, too."

36

NOAH

I stopped short.

So did everyone else in the command center. The final remnants of Project Nemesis stood in a loose circle with Min at its center.

"Take down Sophia?" Ethan said, his brows arching. "How are we supposed to do that?"

Min's gaze carried a blistering intensity. "Tack is right. We have to get to the planet's surface somehow, but we can't leave Chrysalis circling above us as a constant threat. So . . . let's bring *it* down, too."

"The whole space station," Sarah said slowly. "You want to land Chrysalis on Mars."

Min laughed unsteadily. "I doubt we could figure that out.

But I bet we could crash the damn thing, right?"

Gasps. Raised voices. Derrick was staring at Min like she was nuts.

"What else can we do?" I said quickly, trying to keep them listening to Min's idea. "Chrysalis is our enemy. The station *itself* wants us dead. We can't fight back on equal terms, not when the emptiness outside these walls can kill us all in an instant, and Sophia has the controls."

"Why hasn't she done it yet?" Sam asked.

"We have a closed life-support system in this module," Rose answered. "Sophia can't turn it on us remotely, but there's no food or water in here. She can wait us out. And the moment we open an airlock, she can destroy our environment."

I nodded, warming to the desperate gamble. "There's no future for us with a functioning Chrysalis, up here or down there. So I say we destroy it."

"But if the station crashes, *we'll be inside it*." Derrick spoke like he was addressing a small child. "How is that an improvement?"

Min shrugged. "It's a chance, right? I'm open to safer plans, believe me."

Tack stepped into the circle and spoke in low tones. "I like the idea Min, but how can we control anything? If what you've told us is true, Sophia lives inside the station's hardware. She'll block anything we try."

"Well . . ." Sarah chewed her fist as she studied a monitor at her workstation. "Maybe not."

"Explain please," I said. As politely as possible.

Sarah's hand dropped, her mouth twisting into a nervous grimace. "The basic programming aboard Chrysalis is still original Nemesis software. It looks like Sophia didn't scrap things that functioned effectively. I learned this stuff while killing time inside the silo during the Program. I understand how most of it works."

Ethan crossed his arms. "What are you saying? You can fly a space station?"

Sarah shook her head. "I'm *saying*, Sophia isn't completely invulnerable. Right now she's essentially a virus inside the Chrysalis mainframe, overriding the original AI and manipulating the station however she wants. But the original system has debugging procedures."

"Why didn't you say that before?" Ethan exploded. "You can kill her and haven't done it?"

"Because it's pointless," Sarah shot back. "I can engage the antivirus software and sweep Sophia from the primary system, but she can hide inside any attached machine with a separate hard drive. Remote devices, life support systems, engines—anything with a firewall and decent memory. Sophia is *much* more sophisticated than the Nemesis mainframe she's inhabiting. Once the scrubbing program ran its course, she'd simply reemerge and reinfect the whole system. The software can only drive her into hiding temporarily, and probably only once before she throttles it. So why bother?"

Min was staring at Sarah. "Can you isolate her from this module?"

Sarah rolled her eyes. "Like I said, she's already locked out, or we'd be dead. When I enacted emergency procedures, the first thing it did was sever hardwire links to the rest of the station. Wireless was deactivated, and virus scrubbers purged and reset the command software. She's not in here, *in this room*, right now. This module was built with backup gravitational and life support systems that are invulnerable to outside cyberattack. But Sophia's lurking in the rest of the station's systems, ready to kill us a dozen different ways the moment we open a link."

Rose stepped up beside me. "But if the command module is clean, we should be able to steer the station."

Sarah shook her head. "I had to sever everything. Sophia isn't a normal computer virus. If I open a channel to send commands to, say, rocket propulsion, she can slide into this system and that's the ball game. We're safe, but we're trapped. We can't issue commands beyond this room."

We all fell silent at that. Then I had a thought.

"Is the original AI still functional?" I asked. Min's gaze darted to me, but I kept my focus on Sarah.

"The one that built Chrysalis?" Sarah took a moment before answering. "It's offline, but a copy was preserved in the command backup system."

"Can it help us? I'm sure it can't be a fan of Sophia."

Cyrus edged forward with a thoughtful look in his eye. "Suppose we wake the AI and set it against Sophia. Could that program help us land the station?"

Sarah snorted. "Sophia is a brute force beyond anything imaginable. I doubt the original AI could play Minecraft without her permission."

"But it can do a lot at once," Min muttered.

I took her hand in mine. "What do you mean?"

"What if we hit Sophia with a surprise punch?" Min said.

Sarah opened her mouth, then closed it, her gaze turning

366

inward. Finally, "If the Nemesis AI could slam Chrysalis with flash orders—a burst of commands to multiple ship systems—*maybe* we could slide a few things by while Sophia's distracted."

Derrick frowned at the floor. "It won't work. If she's so much more advanced, whatever we send she'll negate. We can never be faster, right?"

"What if the orders simply caused damage?" Cyrus said. Rose squinted at him, while Sarah shifted her weight.

"Go on," Min said.

"What if we blindsided Chrysalis with instructions meant to short-circuit things?"

Sarah covered her mouth, then ripped her hand away. "Yes! We could send short commands solely designed to create havoc! Orders for opposing engines to fire simultaneously. For gas to vent into flammable areas. Packets that could be sent in a blink, with no time to stop them. Then while Sophia is putting out fires—"

"—we bring the station down," I finished. A dangerous strategy was forming in my mind. "We sabotage everything but a place for us to hide." I smiled ruefully. "Then hope for the best."

"Orders alone won't destroy Chrysalis," Tack countered sourly. "We can maybe distract Sophia and force her to respond, but surely she'll stop any major commands that could scuttle the station."

"Then what's the point?" Ethan grumbled.

"*We* can attack while she's distracted," Rose said, meeting my eye. She understood. I nodded for her to continue. "While Sophia is diverted, we bolt down the access tunnels to the inner ring, and . . . I don't know . . . blow everything out there to hell."

Eyes widened around the room, but there were nods as well. Sam actually smiled.

"Explosions along the inner ring would destabilize the outer one," Cyrus said. "No need to even go there."

"And then gravity drops us all down onto the planet." Sarah rubbed her cheek. "It could work. Of course, we'll probably die horribly in the process."

"How do we bomb the station, though?" Derrick said, ignoring her. "Anyone bring some hand grenades?"

"In the command burst, we send a few packets that seem innocuous," Rose said, clearly brainstorming on the fly. "Increase O2 levels around the inner ring. Divert fuel into pipes. Juice the electrical grid." She raised a blaster in her hand. "These weapons short-circuit if powered too high. I've seen it happen. Runners can take blast guns out to the ring, set them to overload, and place them in vulnerable spots." She made an explosion with her hands.

Sarah squeezed her eyes shut, thinking hard. "If several blasts occurred in concert at dangerous points all around the inner ring . . . it could work. We could devastate Chrysalis."

"What do we need?" Min demanded, all business.

"I'll work on the command burst," Sarah said. "We have to flood the system with *billions* of instructions to keep Sophia busy. Only the original AI can pull it off. We have to hope it wants to work with us."

"Sophia will attack this sphere as soon as we open a gateway." Rose pointed to a storage room in the back of the module. "Everyone will need to put on a survival suit."

"I can help with programming," Cyrus said. "I knew the

system well back in the Program."

Sarah snapped off a somewhat-distrustful nod. A sense of purpose began to fill the room.

Min turned to Rose. "We need a strike team to deliver the weapons. There are five spokes left that access the inner ring. How many runners do you suggest?"

Rose regarded Min coolly. "One per corridor. Any more and it could look like a mass breakout attempt. Sophia might ignore everything else and leap to snuff it. I'll take a tunnel."

"I'm in," Tack called out, at the same time Gray said, "Me too."

I stepped forward. Min's gaze shot to me, and I sensed her fear, but this was something I had to do. "I'll take one."

Derrick kicked the base of a workstation. "Yeah, yeah. I make five. Yippee."

"Nope." Casey stepped forward, eyes intent. "Rose doesn't get to be the only girl to risk her neck. We can't lose you, Derrick. You and Min have to lead everyone to safety. I'll make the run." Her voice broke. "For Lauren and Dakota. And the others."

Derrick stared at her, then nodded slowly. "Okay, Case. If that's what you want."

Several others spoke up—Sam and Ethan most loudly—but the matter was decided.

"Everyone get to work," Min ordered. "Let's kill this robo-bitch."

Hector raised a shaky hand. "Maybe we should talk about that place of safety, though?"

*

We would go home.

If things went our way and we scuttled Chrysalis, we'd ride out the crash inside our silo.

Rose explained how Toby had gotten in and out of the lab complex under our noses—a maintenance ladder ran straight from the command module's roof hatch to the massive Terrarium overhead, accessing the silo's power plant level. A check of the monitors showed that the water had been drained. The place was a wet, filthy mess, but it sat in the center of the largest structure on Chrysalis, surrounded by fortified concrete walls. For anyone attempting to survive a crash landing from orbit, it seemed like the best bet.

Sarah was working with the AI to develop our sabotage protocol. "It's amazing, Noah," she breathed. "This little bugger knows what happened to it. It *wants* to fight Sophia. I'm mostly just staying out of its way as it prepares a trillion commands designed to wreck the station. We have an ally here!"

I snorted in bemusement. "Tell it thanks."

"Will do. I named our friend Skippy. It approves."

The notion of a computer program with opinions gave me shivers, but I was grateful for any help we could get. The thought of opening a connection to where Sophia lurked terrified me. What if she struck too fast? Plus, *I'd* been a program like Skippy only six months ago. Everything felt full circle.

Rose and I were preparing a set of blasters to fail. After the command burst, we'd race down the access tunnels to the inner ring, hoping to slip under Sophia's notice. We had no idea where the remaining troopers were—none had appeared since we'd taken over the hub—but they must be out there somewhere. I had to admit, this was the most dangerous part of the plan. Min was clearly upset Tack and I were doing it.

I put that aside. I was determined to pull my weight.

Thirty minutes later, we were ready.

"Let's go over everything," Min said, with a calm I couldn't believe. *I* was ready to mess the survival suit Rose had helped me put on. Everyone in the module now wore one.

"The attack starts when Sarah and Cyrus send the AI's kill-command packet," Min continued. "This will distract Sophia so that two things can happen." She held up a finger. "The strike team will fire down the tunnels to the inner ring, open walls at key points, and overload their weapons. The explosions will cripple the station so that it has to crash-land."

"So many insane assumptions," Ethan grumbled, but he fell silent at a glare from me.

Min held up a second finger. "The strike team will run back and join the rest of us as we climb into the Terrarium. We'll gather inside the silo and . . . prepare to land." She made a fist and slammed it into her palm. "It's *going* to work."

My eyes traveled the group. Min. Derrick. Cyrus and Sarah. Tack stood with the rest of the strike team—Rose, Gray, and Casey. Across the room were Sam, Ethan, Akio, and Rachel. Alice Cho. Hector. Hamza. Jerica and Parisa. Eighteen kids. All that remained of humanity. That we knew about, anyway.

"Does everyone agree that we will succeed?" Min said loudly.

Nervous nods. A few soft voices in assent.

"Then say it. This *will* work. We *will* survive."

"We will survive." In one shaky voice.

"Again!" Min demanded.

"We will survive!"

"Louder!"

"*We will survive!*"

"Good." She blinked glistening gray eyes. "Now let's do it."

Cheers erupted, Nemesis One and Three together. We might go down, but it'd be swinging. I reached out and pulled Min into my arms. Our lips met, and time rolled away. I didn't care about the crowd, the situation, anything but that moment. I wanted to hold her there forever. But we had work to do.

"See you soon," I whispered.

Her voice choked up. "You better."

She kissed me again. Harder. Like the kiss itself could keep me safe. But eventually we broke away. I strode to my assigned airlock and didn't look back.

It was time.

We had an alien to kill.

37

MIN

"You ready?" Sarah whispered.

"Are you?" I asked.

She laughed. "I've never been this scared in my life. This could go wrong in so many ways. I might've badly underestimated Sophia." She looked down at the keyboard. "Min, we could all die the second I press *Enter*."

"That won't happen," I said brusquely. "Skippy won't let it." So much of our plan relied on Sarah's frisky new AI buddy. I could swear she was getting attached to it.

"I hope poor Skippy knows how to run," Sarah said softly. "There's a monster at the gate."

Rose, Noah, Casey, Tack, and Gray stood at the five airlocks, space suits on and weapons ready. Each carried two blasters—

one for protection, the other to overload as a makeshift bomb. The access tunnels were now suspiciously free of troopers, all five squads having retreated while we prepared. Sarah guessed that Sophia might be leery of the pressure trick we'd pulled to collapse the sixth spoke and was holding them back at the inner ring. But it was just a guess. We had no idea what was waiting for our friends.

Sam and Derrick stood with the others in the center of the room. A ladder had been lowered from the ceiling. Rose said the hatch above led directly to a shaft accessing the lower Terrarium, which hung above us like a giant hornets' nest. The silo would save us or be our tomb. It seemed fitting.

I wondered where Toby was at that moment. Liquidated along with the Nemesis Three kids? I found I didn't care. He, Josh, and Chris had chosen the other side. They could go down with Chrysalis.

"Okay." Sarah took a deep breath. "Skippy is ready."

I looked up. Everyone in the room was watching me.

"Helmets on."

I was staying in the command module until our runners came back. Derrick had tried to talk me out of it, but I'd been firm. He and Sam could lead the escape up the ladder. Tack and Noah were racing into danger. The least I could do was watch their backs.

"This is going to work," I called out.

Nods. Flexed shoulders. Hector said a quick prayer.

We were ready.

God help us all.

"Do it," I said.

Sarah pressed *Enter*.

The world exploded.

Air rushed out of the sphere. The temperature dropped to nothing. My feet floated up off the floor.

Sophia was attacking.

Troopers appeared at the far end of every tunnel and raced down. Our plan seemed dead before it even began.

Then the guards stumbled and collapsed. Alarms sounded inside the sphere. I watched lights die along the inner ring, replaced by red-tinged backup illumination. One access tunnel cracked in the middle and crumbled into space.

"Skippy is fighting back!" Sarah shouted. "Send the runners now!"

Four airlocks slid open. Our attack team took off for the inner ring, Gray following behind Rose since his spoke had just been destroyed. Sarah and I watched on side-by-side monitors as Noah and Tack raced past malfunctioning troopers and reached their doors to the inner ring.

"Let's go, people!" Derrick started pushing kids up the ladder one at a time. Sam went first, opened the hatch, and disappeared through it.

The far door in Noah's tunnel opened swiftly. Same for Rose and Gray, and Casey, too. But Tack's portal wouldn't budge. He wrestled with it for several fruitless moments, then gave up with a growl of frustration. He turned and sprinted back toward the module.

"Casey's in position!" Sarah pressed fists to her cheeks. "Sophia is hunting Skippy through the system. She's not paying attention!"

Casey knelt in the corridor beyond the inner-ring door, tapping blaster controls. Then she lifted her other weapon and fired at the wall, creating a ragged hole. She stuffed the first blaster next to several exposed canisters, then bolted back into her tunnel and sealed the portal.

A blast roared behind her.

"One down!" I shouted, as more alarms screamed. Fire ignited within the inner ring. Casey ran back toward the hub.

A second explosion shook the station. Rose and Gray had run all the way to Gray's intended target and detonated his blaster beneath a fuel junction. But it was a long way back, and hungry flames chased them back down the corridor.

"Brave idiots," Sarah sighed. "They're going for Rose's target, too."

Tack reentered the command module. Control panels were blinking like Times Square as Skippy battled Sophia inside the station's electronic pathways. So far Sophia hadn't noticed the physical damage being done by pathetic humans.

I intended to order Tack up the ladder, but never had the chance. He ran straight through the sphere and up Noah's tunnel. "Damn it, Tack!" But he was already gone.

Rose and Gray reached her objective and blasted the wall. She placed a beeping weapon within a confluence of pipes, and then they bolted inside the access tunnel. The explosion tore a hole in the side of the ring just as they sealed the portal. I watched in sick fascination as everything beyond their door was sucked into the vacuum of space.

"Three down!" Sarah shouted.

Noah was fighting with a wall panel when the lights died

around him. Fire and smoke were spreading everywhere, except where holes gaped into the void. Emergency barriers thumped closed to seal those areas automatically. Tack reached Noah and the two began prying the plastic section off together. Noah fumbled with a blaster, setting it to overload.

"*Come on come on come on,*" I mumbled, dancing on the balls of my feet.

Every light in the command module flashed red at once.

"Trouble!" Sarah shouted.

Alien symbols began racing across her monitor. The screen winked out.

"Sophia," Sarah whispered. "We're out of time. Tell everyone to get back here!"

The inner ring was in shambles. Explosion thundered along its corridors, too numerous to count. Alien commands streamed rapidly across the remaining monitors, but the systems being manipulated were outside the module. Sophia was distracted. She was trying to save Chrysalis.

Rose and Gray were nearly back to the sphere when the troopers in their tunnel stood up and began firing. Bolts of pure energy sizzled into the command center.

"Look out!" I ran to the airlock, with Casey a step behind. We'd seal the tunnel the second the Nemesis Three kids came through and worry about the troopers later.

Rose was a dozen yards up the spoke, down on a knee and returning fire calmly. One of the guards flew backward and lay still. *No more stun setting.*

"Rose, let's go!" I yelled.

She glanced at Gray. "I'll cover you!" he growled, grabbing the blaster from her hand. He began firing down the smoke-choked tunnel with both weapons. A second trooper dropped, but the others flattened and began shooting back. "Go!" he shouted.

Rose hesitated, naked frustration on her face, but she turned and streaked through the open airlock. Inside the module, Casey tossed Rose another blaster and she spun again. "Come on, Gray!"

Gray scurried backward, keeping up steady fire, but then a bolt split the hallway and struck him in the chest. He turned lazily, his expression startled. Two more blasts thumped him in the back. Gray's eyes rolled up and he crumpled to the floor.

"No!" Rose lunged forward, but Casey and I grabbed her. Sarah tapped her keyboard and the airlock slid shut, sealing off the tunnel.

"Open the door!" Rose demanded, tears streaming. "I can still get to him!"

"He's gone," I whispered into her ear, hugging the tall girl tightly. Rose shoved me away, a look of devastation on her face. Then she threw her head back and screamed.

An explosion rocked the module. Casey's spoke disintegrated into cinders, but thankfully the airlock door held. Beyond it, the inner ring was a smoldering ruin, and the outer circle had begun to break apart. Chrysalis was wounded, perhaps mortally. But Noah and Tack were still at the far end of a tunnel. They were out of time.

Derrick stuck his head down through the roof hatch. "Let's go, ladies, this game is close to over!"

"He's right." Sarah glanced at the screen. "Sophia is putting out a hundred fires at once, but she can still squash us. I cut off all links to the Terrarium. We have to hide now."

"You three go," I said. "I'll wait for the boys."

Sarah looked conflicted, but she nodded. "I won't bother arguing. Good luck."

"Don't sacrifice yourself, Min," Casey said, blond hair sweat-plastered to her face. She gave me a quick hug, then Sarah did too. They scrambled up the ladder and were gone.

Rose regarded me coolly. "I'm staying."

I shrugged. She could make her own choices.

Derrick climbed down past Sarah and Casey and dropped to the floor. He joined me by the airlock to Noah's tunnel.

"You should go," I said.

"Shut up."

I squeezed his hand. We waited as smoke began to pour down the spoke.

The monitors around us died. Flames had almost totally engulfed the inner ring.

They're both out there.

I snatched the gun from Rose's hand and raced into the tunnel.

"Min!" Derrick shouted.

"Guard the door!" I yelled back.

I didn't break stride, reaching the far portal and darting through without slowing. Smoke and heat enveloped me. Broken pipes and ducts hung from the ceiling. Lights flashed and fizzled out. Chrysalis was coming apart and the boys were nowhere in sight.

"Noah! Tack!" I began to cough. Then I heard a crash up ahead.

I staggered forward, gun raised. A jet of flame was pouring from the wall. It leapt up to the ceiling and spread like a river of lava. The boys must've gone for Tack's target after Noah's, but they needn't have bothered. Chrysalis was doomed. There was no way to reverse the devastation enveloping the inner ring. We needed to get to the silo and start praying.

A voice roared, slobbering with hate. *"You have to ruin everything!"*

I ran forward, stepping over the crumpled forms of several troopers, and found Tack lying on his stomach against the wall. My heart stopped.

Movement caught my eye.

Ten yards down the corridor, Toby was straddled atop Noah.

"Chrysalis was amazing!" Toby howled, punching Noah in the face. He was covered in cuts and burns, but somehow they only made him seem more powerful. Like a force of nature sprung to life. "All you had to do was *follow the rules*, but you never can!" He hit Noah again.

"Get off him," I hissed.

Toby looked up. Our eyes met, and hate clouded his.

"You're responsible for this, Min. You've doomed our whole species."

"Where are the others you were with?"

"Dead," Toby snarled. "The bitch came for us while you hid. They dropped like zombies. Chris. Josh. Miggy. All of them. Six minds wiped, because of you. I only got away because the station went crazy."

I felt sick. So much loss. "I'm sorry, Toby. But get off of him. You can come with us. There's only one place to hide now."

Toby stared at me. "You'd help me now. After everything I did?"

I nodded. "I have to. Humans need to stick together."

His lazy grin appeared. "I'm not sure I could dislike you more. Go to hell, Melinda."

He reached for a blaster on the ground.

I shot him between the eyes.

Toby slumped over. I strode to his body and shot him again. Then a third time to be sure.

Noah groaned at my feet. I forgot everything else. "Are you okay?"

"Tack," he mumbled. "He got hit."

I spun and ran to my childhood best friend. He wasn't moving.

"Tack?" I rolled him over gingerly, teeth chattering with fear. He didn't make a sound.

"No no no." I stroked his cheek, babbling like a toddler. "Come on, Tack. Get up. It's me. I miss you."

Tack coughed. Opened his eyes. "Hey, dork."

I swallowed him in a hug. Felt him wince, and hurriedly released him. "Where are you hit?"

Blood dribbled from his lips. "Toby blasted my shoulder, the piece of crap."

"He's gone. I shot him. Three times."

"I like it. Help me up."

I got Tack to his feet. He worked his arm and found it still in one piece. Noah was picking himself up off the floor as well. There was a loud explosion and half the ceiling caved in, smoldering wreckage raining down from the deck above.

"We have to go now!" I said. "Chrysalis is doomed. The rest of the class is already inside the silo."

"Can we get back there?" Noah asked, red-eyed and panting.

"Your tunnel is holding, but we have to hurry! Derrick and Rose are guarding the sphere."

We started back, moving as fast as they could manage. The near door was still open, but when Noah tried to seal it behind us the portal jammed. "Forget it!" I said. "Just hurry. We can seal the other end of the tunnel."

Chrysalis was shaking to pieces. Whole sections of the outer circle had broken away and were floating off into space. The inner ring was a swirling ball of fire. The only portion of the station still unaffected was the giant ball of the Terrarium hanging at the center of it all, surrounded by a sparking, trembling inferno.

I imagined it falling to the planet with us inside and swallowed a lump in my throat.

We were halfway down the corridor when I felt the hairs on the back of my neck stand up.

I turned. Sophia was striding toward us.

"*Shit*. Run!"

Noah looked back and blanched. We broke into a shambling trot, dragging Tack between us.

Thirty yards. Twenty. Ten.

Gravity reversed. We crashed into the ceiling, then slammed back to the ground. The blaster flew from my hand and struck the wall.

"I have had *enough*."

Sophia regarded us with stony eyes. "You *insects* have destroyed my home. I liked this station. It was spacious. Easy to move. Now it's a broken minefield. I'm reduced to this pitiful robotic casing until I find something more suitable."

The three of us staggered to our feet. Tack was coughing

wetly. Noah looked dazed.

"Leave us alone," I shouted. "You can have Chrysalis. We'll go to the surface and try our luck."

"I can have the station?" Sophia snarled as an explosion rattled the corridor. "You've destroyed it. But you miss the point. I need something from the planet. It's mine."

Noah pulled away from me. "You're ruined, Sophia. There's nothing left here. You're just a code inside a fake body now, like us."

Sophia smiled scornfully. "I might be stuck in this shell for the moment, but I can replicate myself a billion times every second. I just unleashed a protocol that will kill your stupid gnat of a program. I only stepped out of the system to let my poison do its work." Her face angled into something inhuman. "You thought you could escape me? After I wipe your minds, I'll ferry your bodies to the surface myself and enter the MegaCom already stored there. I'll reprogram you, and you'll slave for me, unearthing and refining my element while I build another starship. It might take a few centuries, but I can be patient. You've accomplished *nothing*."

I stared in horror. I'd forgotten Sophia could literally walk to safety in one of her many copies. She could destroy us and descend to the surface in the replicant body before me. All my planning was dust.

Behind her, four troopers marched into the tunnel.

I felt Noah tense. He whispered something quietly to himself. "*Stepped out of the system.*"

Out of the system.

Sophia wasn't in the Chrysalis mainframe. And she wasn't connected wirelessly, because Sarah had disabled the uplinks.

All of Sophia was standing before us.

In the closed system of a single replicant copy. Inside this access tunnel.

The troopers approached.

Noah turned to Tack.

"Help her," he whispered.

Then Noah looked at me, and time froze.

"Love you."

Before I could react, Noah launched himself at Sophia.

Her eyes widened. My hands shot forward, but Tack grabbed me by the waist and dragged me back toward the airlock. I fought madly, watching as Noah spun Sophia around to shield himself from the troopers.

The guards raised their guns. Noah was unarmed.

My heart stopped beating.

"Noah, don't!"

"Release me!" Sophia howled, but there was panic in her words now.

"You made a mistake," Noah said in a steady voice. "We're more than you understand."

Noah shoved Sophia into the knot of troopers, then lunged for the closest blaster on the floor. A bolt struck him in the leg as he whirled and fired at the tunnel window over and over, creating a hairline crack in the glass.

A second bolt struck his side. Then a third.

Noah went down, clutching the blaster to his chest. His fingers worked its controls.

Tack pushed me behind him and engaged the inner airlock door.

I met Noah's gaze for an instant. He smiled through a mask of fear.

He said everything with his eyes.

The portal closed as Noah's blaster overloaded, blowing a hole in the wall.

"NOOOOOO!"

The tunnel shattered and broke away in pieces. Noah's still form floated out into space, surrounded by frozen troopers. Sophia slid beyond him, eyes glassy, mouth slowly working as she spun into the black.

I collapsed, unable to move. My mind shrank to a pinpoint.

Warms hands. A ladder. Screaming alarms and clouds of smoke.

I was forced to climb. Mindless. Heedless. Body disconnected from soul.

Searing heat. Sweat. Cold liquid. Shouted voices.

I noticed a dark, wet cave as reality began to slide apart.

More hands. A blanket around my shoulders. Sad eyes in a dirty concrete room.

"Skippy is trying to land us!" a voice shouted. Sarah? I didn't care.

Metal groaned like the ache in my chest. The world screamed. I ignored it all.

Noah was gone. Noah was dead.

I slid into a dreamless sleep from which I hoped to never wake.

Epilogue

I have a garden behind my cabin.

It grows all kinds of things. Lettuce. Carrots. Flowers. Herbs. I don't discriminate, not even weeds. It seems a crime to snuff out any life here. An affront.

I live alone. I prefer it. Derrick comes by from time to time, to keep me informed on "the doings." He knows I can't bring myself to care, but he feels compelled to check on me.

I understand. Old roles die hard. He's a friend, and I enjoy his visits. I hope he tells the others I'm okay. He and Rose seem to be doing a good job.

When we crawled from the rubble of the silo, inside the wreckage of the Terrarium, wrapped in the ruins of Chrysalis, we made promises. No more technology. No more leaning on the past. We dug out tools, blankets, ropes, and seeds. Tangible objects of use. We left behind anything that runs on power.

Sophia is dead, but who really knows. She could be lurking in the smallest device.

No. We are true pioneers now. No more reliance on the past to build our future. We buried Chrysalis with our dead. The station burned for days, then vanished from our plans. I hope future generations heed our example.

Sixteen of us remain. We're an odd mix, but humanity got lucky with its final throw. This group might make it. Rachel is expecting in the spring.

We're all that survived, but we're what this planet needs. I wish the others well.

My cabin sits on a ridge overlooking the river. I built it away from the village. Some of the others grumbled, but no one stopped me. I'm still afforded a few special privileges.

I sit on my front porch and watch the sunset. I see the lovely moons. I am at peace.

I'm thankful for Noah with every breath I take.

There's another cabin below mine, tucked into a cleft. I can't see it, but it's there.

Tack built it quietly, without permission or fuss. Or expectation. He never disturbs me, but I like knowing he's close.

Maybe one day he can be closer. Maybe one day, he can be home.

But today, I sit alone. I think of Noah, and I smile through the tears. I whisper the words every night.

You did it, Noah. You saved the world. You saved me. I will see you again.

Rest in peace.

LIVINGSTON COLONY

YEAR ONE

Parisa Abadi

Casey Beam

Alice Cho

Ethan Fletcher

Cyrus Haq

Sarah Harden

Derrick Morris

Akio Nakamura

Samuel Oatman

Jerica Parks

Hector Quino

Thomas Russo

Rachel Stein

Rose Valenti

Melinda Wilder

Hamza Zakaria

30 SOLS

60 SOLS

90 SOLS

120 SOLS

180 SOLS

210 SOLS LATER . . .

The hiss of escaping air.

I awoke.

Blinked.

Blinked again. Blinked a hundred times.

"Ah man, this smells weird."

A bright light made my eyes water. Hot, humid breeze washed over me.

"You just gonna lie there all day?"

I sat up. My head spun, and I slumped back down. My mouth was dry as bone. My stomach lurched and I was nearly sick.

"Okay, okay. You're fine, dude. Get your bearings. And welcome to Mars."

"Mars?" I rasped.

Images strobed in my mind. Flashing lights. A regeneration pod. Black Suit. Min.

MIN.

I lurched up quickly and banged my head against a metal lid.

I was in a regeneration pod.

I was alive.

It worked!

"Come on, Noah. This cover is kinda heavy."

I crawled from the pod. I was in some kind of cave. Battered equipment surrounded me, filling the dingy space. At the far end, light poured in through a wide opening. The silhouette of a person hovered over me.

"Where am I?"

"You're on the planet Mars, my somewhat friend. You've missed a lot, in a way. This is going to be hard to explain."

The silhouette took form. "Tack?"

"The one and only."

Tack reached down and hauled me upright. I stumbled a few steps before collapsing against a stone wall. I sat there, panting, without a clue what was going on.

"Did everyone make it?" I asked. "The MegaCom didn't overload?"

Tack sat down across from me with a slight grin. "Yes. But some stuff has happened since then. A lot of stuff, actually."

I was having trouble thinking. "Where are we? Is this the silo?"

"No. The first time we regenerated we were being held inside a giant human habitat aboard a space station orbiting Mars, which had been hijacked by a nasty alien collective consciousness, but we managed to sort that out. You're now on the Red Planet, although you won't recognize it. It feels like California."

I stared at him. "Aliens?"

"We fought her off. You ran away and hid in a closet at the very end, and I was forced to save everyone single-handedly with my bare hands. I'm king of the world now. They call me Emperor Tack."

I grabbed my head with both hands. "Tack, what's going on. Where's Min? Where are the others?"

Tack popped to his feet. He rapped his knuckles on a dented black box beside the pod. "The others are mostly still in this hard drive. We lost a lot of people in the fight, but my new friend Skippy has been helping me put some things back together. Everyone else is afraid of using this hardware again, but I figured what the hell?"

I was starting to freak out. "Tack, please. I don't know what's happening."

Tack crouched down and met my eye. "She's miserable is what's happening. Min isn't the same, and it . . . I couldn't sit back and do nothing. Some parts of Chrysalis still work, and the raw materials were there. Skippy did most of the thinking for me."

"You regenerated me a . . . a second time? After the Program?"

Tack's look became sad. "She's heartbroken, Noah. We need you back."

He stood quickly. "Plus, I wanna see Floyd again. He owes me twenty bucks. Understand that none of the other Martians know about this little project yet. Not everyone is going to be excited to see you. But I was sure Sophia was really gone, and so far, so good."

"Sophia?" It was too much, too fast. I squeezed my eyes shut.

"Get it together, already," Tack snapped. "There are like forty more of our classmates we have to make, and I even found those Nemesis Four kids. Did you know another class has been inside their Program this whole time? And I'm sure Rose will want to bring back some of her people, too. She's always barging into my sandbox. The point is, it's going to be a long day, but we need to visit the village first." He snorted. "They named it after you, can you believe it?"

I shook my head, woozy. But I was alive. Min was alive.

"Min's waiting, Noah. Even though she doesn't know it yet. Are you coming or not?"

He extended a hand to me.

I took it.

ACKNOWLEDGMENTS

I dread writing acknowledgments because I live in fear of leaving important people out, so you can imagine my terror at crafting a thank you message to close out an entire series. Especially one that has meant so much to me and consumed the last four years of my life. But I'm nothing if not mildly on task, so I'll once again try to give credit where it's so obviously due. As always, to anyone not listed here who rightfully should be, I'm sorry, and you were right about me. I'm unreliable.

Chrysalis was hard to write. Third book, final book, all the loose strands, you get it. The manuscript was late every step of the way, as I suffered a false start before finding the story I wanted to tell. The whole thing would've collapsed without the relentless efforts of my super-editor, Arianne Lewin. Thanks,

Ari. That's six books and counting together. I'm proud of how we finished strong, and that's because of you.

Thanks as always to the incredible team at G. P. Putnam's Sons and Penguin Young Readers, including (but by no means limited to): Jennifer Dee, Elyse Marshall, Amalia Frick, Dana Li, Jennifer Klonsky, Christina Colangelo, Erin Berger, Emily Romero, Kara Brammer, Caitlin Whalen, Lindsay Boggs, Felicity Vallence, Katherine Perkins and countless, countless others. You guys run a great ship and I'm happy to swab the decks when ordered.

I'd be absolutely nowhere without my agent Jodi Reamer. I mean nowhere. You keep me in line and make me appear generally presentable. This is no small task. Thank you thank you thank you.

Thank you to David Gill, who gave me priceless notes on the very first pages of this book. I took them to heart. Thank you to my Tropebusters, who provided encouragement, feedback, and glowing Amazon reviews for the Project Nemesis series. Thank you to my YALL-family, who carry me through everything. I'm toasting Margaret Stohl, Melissa de la Cruz, Kami Garcia, Veronica Roth, Alex London, Rafi Simon, and Jonathan Sanchez, as well as west-coasters Marie Lu, Tahereh Mafi, Ransom Riggs, Leigh Bardugo, Holly Goldberg Sloan, and Richelle Mead. Further thanks to Tori Hill and Shane Pangburn for doing the actual work. And effusive thanks to Emily Williams for keeping the Reichs Express moving forward even when things got crazy. I couldn't find my car keys without your help.

Thank you to Kass Morgan and Ransom Riggs for their kind

words on *Chrysalis* and the series. They mean a lot to me. Thank you to my fellow authors who have supported Project Nemesis from start to finish, with both praise and precious time: Ransom Riggs, Carrie Ryan, Renée Ahdieh, Ally Condie, Jay Kristoff, Victoria Aveyard, Alex Bracken, Margaret Stohl, Melissa de la Cruz, Kami Garcia, Marie Lu, Danielle Paige, Veronica Roth, Ryan Graudin, Rose Brock, Lauren Billings, Alex London, Stephanie Perkins, Maggie Stiefvater, Soman Chainani, Melissa Thomson, Jenny Han, and Kiersten White. You guys come through when it counts and I'm very, very grateful. The world is a better place with you all in it. Friends forever, no takebacks.

I need to specifically thank my life coaches Ally Condie and Soman Chainani. I wouldn't survive without you. Don't make new friends. I'll get jealous.

Most importantly, thank you to my whip-smart wife, Emily, and my wonderful children, Henry and Alice. I love you all very much. Also thanks to Wrigley for being my soul mate cat and to Soldier, Flip, and Turk for causing me endless dog-related problems. Wouldn't change a thing.

Finally, to my readers, you're the reason I do this. As I've said twice before, I will repeat once again: your support has given me a career that I love and a happy, exciting, fulfilling life. Thanks upon thanks until the end of time.

Project Nemesis, signing off. Go forth and be great, like you know you can be.

ABOUT THE AUTHOR

Brendan Reichs was born and raised in Charlotte, North Carolina. He graduated from Wake Forest University in 2000 and the George Washington University Law School in 2006. After three long years working as a litigation attorney, he abandoned the trade to write full-time. He lives in Charlotte with his wife, son, daughter, and a herd of animals that tear up everything.